Life in Plan B

By

Jennifer Vessells

ISBN: 0615852491
ISBN-13: 978-0615852492

DEDICATION

This book is dedicated to two amazing people: my mother, Jody Leiter, who spent countless hours scrutinizing each draft as if the book were her own, and my wonderful husband, Michael, whose encouragement and sacrifice helped me accomplish my dream of writing a book. I can't imagine going through this process without your support. I love you both so very much.

CONTENTS

ACKNOWLEDGMENTS

I completed this, my first book, with the support of many friends and family members, a lot of whom, spent their time and efforts reading, editing, and bettering each version of this book out of the goodness of their hearts. To all of you who helped me through this process – by reading, editing, or simply offering an encouraging word here and there – I thank you from the bottom of my heart. Your support means the world to me and I will never forget it.

1 TOMATO JUICE

I rolled over and groaned when my phone alarm blared from across the room. I wasn't particularly tired, but I had no desire to leave the oversized mattress and down pillows that had consumed me a mere six hours earlier. In a bratty act of refusal, I grabbed a pillow and wrapped it around my ears in hopes of drowning out the noise. Much to my dismay, it was no use. The alarm easily penetrated the pillow's feathers as it grew louder, threatening to arouse the hotel's other guests.

Defeated, I threw the pillow across the room and stared at the ceiling, silently encouraging my body to move. After a few seconds, I managed to swing my feet from beneath the plush sheets onto the hotel room floor below. Although the bed had been heavenly, the hotel carpet felt scratchy and uncomfortable on my bare feet. Frowning and rubbing my eyes, I stumbled across the room to turn off the alarm, glancing back longingly at the warm, disheveled bed. Flouting my usually lazy Sunday morning routine, I couldn't dive back into bed for an extra hour of sleep. I had a plane to catch.

I have always struggled to get out of bed in the morning, even as a child. My mother tried everything she could over the years to get me up for school, but nothing ever really worked. I was almost always late to the bus stop, running around the house, trying in vain to reach the end of the driveway in time.

However, as much as I hated waking up, I loved the rare mornings in my

3

childhood when Dad had weekend wake-up duty. Those mornings were my absolute favorite. On those mornings, I didn't mind waking up. When it was well past time for me to join the rest of the world, Dad would sneak into my room and begin quietly chanting the ominous "shark attack" tune from *Jaws*. His voice would start out low and slow, getting faster and louder as he approached my bed.

Although I would always wake up in the beginning of the chant, I would keep my eyes closed as he approached, clutching my pillow tight and giggling uncontrollably as he closed in. When he reached my bed, I would tear my eyes open and squeal, flailing my limbs and trying desperately to stay atop my mattress as he shook and tipped it to try to flip me out of bed. Breathless from laughter, I would fling my arms around him and make him carry me out of my room. He would always whisper, "I love you, Beezer," and smile sheepishly at my mother, as she rolled her eyes in disapproval. Beezer was a far cry from Haley (and a little embarrassing as I grew older), but I loved when he called me it all the same.

A pang of grief gripped me in the stomach as I thought about those mornings. I had loved them; I had loved him. And oh, how I'd missed those mornings once they were gone.

Stepping into the hot shower did wonders to wash away my sleep – and my memories. The warm water and lavender soap soothed me as I bathed, providing a calming, warm escape from the painful remembrances of my late father. I took my time washing my long, chestnut hair, being sure to condition the ends that now reached the middle of my back effortlessly. I only emerged from the shower after my fingers were wrinkly prunes and my back was red from the water's heat.

Checking the time, I wrapped myself in one of the white hotel towels and began drying my hair. It had been an enjoyable and successful business trip, but I was ready to be back home to the quieter brick streets of Victorian Village – my little piece of the world in Ohio's capital city.

I paused for a moment and peered at my reflection through a small circle in the mirror where I had wiped off the fog. It was hard to believe that it had been almost four years since I'd left Manhattan and returned to my home state.

Sometimes my life in New York felt like a faraway dream, but today it seemed like only yesterday that I had given up on Manhattan and retreated back to the Midwest.

I sighed and continued drying my hair. On the one hand, I was proud of myself for taking the plunge after college and moving to New York, grateful for the experiences I'd collected while living like a sardine and trying to break into the exclusive world of fashion. On the other hand, however, my time in New York seemed like a needless waste. I'd failed to snag a decent job during the two years I lived there, notwithstanding my new, glistening Bachelor of Science in Fashion Design. Instead, I'd spent most of my time bartending in the East Village and begging small-time designers to let me work for free. I feared that my failure to 'make it' like I'd always dreamed would haunt me for the rest of my life. Somehow, I had failed Life Plan A and would forever live my life, a little bit less fulfilled, in Plan B.

****

I stuffed the last of my belongings into my carry-on two minutes before the car service was due to pick me up from the hotel. Rolling my luggage hurriedly behind me, I stopped on my way out the door to look into the mirror one last time. I'd gathered my wavy brown hair into a lazy bun and hastily applied a thin layer of makeup to give my pale, round face a false hint of color. My full lips were especially dry from the early spring weather, and the dark circles popping out from under my big, too-close-together green eyes were especially prominent. Cringing, I made a mental note to get more sleep.

Tilting my head while assessing my outfit, I smoothed over a few wrinkles in my new cream cashmere sweater. The sweater had been slightly overpriced, but its simple, soft elegance had been too much to resist. It felt decadent on my bare skin, caressing me like a warm lotion. I was glad I'd purchased it and excited to debut it during my trip home.

I paired my new sweater with my favorite pair of thick black cotton leggings. They featured golden zippers up the sides and disguised my saddlebags more successfully than spandex. Although I'd transformed from an uncoordinated, gangly theatre kid into a slender (but still uncoordinated) woman, I battled thigh dimples like any normal female.

I completed my travel outfit with a pair of patterned black flats. I found them a few months ago on the clearance rack while scavenging in my usual warehouse discount store, buried under boxes like a hidden gem beneath the sand. Made of soft leather with a diamond pattern subtly embossed into their skin, I had fallen for the shoes instantly. I wore them so frequently, that they had already been resoled.

I had an almost unhealthy obsession with shoes – an obsession that could be traced back to the time I wore a pair of transparent princess heels as an eight-year-old Cinderella. I was enamored with the story of how Cinderella found her prince, insisting, from that moment on, to always be wearing a fabulous pair of shoes. Shoes fascinated me. Each pair was so different; it was like they had their own complicated stories full of successes, failures, and endless life experiences.

I empathized with the bulky, ugly shoes, and imagined how depressed they must be, constantly staring and envying the gloriously fashionable ones around them. I loved the way leather shoes smelled and imagined the shock they first felt upon discovering shoes made of pleather. I loved shoes with buckles, shining with importance and purpose. I even loved the way my grandmother's heels shuffled along, hideous though they were. It was as if they were trying to achieve the ultimate balance of support and style, failing miserably to achieve either. Shoes had enthralled me for twenty unfaltering years, and my patterned black flats were no exception.

****

I felt myself begin to relax when I was safely tucked away in the Lincoln Town Car that had been waiting for me in front of the hotel. No matter how laid back the trip, my visits to New York never failed to cause me anxiety. The anxiety would take hold in my chest almost immediately upon my arrival into the city and wouldn't loosen its grip until I was safely on my way out of town.

A loud bang startled me from behind, interrupting my relaxation. Annoyed at having been made to wait for more than thirty seconds, the chubby driver had carelessly slammed my suitcase into the trunk and was now forcefully stuffing himself back into the car, causing it to rock as he wriggled into his seat. His cheeks were flushed pink from the exertion, and he glared at me in the rearview mirror while catching his breath.

"LaGuardia?" He asked in a thick, New York accent. It wasn't often I traveled with a driver born and raised in the United States. I normally rode with drivers from interesting and faraway places, filling my trips with stories about how they'd ended up in the nation's biggest city. This morning's drive wasn't promising the same interesting conversation.

"Yes. Terminal C, please," I responded, not unkindly. Grabbing my earbuds out of my purse and plugging them into my phone, I closed my eyes and escaped into a world made possible by Dave Matthews Band – my favorite artist since the sixth grade. Not long after I had closed my eyes, however, my musical heaven was cut off by an incoming call.

Glancing down at my phone, I saw that it was Alex. Alex was one of my best friends, and also my employer. I had entertained an important potential client last night, and although we'd agreed to discuss the meeting when I'd returned to Columbus, Alex's patience appeared to have run thin. Frankly, I wasn't the least bit surprised. Alex had never been capable of much patience. "Hello, Alex," I greeted, taking a slightly patronizing tone.

"Haley Blythe Simpson," he started anxiously, "I can't take it anymore! How did it go?! The meeting? Dinner? Tell me everything, for Christ's sake!" Although normally high-strung, I could tell Alex's blood pressure was at unusually high levels as he waited for an answer, panting loudly into the phone.

"Oh, it went okay, I guess," I said vaguely. The meeting had actually been a giant success, but I couldn't resist the opportunity to tease him. "Naresh was reserved about the deal like always," I continued. "At the start of dinner he told me he needed to think it over and perhaps see more of your fall line before committing to anything long-term."

As I spoke, I could hear Alex's hope escaping him like an untied balloon. Teasing him any longer would be downright mean. "However," I continued more eagerly, "thanks *entirely* to my unmistakable wit and charm and not at *all* to your genius design talent, Naresh was sold by the end of dinner. *De Alexia* will be showcased for one year starting this summer in one of New York City's hottest boutiques, directly on Spring Street! Someone from Resh+001 is faxing the paperwork over first thing tomorrow." There was such a long pause after I'd finished, I was afraid we'd been disconnected. And then my eardrums exploded.

"OHHHHH MY GODDDD!!!!! OH MY GOD, OH MY … HOLY MOTHER OF … I CAN'T BELIEVE IT, HALE!!!! OHHHHH MY GOOODD!!!!" Alex's screaming became indiscernible after a while, but even through the noise, I could make out his partner, Patrick, screaming along with him in the background. I was glad Patrick was there to share the moment. Having no one to share good news with always seemed to make happy moments a little bit depressing.

"Okay!" I yelled, trying to catch Alex's attention amidst the screaming. "I'm hanging up now . . . I'll see you tomorrow!" Unsure as to whether Alex heard me, I hung up the phone, grinning. The driver was back to glaring at me through the rearview mirror, but I didn't care. Alex and I had been courting Naresh's boutique tirelessly for months. A deal with Resh+001 was like a dream come true for Alex's business.

Almost three years ago, Alex started a men's boutique in Columbus, Ohio's Short North area, stocking it with clothing only he designed. He named the boutique *De Alexia* after his bossy, dramatic, and creative female alter ego, whose passion for design had inspired me since our geeky teenage community theatre days. Thanks to Alex's (or Alexia's) talent, it hadn't taken long for the boutique to become a success in Columbus. Now, after a couple of years of endless promotion, marketing, and hustling, we had broken beyond Ohio's borders and gained interest from some of New York City's most exclusive stores. Naresh's boutique on Spring Street, Resh+001, was our biggest account yet.

Born in the United States to Indian parents, Naresh possessed a unique mixture of cultural passions. Although he appreciated cricket and Bollywood more than the average American, Naresh's fashion interests were not inspired by India's classic, Bohemian style. Instead, Naresh had an incredible eye for new, chic, cutting edge men's fashion – an eye that had earned his boutique prominent features in many popular fashion magazines. Getting Alex's clothes into Resh+001 was huge for the future of *De Alexia*.

While I was ecstatic over the boutique's success, a small, dark, and contemptible part of me felt resentful toward Alex for his achievements. I had worked with Alex side-by-side since shortly after the boutique opened, but it still didn't quite feel like *De Alexia*'s success was our success. Rather, it felt like Alex's success – one I helped achieve, but his all the same. And although I had been working hard to help Alex live his dream, in the end it was *his* dream. Not mine. When I left New York a few years back, it was as if my dreams had stayed behind. Now, in the wake of Alex's achievements, my dreams seemed long forgotten.

****

Looking out the window, I noticed the driver pull up to the terminal. I unfastened my seatbelt and signed the bill, eager to get out of the car and into the airport where I could finally eat some breakfast. When I opened the door, the cold spring air came rushing in, making me wish I had worn my coat. Vainly, I had decided to pack my coat and suffer without in order to prominently display my new sweater. It had been too long since my last date, and I figured it couldn't hurt to look nice at a New York City airport.

As the cold wind blew through the cashmere with ease, I cursed at myself for choosing cuteness over comfort. Who was I kidding? Single people in their late twenties no longer met people in real life. I should have saved the sweater for the debut of my online dating picture.

The security line at the airport was atypically long for a Sunday morning at LaGuardia, torturing my empty stomach with every minute that ticked by. After an agonizing fifty minutes, I finally reached the TSA checkpoint. Flinging off my shoes and placing my computer a little too harshly into the bins, I rushed through the metal detector as fast as I could, trying not to move so fast as to earn myself an intrusive pat down. Once through, I bee-lined to the food court and purchased a breakfast burrito and a coffee, making my way to the gate with fifteen minutes to spare before boarding.

Halfway through my burrito, a voice came booming over the loudspeaker, beckoning me to see a flight attendant at the gate: "Flight Number 5997 traveling to Columbus, Ohio is paging passenger Haley Simpson. Haley Simpson, please approach the customer service desk at Gate C18." I wiped down my greasy hands and face hastily, eager to see whether I'd been upgraded to first class. I traveled to New York frequently enough, that my loyalty miles earned me free upgrades if seats became available. As I approached the desk, one of the stone-faced gate agents turned to address me, without even the hint of a smile.

"Can I help you, ma'am?" She asked monotonously, her face remaining expressionless. Something about her stoic stature was strangely impressive.

"Uh, yes." I responded, hesitantly. "I'm Haley Simpson – I was paged." With no sign of recognition, the gate agent tapped lifelessly on the computer in front of her. Reaching over to the printer, she pulled out a ticket and handed it to me over the counter.

"You've been upgraded, Ms. Simpson. Have a nice day." And with that, she turned and continued staring at the screen with which she had been engaged before my interruption. I thanked her, despite her disinterest, and then sat back down in the gate area to await priority boarding.

Although the flight was only over an hour, an upgrade to first class always made it a little bit better. It was nice to settle into a slightly bigger seat with a complimentary blanket, knowing that instead of a bite-sized packet of peanuts or pretzels, I would be snacking on bananas, chocolate, and shortbread cookies. It's the small things in life, I guess.

Once boarded and comfortable, I wrapped my upper body with the blanket, ordered a tomato juice, and closed my eyes as the rest of the plane boarded. The cabin was uncomfortably chilly, making me grateful for the blanket. Before long, I heard the flight attendant clearing her throat, and assumed she had brought me my drink. Opening my eyes lazily, I saw her standing over me, fidgeting, with no drink in sight. Naturally, I assumed she had forgotten my order. Smiling politely, I pleasantly re-requested my tomato juice. She didn't budge. Hovering awkwardly in the aisle, the flight attendant looked at me apologetically.

"Actually, Ms. Simpson, there has been a mistake," she whispered softly, shuffling and glancing toward the flight deck, looking for someone to come to her rescue. "I know the ticket counter indicated you had been upgraded to first class, but there aren't enough seats after all. We will need you to take your original seat assignment in coach. I apologize for any inconvenience." By the time she finished talking she had regained her resolve and spoke loudly and clearly – loudly and clearly enough for the whole plane to hear her banish me to coach. Behind her stood a smug, chubby bald man waiting anxiously for me to vacate what was rightfully his.

"Of course," I replied, embarrassed. I didn't know why I felt so awkward, but as I rose from my seat, I felt as if all of the passengers were staring at me, judging, assuming I had tried to obtain a first class seat by trickery. Surrendering the blanket, I made my way sheepishly down the aisle, wondering whether I would ever reach row twenty-eight.

It was a long, dramatic walk, and I was relieved when I finally made it to my seat at the back of the plane. Shoving my beautiful Cole Haan spring bag into the overhead compartment, I looked down into the cramped row of seats. Although I had been assigned a middle seat, any internal temper tantrums that may have been building inside of me quickly faded when I noticed the cute male passenger sitting on the aisle. Focused on his Kindle and oblivious to the outside world, I tapped him lightly on the shoulder.

"Excuse me, that's my seat," I said in the sweetest voice I could muster. I squeezed slowly by him, not unhappy when my back brushed against his arm. Sitting down, I waited impatiently for the ideal moment to covertly scope out his left hand for a ring. After glancing nonchalantly, I raised my thin eyebrows in pleasant surprise. No ring.

While my neighbor focused intently on his book, I took the opportunity to study him more closely. To my girlish delight, he was even more attractive than I originally thought. He had brown, chestnut hair like mine, coifed into a stylish, messy do. He bore a striking resemblance to Colin Farrell: bushy eyebrows, light hazel eyes, and boyish features, masked under a five o'clock shadow.

Wriggling into my seat, I felt the rush of adrenaline usually reserved for young high school girls when they develop a new crush. Suppressing the normal fit of giggles that typically accompanies such a rush, I coughed and stretched out my hand to introduce myself. "Hi," I offered as confidently as I could manage, "I'm Haley." He smiled, but before he could respond, the flight attendant from the first class cabin appeared in the aisle to interrupt.

"Ms. Simpson, I do apologize about the seat mix-up," she said apologetically, extending me a cup filled with tomato juice. "Here's your drink. Please let me know if you'd like anything else." I looked up at her and nodded politely, trying to mask my annoyance at her intrusion. Once she'd left, however, my neighbor put down his book and nodded toward my drink, undeterred by the interruption.

"Tomato juice, huh?" He inquired. I smiled at him in response, encouraged by his returned attempt at conversation. I nodded with as much charisma as I could muster. "Tomato juice also happens to be *my* airline drink of choice," he shared. "I'm Nick." He reached his hand out and smiled at me, his hazel eyes filled with genuine warmth. Ignoring my growing nerves, I reached out to give his hand a firm shake.

"Haley," I responded, reintroducing myself. His hands felt rough in my own. Not unpleasantly rough, but just the right amount of rough you'd expect from the perfect man. "What are you reading?" I asked, referring to the book with which he'd been engrossed before my interruption. He looked down at his Kindle as if he had forgotten it was there.

"Oh, well, I'm reading a child's book about rescuing Santa, if you can believe it," he replied, laughing. His smile was intoxicating – I watched as the corners of his eyes crinkled in response to his rising cheeks. "My six-year-old niece just started reading it, and it's all she wants to talk about. I figured that if I ever wanted to relate, I should check it out."

"Wow, that's sweet," I responded, impressed. I wasn't particularly interested in kids, but the way Nick talked about his niece was definitely attractive. I sat there, half-listening to Nick talk about his niece, half-staring at the way his mouth moved as he spoke. I wished we were on a longer flight. I wanted more than just an hour with this adorable man.

Before long, the snack cart arrived in the aisle to interrupt our nonstop chatting. The same flight attendant who had brought me my drink asked politely if we would prefer cookies, pretzels or peanuts. "Cookies," I informed her cheerily. It was easy to be nice to her now. This was turning out to be the best flight of my life.

I reached across Nick to grab my cookies, reveling in our forced physical closeness. This was the one time I didn't hate the claustrophobic quarters of coach. I could get intimately close to Nick's neck, smelling the delicious aroma of his cologne, without being inappropriate. Unfortunately, however, my flirtatious fantasy didn't last long. As I pulled my arm back from the flight attendant, cookies in hand, my arm bumped the tomato juice resting on the wobbly tray in front of me. My heart stopped for a moment as my drink, still halfway full, tipped slowly off of the tray's edge and fell into my lap, leaving a bright red stain on my cream colored sweater.

"NOOOOOO!!" I could hear myself yelling, but my voice sounded distant and muffled, like I was having an out of body experience. The passengers in the other rows were turning to stare, but I didn't care. I continued to yell, forgetting where I was and who was sitting next to me. "I just bought this!!" I exclaimed to no one in particular. "This is cashmere! Brand new cashmere!!!" Frantic, I turned to the flight attendant and asked for some club soda. It was clear from her response that she did not appreciate my panic.

"We'll be around with beverages in a moment, dear," she said carefully, looking at me hesitantly, her eyebrows raised in response to my sudden outburst.

"I don't want it to *drink*," I responded angrily, "I want it to save my sweater!" Without giving her a chance to respond, I unbuckled my seatbelt and flung myself clumsily over Nick's lap. I guess I could have asked him politely to move, but in the moment, every precious second seemed to count. In a brief state of insanity, I began to open drawers and unlock carts, trying to find the coveted club soda.

"Ma'am!" One of the other flight attendants had followed me and was now attempting to barricade her body between the carts and me. "Ma'am, you cannot DO this – please, let me get you what you need." Glaring at her like a rabid dog, I managed to spill what I desired.

"Club soda," I gasped. Exasperated, the flight attendant reached into a drawer and pulled out a club soda, staring at me as if I had leprosy. I immediately peeled off my sweater, revealing the worn camisole underneath, and started scrubbing it frantically. Amazingly, the stain began to fade – the club soda was actually working!

The next few minutes were a blur. Nothing else mattered. Scrub, rinse, pour, repeat. Scrub, rinse, pour, repeat. Finally, after using what seemed like the airplane's entire supply of napkins, the stain had disappeared. I was so happy I was near tears. "It's gone!" I exclaimed. Looking up, I realized that the flight attendants and some of the passengers were staring at me the way normal people stare at crazy people. My heart sank into my feet once I realized what I'd done. What had come over me? I had just hurdled myself over a very good-looking man – a man who had been flirting with me for a solid thirty minutes – to salvage a cashmere sweater. I was horrified. Even Alex wouldn't believe it when I told him what I'd done.

Slinking slowly back to my seat, sweater in hand as everyone gaped at me, I reached row twenty-eight, where Nick was staring at me warily from the aisle. Although I didn't know exactly what he was thinking, the expression on his face indicated it couldn't be good. "My stain," I muttered, almost too quietly for him to hear. "It's gone." I smiled hopefully. Nick's expression did not change.

"I'm glad?" He stated it almost like a question – as if he wanted to tell me I had overreacted, but thought better of crossing a woman who had used him as a hurdle and freaked out over a tomato stain.

"It was new . . ." I trailed off into a whisper, my happiness fading, realizing I no longer had a chance in the deepest rings of hell to ever be more to Nick than a crazy girl he met on a plane. Devastated, I looked down at my sweater. The corners of my mouth turned slightly upright again as I saw the soppy wet portion of the cashmere I had saved from an early and tragic death.

Politely excusing myself to get to my seat, I shimmied past Nick and reached above my head to turn the air on as high as it would go. Continuing to ignore the stares, I placed the soppy part of my sweater directly underneath the blast and held it there to dry. Nick didn't talk to me the rest of the flight. All I could do was sit there in silence, my hands over my head under the blast, and pray desperately for the plane to land.

2 CLASSIC HALEY SPECIAL

I hustled off the plane as if the grim reaper himself were chasing me. Mentally thanking whatever gods had subconsciously encouraged me not to check a bag, I sprinted straight to the parking garage where I'd left my car. I was mortified by my actions on the plane and anxious to get home where I could shelter myself from everyone's judgment.

Shivering as the elevator opened to the outside world, I paused, trying to remember where I had parked. The wind was blowing relentlessly even in the garage, blurring my vision as my green eyes watered from the chill. After several trips up and down different parking rows, I finally found my little blue sedan waiting faithfully for me between two oversized trucks. The sight of it warmed my insides a little, reminding me that I was almost home.

Although it wasn't exactly aesthetically pleasing or sporting the latest technology, I adored my car. Sure, its royal blue coat of paint and gray cloth interior were faded from years of use, dark coffee stains covered the passenger side carpet, and a couple of scratches marred the driver's side door, but otherwise, my little blue car was in tip-top shape. Its imperfections gave it character; a cool, vintage look.

In an uncharacteristic act of generosity, my mother gave me the car when I first returned home from Manhattan. Knowing that I had no job and no assets to speak of, she was determined to at least give me means by which to get out of the house. Since that time, my car had carried me unfailingly wherever I needed to go. And the absence of car payments made it all the more lovely.

While the sedan's radio rarely picked up a signal with its broken antenna, the car had an archaic, but functional cassette player – arguably, its most endearing quality. I used the cassette player often to listen to the MC Hammer tapes Dad had given me at the ripe old age of seven. Every time I listened to them, I was flooded with unforgettable memories of family vacations and spontaneous dance offs to *U Can't Touch This*.

In light of these memories, my brother and I played *Too Legit to Quit* at Dad's funeral, to my mother's consternation. Although they reminded me of Dad, listening to those tapes always made me deliriously happy, even on my most miserable days. I was anxious to start the car and pop in one of the tapes to help me forget the past embarrassing hour of my life.

After the quick, fifteen-minute drive from the airport – "Hammertime" in full swing – I drove the streets around my apartment, searching for a parking spot. Finally snuggling my car between a station wagon and a beat-up pick-up truck, I reached into the backseat to gather my luggage, still thinking painfully about the morning.

Thankfully, the short walk to my front stoop caused me to temporarily forget about the plane debacle as I soaked in the cold, but beautiful day. The giant trees lining the sidewalks were all in bloom, hovering over the streets to form a colorful, shady tunnel. The sun was peeking sneakily through the wind-blown trees, leaving vigorous dancing shadows on the pavement. Bikers, runners, and people walking their dogs filled the sidewalks, out enjoying the Sunday afternoon. I felt like I had fallen into a painting.

Turning toward my apartment, I stopped short of my porch when I spotted the skinny, overly bundled blond grinning down at me from the top step, a bottle of my favorite Moscato in his right hand. *Alex.* Alex had dressed his beanpole frame in his personally branded skinny jeans and a high-collared sweater that he'd zipped up all the way to protect himself from the breeze. He wore thick, oversized, black-rimmed glasses and black high-top sneakers with a white one-inch sole so bright that it almost reflected in the sun. His blonde hair was cut short, just longer than a buzz, and his long, sunken face was half-covered in a dark, navy scarf that matched his militaristic jacket.

Although Alex had a good appetite, he always looked gaunt, especially in his face. Whenever he dropped any weight, his cheekbones jutted out prominently, causing his cheeks to look unnaturally sunken. I pretended that his presence annoyed me.

"What are *you* doing here?" I inquired, exaggerating my sarcasm. "I work weekends for you, travel for you, schmooze clients for you – which, you know, is my least favorite thing on the planet – and now you are here to monopolize my Sunday afternoon. Are you incapable of leaving me alone to enjoy a little peace and quiet?" Smiling widely, we stood there looking at each other for a moment.

Then, in a fit of ecstasy, Alex came bounding down the stairs and wrapped me in his arms, causing me to drop my luggage on the sidewalk. His embrace was slightly too hard, but it felt good. It had been a long time since someone had held me that close, and after the awful plane ride, I needed the affection. Breaking the embrace, Alex grabbed me by the arms and pulled away so he could see my face.

"Hale, you are incredible, amazing, perfect . . . where would *De Alexia* be – or rather, where would *I* be – without you?" He hugged me again, this time being more careful not to crush my ribs. "We are celebrating this afternoon," he announced, "just you and me. Chick flicks, wine, salty caramel ice cream, you name it. No excuses." He released me once again and smiled at me devilishly. "We both know you don't have any plans." He knew full well his tease would ruffle my feathers. I frowned and looked at him indignantly.

"I could have plans!" I protested.

"Oh yeah?" he questioned. "Who with?" Although I knew he was joking, there was truth to his feigned doubt. I had very few friends – all of whom Alex knew well – and if I had an upcoming date, Alex would have been the first to know.

"Maybe I'm meeting Lindsay for dinner," I lied, wishing that my lack of plans hadn't been so predictable. Lindsay and I had been close friends since elementary school. Always the smarter of the two of us, Lindsay was a lawyer working obscene around-the-clock hours at a big, local firm. She was the yin to my yang, and I loved her dearly.

Smiling at me knowingly, Alex picked up one of my bags, put his arm around me, and steered me toward my apartment, the wine bottle flailing dangerously close to my face.

"I'm sure you have plans with Lindsay, honey," he replied, patting my shoulder. "But until then, let's see how many bottles of these we can get through while watching *Love Actually*." Without further discussion, I unlocked my apartment door and headed straight for the kitchen.

Although I had only been gone for two days, the cold apartment smelled musty and unlived in when we walked through the door. The building, which housed two other apartments, was a former mansion built in the late 1800s. While historic and beautiful, the building had a unique set of problems. Without daily cleaning and fragrances, it quickly became stuffy and airless, exacerbating what few allergies I possessed.

Turning on the radiator and flipping on the kitchen light, I dropped my bags on the floor and reached into the cabinet over the sink for some wine glasses. I had little doubt that the apartment's unpleasant antique odor could be overcome by healthy quantities of Moscato.

"I don't think it looks that weird, Hale!" Alex called to me from the next room. I leaned over the stark white countertops to see what he was talking about. The ground floor of the apartment was an open floor plan with a great room, a kitchen, and a half bath, so there were no walls separating the kitchen and family room.

"Oh, that," I responded in recognition, sliding back off of the counter. Alex was referring to the mobile closet I purchased to house my ever-growing clothing collection. The loft upstairs – allowing just enough room for a bed, nightstand, and a small dresser – had only a tiny coat closet to fit my wardrobe. Tired of stacking clothes into piles on the floor, I had recently splurged for a mobile closet that found its home in the corner of my great room.

"I mean, it looks like a mobile closet," Alex admitted, "but it isn't an eye sore. It certainly looks better than the piles of clothes you had sitting all over the apartment."

"I guess," I agreed, although what I really desired was a bigger closet. I was no gifted decorator, but a mobile closet sitting in my family room was a slight affront to even *my* mundane interior design sense. Frankly, I didn't have much choice. It was either live in Victorian Village and put up with my mobile closet, or move to a less desirable suburban area where I could afford a large, one-bedroom apartment. Given that I would never voluntarily leave the artistic urban area of Vic Village, my mobile closet would simply have to do.

Opening Alex's bottle of wine, I made my way around the kitchen counter and plopped eagerly into my favorite spot on the couch. I had a strange love for decorating with primary colors, so my couch was a bright solid red. I purchased the couch and matching oversized chair at a furniture outlet between Columbus and Cincinnati almost immediately upon getting my own apartment. They were my favorite things in the whole place, other than the framed picture of Dad hanging on one of the painted blue pillars dividing my kitchen and family room.

Seeing that the wine was ready for consumption, Alex took a seat in the chair, propping his legs up comfortably on the ottoman. By the time I had finished describing the traumatic plane scene, wine seemed to be leaking out of every hole in Alex's face. Laughing and crying hysterically, he finally calmed down enough to manage speaking.

"Hale," he sputtered in disbelief, "that is one of the most amazing things I have ever heard. You can't make that shit up!" When he started to laugh again, he held his sides in exaggerated agony. "Oh, it hurts to laugh! I *can't wait* to tell Patrick." Sighing dramatically between his slowing laughter, he looked over at me, tears continuing to stream down his face. I was not amused. "Oh, come on, Hale," Alex pleaded, encouraging me to see the humor in the situation. "What's-his-face . . . Nick . . . is probably some creep who reads kids books to relate to children so he can lure them into his van. Don't beat yourself about this, it's an incredible story." Continuing to stare back at him with disapproval, I shook my head and poured myself some more wine in an attempt to forget my lingering humiliation. "Plus," Alex added, "it *is* a very nice sweater."

"Okay, okay," I said, putting my hands up in surrender. "Can we stop talking about my embarrassing ordeal today and instead focus our attention on the boutique?" I looked at Alex, my eyes pleading with him to change the subject. Stifling more laughter, Alex nodded his head in concession.

"Fine," he said, with a hint of disappointment. "But you have to give a toast first! You just landed a huge deal for us; it's only appropriate." I cocked my head to the side and pursed my lips in thought, raising my glass slowly as I considered what to say. I was happy to oblige, eager to switch the focus away from my recent traveling experience.

"To *De Alexia*," I began diplomatically, refocusing Alex's attention. "May its success fill us both with inflated senses of importance and make us embarrassingly rich for the rest of our days;" Alex giggled, doubling over dramatically in the chair. "To Alex," I continued, turning on him playfully, "may he continue to design inspiring men's fashion, and may he always find my pathetic life humorous and entertaining." Alex looked as if he might protest, but I continued before he could defend himself. "And to me," I started, unsure of where my mind was taking me. "May I forever ride Alex's coattails into success . . . and when dying alone as an old maid, leave my earthly possessions to those who did not treat my joke of a life as their personal sitcom." Smiling, I raised my glass toward Alex, who stared back at me with defiant eyes. After a few seconds, however, he was back to giggling like a little girl in the oversized furniture. Raising his glass in response, he smiled widely.

"Cheers!" He exclaimed, and we downed our glasses.

****

I woke up with an excruciating headache the next morning. Dehydrated from the plane ride and the couple bottles of wine I'd consumed with Alex the day before, it felt as though a small elephant had trampled my skull and then used it as a hammer.

Blinded by discomfort, I winced and reached for my phone. Nine o'clock in the morning. Why on earth was I awake? I had planned to sleep in all morning, dragging myself into the boutique sometime early in the afternoon. Groaning, I rolled over in my yellow cotton sheets and closed my eyes, trying to drift off once again. Making an effort to clear my mind, I became distracted by the faintest of noises: a bird chirping, the radiator humming, people chatting loudly as they cruised along together during their morning jog. It was no use. I couldn't fall back asleep.

Turning over slowly so as not to exacerbate the splitting pain settling in between my eyes, I stared at the ceiling. I needed to get up. The sooner I was up and about, the sooner I could justify a nap. Reaching over to my nightstand once again, I grabbed my trusty water bottle – always filled right before bed in anticipation of mornings like these – and a bottle of aspirin to cure the pounding in my brain.

My restlessness this morning was likely due to *De Alexia*'s pending deal with Resh+001. Like all of the boutique's deals, I would be anxious until the paperwork had been received and signed. Naresh was a straightforward, no bullshit guy, but you could never be one hundred percent sure that what a man says is what he actually means. Unfortunately, I have found this to be true in both business and personal relationships.

Managing to hoist myself out of bed, into the shower, and into some clothes, I readied myself for the public. Hair dried and make-up on, I rummaged around in my bedroom closet to find the turquoise pair of peep-toe wedges I had purchased during a recent trip to New York.

Although the temperature was still in the low fifties, I could no longer wait for the weather to catch up while my fabulous new shoes sat lonely in my closet. Removing them slowly from their box, I slipped my new wedges on with glee. The fabric stretching snugly across my feet felt a little stiff, but I knew it wouldn't be long before the shoes would be one with the contours of my feet. The soles were soft, yet firm, making my feet feel as if they were walking on springy clouds. The rest of me may have looked a mess, eyes puffy from a night of restless sleep, but the wedges would steal the show. Feeling better instantly, I carefully descended the stairs and left the apartment, mentally preparing myself for the three-quarters of a mile walk to the boutique.

****

De Alexia was situated quaintly between an antique lamp store and a specialty pet store on Columbus's popular High Street. In recent years, revitalization efforts in the city led to a new array of upscale apartment buildings, condos, and restaurants in the neighborhood, driving up the prices of the already expensive specialty stores that had always called the Short North area their home.

Although we were newer than most of the clothing boutiques, *De Alexia* fit in well with the cozy, eclectic storefronts of old. Set in cursive on an iron plate, the boutique's name reinforced the store's expensive and upscale feel. The mannequins in the two front windows were styled fashionably for summer, striking fierce poses in Alex's cropped pants, shorts, tees, and tanks. I smiled as I reached for the door, wondering whether Naresh would display the clothes in a similar fashion.

I entered to find one of the store's employees, Dominic, folding jeans for the front table display. The boutique looked neat this morning, clearly not yet having to host more than a couple of customers. The old wooden floors had been swept and the front racks appeared recently organized. Alex had a particular eye for the style and layout of the boutique, continuously demanding a crisp and obsessively clean look throughout the store, no matter how busy the day. He felt as though the organization of the store reflected the fresh, tailored look of his line, and would freak if he found the store unkempt and disorganized.

Raising his head as the bell rang to announce my entry, Dominic gave a gruff, "Hey Hale," and quickly refocused on the task at hand. I chuckled a little too loudly when I saw his hairy face scrunch up in confusion, as if mastering jean folding was as difficult as solving a calculus equation. Dominic wasn't the sharpest of tools, but he was well liked, always showing up to work on time and entertaining everyone with his slightly dimwitted antics. Dominic worked at *De Alexia* part-time, trying to save money in his last year of college. No one quite knew what he was majoring in, but he had been preparing for his graduation later this spring for some time.

Dominic's thick, curly brown hair was as long as I'd ever seen it, dangling almost low enough to block his vision. He was probably about twenty pounds overweight for his 5'10" frame, but nevertheless had squeezed himself into Alex's most popular pair of Euro-style skinny jeans. Thankfully, the wanna-be-grunge Guns N' Roses t-shirt he was wearing was long enough to cover up his waistline, preventing any plumber-style mishaps. I chuckled again, this time wincing as my head pounded angrily in response. Rubbing my temples, I glanced up and asked Dom if he wanted any coffee from up the street.

"Nah," he responded, eyes not moving from his folding project. "I had a Mountain Dew earlier, I'm good." I cringed at the thought of shocking my system with that much sugar in the morning and made my way to the back of the store to find Alex.

Passing the unmanned register, I slipped through the office door to find him on the phone, sitting in the red, patchy office chair we had picked up at a Springfield flea market a few months earlier. He turned as he heard me come in, a smile plastered on his face. Winking, he held his finger up, indicating he'd only be a few more moments.

"Great! Sounds good, man," Alex responded into the receiver. I could tell he was wrapping up his conversation. "Okay . . . yup . . . great . . . talk to you soon." Leaning over the messy desk to hang up, Alex turned and looked me up and down in amusement. "You're up bright and early!" He exclaimed, in mock surprise. I smiled, rolling my eyes, and glanced curiously at the phone. "Nice shoes," he added, more seriously. I ignored the compliment, more interested in whom he'd been talking to.

"What gives?" I asked, secretly hoping it hadn't been Naresh explaining there was a 'delay' in the paperwork.

"Oh, that was Naresh," Alex announced, confirming my fears. "He wanted to make sure I was here to receive the contract, wanted to know if I had any questions, blah blah blah." He waved his hands impatiently as he trailed off, obviously unconcerned by the phone call. I hoped he wasn't leaving out anything important with his 'blahs.' Alex wasn't the best listener. "Anyway, Hale," he continued, turning in the chair, crossing his legs, and intertwining his long, bony fingers, "once I receive the paperwork I'm going to pop down to Charlie's office so he can give everything a look-see." Charlie was *De Alexia*'s lawyer, someone who Lindsay had recommended on the cheap. "And you, my love," Alex stated, his expression turning into a half smile, half grimace, "are going to have to schedule another flight to New York, leaving sometime Wednesday morning." He winced and leaned back as if he thought I might slap him. I wasn't a violent woman, but part of me did feel like hitting him. I didn't mind traveling, but I'd been living out of a suitcase for nearly a month.

"Why do I need to schedule such an urgent flight, may I ask?" I inquired, haughtily. "I just got back yesterday!" I tried to keep a calm demeanor about me, but I could feel my large green eyes getting wider by the second, bulging menacingly in Alex's direction. I had my dad's eyes. Whenever he had been angry, his big green eyes would pop out as if trying to escape their sockets. 'Bug eyes,' my brother and I had called them.

"Now, don't get mad at me yet," Alex pleaded defensively, both hands up in front of him for protection. "It was Naresh's idea." I looked at him quizzically, silently encouraging him to explain. "Naresh thinks, like we both do, that my line could benefit from a couple of pairs of shoes."

Shoes were the only accessories Alex didn't design. In the past, we had considered hiring a designer to collaborate with Alex and create unique shoes for *De Alexia*, but we had had difficulty locating a designer that meshed well with Alex's style and who would work with us for a reasonable price. The Columbus shoe designers had turned out to be serious divas.

Alex put his hand up as I opened my mouth to speak. "Let me finish," he stated, firmly. "I told Naresh that we've been down this road before, unsuccessfully, and aren't exactly keen on going through the process again. He completely understands, but told me that he knows an incredible shoe designer in New York who would fit well with our style and who would be fairly cheap because the designer owes Naresh a favor. If we meet the designer soon to work things out, Naresh is hopeful that we can put a couple of pairs together, if not for the summer collection, but for the fall."

"And this is where I come in," I replied unenthusiastically.

"Yes," Alex answered, "you're our New York liaison and Naresh loves you. He has a dinner set up for the three of you Wednesday evening. Please????" Alex batted his eyes and looked at me with a pathetic begging expression. My head was pounding too violently to put up a fight. Plus, Naresh was right. We really could use some shoes for Alex's line.

"Fine," I agreed in defeat. "Now, I'm going to go get some coffee before I pass out and die. Want anything?"

Back to grinning like an idiot, Alex relaxed back into the chair, confident he was no longer in danger of being physically accosted.

"Chai latte, please!" He requested, a little too happily. Frowning, I nodded, and turned to fetch my much-needed caffeine fix.

****

After a couple of coffees, a nap, and a shower, I met Lindsay for dinner, feeling much better than I had when I'd first woken up that morning. I was excited to tell her about *De Alexia*'s deal with Naresh – the papers had officially been reviewed and signed – and about the possibility of collaborating with a New York shoe designer for Alex's line. I was also fully prepared to whine about having to travel again. How was I supposed to meet a man in Columbus without actually *being* in Columbus? Maybe Lindsay would have an answer. She would at least indulge in my complaining.

Lindsay and I planned to meet at our favorite sushi place a few blocks from my apartment. Although I found myself running a little late on account of my extra long nap, I ended up walking into the restaurant at the same time as Linds. She looked more frazzled than usual, her dirty blonde hair pulled up haphazardly into a messy bun and her grayish blue eyes drooping as if she hadn't slept in a week. She was normally very striking – having grown out of the uncoordinated, gangly stage a little more gracefully than I – but tonight looked shockingly downtrodden and beaten.

Once we had been seated and served with two dirty martinis, I asked her if anything was wrong. Taking a long, drawn out gulp of her drink, Lindsay sighed and looked at me apologetically. "I'm sorry I look like such a disaster," she apologized. "Work has not been treating me well, lately." She stopped to take another long swig of her drink.

"Did anything happen?" I asked concerned. She looked back at me and smiled tiredly, taking another gulp of vodka and olive juice.

"No," she assured me. "Nothing particularly awful. I've just been swamped and unable to do much of anything other than work. I almost cancelled on you for dinner again, but figured you may not have forgiven me for flaking on you three times in a row." She raised her eyebrows, daring me to disagree.

"I would have forgiven you . . . eventually," I joked. Sighing, Lindsay took another big gulp of her drink and quickly took the focus off of her job.

"So, Hale," she stated. "Please tell me what's going on in the totally different and usually way more interesting world of *De Alexia*. Anything new?" She smiled at me encouragingly, but I couldn't help but feel weird sharing the boutique's exciting news after hearing that work was giving her such a shit time. Sighing, I looked at her thoughtfully.

"The boutique continues to be busy," I responded vaguely. "I'm going to

New York again on Wednesday morning to meet someone who might be able to design shoes for Alex's line."

"You're going to New York again?" Lindsay asked, surprised. "I feel like you're never here!"

"Me too," I said, nodding in agreement. "But finding a good shoe designer would be huge for the boutique. Plus, the constant travel will give me an excuse not to date. My self-confidence could really benefit from a period free of constant disappointment and rejection." Lindsay laughed at my self-deprecation.

"Yes, yes," she said, still laughing. "You poor, homely, woman. You know, you might as well give up on dating now while you're ahead. Once you embrace your doom as a husbandless old maid, you'll be much happier." It was easy for her to mock me and laugh at my dating misery. She and her boyfriend, Trevor, had been together for almost five years, and would soon be engaged. Someone like her couldn't possibly understand the struggles I faced when trying to date. I told her as much, which caused her playful mocking to turn into harsh scolding.

"Haley Blythe Simpson," she started, "I realize it's not easy to date, and I realize that you've been scarred by a bad past relationship, but I swear, if you don't start appreciating the fact that you are beautiful, kind, gifted, and artistic, how is anyone else ever going to see it? You don't let anyone in! You hide behind your belittling humor and then you tell me you can't meet anyone who appreciates you for you. C'mon, Hale, *you* don't appreciate you for you!" Flustered, she took a last gulp of her drink, and signaled the waitress for another. Peering sheepishly at her across the table, I took a long sip of my drink as well. I hoped the vodka would take the sting out of her words of tough love.

"Too bad you're taken," I joked uncomfortably, trying desperately to avoid another blitz attack. Exasperated, she ignored my attempt to diffuse the situation.

"All I'm saying, Hale, is that once you meet the right guy and actually open up to him, you'll be fine. You make dating a joke. And by doing that, you don't have to put yourself out there and risk getting hurt." I knew she was trying to encourage me, but I felt as if we were always having the same conversation. I was tired of talking about why I didn't have a boyfriend. The look on my face must have telegraphed my thoughts because almost instantly, Lindsay's expression softened. "I'm just saying, Hale," she said quietly, reaching over the table to grab my hand. "You are so wonderful – you have to give someone a chance to see it."

"Thanks Linds," I said, my mind going almost immediately to Sunday's plane incident. "You know, maybe if I share my recent attempt at dating, you can give me some advice on what I should have done differently." I did my best to sound sincere.

"Of course," she said, taking the bait. "Anything." Stifling a chuckle, I began to tell her of Nick and the recent stain debacle. When I had finished, she looked mildly horrified, allowing for a long, awkward silence. Fidgeting in her chair and staring blankly at her drink, her expression slowly changed as she tried to hold back the laughter building up steadily inside of her. "Well, Hale," she started, blinking her gray eyes thoughtfully, "I'm no expert, but maybe next time, try not to use the man you're flirting with as a track prop." We both burst out laughing, reveling in the ridiculousness of my recent adventure. She may have been right about most of my past dating experiences, but this particular failure was a classic Haley special; one that not even Lindsay could reason away.

3 THOSE SAPPHIRE EYES

Being on a plane again felt strange and uncomfortable so soon after Sunday's disastrous trip. As I walked down the aisle toward my seat, I scanned every passenger and flight attendant's face, praying that none of them had been on my flight three days ago. I was a mess of uncontrollable nerves, but luckily, I didn't recognize anyone. Nor did anyone seem to be giving me an unusual look. Nevertheless, it was hard to forget how mortified I had felt on that plane ride home. Had the passengers told their families and friends about the crazy woman on their flight to Columbus? Imagining them laughing at my expense was torturous. I was used to being the brunt of my friends' jokes, but I couldn't stand the idea of being talked about and laughed at by a number of faceless strangers.

After what seemed like days of travel and mental anguish, I finally made it back to my usual hotel. No one had given me a second look or a knowing glance during the trip, but for whatever reason, I couldn't let myself relax. It was only when I was ensconced in my hotel room and sprawled out across the bed, did I let myself breathe. Glancing at the clock, I was annoyed to see that it was only noon. I had eight hours to kill before meeting Naresh and the shoe designer for dinner in the Flatiron District.

I rolled onto my back and interlaced my hands across my stomach, considering how to spend my day. I had many enticing options, the most compelling of which included putting on some sweats, ordering room service, and watching mindless day television for several gluttonous hours.

Forcing myself into a sitting position, I sat on the edge of the bed and put my head in my hands. I wasn't sure whether it was the recent increase in my travel or the lingering embarrassment from Sunday's flight, but I felt a little depressed. Lying around the hotel room would only make my darkening mood worse.

I stood up and walked across the room to turn on the shower. When I felt down, there were a couple of things that always seemed to make me feel better. One included sitting around Alex's apartment in pajamas, watching old videos of our community theatre days. The other, of course, was shopping. Seeing as how I was in New York City – one of the best shopping cities in the world – and a few hundred miles away from Alex's apartment, my plan for the day was obvious. A shopping extravaganza at some of SoHo's most avant-garde boutiques was just what I needed to get me out of this funk.

****

After a quick lunch on Lexington Avenue, I took the Southbound 6 Train to Spring Street. The train was fairly empty in the early afternoon, and I was thankful for the chance to sit. I abhorred having to grip the germ-infested poles to stabilize myself while standing on the subway. I wasn't a clean freak by any stretch, but I also wasn't eager to share whatever organisms the millions of others riding the train may be carrying.

Stepping off of the train when it reached my stop, I was temporarily mesmerized by the early twentieth century mosaic tiles announcing my arrival at Spring Street Station. Blues, greens, and oranges dominated the sign, forming a decorative triangular border at the bottom of the stark white "Spring St" letters on the subway wall. Mosaic signs marked most, if not all, of New York's subway stations, and all were strikingly beautiful, especially given the fact that they existed in the dank, smelly underground. Although I'd seen them hundreds of times before, their unexpected grandeur never ceased to impress me.

Climbing up the stairs from the subway station, I felt a rush of excitement as I emerged onto the street. SoHo was alive with people, all dressed in outfits more interesting than the last. One woman passed by in a purple strapless maxi dress, paired with a short denim jacket and peep-toe leather print pumps. Her dyed blond hair was pulled together in a long, relaxed braid, and her white Prada handbag was swaying back and forth as she marched down the street, chatting loudly on her phone.

To my left, I noticed a middle-aged couple holding hands as they waited on the corner to cross the street. The man was dressed in fitted, cuffed jeans, a corduroy, brown jacket, and a neutral colored scarf wrapped loosely around his neck to keep out some of the cool spring air. His curly dark hair was tied back in a low ponytail. Although his back was turned to me, I could tell from his hands he had smooth, olive skin. His partner was equally well put together and had the same beautiful skin color. She had long brown hair that fell easily past her shoulders in loose curls. She wore a pair of black skinny jeans, paired with an oversized, light blue sweater that peeked out beneath her cropped beige jacket. Her flat-heeled boots, made of brown distressed leather, covered her to her knees. I could tell they weren't from New York. Although their foreign language initially gave them away, their reluctance to jaywalk was also a clear sign that they were visiting. No cars were coming from either direction, but the couple didn't move until the signal beckoned them across. No New Yorker worth his or her salt would have stood there for more than a couple of seconds before bolting across the street.

As I watched them cross, I felt an unexpected twinge of jealousy. It was clear they were in love. I watched them saunter casually across the street, holding each other tightly. Once safely on the other side, the man pulled the woman in close for a kiss. It was quick, but passionate. Smiling as she pulled away, the woman let go of her lover's hand to touch him lightly on the cheek. He put his hand over hers affectionately in response and intertwined their fingers once again. Turning their backs toward me, they continued walking together down the sidewalk, hand-in-hand, until they disappeared from view.

I caught myself daydreaming as I watched them fade out of sight. I imagined myself in her place, walking hand-in-hand with my own gorgeous man who couldn't walk too far without bringing me in close. I found myself longing for that companionship, that easy love.

My thoughts were interrupted when someone bumped into me, trying to squeeze past me on the sidewalk. Only then did I realize I was still half-blocking the entrance to the subway. Moving to the corner of the street, I glanced back and forth, considering which direction to go, refocusing my wandering attention on my glorious surroundings.

SoHo (named after its location south of Houston Street) was not only known for its unique infusion of artists, designers, and musicians, but also for its historic cast-iron buildings. Much of SoHo was designated historic in the early 1970s, guaranteeing that the beautiful buildings would forever be preserved. Along with the cobblestone streets, the old buildings played an integral part in SoHo's artistic vibe. The fascinating history and scenery made shopping in the area all the more enjoyable. Unbuttoning my jacket to let in the cool breeze, I decided to turn north toward Prince Street, which housed some of my favorite shops. Prince Street had a good mix of internationally known stores and some unique designer-owned boutiques.

It was the perfect place to begin my shopping trip. Thinking about the affectionate couple again, I started up the street, eager to reach the first store. Shopping would be a welcome temporary escape from life's everyday reminders that, although surrounded by people, I continued to be alone in the world.

****

I flopped onto a bench in Madison Square Park, exhausted. Every inch of my body ached from the past few hours. My lower back ached from being on my feet all day, my feet ached from carrying me relentlessly from store to store, and my arms ached from carrying the four large bags I had accumulated during my shopping spree. Notwithstanding the aches, however, I thoroughly enjoyed my afternoon. I even interrupted my shopping to stop into a few men's boutiques to do a little marketing for *De Alexia*, eager to spread the word about our deal with Resh+001. I was anxious to see whether our partnership with Naresh would gather interest from other New York City designers and boutique owners. Boutique owners, especially those in areas like SoHo and Tribeca, were in a constant struggle to fight against the mainstream, while also providing clientele with the styles and brands they demanded. I hoped that providing people with options from *De Alexia* would strike the appropriate balance. Only time would tell.

I hugged myself tightly as a cold breeze sent chills up my spine. It was getting colder as the sun set beneath the buildings, casting brilliant pinks across the sky above. Rifling through my bags, I pulled out a blue and beige printed scarf and wrapped it around my neck. The scarf provided that extra layer I needed to stay comfortable. My stomach rumbled impatiently, reminding me that it was nearly time for dinner. Taking a deep breath and standing from the bench, I picked up my bags and headed the one block south toward 23rd Street, anxious to reach the rooftop restaurant and beer haven where Naresh had made reservations.

The restaurant was located on the rooftop of one of my favorite Italian markets. The market's giant first floor was divided into different restaurants and grocery departments, providing a unique shopping and dining experience at every corner. I hung out at the market frequently during the period of time I lived in Manhattan. I enjoyed devouring a cheese plate and a glass of wine from the market's enoteca while watching the crowds mull in and out of the market's various sections. It was an excellent place to people watch.

Bags in hand, I entered from Fifth Avenue into the gelato and coffee area. Passing by the bustling espresso stations and heading toward the seafood section, I noticed signs directing me toward the trendy rooftop restaurant. I had never eaten there before and was excited to try the restaurant's Austrian-inspired food and homebrewed cask ales.

Approaching the hostess, I asked whether anyone from our party had arrived. To my delight, the hostess confirmed that two people were already upstairs waiting for me. Butterflies fluttered in my stomach as I headed toward the elevators and up to the roof. Shopping had kept me from dwelling on the importance of this meeting, but now, the weight of it all fell heavy on my shoulders. I hoped desperately that Naresh's designer could contribute to Alex's line. It was not only important to please our newest and biggest client, but the addition of a shoe designer to Alex's team could help open doors that, as of now, remained stubbornly closed.

I loved the rooftop restaurant the moment it came into view. Although the retractable roof was in use to shelter the restaurant's diners from the cold spring evening, views of the surrounding buildings, including the Empire State Building, were still prominent. Casks of beer lined the long, packed bar on the north side of the restaurant, while the rest of the floor was littered with blood red tables filled with large groups of people sharing cheeses, meats, and olives. The ambiance screamed fancy German beer garden.

Scanning the roof, I spotted Naresh and raised my bags to snake my way carefully between the tables. Setting my bags down with a huff, I turned toward Naresh, who had risen to give me a quick hug.

"Haley, I'm glad you could come again on such short notice," Naresh said, warmly. "And I see you had a productive day." He pointed and smiled at my bags. I laughed in response. Much to my delight, Naresh had turned out to be one of the more down-to-earth boutique owners I'd met – something I didn't usually find in the often-artificial world of fashion. For some reason, the fashion world had developed into a community of business owners, designers, and fashion writers, who, in large part, projected shallow and overly bombastic personalities. Naresh was a welcome change from the double cheek kisses and the excessive "OMG"s with which I had been forced to grow accustomed. After months of meetings, we could almost be characterized as friends.

"I'm sorry I didn't think about doing this while you were in town over the weekend," Naresh continued. He looked at me with his dark brown eyes, genuinely apologetic. "I'm sure you weren't thrilled to get back on a plane so soon." Smiling back at him while I took my seat, I suppressed my true feelings and offered a polite white lie for the good of *De Alexia*.

"Nonsense," I replied. "Alex and I are both eager to make this relationship work, and are thrilled to meet the shoe designer you recommended." As I finished, I glanced quizzically at the empty seat across from me. "Speaking of this designer, the hostess indicated both of you had already arrived. She must have miscounted."

"No, she was right." Naresh assured me. "Keegan had to use the bathroom. Ah, here he is now!" Turning toward the entrance of the restaurant, I followed Naresh's gaze. Instantly, my heart somersaulted in my chest when I spotted the tall, muscular, wavy-haired brunet strolling toward us. Dressed in a fitted brown sweater and relaxed jeans, he looked like a Ralph Lauren model. He put his hand up in acknowledgment when he saw me staring. Unable to respond, I found myself lost in his sapphire eyes, gaping at him like an idiot as he approached. Just like the market's Austrian rooftop restaurant, Keegan entranced me instantly.

Pulling my jaw off the floor, I cleared my throat and shuffled nervously as Keegan took his seat at the table. Smiling at me, he waited patiently for Naresh to introduce us. Agonized by his perfection, I could have sat there in silence for the rest of the night watching him smile. He had a dimple in his right cheek and his teeth were straight and unfathomably white. His lips were perfect, moist and full, curling up more prominently on the right side than the left. I imagined what it would be like to grab his thick brown hair in the heat of passion and let him envelop me with his mouth.

"Haley," Naresh started, snapping me out of my improper daydream, "this is Keegan Bransford; the designer I told Alex about the other day." Tingling all over, I extended my arm and gave Keegan's strong hand a limp shake. I looked shyly into his eyes, barely able to hold his gaze for a second before blushing stupidly.

"Hello," I managed, trying my best to get a grip. I was dangerously close to making a fool out of myself – and *De Alexia* – in front of one of our most important clients. Taking slow, measured breaths, I rubbed my sweaty palms on the legs of my pants and tried to think of something intelligent to say while I regained my composure. I imagined that Keegan was used to making women melt – he was exquisite. Finding my voice again, I turned back to Keegan and smiled. "I'm really excited about our potential partnership," I blurted. Mortified that he might be able to read my salacious mind, I stammered to explain. "Well, I mean, on behalf of *De Alexia*, not myself, of course . . . "

I closed my eyes in embarrassment and took a deep breath to center myself. I felt like I was losing my mind. When I opened them up again, Keegan was watching me in amusement. I didn't dare look at Naresh. "What I mean," I said, more carefully, "is that Alex and I are very excited about your ideas for *De Alexia*'s line. And we are hopeful that this could turn out to be a successful partnership." I was furious at myself for acting like an awkward floozy, but tried to shrug it off as if my behavior wasn't a big deal. Keegan crossed his arms on the table and leaned forward.

"I'm excited, too," he replied, smiling at me with his eyes. I felt my neck flush with desire. I couldn't remember anyone ever affecting me this way. It was both frustrating and thrilling at the same time. "After Naresh told me about the line over the weekend, I looked at the samples and put some ideas together for *De Alexia* footwear," he informed me. "At this point, all I have are preliminary sketches and suggestions, but I'm dying to know what you think." For a moment, our eyes locked, and my heart skipped wildly in my chest. I dropped my gaze coyly and felt myself grow hot as Keegan continued to stare across the table.

"You've got to be kidding me." Naresh muttered quietly at my side, interrupting my internal meltdown. I was grateful he'd broken Keegan's trance, at least for the time being. "I am incredibly sorry," he said, staring at his phone with a concerned expression. I furrowed my brow in confusion. "I need to run to the store," he claimed obscurely, "some kind of mix-up with an order." Without looking at Keegan or me, Naresh began to gather his things, staring at his phone in growing frustration. Realizing he was about to leave me alone with this indelible Greek god, I began to panic.

"You're going now?" I tried to hide the alarm in my voice. Naresh shot me an apologetic glance, but didn't respond until he'd sent a couple of frantic texts.

"I'm sorry," he said again, standing from the table. "Retail emergency. I must go. Please eat without me." I felt my stomach flip as I watched him prepare to leave. I wasn't sure that I could handle Keegan on my own. "Hale, let's catch up sometime tomorrow," Naresh suggested. "Call me when you get a chance. And again, I'm sorry for my sudden and rude departure. Please forgive me."

"Okay," I managed, my nerves gathering into a lump in my throat. And with that, Naresh was gone.

For a moment, Keegan and I sat in silence, surprised by our abandonment. Shifting awkwardly in my seat I tried once again to think of something to say. All I could manage to do, however, was study my utensils for food stains, hoping that Keegan would end the silence. Luckily, it wasn't long before the waiter approached the table for our drink orders. Glancing down at the menu, I realized I hadn't even considered what I wanted to drink. From the moment I'd first laid eyes on Keegan, behaving like a functioning adult had been my only focus. And now, all I could think about was the fact that I was alone on a rooftop, about to dine with a breathtaking model of a man, who was not only out of my league, but who continued to stare at me across the table in a way that flipped my stomach and tied my throat into knots. I was a mess. I had to somehow remind myself that the dinner was a business meeting and that my focus should be on determining whether Keegan was a good shoe designer for *De Alexia*. Not whether he was a good fit for me.

"I'll have one of your pale ales," Keegan requested. "Whatever you recommend." Scanning the menu in desperation, I nodded in agreement.

"Me too," I added, my voice unusually hushed. "A pale ale sounds good." I wished I hadn't copied Keegan's order, but I didn't feel capable of making any substantial decisions on my own. Once the waiter was gone, Keegan turned and continued our conversation as if Naresh had never left.

"Well, I'm glad that at least you and I are able to do this," he said, getting back to our business discussions. I nodded, trying to remain calm and impassive. "I know Naresh is anxious to get some shoes out with Alex's clothing and other accessories, so I brought my designs with me if you're interested in looking at them." Reaching under the table, he pulled out a dilapidated, but fashionable brown briefcase. I could tell from the worn leather shoulder strap that he had used it for years, and imagined how cute he must look walking down the city streets, the briefcase strapped across his muscular shoulders.

"Sure," I agreed slowly, starting to regain control over my flighty demeanor. "The sooner the better. Alex will want to know whether I think your ideas will work well with his style." Grabbing the designs Keegan was offering me, I looked thoughtfully at the first sketch. Its quality quickly transported me back into business mode. It was good. Really good.

He had developed a white gym shoe with a thick white sole and rounded toe. The shoelaces were thick and interlaced loosely across the top, leaving me to admire the subtle, but edgy lines he had designed on the sides. The pattern was simple and sharp, which worked well with *De Alexia*'s clothing. Alex would be pleased. Out of all the designers we had courted in Columbus, not one had come close to fitting the boutique's simple, yet forward style. It was impressive that Naresh was able to find a match almost immediately.

I tried to remain stoic as I perused Keegan's sketches. If he knew how I actually felt about them (or him, for that matter), our negotiations could be extremely lopsided in his favor. Flipping through the few designs he had handed me – one as good, if not better, than the next – I forgot about my awkward inner teenager and fully assumed my role as *De Alexia*'s New York City representative.

"Your sketches are interesting," I commented vaguely, handing them back over the table. Keegan laughed, flashing his glistening white smile.

"Well, that certainly tells me nothing," he replied, grinning. The waiter brought us our pale ales and set them delicately on the table. Realizing that neither of us had looked at our menus, he hustled off again without a word. Picking up the beer and taking a refreshing sip, I focused hard on the business at hand and considered my words carefully.

"Look," I started, careful not to meet his eyes, "the reason Alex sent me to this meeting was to make sure your designs didn't completely miss the mark." I took another swig of my beer as Keegan regarded me suspiciously from across the table. "Alex has a particular vision for *De Alexia*, and needs someone who sees that vision as clearly as he does."

"I understand that," Keegan stated. "Do they miss the mark?" Smiling politely, I ignored his question, continuing to avoid his gaze.

"Alex also sent me to this meeting to feel you out to make sure he would like working with you. We've had bad experiences with designers in the past." I looked at him playfully. He was beautiful, and I was feeling more relaxed with each passing minute. Leaning in once again, Keegan locked his sapphire eyes with mine, sending my heart into spastic palpitations.

"Well, then," Keegan responded. "You've seen my designs. Although there are only a few, I think you can at least get an idea of how I envision Alex's line." He leaned back and broke our eye contact to scan the menu, leaving us to linger in silence.

"The rest of our evening," he continued casually, still looking at the menu, "can be used then, to 'feel each other out.'" He looked up at me, a telling smile creeping slowly across his face. My stomach churned with nervous anticipation as I smiled back. Crossing my legs and leaning over the table, I raised my glass, finding a surge of unexpected confidence.

"Here's to 'feeling each other out' then," I toasted, trying to appear cool and collected while my insides melted like chocolate in the hot sun. Keegan raised his glass in response and grinned, his sapphire eyes burning into mine.

"Cheers," he said, clinking my glass, never once blinking.

4 A WALK IN THE PARK

Keegan Bransford was nothing short of irresistible. I could have listened to him regale me with bits and pieces of his life story all night, watching the dimple in his cheek disappear and reappear as he spoke. "I'm not really sure how it happened," he was saying, referring to his illustrious career, "but at some point in the last thirteen years, my role in the design world has morphed into a freelance/consulting gig. Essentially, I'm hired to help other designers find inspiration for their lines." I shook my head in response to Keegan's success story.

"I'm completely jealous," I admitted, leaning back comfortably in my chair. Over the course of the evening, I'd finally managed to relax in his company, though certain movements of his lips still sent involuntary charges through me like pleasurable bursts of electricity. "I think that every artist – whether it be a painter, designer, or poet – dreams of being 'discovered;' having someone stumble onto their work and making them an immediate success."

Unbelievably, that's exactly what had happened to my gorgeous dinner companion. After graduating from high school, Keegan snagged a job at a Tribeca art studio owned by his best friend's father and started saving money for design school. After a couple of years at the studio, Keegan's life was forever changed when a client happened upon his personal portfolio of design sketches. Immediately impressed, the client put him in touch with some leading New York designers. The rest, Keegan told me, was like a blur, and along the way he was somehow skyrocketed into an enjoyable, lucrative, and successful career. I wished I could be so fortunate.

"I was one of the lucky ones, I guess," he said, shrugging. I scolded him for his modesty.

"I'm sure it had nothing to do with your talent," I said sarcastically, encouraging him to take a little credit. Keegan shrugged again.

"I felt pathetic," he confessed, crossing his arms on the table and peering up at the lighted buildings surrounding us in the dark night. "Carrying around those sketches like I was already a designer." He laughed. "I almost gave up on it, you know – my sketches. I can't even remember why I had my portfolio at work that day." I nodded slowly in response, watching as he drifted off into his thoughts. I could empathize all too well. Like Keegan had before his big break, I too carried personal design sketches with me at all times – most of them, designs of shoes, actually – hoping that one day they might become more than scribbles on recycled paper. I realized it was silly to think that someone would take to my sketches like they'd taken to Keegan's. As exemplified by my failure to "make it" in New York City, my talent paled in comparison to his. Nevertheless, I held on desperately to this last piece of my dream. I knew my sketches weren't good enough to share, but I felt that as long as I kept sketching and honing what little skill I possessed, I could delay the day on which I would have to admit I would never be a designer. Maybe Keegan was right. Maybe it *was* pathetic.

Finished with his dinner, Keegan pushed back his plate and set his napkin on the table. Leaning back in his chair, he grinned at me silently. Able to hold his stare for only a few seconds, my eyes darted to the floor in blissful discomfort. My heart was pounding so hard that I feared Keegan might be able to see it beating through my jacket. Just when I would pull myself together, Keegan would throw me a look that would render me capable of only basic life functions.

"Did we leave any room for dessert?" I jumped dramatically as the waiter popped up suddenly to my right, bouncing up and down impatiently. Keegan chuckled at my skittishness and looked at our server noncommittally.

"Maybe," I responded uncertainly, embarrassed by my edginess. I looked at Keegan, seeking more guidance. None was forthcoming. "I guess there's no harm in taking a look at the menu," I decided finally. I didn't usually eat dessert, but at this point, I would do anything to extend my night with Keegan.

"I'll be back with the dessert menu, then," the waiter announced quickly, and darted off into the restaurant. After he'd left, Keegan refocused his sapphire eyes on me, still grinning.

"A little on edge, are we?" He kidded. I blushed in response.

"I was lost in my thoughts," I confessed. "Forgot where I was for a second." Continuing to smile, Keegan leaned in and before I knew it, had placed his hand casually on mine, squeezing it lightly.

"You know," he started, his hand still clutching mine. "There's no question that the dessert here is pretty awesome." He leaned back and let go of my fingers, continuing our conversation like he'd never touched them. "*However*, there is a cool little place in Madison Square Park – the park right across the street from here – that makes the best shakes on earth." I stared at my hand, willing it to move. Keegan's superpowers had frozen it in place, rendering me incapable of using it. "What do you say?" Keegan seemed completely unaware of my mild paralysis. "Are you up for a shake and a little walk in the park after hours?" I wanted nothing more.

"Uh, sure," I agreed, trying not to sound overly enthusiastic. Although I'd been to the shake shack in the park several times, I didn't feel it was necessary to tell him. He seemed so excited to share one of the city's treasures with me. I wasn't going to ruin things by telling him that I'd already experienced it. In fact, I hadn't even told him I had lived in New York for two years. I wasn't sure why, but I think it had to do with the passionate way he spoke about the city, as if he wanted me to see it through his eyes. If he knew that I'd lived here for a couple of years, I supposed he wouldn't enjoy telling me about his favorite places and experiences nearly as much. I didn't want that to happen. I wanted to sit here forever and listen to Keegan share his world with me.

I glanced up as the waiter brought us the dessert menu. "Actually," I told him, apologetically, "we've decided to skip dessert. All we need at this point is the check." Obviously annoyed, the waiter puckered his lips.

"Of course," he responded, coolly. And with that, he was off again to fetch the bill. Once he'd left, I turned back to Keegan. He was gazing around the restaurant, watching the growing crowd of people amassing at the bar.

During our meal, the rooftop restaurant had slowly turned into a trendy bar scene rather than a hotspot for dinner goers. Most of the drinkers were in suits, clearly eager to have escaped the daily grind for a midweek beer.

"I can't imagine working in an office every day," Keegan pondered, still watching the crowd. I nodded my head in agreement.

"My friend, Lindsay, is a lawyer in Columbus," I shared. "She can't stand the fact that she sits at a desk all day. She said she gets restless if she doesn't at least walk to get lunch." Keegan shook his head and sighed.

"I could never do that," he declared.

"Me neither," I agreed. "Not only would it be miserable, but I would get so fat sitting around all day!" Breaking his gaze, Keegan turned and looked at me doubtfully.

"You?" He questioned skeptically. "I can't imagine you ever being fat. You are so naturally thin; I can tell by the tiny size of your wrists." He grabbed my arm again, this time putting his forefinger and thumb around my wrist to dramatize its small size. I should have been offended by the uninvited contact considering our meal was supposed to be a business meeting, but any thoughts about formality or *De Alexia* had long been forgotten. Instead, I relished every flirtatious moment, hoping that Keegan saw me as more than a potential business partner. Letting go, he put his measurement on display, peering through the small hole he'd made with his fingers. "I mean, look how small they are!" He exclaimed. Blushing and rolling my eyes at him, I looked up as our waiter approached the table once again.

"You all have a wonderful evening," he offered curtly as he placed the check onto the table.

"You too," I responded, reaching for the bill. Keegan looked at me disapprovingly.

"Nonsense," Keegan said, also reaching for the check. "Dinner is on me." I wasn't sure how to handle his offer. Because the dinner had been held to discuss business for *De Alexia*, I had planned to pay for it all along. Usually, clients didn't even pretend to foot the bill.

"No," I responded, firmly. "This is a business dinner for *my* business. Please let me pay on behalf of *De Alexia*." Before I had finished, Keegan snatched up the check and smiled at me devilishly.

"If you're really that torn up about it," he stated, "you can pay for our meal the next time around." I looked back at him with anticipation. Did he mean our next business meal? Or was he suggesting something more – more intimate, perhaps? Either way, I smiled at him, glad to hear that he expected to be seeing me again.

"Okay," I agreed, without further argument. Sinking into my chair as he reached into his back pocket, I imagined what life would be like if Keegan were mine. Throughout dinner I had noticed women sneaking glances in our direction to get a glimpse of my handsome dinner guest. What were they thinking, watching us enjoy a dinner for two? Did they think we were together? I snickered at the thought. Keegan was unbelievably hot, and I was . . . well, me. That should be enough to allay their suspicions. Nevertheless, it was sweet to pretend we were together, even if only for an evening.

While Keegan pulled out his credit card, I checked my phone to see whether Naresh had texted me about meeting up later in the week. Although I had no messages from Naresh, I had four text messages and a missed call from Alex. True to form, Alex was desperate for information on Keegan. I figured I should call him sooner rather than later before he developed an ulcer. If anything, I would be doing a kindness for Patrick, who by now must be at his wits end watching Alex pace relentlessly around their apartment.

"If you'll excuse me," I requested, shoving my phone into my pants pocket. "I'm going to use the ladies' room before our little adventure in the park." Nodding in response, Keegan leaned back casually, indicating he was in no rush.

"Take your time," he replied. Smiling appreciatively, I stood to make my way toward the bathroom. I felt a little unsteady, having consumed a couple of pale ales and two glasses of wine over the course of the evening. It probably didn't help that I'd changed into the pair of black high-heeled wedges I'd purchased during the day's shopping trip, but they were too lovely not to wear to such an important meeting. In this line of work, your appearance was ninety percent your credibility at first blush. If you couldn't dress yourself like you understood design, how could you make business decisions that directly affected fashion?

Trying not to wobble, I started weaving through the tables until I made my way into a hallway out of Keegan's line of sight. Pulling out my phone and dialing Alex, I waited patiently as it rang, excited to tell him about Naresh's excellent choice in designers.

"Hale!" Alex shrieked on the other end of the phone. "I didn't think I'd hear from you for at least another hour." Chuckling, I shook my head.

"Well then why did you text me a hundred times?" I asked him. "It's like you thought I'd forget to call you."

"Never!" He responded, pretending to be offended by my accusation. "I was just . . . excited. Okay, enough chit chat, did you meet the designer?"

"Yes," I confirmed, ignoring his pushiness. "And I also saw his initial sketches. Which were amazing, by the way."

"His?" Alex questioned. "For some reason the way Naresh talked about him I thought he'd be a woman."

"Nope, he's definitely a guy," I responded, too fervently. Catching onto my tone, Alex suspected my attraction immediately.

"Wow, and a cute one at that, huh?" He inquired. Blushing, I was relieved we weren't having this discussion face to face. It was annoying how well he could read me.

"Well, sure," I admitted, trying not to reveal my true feelings. "But more importantly, Alex, I think you'll like him. Naresh really hit the jackpot with this guy."

"AH! I'm so relieved." Alex's breath escaped him as if he'd been holding it in for hours. "With our track record, I didn't have the highest hopes. And the last thing I wanted was to reject a designer who comes personally recommended by an important client."

"I know," I agreed. "You won't have to worry about rejecting him. He has some really great ideas, and he's also totally normal, which is a huge bonus. Look, I've gotta go," I told him, urgently. "I'm still having dinner with him, but I wanted to give you an update so you wouldn't freak out while waiting for me to call."

"Oh! Go, go, go," he responded. "Call me when you leave, though. I need to hear more."

"Okay," I agreed, as two women in their early twenties passed by me giggling raucously. "We're actually just about to pay, so it won't be too much longer."

"Alright, Hale." I could tell Alex was a little disappointed about having to wait for my next call. "By the way, what's his name?" He asked.

"Keegan Bransford," I shared. I liked the way his name sounded on my lips.

"Hmm, I've never heard of him," Alex said thoughtfully. "Well, anyway, Hale. I'll talk to you soon." I bid Alex farewell and hung up the phone.

On my way back to the table, I watched as Keegan leaned back in his chair, his hands crossed casually behind his head, surveying the bar scene with mild interest. He was patient and calm as he waited for his dinner guest to return. It was like out of a dream that I was the one for whom he was waiting.

"Ready?" Keegan asked as I approached the table. His eyes lit up when he spotted me.

"Ready," I confirmed, reciprocating his energy with a big smile. I grabbed my jacket and stuck my phone in the pocket. Keegan pointed to my shopping bags as he stood.

"I didn't notice those before," he said, raising his eyebrows. "You had an impressive shopping day, I see." I reached down for them, embarrassed that I hadn't returned to the hotel before dinner to leave them.

"Yes, I meant to drop them off at the hotel," I confessed, "but it's easy to lose track of time in this city." Keegan nodded knowingly and motioned for me to go ahead. As I passed him, he placed his hand on my lower back to guide me through the small space between him and the neighboring table. Although it was a brief touch, it was enough to send chills up my spine. I glanced back at him and smiled. He winked at me with his beautiful blue eyes. After that, it was a miracle I made it through the crowded restaurant without falling on my face.

As we approached the elevator, I realized that for the first time tonight, we were completely alone. Feeling my anxiety increase with each passing second, I focused on breathing evenly and prayed that my face was not as deep a red as it felt.

Pressing the button to call the elevator, Keegan looked at me with a concerned expression. "You okay, Haley?" He asked. "No offense, but you don't look like you feel so hot." I shook my head and waved my hand, dismissing his concern.

"I'm fine," I assured him, gulping down my nerves. "I'm not a huge fan of elevators." The lie came to me easily.

"Yeah," he agreed. "I'm not the biggest fan, either. We'll get through it together." He smiled and once again put his hand on the small of my back to guide me into the elevator. With the bulk of my bags, the two of us remained close as the elevator doors closed, but neither of us said a word. I tried not to concentrate on the heat of his breath or the heavy thumping in my chest. Instead, I watched as the numbers of the floors decreased as we descended, almost as if they were counting down our time alone together. Although I liked being close to Keegan, I was relieved when the elevator doors finally opened. The close quarters and tense silence were making me uncomfortable.

"After you," Keegan said, holding the door like a gentleman as I gathered my things. I smiled coyly and stepped into the market's maze of Italian food. "This way," Keegan directed from behind me, pointing toward the same doors through which I'd entered earlier.

Having forgotten that it was still early spring, I shivered dramatically when we stepped out onto the sidewalk, the brisk chill in the air catching me by surprise. "Oh, it isn't that bad." Keegan poked at me playfully.

"I know," I responded defensively, "but eating on the rooftop tonight threw me off. The heaters made me forget it was still so cold outside." I shivered again as a strong breeze came barreling down the street. Dropping my shopping bags, I rubbed my arms for some heat. "I don't understand why they call Chicago the Windy City," I complained. "New York is just as bad, if not worse." Grunting, I tightened my scarf around my neck and buttoned the top button of my jacket.

"Well, where we're going also has heaters," Keegan reassured me, pointing into the park. "The faster we get to that little building in the park, the faster you can be warm again." I nodded and drew in a deep breath, refusing to let a bout of chilly weather put a wrinkle in our evening. Grabbing some of my bags with his right hand, Keegan walked up to me and extended his left arm for me to take before crossing the street. "In the meantime, I'll do my best to keep you warm," he said softly. I smiled back at him more suggestively than I'd intended and intertwined my arm in his. I leaned against him as we crossed the street, huddling close to his warm body. Our contact felt quite intimate. It excited me, but I was unsure of how to act. I didn't want our potential business relationship to take an inappropriate turn, but I also didn't want to miss out on what was continuing to feel like a successful first date.

I shivered again once we were across the street, our arms still intertwined.

"You sure you want a milkshake?" Keegan asked, his face close to mine. "It won't help you get any warmer."

"Oh, I'm sure," I confirmed adamantly, matching his steps. "I haven't had a shake from this place in years!" Stopping suddenly, Keegan slipped his arm out from under mine and looked at me.

"You've already been here?" He asked, taken aback by my unintended admission. "Why didn't you say anything when I was talking about it?" I looked at him sheepishly, not quite sure how to explain myself.

"Well," I started guiltily. "You seemed excited about sharing it – I thought it was cute." I bit my bottom lip, afraid that I had gone too far, but Keegan's confused expression quickly turned into a playful smile.

"Cute, huh?" He asked presumptively. He took a step toward me, moving dangerously close. Laughing nervously, I tried to diffuse the situation by confessing the other things I'd withheld throughout the evening.

"You know," I started, heading determinedly toward the back of the park again, "I actually lived here for two years right out of college." My attempt to distract him worked.

"You did? Why didn't you tell me?" He asked, again surprised that I hadn't mentioned it during dinner.

"I don't know," I admitted softly, looking at the ground in shame. "I was embarrassed, I guess. I . . . I moved here to follow a boy." The words spilled out before I had a chance to stop them. I didn't know why I was suddenly opening up to Keegan about my past. I normally didn't speak of it to anyone.

"Why would you be embarrassed?" He inquired. "A lot of people move for their significant other." I scoffed.

"Yes, well, not always a wise decision," I said, my voice flat and bitter. I'd moved to New York to follow my then-fiancé, Brayden, a musician. About a year later, on my birthday, I'd arrived home to find Brayden fondling an aspiring brunette model in our bed.

"I'm sorry," Keegan said from behind me. I wondered whether I'd been talking out loud.

"About what?" I asked, feigning innocence, trying to steer the conversation away from Brayden. The two of us had had such a wonderful evening. I didn't want to tarnish it with a discussion about my past. Keegan gave me a knowing look, but let it go as I turned back toward the shack. He placed his arm around my shoulders to bring me in close once again, but didn't say anything else about it. It felt good to be in his arms.

"Shit." Keegan cursed in disappointment as we approached our destination. There were still people eating and talking at the surrounding tables, but the restaurant was dark and the order window closed. "I didn't think it closed until after eleven." My hope for a shake fading, I looked at my watch. It was 11:15 p.m. How had it gotten to be so late?

"We were at dinner for well over three hours!" I exclaimed in disbelief. "I hadn't realized." Kicking the gravel, Keegan looked at me apologetically.

"I'm sorry," Keegan offered, removing his arm from my shoulders. "I didn't know it was that late, either." Standing together in awkward silence, I started to rock on the balls of my feet, disappointed that our night was coming to too soon an end.

"There's gelato back in the market," Keegan suggested hopefully, trying to salvage our dessert plans.

"No," I responded, defeated. "I noticed the gelateria was closed when we were walking out." Glancing at him regretfully, I knew the night – my little fantasy – was over. "I should go," I told him reluctantly. "It's getting late and I'm not really sure whether I'm flying out tomorrow." I had booked a departing flight for noon, but didn't know whether Naresh would want to meet again before I flew back to the Midwest.

"Okay then," Keegan responded. It lifted my spirits to hear him sound equally defeated. "Let's hail you a cab." Making our way toward the curb, Keegan placed his arm on my lower back to guide me yet again. He left it there until we reached the street. I glanced up at him affectionately, wishing I could bottle up the moment and keep it with me forever.

Looking down the street, Keegan raised his arm high at an empty van taxi making its way toward us. "Maybe you'll be on cash cab," he joked, lowering his arm as the taxi slowed. I laughed.

"I'll split my winnings with you," I promised. I turned and looked at him more seriously. "Thanks for a really great night, Keegan." He smiled fiercely.

Clearing my throat, I tried to end on a professional note to remind us both that this had been a business meeting, after all. "I think Alex will really like your sketches," I said, as the cab pulled up to the curb. "We should get you two together. I'll get in touch with Naresh. Hopefully we can arrange something soon." Smiling at me placidly as I opened the sliding door, Keegan said nothing. Sad to be leaving him, I piled my bags into the van and reached to pull the door closed.

"Haley, hold on a second," Keegan said, stopping me. "You forgot something." Thinking I had left one of my shopping bags, I counted them in the cab. All accounted for. Turning back to the opening in the door to see what I could have left behind, I found Keegan so close to me our faces were almost touching. Frozen in place, I gaped at him as he brushed my hair lightly away from my mouth. Running his finger along my cheekbone, he whispered, "I've been waiting to do this all night." I sat in shocked silence as he reached his hand behind my head and pulled my lips to his in a forceful and passionate kiss. In that moment, Alex and *De Alexia* were instantly wiped from my thoughts. The exhilarating feel and unforgettable taste of Keegan Bransford were all that remained.

5 CHEERS

I woke up to the sound of knocking on my door. "Housekeeping?" A woman inquired. In my state of confused elation last night, I must have neglected to hang the 'Do Not Disturb' sign in the hall. Groaning, I turned over to look at the clock. It was only 8:30 in the morning. My alarm wasn't set to go off for another hour.

"I'm still sleeping!" I called, a little too angrily. Although I loved this hotel, I hated how early the cleaning staff started making their rounds.

"Okay, we'll come back later," the woman announced politely, and moved on to a neighboring door to repeat the cycle with another unsuspecting guest. Turning on my back, I shut my eyes tightly, trying to stave off the flood of thoughts rushing to my head. I had hoped that once I finally managed to sleep, I would wake with newfound clarity. Unfortunately, however, I woke just as overwhelmed, if not more so, as I was when I'd gone to bed last night.

Of course, I was surprised and excited by Keegan's passionate kiss. It had been a long time since anyone had electrified me in such a way, and I had never kissed someone as attractive as Keegan. But his kiss also introduced undesirable complications. I worried that I'd succumbed to my feelings for him too willingly, and that our exhilarating, but brief bout of intimacy last night would impact his potential relationship with *De Alexia*. Similarly, I was concerned about what Alex might say. I wondered whether I should tell him. Pressing my hands to my head, I gripped my hair to relieve some of the tension in my scalp. It was all so overwhelming. I wasn't sure what to do.

As I tossed and turned in bed, my phone buzzed from the other side of the room, indicating I had a new message. I popped out of bed more willingly than usual, anxious to see who was texting me. I hoped it was Keegan, confirming that he, too, was reeling from the way our night together had ended. Sadly, however, my hopes were not to be fulfilled. Over the course of the night and early morning, I had received four texts, a missed call, and a voicemail, none of which were from Keegan. Disappointed, I grabbed the phone and carried it back to the warm bed, sliding comfortably back between the sheets.

Scrolling through my messages, I smiled to see one from Lindsay, expressing her hope that dinner last night had gone well. I grinned stupidly, remembering the way Keegan's lips had felt on my own. Not sure yet how to respond, I moved on to the other texts.

The second was from Naresh: *Sorry I had to bail last night. What did you think of Keegan? If you liked him, we should set up another meeting soon.* My grin dropped quickly into a concerned frown as I worried about Naresh finding out what had happened last night. He was *De Alexia*'s biggest and most important client, and although we were friends, I couldn't imagine he would appreciate the unprofessional end to my meeting with Keegan. Developing footwear for Alex's line was almost as important to Naresh's business as it was to ours. Riddled with guilt, I texted Naresh that I would call him within the hour.

The last two text messages, not surprisingly, were from Alex, scolding me for not calling after dinner as I'd promised. Sighing, I rested the phone on my chest and stared at the ceiling. I had to call him, but I wasn't sure what to say. Alex was one of my best friends, but he was also my boss.

As a friend, I wanted nothing more than to spill all of last night's juicy details without reservation. But as an employee, I wanted to hide my lack of professionalism and act like nothing had happened. The idea of lying to Alex was unsettling, but I knew he'd blow the situation out of proportion. Not wanting to deal with his overreaction, I decided not to tell Alex about the kiss until after Keegan's relationship with *De Alexia* was more secure.

I looked down as my phone buzzed again. Naresh had responded quickly. *No need for a call*, the message read, *as long as you can meet me for drinks tonight.* I wondered whether he intended to include Keegan in the meeting. My heart skipped excitedly at the thought.

Where and when? I inquired.

9:30. Wine bar on Stone Street. I was surprised by Naresh's choice of location. Stone Street was located on the southern tip of the island in the heart of the Financial District. It was a serious hike from my hotel in Midtown and far enough from Naresh's boutique in SoHo to require a train or a cab. It also wasn't exactly known for its raging nightlife. I thought it was a strange place to meet, but didn't ask any questions.

I'll be there, I confirmed.

****

Hanging up with the airline, I rubbed my temples soothingly in efforts to relieve the unpleasant headache I'd developed. I'd been on the phone for an exhausting half an hour trying to change my flight to the next morning – a conversation that should have taken two minutes. I shook my head, trying to understand why certain things were always so difficult. It was as if the airlines, credit card companies, and cable providers had entered into a contest to see who could provide the most painstakingly mind numbing customer service experiences. After my phone call, the airlines had catapulted comfortably into the lead.

Continuing to massage my temples, I set my phone onto the bed, trying, without success, to gather the courage to call Alex. Welcoming any distraction, I realized I hadn't yet checked my voicemail. My only missed call was from my brother in Nashville. Curious to hear why he was calling, I scrolled to the message and pressed play. The familiar sound of his deep, happy voice rose to greet me immediately.

"Hey Hale. It's Michael. Been a while . . . so I'm sure you already know, but the anniversary's coming up. Wanted to confirm our regular plans – the beer, the lawn chairs, etcetera. Call me back and let me know what to bring this time. Love you." The swirl of emotion stemming from Keegan's kiss was quickly displaced by feelings of nostalgia and grief.

I erased the message and put the phone down slowly as I leaned back on my pillow, folding my arms across my chest. With all of the craziness going on with *De Alexia* I had completely forgotten that the anniversary of Dad's death was in two short weeks. I hadn't thought about it once. Angry with myself for not realizing it was so near, I looked at my calendar. Thankfully, the day was free of any meetings or trips. I could continue our family tradition unencumbered.

Every year on the anniversary of Dad's death, my brother and I would meet at Dad's grave in Cincinnati, no matter the cost or inconvenience. We hadn't skipped an anniversary once in almost fifteen years. In the early years, as a couple of lost preteens, we would stand in front of his grave and mourn for an hour, trying to figure out how to remember and celebrate our dearly missed dad. As we grew older, however, our visits turned into a glorified tailgate of sorts, complete with food, beer, and music.

Now, every year at noon on April 21st, my brother and I would plant our lawn chairs next to Dad's headstone and crack open some beers. Rain or shine, our visits usually lasted for hours, rendering both of us way too drunk to drive home. There were a couple of years it was so stormy that we had almost given up. But no matter what the weather, we always pulled through for Dad.

Sometimes we would reminisce about him, sharing our favorite memories until we were too tired to laugh or cry. Other times, we would chat about what was going on in our own lives, catching up as if we had met for coffee on a random afternoon. Our tradition was actually a great way for us to spend some uninterrupted time together. And I liked to think that Dad enjoyed the time we spent updating him on our lives.

Mother had participated in the early years – mostly out of necessity because neither Michael nor I could drive. But as the years passed and Michael and I were able to operate a car on our own, Mother 'moved on' and stopped coming altogether. I doubt she had been to Dad's grave for nearly a decade. Although I liked visiting Dad without her, I had a hard time forgiving her for forgetting him. It was like she had tossed that part of our lives aside while she was busy becoming Mrs. Whomever whenever the mood was right. To date, she had been married and divorced three times since Dad's death.

The first marriage came only five years after he died, to a man she met during grief counseling. She told me she would never remarry, only to renege on that promise when I was seventeen. Their wedding invitations featured the catchphrase, "It's never too late for happily ever after." It made me sick. Watching her marry man after man then toss them aside left me wondering whether she would have done the same to Dad had he lived.

Sighing, I rolled out of bed to use the bathroom. Although I was a little distracted by anger and grief, thinking about my family had cleared my head a bit. For the first time since I'd met Keegan, I didn't feel as if the world were spinning like an out of control Merry-Go-Round. I felt more grounded and in control. Now was the perfect time to call Alex.

"Well, you're up and at 'em this morning!" Alex observed enthusiastically when he picked up the phone. As expected, he seemed surprised to be hearing from me this early in the morning.

"Yes, well, I didn't sleep all that well," I admitted, preparing to blame the alcohol.

"Yeah, sorry you've been in hotels so much lately," Alex replied apologetically. "But hopefully, after this shoe business is taken care of, you can take a bit of a break from New York City."

"That would be nice," I responded. I was tired of traveling, even though traveling was what had ultimately led me to Keegan.

"Sooooo Hale, tell me about this designer. I want to know every little detail." I hesitated, but not for long.

"Ah, yes, Keegan," I began. I felt my face flush, grateful for the hundreds of miles that separated me from my excitable friend. "Alex, he's perfect. His designs are dead on, he's normal, he's easygoing, and he's excited about helping out Naresh – and us. I think you'll really like him."

"Wow." Alex seemed stunned. "That's a pretty strong endorsement, Hale. Shocking positivity from a seasoned cynic." Alex laughed, but his observation suddenly made me nervous. I barely knew Keegan, and here I was endorsing him and his designs like I'd known him for years. Alex was the only other person I'd ever talked about like that. I was concerned that my attraction had obliterated my objectivity. "He must have really made an impression," Alex added.

"Well, I mean, I had one dinner with him, Alex," I said, backtracking. I hoped desperately I hadn't let my feelings for Keegan influence the way I did my job. Nevertheless, I couldn't go back on my endorsement of him now. "But hands down, this guy is leagues above anyone else we've ever tried to work with." I stated it confidently.

"Okay then," Alex said, matter-of-factly. "I trust you." I gulped. He shouldn't trust me. Not after last night. "So what happens now?" He asked. "What did Naresh say after the meeting?" Shifting uncomfortably, I forgot I hadn't mentioned Naresh's absence.

"Well I'm actually staying another day to meet Naresh for drinks," I replied. "He had to leave in the middle of dinner for some emergency at Resh+001 . . . he wants to talk about next steps this evening."

"Gotcha," Alex stated without a hint of suspicion or concern. "Well, let me know what he says. Obviously we don't want to make any promises to anyone until I've met this supposedly brilliant shoe designer."

"Obviously," I responded, sitting down at the edge of the bed. "How's Columbus? Anything exciting happening at the store?" I jumped at the chance to change the subject.

"Nothing crazy," Alex replied. "We do need to start thinking about hiring another associate to replace Dom, though. He told me he plans to stop working soon after he graduates. It's only about a month away." I groaned, hoping Alex wouldn't ask me to help with the hiring process. Alex chided me immediately. "Oh, cut it out, Hale," he scolded. "Patrick is going to handle it. Unlike other people, P is willing to help me because he loves me."

"Oh, shush," I protested. "You know I'm willing to help, but I hate interviewing all of those people. And you know how bad I am at first impressions – I never read people right."

"Oh, I know," Alex stated, agreeing with my self-assessment. "Which is why I'm slightly nervous about your firm endorsement of this Keegan dude." I cringed, disappointed we were back to talking about him.

"Well, like you said, Alex, you'll meet him before anyone makes a blood oath." Alex laughed.

"This is true," he said. "Which is why I'm anxious to meet him."

"You will soon enough," I assured him. "I'll call you after drinks with Naresh tonight if it's not too late."

"No," Alex replied. "I don't care how late it is – call me no matter what. It was torture enough to wait on you last night; don't forget me this time!"

Confident that my meeting with Naresh wouldn't end like my meeting with Keegan, I assured Alex I would call.

"And then I'll see you tomorrow afternoon," I stated. "In person."

"Okay, love," Alex replied. "Thanks for everything. You're amazing." Although his gratitude made me smile, I also felt guilty. If he'd known what happened last night, he probably wouldn't want to thank me for *everything*.

"You're welcome, Alex. I'll talk to you tonight." Hanging up the phone, I crawled into bed for more sleep, trying to ignore the guilt and shame tugging lightly at my conscience.

****

Stepping off the 4 Train and into the Wall Street subway station, I tied the belt on my jacket as tight as it would go. It was unseasonably cold for an early spring night, and I hadn't packed accordingly. I was dressed in neutral peep toe stilettos, a cropped turquoise sweater, and a pair of light skinny jeans, which did little to protect me from the cold northeastern air. Regretting my decision to lay around the hotel all day instead of shop for warmer clothes, I climbed the stairs to street level, bracing myself for the short walk to Stone Street.

Emerging onto the sidewalk, I surveyed my surroundings to get my bearings. I knew where I was almost immediately when I saw the high, triangular steeple of Trinity Church. The Episcopalian church – a New York City landmark and beautiful embodiment of Gothic Revival architecture – marked the location of Wall Street with pride and importance. Stone Street (more officially known as Pearl Street) was only a block or two away.

Making my way carefully down Wall Street's cobblestones, I realized I had never been to this part of Manhattan when it wasn't overcrowded with people in high-priced suits rushing around the streets like the world was on fire. Almost 9:30 at night, Wall Street was eerily still, the New York Stock Exchange having closed several hours earlier.

Unlike most other parts of Manhattan, the Financial District didn't offer substantial evening dining and after-hours establishments. People commuted to the southern most part of the island to work, and then commuted back to

New Jersey, Brooklyn, Upper Manhattan, or wherever else they called home. It was weird to feel alone in a place that, during the day, was normally teeming with people. The deserted feel of it gave me the creeps.

Turning down Stone Street, I was relieved to finally sense life again pulsating from the various bars and restaurants that lined the City's oldest street. This particular section of Pearl Street was pedestrian only, usually providing a break from the fast-paced and busy surrounding roads. While the cobblestone street and historic brick buildings gave the area an appealing early twentieth century feel, the stones made it difficult to navigate in heels. Thankfully, I reached the wine bar without any mishaps, with one minute to spare.

When I walked in, I spotted Naresh sitting alone at the bar guarding an empty seat to his right. There was no sign of Keegan. His absence both disappointed and relieved me, my stomach churning with a confusing mix of emotions. Seeing me almost immediately, Naresh waved and motioned for me to take a seat on the stool next to him. As I walked toward the bar, resigned to the fact that it would be just the two of us, I absorbed the scene around me.

The wine bar's modern vibe was drastically different from the old world feel of the street outside. Decorated in a clean modern style, the bar had a luxurious, upscale feel but gave off a stuffy aura – one I didn't particularly like. To be honest, I was surprised to be meeting Naresh in such a place. He was as far from a snob as anyone I'd met in the industry. I didn't expect he would enjoy a place like this.

"Hi!" I exclaimed, greeting Naresh with a hug before settling into my seat.

"Hey, Haley. Good to see you," he responded warmly. Holding up his phone and exaggerating its placement in his pocket, he smiled at me. "No retail emergencies tonight, I promise." Looking at him warningly, I scolded him for jinxing his luck.

"You never know Naresh – disasters can happen at all hours of the day. You shouldn't put it away where you can't hear it." Nodding his head in agreement and chuckling, he took a quick sip of his drink.

"This is true. Very true." Peering up at the bartender as he approached, Naresh asked me what I was drinking. Thinking about it, I leaned over to take a whiff of his nearly empty glass. The scent of mint wafted toward me invitingly.

"I think the more important question is, what are you drinking?" I asked him. "Whatever it is, it smells amazing." Picking up his drink, he held it out for me to taste.

"Have a sip," he offered. "It's a mint julep. Delicious." Obliging him with a small sip, I nodded my head in agreement.

"I think I'll have one as well," I concluded.

"Excellent!" Naresh responded, turning toward the bartender to order two more drinks. Although he always looked well put together, Naresh looked especially dashing this evening, dressed in smart navy blue suit pants and perfectly polished black dress shoes. His winter coat was draped carefully over the bar stool, revealing his matching suit jacket, pink shirt, and dark navy tie.

"You're awfully dressed up for the occasion," I observed, wondering where he'd been. Looking down at his suit and rolling his eyes, Naresh loosened his tie again as if it were suffocating him.

"Yes, I came straight from a benefit," he said. "Normally I love benefits; free booze, good causes, good people. But tonight was more obligatory than anything. It was a benefit for the American India Foundation. I normally love the foundation, but tonight I was asked to babysit the keynote speaker, who turned out to be your typical diva CEO. After seventy-five requests for different kinds of sparkling water, I was ready to get out of there." I laughed and grabbed the mint julep the bartender was offering me.

"I'm sorry it was such a crummy night," I offered, taking a drink. "Who was the speaker?" Waving his hand to indicate it didn't matter, he too took a sip of his newly made cocktail.

"Some Indian CEO of a communications company – you wouldn't know him." Slightly offended by his assumption, I narrowed my eyes.

"Try me," I dared. Turning to me with curiosity, Naresh shared his name. "Nope," I responded. "Don't know him." Laughing, Naresh shook his head and took another drink.

"So I'm dying to know, Haley," he started, getting down to business. "How did last night go after I left?" Looking at me expectantly, he waited for me to respond. I blinked dispassionately, trying to give nothing away that might hint toward the night's exhilarating, but inappropriate ending.

"It went really well!" I exclaimed as positively as possible. "Keegan is easy to get along with and after taking a quick peek at his initial designs, I think he'll be able to create some really great shoes for the line." Clearly pleased, Naresh clapped his hands together in triumph.

"I knew you'd like him!" He gushed. "Keegan told me you two got along really well, but I wanted to make sure you felt the same way." Blushing a little, I wondered what else Keegan had told him. At this point, it didn't seem to matter. Judging by Naresh's excitement, he was pleased by whatever news he'd received.

"Yes," I admitted. "We got along great. The only final piece of the puzzle is getting Keegan and Alex together to make sure *they* can work together. If that goes as well as it should, we can get a deal on the books and get production rolling for the summer and fall lines." Still smiling, Naresh nodded in agreement.

"I'll call Keegan immediately and try to get him on a flight to Columbus within the week," he stated. "I think it's aggressive to plan to get a shoe or two out for the summer, but we can always try." He pulled out his phone. I was surprised that he would suggest a meeting in Columbus. Even the most down-to-earth people in New York assumed that any important business meeting would happen in Manhattan. Nursing my drink, I watched Naresh as he waited patiently for Keegan to pick up.

"Hey, Keegan, it's Naresh – what's up?" Smiling, he chuckled at the way Keegan responded. "Well, all's clear if you'd like to join us," he continued. A feeling of dread and excitement washed over me like a heavy blanket. "Okay, buddy," I heard him say. "See you in a few minutes." Hanging up, he turned to me and smiled.

"Is he meeting us?" I asked, trying not to sound anxious.

"Yup," Naresh responded, like it wasn't a big deal. "That's why I decided to meet down here. He lives in the Trump building on Wall Street, right around the corner. I figured if you were interested in moving forward with the deal – or at least willing to get Keegan and Alex together – we should all celebrate!" Feeling a little woozy, I concentrated hard on keeping it together for Naresh. I didn't know what it was about Keegan Bransford that made me fall to pieces, but just thinking about his presence sent my blood pressure to the roof.

"Great!" I exclaimed, gulping down my anxiety with a swig of my drink. "Well, that explains why you wanted to meet down here," I continued. "It's shocking how dead it gets at night – walking down Wall Street is creepy when no one's around!" Naresh nodded.

"I know, it's weird," he replied. "Keegan claims he likes living down here because it's quiet at night. It's surprising for a guy who loves to party." He laughed and swirled his drink in tight circles to mix the ingredients. I raised my eyebrows, interested to hear more.

"How long have you known him?" I asked. But before he could respond, someone he knew interrupted by slapping him on the shoulder with a raucous, 'Well look who it is!' After a brief introduction, I sat there awkwardly as they chatted about people I didn't know and parties I hadn't attended.

I was uncomfortable being the odd man out, but I only had to sit there for a couple of minutes before Keegan walked into the bar. Although I didn't think it possible, he looked even better than he had the night before, dressed in a navy wool jacket and gray jeans, his bright blue eyes somehow sparkling in the dark. As he approached, he winked at me in acknowledgment and pointed to the two men having a conversation at the bar to my left with curious interest. I shrugged and smiled, watching as Keegan interrupted their conversation to give Naresh a quick hug. Their interaction was brief, but nevertheless hinted that they were more than just colleagues. I wondered how close the two of them were outside of work. Turning toward me, Keegan smiled knowingly, as if he and I possessed a secret no one else in the world knew. I suppose we did. I smiled back shyly, weakened by the power of his stare.

"Haley, it's great to see you again so soon," he said, leaning in to give me a kiss on the cheek. The feel of his lips against my skin made me breathless.

"You too," I said as matter-of-factly as possible, avoiding his eye contact.

"Well I see you two have started without me," Keegan observed, rubbing his hands together. "Do you need a refill?" Glancing down at my drink, I realized I had drained it. It was like my comfort blanket, giving my mouth and hands something to do while I sat alone at the bar, waiting for Naresh to finish his conversation.

"Yes, please," I responded. "Mint julep."

"Ah," Keegan said. He looked at Naresh, who had finally refocused his attention on Keegan and me. "I see you've taken a liking to my friend's favorite drink." Naresh smiled.

"She has amazing taste," he joked, turning to me to apologize for the previous interruption. I told him it wasn't a big deal.

"One mint julep coming up, then," Keegan declared. "However, if we're celebrating tonight, how about some tequila shots as well?" Keegan looked at me and raised his eyebrows, gauging my reaction. Staring back at him stoically, I tried hard to hide my displeasure. I had no interest in taking shots. Shots did *not* agree with me, especially tequila. When I didn't say anything, Keegan turned to Naresh. "Whaddya say, my friend?" Naresh smiled with approval.

"Tequila it is!" He responded enthusiastically. My heart dropped a little and I gulped as stomach bile began to rise in my throat. I wanted desperately to bow out of the celebration, but was ultimately more concerned about what Keegan and Naresh would think if I refused to participate than the negative effects of the liquor. I knew it was juvenile, but I wanted to belong. Passing on the tequila might make me seem lame or judgmental. I didn't want to appear that way, especially in front of Keegan.

As Keegan approached the bar, Naresh looked at me and leaned in, checking to make sure I was okay. "No worries if you're not up for it," he said quietly. It was as if he could sense my reluctance.

"No, no," I said quietly, dismissing his concern. "We're celebrating!" I smiled with as much gusto as I could muster. I couldn't believe I was agreeing to this.

After our three shots of top shelf tequila were served, the three of us turned to each other and held up our liquid fire. I stared at it ominously, reassuring myself that it was only one shot. I could do it. One little shot. "To our potential partnership!" Naresh exclaimed, interrupting my internal pep talk. "Well, I guess, more accurately, partnerships." Looking at him with consideration, Keegan raised his shot glass above the rest.

"Here, here!" He exclaimed. "To our potential partnerships!" He smiled at me devilishly, his attractiveness at an all-time high. I raised my shot glass in response, thinking of something clever to say in return.

"Cheers!" I declared, failing to devise much else. Tapping our glasses together in conclusion, we all took our shots, grimacing as the tequila burned menacingly down our throats.

6 ONE HELL OF A HANGOVER

I woke up in a daze as my phone rang loudly from the nightstand. I grumbled softly, my head splintering as I turned over to reach for it, wanting nothing more than to silence the awful noise. My stomach churned menacingly with the slightest movement. Blurred images of dancing and taking shots flashed across my mind. I cringed, dreading the unpleasant day that lay ahead.

Hands down, my least favorite part of my job had become partying with the boutique's clients. Don't get me wrong; I loved to go out to bars, have a few drinks, and sometimes get a little drunk before calling it a night. But to the crazies in the design world, my version of a night out was their version of a night in. Most designers, especially in New York, hit the party circuit hard and refused to stop until the sun came up. Naresh and Keegan had proven to be no different. Unfortunately for my weak stomach, I was in for a hell of a hangover for at least the next twenty-four hours.

Annoyed and delirious, I squinted at my phone screen to see who was calling. "Oh, great," I murmured, realizing that it was the taxi service calling to tell me which car would be picking me up for the airport. I was thankful the car company had called because I obviously hadn't thought to set an alarm last night.

I let it go to voicemail and checked the clock, realizing that I only had fifteen minutes before I needed to be out of the hotel. Gingerly pulling my legs out from under the sheets and setting my feet on the floor, I sat up, grasping my throbbing head in my hands. Although I should have been frantically getting ready to leave, the thought of doing anything besides lying in the bed was excruciating.

Pressing my pulsating temples, I looked at my phone again, this time noticing that I had several missed calls and text messages from Alex. It appeared as though I had forgotten to call him for the second night in a row. By now, he was probably pretty pissed at me for blowing him off.

Grabbing the phone and dragging myself into the bathroom, I started to scroll through Alex's messages as I sat on the toilet and prayed for my head to stop throbbing. Still operating in a daze, I was perplexed as I read Alex's texts.

1:26 AM: *Hale, you promised you'd call. Did you forget? Are you sleeping? Don't make me slap you.*

1:56 AM: *Okay, I'm officially annoyed at you unless you call me right now.*

2:01 AM: *Hale! WTF!? Who are you with? I'm worried. You're hammered. Call me back! Could NOT understand a single thing you just said.*

2:13 AM: *Hale – definitely not funny. I am calling the hotel in T minus 5 minutes if you don't call me.*

2:25 AM: *Um, hotel said you're okay, but wouldn't tell me whether you have company. Who the hell is with you!? HALEY BLYTHE SIMPSON . . . WHAT IS GOING ON!?*

7:15 AM: *Call me as soon as you wake up. If you don't, I will fire you. And then punch you in the face.*

In a state of utter confusion, I read Alex's text messages again. I couldn't remember much of the night, which wasn't entirely surprising given the fact that I'd taken three shots of tequila at the wine bar in a span of twenty minutes. I checked my call log. Sure enough, I had called Alex at two o'clock in the morning. No wonder he'd been worried. At that point in the night, my sentences had probably been incomprehensible. He must have panicked when he heard Naresh and Keegan's voices in the background of wherever the hell we were. I hoped that when I explained the situation, he would understand.

Slowly, I stood to make my way back into the room to pack. The shower was heating up and fogging the bathroom mirror, but I wasn't confident I'd have the time to jump in before I needed to leave. Rubbing my eyes, I walked back into the room to find my suitcase. As soon as my eyes were able to focus, I panicked when I saw a man's naked body sprawled haphazardly on the other side of the bed.

Stifling a scream, I scurried frantically back into the bathroom to hide. I crumbled to the cold tile floor, clutching my cell phone to my bare chest and breathing heavily in panic. Almost instantly, memories from the night came rushing back to me like a flash flood. Careful not to make a noise, I held my breath and craned my neck around the bathroom door to confirm my foggy memory. Whipping my head back inside the bathroom, I closed my eyes in disbelief. I had slept with Keegan Bransford.

Paralyzed in a state of temporary shock, I racked my brain, trying desperately to figure out what to do next. I couldn't believe what I had done. Sure, Keegan was incredibly attractive and intoxicating, but I had only known him for two days! Not to mention the fact that he was an important potential business associate of *De Alexia*. I'd felt mildly guilty about kissing him the other night, but sleeping with him in a drunken stupor was a whole new level of irresponsibility. If I wasn't panicked about my imminent plane departure, I was certainly panicked now.

I searched my fuzzy memories, trying in vain to put the pieces of the night back together. I tried to remember what Naresh might have seen, but unfortunately, couldn't recall much of the evening after leaving the stuffy wine bar on Stone Street. I hoped Naresh hadn't witnessed anything inappropriate between Keegan and me, but given my uninhibited state, it was unlikely. I punched the tile floor in frustration. I would never forgive myself if Naresh's faith in me had been weakened to the point where he questioned the general integrity of *De Alexia*.

The possibility of screwing up the boutique's relationship with Naresh made me even more nauseous. Leaning my head back against the bathroom wall and closing my eyes, I thought about what Alex would say. Not wanting to consider the possibilities for very long, I glanced down at my phone to check the time. My car was scheduled to arrive in just under ten minutes. I felt defeated and sick on several levels. There was no way I could pack, get ready, and get out the door in such a short amount of time. And, of course, there was also a gorgeous naked man in my bed of whom I needed to dispose.

Pulling myself slowly off of the floor and turning the bathroom corner, I approached the bed awkwardly in search for some clothes. Hastily throwing on an old t-shirt and athletic shorts, I stood at the edge of the bed watching Keegan, my phone still clutched to my chest. As I stood there watching him sleep, I couldn't help but feel a little excited that he was here. The memory of my night was blurry and disconnected, but there was no forgetting Keegan's charm. He had held doors, feigned jealousy if men talked to me at the bars, and looked at me with those sapphire eyes as if he'd never be whole again unless we were together. For the first time since Brayden, I had felt attractive and wanted. It was an unfortunate aligning of the planets that the man making me feel this way was an important business contact.

Clearing my throat, I tried to stir Keegan from his coma, keeping my eyes focused determinedly on his face. Although we'd slept together last night, having to witness his full frontal in the sobering light of the morning made me very uncomfortable. When a few subtle "Ahems" didn't wake him, I started poking his foot with my right index finger, afraid to get any closer. I stopped jabbing him when he started to moan. Slowly opening one eye, Keegan smiled when he saw me standing anxiously at the foot of the bed.

"Good morning, beautiful," he whispered. Even now, Keegan's charms flustered me. All the blood rushed to my head, increasing my throbbing headache tenfold.

"Hi," I responded sheepishly, trying to ignore the pain while thinking of what to say.

"Come back to bed," he encouraged, sitting up and grabbing at me playfully. I stepped out of his reach and tried to focus on the task at hand. I would be lying if I didn't admit his offer was enticing.

"I can't," I told him regretfully. Keegan looked at me doubtingly.

"Are you trying to get me to beg?" He questioned playfully, sitting up and resting his hands behind his head, completely unashamed of his nudity. Avoiding his gaze, I powered through my emotions, now almost thankful for the hangover. The nausea and shooting pains in my head numbed the excitement and passion I would have likely been feeling otherwise.

"No," I assured him, embarrassed. "I have to leave here in . . . oh, look. Five minutes." Keegan sat there assessing my seriousness for a few seconds and then moved to get out of the bed. Facing away from me as he stood, he reached to grab his clothes from the floor. Trying to remain strong in my conviction, I couldn't help but notice that Keegan looked just as good from behind as he did from the front. A part of me melted as I watched him put on his boxers and pants, almost drooling as I stared at his perfect body. He was delectably fit and the perfect amount of hairy. I found myself longing to rub my hands on his chest and push him back into the bed for a quick romp.

"Shame you have to go," Keegan stated, putting on his shirt and snapping me back to reality. "I was looking forward to waking up with you this morning." I stared at him as he continued to put on his remaining clothes. I had woken up panicked, embarrassed, and confused, but Keegan had woken up as if nothing were out of the ordinary.

"I wish I could stay, too," I found myself admitting. What was I doing? "But I have to go back home and set up your meeting with Alex." The thought of telling Alex about what I'd done made me ill.

"You know," Keegan suggested, turning to face me, "you shouldn't tell him about us." I looked at him with confusion, half-wondering whether he'd read my mind.

"Why not?" I asked.

"He may not understand at first," Keegan explained. "We should just wait until the business relationship is off the ground before we ease everyone into the idea of you and me." *You and me.* His words echoed in my head like a broken record.

"Uh, okay," I responded, unsure how I should feel. He was asking me to lie to my employer and one of my best friends, but in doing so, he was also hinting that he expected the two of us to have some kind of future. *You and me.* It was both disturbing and exciting. Fully dressed, Keegan walked up to me and put his hands on either side of my face.

"I had a great time last night," he whispered, his breath somehow still fresh and sweet, his cologne still lingering on his clothes. Pulling me in close, he kissed me passionately, erasing my hangover symptoms for a brief moment. His lips felt warm and soft against my own. I suddenly wanted to beg him to stay, but thought better of it before he released me. I had too much to think about and I needed to be alone to clear my head. "Oh, and the same goes for Naresh," Keegan added, as he headed for the door. "He and I are friends, but we should definitely not tell him about this until the time is right." Blinking in disbelief, I found my voice again.

"Did he not suspect anything last night?" I asked, hopefully.

"No way," Keegan responded with confidence. "He left pretty early – don't you remember?" Ashamed that I had gotten so drunk so quickly, I pretended as if I had forgotten.

"Oh, right. I remember," I lied, relieved that Naresh remained ignorant of our indiscretions. Keegan stood at the doorway. He looked like a model in a catalogue, one hand in his pants pocket and one on the door, his cute brown hair messy from the night. I couldn't believe that this man was the least bit interested in me.

"I can't wait to see you again, Haley." Keegan flashed his dimple in my direction. Lingering for a moment in the doorway, he finally disappeared into the hallway and out of my sight.

When he'd been gone for about a minute, I let out an audible sigh and crumpled onto the bed to try and control my dizziness. I couldn't think, I couldn't breathe, and I couldn't stop spinning. After about a minute I realized there was no controlling it. Holding my stomach as I charged to the bathroom, I took a quick glance at the bedside clock. I wasn't sure of much, but two things seemed rather certain: 1) I was going to be sick; and 2) for only the second time in my life, I was going to miss my flight.

****

It cost me fifty bucks and some ridiculous fees with the car company to catch a plane two hours after my originally scheduled flight. Even though I literally bought myself some extra time to quell the queasiness of my hangover, I still used the plane's barf bag several times, much to the chagrin of the kind gentlemen sitting next to me.

Dealing with nausea, however, was the least of my problems. Thoughts about Keegan consumed my entire trip home. I dwelled on his suggestion to hide everything from Alex, wondering whether it was the right course of action. Neither Alex nor Naresh knew what had happened, and if I refrained from saying anything, it would stay that way. But at what cost? Other than my kiss with Keegan the previous night, I had never kept anything from Alex. I felt ashamed by my dishonesty, and uneasy about extending the lie. But if Keegan planned to commit to business with the boutique, notwithstanding our relationship, I didn't see any upside to sharing it, other than to clear my conscience. Maybe Keegan was right. Maybe it was best that our hook-up remained a secret for the time being. What harm could really come from this temporary omission?

As we landed in Columbus, I sent Alex a text indicating that I would head straight to his apartment from the airport. Although I'd decided to hold my tongue about Keegan, I still had a lot to explain. Alex had apparently heard me with Keegan last night and was fuming at my lack of communication over the past couple of days. I couldn't remember him ever being so mad at me.

Looking down at my buzzing phone, I saw Alex respond, *Great*. I knew that he meant it in the 'I would rather jump out of a plane without a parachute than see your face right now' way, but I had to let him know – from a business perspective at least – how the last couple of days had gone. Perhaps after hearing that Keegan wanted to meet him and get started on designing shoes, Alex would forgive my flakiness.

I made it quickly through the airport to avoid the stares of those who had witnessed me puking on the plane. Rushing out of the terminal from embarrassment was beginning to seem like the norm. After picking up my car, I drove toward Victorian Village with a heightened sense of anxiety. Confrontation was not my strong suit, and I knew that facing Alex would be unpleasant, at least initially.

Pulling over in front of Alex's place, I turned off my little blue car and laid my forehead on the wheel to try and find some relief from the horrible aching in my head and neck. In addition to my anxiety, my body was completely ravaged. My legs were swollen from the flight, and my head and neck ached from dehydration. I hadn't slept, I hadn't eaten, and I felt as if my thick lips would crack at a moment's notice.

Sitting in my seat, I wanted nothing more than to open the car door and lay face down in the cool spring grass. Lying peacefully in front of Alex's apartment, however, was not in the cards. Like a hawk perched patiently in wait for its prey, Alex had been waiting for me to arrive – a fact made clear to me when he suddenly banged his fist on my passenger side window.

"Are you dead?" Alex asked viciously, the car window muffling his inquiry. "I hope you're dead." Moving my head slowly in agony, I looked at him to prove that I was not yet dead. Studying my face, Alex quickly changed his look of exaggerated anger to exaggerated disgust. "Ew, Hale," he commented harshly. "You certainly *look* dead." I laid my forehead back onto the wheel and motioned for him to go away.

"Give me a second," I managed, distressed. I was feeling worse by the second. Impatient for answers, Alex ignored me and opened the passenger side door.

"Seriously," he started, leaning into the car to get a closer look. "What the hell happened to you the last couple of days? You look like complete shit. We need to talk. Get in the freaking house!" Slamming the car door, Alex waltzed his bony beanpole body back up the sidewalk and into his apartment, leaving the door open for me to follow. I had no choice but to go into the apartment and explain why I'd been irresponsibly unresponsive during my recent trip.

Willing my body to move and promising myself that I'd curl up into a ball as soon as I stepped in the door, I hoisted myself out of the car and painfully made my way to the modern black couch in Alex's family room. Alex was nowhere in sight.

The apartment was as neat and clean, if not more so, than the boutique. Alex's no-fuss, straight-edged style was apparent from the moment you stepped into the apartment. If you hadn't seen his clothing line, you would certainly be able to pick it out of a line-up upon seeing the apartment. Alex's decorative tastes reflected the same straight lines and sleek, expensive feel of his clothes. The only aspect of his clothing line that the apartment didn't adopt was the color scheme. Unlike Alex's colorful tees and tanks, the apartment was decorated with neutral colors and modern furniture. The only allowances of color came from the reds and oranges in the unique contemporary painting above the fireplace. My brother, Michael, painted it for Alex after visiting one weekend, insisting that he allow some color into the apartment. Although Alex had pretended to be annoyed, he beamed whenever anyone commented on the piece. He loved to tell people that the painting was made personally for him by an up-and-coming Nashville artist. Michael was pleased that it was prominently displayed in the living room.

Alex somehow made modern feel clean and futuristic, but also homey and comfortable. At the moment, I was particularly grateful for his attention to comfort. Lying on his couch was like falling into a cloud designed by mattress gods. It was airy, but firm in all the right places. Unless Alex eventually kicked me out, I wasn't moving for the next couple of hours.

"Haley, my lord, are you okay?" Patrick's concerned voice stirred me from my facedown position on the couch. I turned over and looked up to find his short, stocky frame making its way toward me, a wet cloth in his hand. Sitting on the edge of the ottoman and putting the cloth on my forehead, he tisked maternally. His square jaw was tensed with concern, and his thick eyebrows furrowed together in worry over his soft brown eyes. Patrick was sweet; there was no mistaking it. But sometimes, his caring and overly sensitive nature was a little annoying.

"Patrick, I'm not four," I groaned, looking around the room for Alex. Although I was complaining, I didn't take the cool cloth off of my forehead. I hated to admit it, but the cloth felt nice. It was relieving some of the throbbing in my brain, which I didn't think would ever stop.

"I know, Haley Blythe," Patrick said, stroking my hair. "But it still doesn't mean we can't take care of you." I laughed too hard, sending a sharp pain through my skull like a knife. Wincing, I squinted at Patrick, who was still looking at me like I was an infant with a fever.

"I don't think Alex really wants to take care of me at the moment," I observed. "He seems a little pissed." Before Patrick could dissuade me of such notions, Alex's voice came bellowing from the hallway.

"You're damn right, Hale!" Alex yelled. "I'm not coming in there until you're ready to tell me what the hell happened in New York. And don't think that you can bullshit me because I heard someone with you last night!!" Annoyed by Alex's childish behavior, I temporarily forgot that I was the shitty friend in this scenario.

"Alex, stop throwing a temper tantrum and get in here so we can talk!" I exclaimed. "I happen to be hungover because Naresh and Keegan wanted to take shots and party to celebrate their future partnership with YOU!" Alex didn't respond. "I'm setting up an appointment for you and Keegan in Columbus this coming week, Alex. This is actually happening!" Hesitating, I continued, searching for a lie to cover my night with Keegan. "And the dude last night, Alex? Just some guy I met out." Stomping in from the hallway, Alex finally came into view, looking furious.

"Haley," he started, trying to keep his anger under control. "Please tell me you didn't whore yourself out in front of Naresh and Keegan." Angry at his choice of words, I sat up, ignoring the splitting pain in my head.

"Whore myself out? I'm sorry, Alex, but you've had plenty of one-night stands, and I have NEVER judged you for it." Patrick shifted uncomfortably on the couch but didn't say anything. I hoped he knew I was talking about Alex's life before the two of them met.

"This is different," Alex argued, not faltering. "You chose to do this when hanging out with two HUGE business contacts, Haley! MY potential business partners! Not sure if you remember, but this IS a job – not an excuse to gallivant around New York to shop and sleep around!" He started to pace, flashing me angry looks every time he passed. I was temporarily stunned by his maliciousness. "Haley, don't you get it? What if Naresh is offended that you took home some random guy last night? Do you not understand what's at stake!? This is my dream – something I've wanted my whole life. I can't lose it because you got some guy to sleep with you." Shocked, I looked at Alex angrily, hurt by his outburst.

"Oh, I get it!" I yelled defensively, boiling with anger. "Don't you worry your pretty little head, Alex. I would NEVER do anything to jeopardize *your* dream and *your* business." Standing up and ignoring the nausea, I stormed toward the door. "Naresh and Keegan were long gone before I met the guy," I yelled, lying shamelessly through my teeth. "He was staying at the hotel and I met him at the hotel bar when I went down for another drink. Your precious dreams are safe and sound from my 'whoring.'"

I slammed the door behind me as I left, hot, wounded tears streaming down my round face. I was too mad to feel guilty about my brash fabrication. It was clear to me that Alex only cared about himself and the future of *his* business. I was glad I hadn't told him about Keegan. Sitting on his high horse, focused solely on himself, he would have never understood.

7 BREAKFAST SURPRISE

Sitting at a corner table at my favorite breakfast place in nearby Grandview Heights, I stared at the smudges on the napkin holder as I waited for Linds to arrive. I'd called her after leaving Alex's apartment yesterday to schedule an emergency breakfast summit this morning. I needed to talk to someone about what had happened with Keegan and Alex, and the situation that was starting to unfold as a result.

Sensing my distress, Lindsay had agreed to meet me this morning at 9:30 sharp. She was an amazing friend and one of the most unfailingly loyal people I had ever met. Unlike Alex, whose ability to keep secrets was as stellar as a pig's ability to fly, Lindsay protected secrets like a bank vault. I was thankful to have her in my life.

Taking my attention away from the napkin holder, I peered around the restaurant impatiently. Tucked away in a strip mall just a quick five-minute drive from my apartment, it was normally crowded with families, elderly couples, and people trying to cure a hangover. Today I had been lucky enough to acquire a table shortly after arriving without having to endure the usual wait.

Decorated with shiny silver tables and matching silver chairs, it had an almost unintentional 1950s vibe. Like most places in Columbus, however, the café displayed a nauseating amount of Ohio State University football gear. An obnoxious array of pictures, jerseys, and posters plastered the walls, exhibiting the city's obsession with the college's most well known sport. College football season in Columbus was the worst, as far as I was concerned, and unfortunately, I lived in the epicenter of college football mania – Victorian Village sat just south of the university's campus. Rambunctious tailgaters parked their trucks on the streets surrounding my apartment and stumbled into the area bars after the game to gloat about the victory with which they had absolutely nothing to do. Grandview Heights, located a few minutes west of campus, was no different.

Lost in my increasingly murderous thoughts about football season, I didn't notice the waitress approaching the table until she had popped up next to me for my drink order. "Would you like any coffee while you wait?" She asked politely.

"Yes, please," I confirmed, requesting that she also bring some cream and sugar. Twiddling my thumbs, I looked down at my phone to check the time. I was anxious for Lindsay to arrive. It was only five minutes past 9:30, but I had already been up for three hours this morning. It seemed as if I'd been waiting on her for ages. I'd tried to stay awake as long as possible yesterday, but my body had given up at about six o'clock in the evening. I was thankful for the twelve hours of sleep that had helped me recover from Thursday night's events, but was annoyed that I had to wait over three hours for my breakfast with Linds.

Watching the front door, I finally saw Lindsay making her way inside, hauling what looked like a company-issued computer bag. Smiling and nodding when she saw me at the table, she made her way toward me, bumping fellow patrons accidentally with her bulky luggage as she passed. Flopping down into the seat across from me, she shoved the bag into the corner and struggled to take off her jacket, which fit tighter than usual due to the thick wool sleeves of her sweater. After hanging her jacket on the back of her chair, she turned to me and smiled.

"Hi," she said, almost laughing at her bumbling entrance. I was happy to see her. I nodded curiously toward the computer bag she had dropped carelessly on the floor beside her.

"Do I even want to ask about the computer bag?" I inquired.

"No," she answered definitively, fussing with the loose strands of blond hair hanging in her face. "I have to work this weekend, so I figured I'd pick up my computer while I was near the office. I didn't want to leave it to freeze in the car." Offering no further explanation, Lindsay took her hair down and gathered it again in a loose ponytail.

"Ah," I responded in acknowledgment, watching her beautiful blond hair gather effortlessly back into place. "The trials and tribulations of a high powered attorney." Although I kidded with her about her job, I knew it was wearing on her with each passing day. I worried about her stress levels, but she hated to talk about it. I figured it was best to keep joking with her until she was ready to unload her troubles – if that day ever came. She waved her hand at me impatiently like usual.

"I hate talking about work," she said dismissively. "You know that as well as anyone. I'm here because you sent me a 9-1-1 text yesterday and then disappeared off of the face of the Earth."

"Sorry," I responded apologetically, realizing that I had been slightly cryptic about my troubles before falling into a coma. "I was really hungover and mentally exhausted from the week," I explained. "I passed out pretty early."

"I almost came over when you didn't answer my calls," Lindsay scolded. "But I figured that you would have actually dialed 9-1-1 if you were in a life or death situation." Nodding my head in confirmation, I took a sip of the coffee that the waitress had placed in front of me.

"Would you like some coffee as well?" The waitress asked Lindsay, finding a good time to interrupt.

"Yes, please," Linds replied. "Just black is great." After watching the waitress flip her dyed red hair as she turned away from the table, Linds looked back in my direction expectantly. "Well?" She asked impatiently. "What's going on, Hale?" Leaning my head back, I took a deep breath and looked at her nervously.

"I honestly don't know how to start," I confessed. I was more anxious to tell her about Keegan than I'd realized. I knew she wouldn't tell Alex, but I was slightly worried she would judge me. Lindsay was normally good about dispensing helpful advice and listening without opinion, but when it came to my relationships with men, she seemed to have less patience.

"How about you start by telling me what's going on because you're freaking me out right now," Lindsay said, a worried look creeping across her face.

"It's nothing you need to be worried about," I assured her, "I just – I don't know. I've never asked you this before, but this is something you can't tell Alex, okay?" Studying my face curiously, Lindsay sat across the table silently as the waitress set her coffee on the table. Putting her hand on her chin, Lindsay raised her eyes at the waitress for an instant, still seemingly lost in thought. "We're going to need a few minutes," she told the waitress before she could ask whether we were ready to order.

"Take your time, ladies," she replied politely, turning to leave us alone once again.

"Okay, Hale. I won't tell Alex," Lindsay stated matter-of-factly, turning her full attention back in my direction. "Now will you tell me what's going on?" Gulping, I shifted uncomfortably in my seat.

"So I told you at dinner Monday that I was going to meet a shoe designer this week for *De Alexia*, right? Someone Naresh recommended?"

"Yes . . ." Lindsay replied, waiting for me to continue.

"Well, he turned out to be gorgeous and sexy and, well, irresistible."

"Yes . . ." Lindsay said again, her eyes narrowing in anticipation.

"And, to cut to the chase here, I, uh, I slept with him." I braced myself for the worst, but Lindsay looked at me blankly, trying to hide her shock. "Alex doesn't know," I explained quickly before she could react and start asking questions. "Neither does Naresh. And I like this guy and I shouldn't have slept with him – I just, I just don't know what to do." Speechless, Lindsay started to shake her head as she wrapped her brain around my news.

"Slow down," she finally managed, closing her eyes to organize her thoughts. "I mean, how? When? What the hell happened? You were only there for two days!"

"I know, I know," I said, a little embarrassed, "he's just . . . we just clicked, I guess." Lindsay sat there, looking at me almost dumbfounded, waiting for me to tell her the details.

"I'm listening," she said, raising her eyebrows, encouraging me to go on. Obligingly, I began a detailed account of my two days with Keegan.

Lindsay didn't say a word while I recounted my torrid affair. I tried to read her reaction as I explained how I felt about him and how he had so romantically initiated our first kiss. Stoic and attentive, Lindsay sat on the other side of the table listening, waiting patiently for me to finish. "And I was going to tell Alex yesterday when I got home and try to figure this whole mess out," I explained to her, "but Keegan thought it was best to keep it between the two of us until his business relationship with Alex and Naresh is more concrete. As it turns out, it was good I didn't tell him." I gave Lindsay a quick recap of yesterday's drama at Alex's apartment.

"Do you agree with Keegan?" Lindsay asked after I'd finished my story. Her grayish blue eyes surveyed me interestedly.

"What do you mean?"

"Do you think it was really best to hide it from Alex?" Gauging her tone, she didn't seem to think it was best. I wondered why she was focusing on that part of my story instead of the cruel things Alex had said to me yesterday.

"Well," I started, a little defensively, "after our fight yesterday, I can't really see the point in telling Alex now!" Lindsay sat there, continuing to study me for a moment. I shifted in my seat, waiting for her to respond.

"I mean, it's always a good decision to tell the truth," she replied. I widened my eyes at her in annoyance.

"Oh, come on, Linds," I pleaded. "You know it's not that simple. If I tell him now it will only make things worse between us. Plus, I'm not sure he deserves to know after freaking out and basically calling me a whore yesterday." Lindsay grimaced.

"I just don't see any good coming out of you hiding it," she replied. "Alex will find out about this eventually, you know he will. And the longer you lie, the worse it will be when he does." I rolled my eyes even though a part of me knew she was right. "I *am* sorry about yesterday," she added. "He was mean and unfair. But nevertheless, you should consider his point of view. Although you didn't, you could have really screwed things up for the boutique." I flashed her an angry look.

"Yeah, that's already been pointed out to me, thanks," I responded, the irritation in my voice palpable. I started to regret telling her about Keegan. I came here for her advice, but it felt more like a lecture. I was disappointed that she wasn't the least bit excited to hear I'd met someone.

"Don't be upset with me," Lindsay requested softly. "I'm only trying to come at this from an outside perspective. If you wanted to talk to someone who would ignore the problems this poses and jump up and down at the mention of kissing a boy, then you shouldn't have called me. Unlike the brainless cheerleader you so desire, I desperately want you to be happy – and it would be amazing if this situation with Keegan works out. But look at it from my point of view: You slept with a man who is getting ready to pitch designs to *De Alexia* and have agreed, at his suggestion, to hide it from everyone. I don't know, Hale. It makes me nervous." I sighed.

"I get how it looks," I muttered. "But do you understand at all where I'm coming from? Alex was horrible to me yesterday. And even if he hadn't been, at this point, telling him about Keegan would cause more harm than good. Plus, Keegan's a really nice guy. You'll see when you finally meet him. I think I might have real feelings for him, Linds." She looked at me thoughtfully.

"Just be careful," she advised. "And keep your wits about you. Don't let your feelings for him trump your common sense."

"Thanks Dr. Phil," I replied sarcastically. She looked at me in protest. Feeling bad about mocking her, I looked at her apologetically and leaned forward on the table. "No, seriously, Linds," I added, genuinely. "I really do appreciate the advice." Although I hadn't appreciated its content, I did appreciate her for listening and sharing her honest opinion. "I think I'm done talking about this now, though," I said. "Let's forget about it and enjoy breakfast, shall we?"

"Fine by me," she responded, picking up her menu and changing the subject as if we'd never discussed it. "Are you going to get that eggs and avocado thing you got last time? That looked good; I think that's what I'm getting." She scanned the menu for a moment, pursing her lips together as she considered her other options. "Although I could get a little crazy and order some pancakes," she said. "You know, we really should carb up for our 5K walk tomorrow morning." Groaning, I smacked myself lightly on the head.

"I totally forgot about that!" I declared. "I'm glad you said something, I would have stood you up for sure." Shaking her head, Lindsay didn't look the least bit surprised.

"It's a wonder that you're able to feed and bathe yourself," she joked. "Why are you incapable of checking your calendar on a daily basis? It's not hard. It takes two seconds."

"Shut it," I responded. "This coming from the woman who wants to carb up for a three-mile walk. Go ahead and have those pancakes – it will only take you about a month to walk them off." Throwing her napkin at me, she laughed.

"I will have you know that my participation in any physical activity requires an extreme increase in my calorie intake," she said. "I'm so used to being chained to my desk all day that any movement in addition to walking to my car at night is far beyond anything my body is capable of. By the way, is Patrick still coming with us? And that sweet, curly-haired kid from the boutique? I know I've met him a few times, but I can never get his name right – Rick? Or something. What is it?"

"Nick . . ." My voice was almost a whisper as I stared fixatedly at the two men walking through the café door. I knew Lindsay was talking to me, but I had stopped listening.

"What?" Lindsay was oblivious to my sudden distraction. "No, it's not Nick. It's Dominic! Wait, is that what you call him now? I thought you called him Dom?"

"No!" I yelled in a hushed whisper, grabbing her hands to make her focus. "It's Nick! Remember – the guy from the plane who I hurdled over to get club soda after spilling tomato juice on my sweater? He just walked into the restaurant!" Without thinking, Lindsay spun around in her chair while I leaned back in mine, twirling my hair, trying to behave normally. I couldn't believe he was here.

Unfortunately, Lindsay's obvious staring and my not-so-normal hair twirling drew Nick's attention almost immediately. Looking over at our table, he squinted in faint recognition and then smiled as he remembered me – the crazy lady from the plane.

"Great, Captain Obvious," I whispered through clenched teeth as Nick walked toward our table. "Now he's coming over here. This is freaking embarrassing." I smiled and waved stupidly as Nick approached. Never in a million years did I think I'd have to face him again. Lindsay turned to me, trying to stifle her laughter. I glared at her menacingly. There was nothing funny about the man approaching our table. Only mortifying.

"I see you decided to skip the tomato juice this morning," Nick said in jest as he reached our table. Lindsay snickered and I blushed in embarrassment.

"Yes, I recently had a falling out with tomato juice," I replied, shooting Lindsay another glare. Nick chuckled. Looking down at my napkin, I winced, painfully recalling our plane ride together. "I think it's safe to say that our flight on Sunday made my top five most embarrassing moments list." Nick chuckled again and stretched out his hand to reintroduce himself.

"It was definitely my most interesting plane ride yet," he admitted. "It's Nick – not sure if you remember."

"I remember," I told him, grabbing his hand. "Haley." His hands felt just like I remembered them: the perfect amount of rough.

"Ah, yes," he said in recognition.

"And I'm Lindsay." Lindsay interjected from the other side of the table, stretching out her hand.

"Yeah, sorry – my friend, Lindsay," I said, gesturing in her direction.

"And that's my buddy Mark," Nick said, pointing back to the door where his friend was waiting. Completely uninterested in Nick's whereabouts, Mark stared unmoving at his phone as he waited for a table. "He's in town for the cancer walk tomorrow," Nick explained.

"We're doing that, too," I told him quickly, happy to be talking about something other than last Sunday's flight. "Lindsay and I were just now discussing how we should carb up. We were thinking that three pancakes each should do the trick."

"Oh, are you doing the half-marathon race before the walk?" Nick asked, impressed. Shaking my head vigorously, I was embarrassed he hadn't picked up on my joke. His hazel eyes regarded me intently.

"No, no," I assured him. "We're doing the walk – really we're just looking for an excuse to increase our calorie intake without feeling bad about ourselves later."

"Oh!" Nick said, laughing. "Three pancakes sounds about right, then. Maybe you should add some French Toast to be safe." I smiled politely, once again finding myself a little embarrassed. Nick had to think I was some sort of superficial lunatic. Sunday, I freaked out over a cashmere sweater stain, and this morning, I was talking about counting calories. I was coming across beautifully. "Are you guys walking for someone special tomorrow?" He asked, not sensing my humiliation.

"We're doing the walk as part of a charity outreach program for my work," I told him. "We allot a certain amount of money to donations every year. We figured that the walk would be a good way to get some exercise and donate to cancer research. How about you?"

"My mother is a breast cancer survivor actually," Nick replied proudly. "I do the walk with her every year." He puffed out his chest a little and smiled fondly. It was obvious he loved his mom very much. I found myself suddenly envious at the thought.

"Wow, that's great!" I said, ashamed by the unexpected flicker of jealousy. As I finished my sentence, Lindsay kicked me violently under the table. I flinched and looked at her sideways, trying to figure out what had gotten into her. She was staring at me, her gray eyes bulging with a message I didn't understand. Nick noticed the exchange, too, and shuffled his feet awkwardly.

"Well maybe I'll see you guys out there," he suggested, glancing at Lindsay one more time as he backed away from the table. "It was nice running into you, Haley."

"You too," I said, nodding at him as he left. He looked back at me and put his hand up in short wave. When he was barely out of earshot, I turned to Lindsay.

"What the hell was that for!?" I asked her. "That hurt!"

"What was that *for*?" She asked, repeating my question. "He was totally flirting with you! Why didn't you ask for his number? Or suggest walking with him tomorrow?" I couldn't believe she was trying to set me up right now.

"Oh, I don't know," I replied, in mock wonderment. "Because I just spent the last ten minutes talking to you about how I slept with another man for whom I have feelings. Or maybe because the last time I saw him I used him as a track prop and had a nervous breakdown over a tomato stain! I highly doubt that Nick wants my number. He came over here because he saw you staring." Lindsay leaned back in her chair and put her hands up in surrender.

"Fine, Haley, but he is incredibly cute and I think you're an idiot for not asking him out. There's no harm in having options."

"Think what you want," I told her. "But for now, can we concentrate on eating, please?" Nodding her head curtly in response, Lindsay closed the menu and stared at me with an annoying 'I'm-not-going-to-say-anything-but-you're-making-the-wrong-decision' look on her face. Much to my dismay, she stubbornly maintained that look for our entire meal. I wasn't sure if it was just about Nick, or also about Keegan. I was relieved when it finally came time to give up on what remained of our pancakes and leave the restaurant.

After paying the bill and gathering our things, Lindsay and I made our way through the café directly past Nick's table where he was chatting with Mark over some eggs and bacon. Catching his eye as we passed, I smiled and waved, acutely aware of what Lindsay must have been thinking behind me.

I was thankful when we reached the door. Pulling it open, I cringed as a rush of cold air blasted me in the face. Although I was wearing a jacket, I only had a thin cotton t-shirt on underneath. Apparently my attempt at pretending the weather was warmer hadn't made it so. I turned to Lindsay to give her a quick hug good-bye so I could retreat to the shelter of my car.

"See you tomorrow morning," I said, hugging her. "You still planning on picking me up?"

"Of course," she replied. "Be at *De Alexia* at 7:30 – the walk gets packed pretty quickly, so we need to get there early. I'll text Patrick to make sure he and Dominic are still coming."

"Fine," I said whining a little. Another early morning was not my idea of fun. "But don't expect me to be chipper."

"I never do," she jabbed, making her way to her car. "Until tomorrow!" Waving, I turned and headed in the opposite direction toward my blue sedan.

"Hey, Haley! Hold on a second!" I stopped and turned around again in time to see Nick walking hurriedly toward me from the café's doorway, a piece of paper in his hands. Confused, I watched him approach without saying a word. Shivering, Nick handed me the paper, a shy smile creeping across his face as he shrugged. "You should join us for the walk," he suggested, still trying to shake the cold weather. "We have a big group this year; a few friends, extended family members, and my mom of course." Peering down at the paper, I noticed he'd scribbled his name and telephone number on it. He had terrible handwriting. "That's my number," he continued, watching me stare at it. "In case you can't find us. We're meeting in the back left corner of the registration tent." Realizing I still hadn't spoken, I blinked my eyes and nodded my head in agreement.

"Sounds great," I said without thinking. "I'll see you tomorrow then." Smiling, Nick looked back at the restaurant, clearly desiring to get out of the cold.

"Great!" He said. "Make sure to dress warmly tomorrow. It's supposed to be around the same temperature as today. Gotta love unpredictable Ohio spring weather!" Waving as he jogged back to the restaurant, I stood in the middle of the parking lot as he disappeared from view. As soon as he was gone, my phone rang. It was Lindsay.

"I saw the whole thing!" She shrieked. "Did he ask you out? Did he give you his number?"

"He wants to meet up for the walk tomorrow," I told her, still processing what just happened through my surprise. Turning mindlessly toward my car, I opened the door and climbed in, relieved to be protected from the relentless gusts of cold wind outside.

"I knew he was flirting with you," Lindsay gloated. I turned my key in the ignition.

"I guess," I replied, not really knowing how to feel. Nick was an extremely good-looking guy and seemed really sweet, but the image of Keegan's face kept flashing obtrusively in my mind. "We can decide whether to meet up with Nick when you pick me up tomorrow morning," I said, unable to match her enthusiasm. "Until then, I'm going to turn up the heat in my apartment, watch bad movies all day, and try and relax after the crazy freaking week I've had." Pulling out from the parking lot, I heard Lindsay sigh in frustration.

"Okay, Hale," she agreed reluctantly, "but I'm disappointed you aren't more excited about this. He's really cute – you even described him as dreamy when you told me about meeting him on the plane."

"I know," I admitted. "I just have a lot on my mind. This comes at an inopportune time, Linds."

"Well get some rest," she suggested. "You'll feel better about it in the morning." I raised my eyebrows skeptically as she hung up the phone. Lindsay was right. I should have been ecstatic about getting Nick's number. But surprisingly, I wasn't. In fact, I didn't really feel much at all. I couldn't shake Keegan from my mind. I began to wonder nervously why he hadn't called since our Thursday night tryst. Had I been simply a conquest? Someone he'd cast aside after so easily luring into bed? Frowning at the unsettling notion, I hoped Lindsay was right in suggesting my thoughts would be clearer in the morning. For some reason, however, I doubted it. I feared it was going to take a lot more than Nick's messily scrawled number and a good night's sleep to forget the electrifying, spellbinding appeal of Keegan Bransford.

8 DON'T CALL IT A DATE

It was only 7:20 in the morning, but there I was, freezing like an ice cube tray outside of *De Alexia*. I was irritated that I hadn't thought to bring keys to the store. Waiting inside, even with the heat turned down low, would have been much more pleasant than facing the blistering winds on the sidewalk. I winced as another chilly gust came by. I longed to be back in my apartment where it was warm and cozy. Yesterday, I had cranked the heat up to seventy-five degrees and curled up on my comfy red couch in my favorite flannel pajamas. As I stomped my feet and hugged myself tightly, I felt as if I would never be warm again.

"Cold?" A voice called to me from across the street. Looking up to find the source of the voice, I waved when I saw Dom, nodding in response to his question. Waiting for an opening in the traffic, Dom hurried across the street, his hands tucked away in his gray hooded sweatshirt, his messy brown hair hidden under the hood.

"Do you have keys to the store?" I asked hopefully as he approached, my teeth chattering.

"Nah," Dom replied. "I'm not a key holder."

"Crap," I declared, shivering. "I was hoping we could sneak in for a bit to warm up." Looking at him for a moment, I realized Dom was wearing gym shorts, with no pants to keep him warm. "Aren't you cold!?" I asked, shocked that he was so underdressed.

"A little," Dom said nonchalantly, "but not too bad." Staring at him in disbelief, I shook my head. He reminded me of the college guys you saw on television at football games in subzero temperatures without a shirt on. I never understood that. But then again, I didn't understand the allure of football, either.

"You do anything last night?" Dom asked, trying to strike up a conversation.

"No, I stayed in," I said, trying hard to focus on something other than my frozen toes. Dom nodded in response. To a senior in college, I must have seemed pretty boring. "I've been traveling a lot lately," I explained, "and really needed a good night of doing nothing. So that's exactly what I did. Yesterday was a whole lot of nothing." Dom nodded in response again, continuing to watch the street for Lindsay and Patrick.

"Yeah," he finally commiserated. "Sometimes it's good to recharge your batteries and relax." I smiled in agreement and hugged my arms close as another blast of cold air permeated my clothing. Although yesterday *had* been relaxing, thoughts about Keegan, Alex, and Nick circled obnoxiously in my head, prohibiting me from fully rejuvenating. Mostly, I had struggled terribly with my feelings of guilt for lying to Alex on Friday. My guilt increased tenfold when I found a bouquet of purple calla lilies and an apologetic note on my doorstep upon arriving home after my breakfast with Linds. I knew I should have called or texted Alex in response, but I had no idea what to say. What *could* I say? Accept an apology from him while lying through my teeth? It didn't feel right.

"Did you do anything exciting last night?" I asked Dom, trying to shake the stressful thoughts about Alex out of my head.

"Just the usual," he said, nonplussed.

"What's the usual?" I inquired.

"Went to this small, Irish bar south of campus," he replied. "It was only a couple of the guys. Exams are coming up next week, so a bunch of the dudes were studying." The Irish bar he was referring to was likely the hole-in-the-wall south of campus where students and even young professionals from Victorian Village would go to enjoy a low-key night out. It was hidden from street view and therefore not as popular as the other campus bars, giving it an unintended feeling of exclusivity.

"Why aren't *you* studying?" I asked him. He shrugged.

"I'll be fine," he said calmly. "I already scored a job after graduation – I just need to pass, really." I looked at him in bewilderment. He seemed completely unconcerned about blowing off his exams. Even if my grade had absolutely no bearing on my future, I could never do that. Studying any less than I was physically capable made no sense to me. I was jealous that he could be so relaxed.

"Where did you get a job, Dom?" I asked, interested. This was the longest conversation I'd ever had with him that didn't involve *De Alexia*. I was curious to find out what he'd been studying.

"The local power company," he said monotonously. "I'm going to be working on substation design as an engineer." I was floored. I had no idea that Dom was even capable of spelling the word 'engineer.'

"That's great!" I exclaimed, shaking my head in shock. I immediately felt guilty for misjudging him. Why had I assumed he wasn't smart? I had made seriously incorrect assumptions about this sweet, unassuming co-worker with whom I'd been acquainted for almost a year. I felt pretty self-centered and shallow.

"Friends!!!" Patrick's voice called from around the corner, interrupting my harsh self-assessment. His short, boxy frame appeared around the building a few seconds later, dressed in sweats and a white t-shirt with "*De Alexia*" printed on the front. His short brown hair, normally parted to the side, flew haphazardly in the wind.

"Hey, Patrick," I responded. "Are those the shirts? I like them!" Smiling, Patrick reached into the small duffle bag he was carrying and pulled out two more.

"Yes, ma'am," he confirmed, throwing the smaller one in my direction. "Alex and I made a t-shirt for everybody. Wear them proudly!" Despite my lack of coordination, I managed to snatch the shirt before it hit the ground and held it out in front of me, nodding in approval.

When I'd told Alex about the 5K a few months ago, he'd immediately seen the event as a marketing opportunity. Although it felt a little wrong to abuse the charity walk for commercial promotion, Alex had eventually convinced me that it was not uncommon for businesses to promote their charitable contributions. Notwithstanding my feelings about the self-promotion, I had to admit, I liked the shirts. Similar to Alex's line, they were sleek, simple, and chic – if a t-shirt could ever really be described as chic.

As I admired the t-shirt, I wondered how much input Patrick had had in designing them. His tastes were generally flashier than Alex's and his feelings were easily hurt when Alex disagreed with his opinions. Alex's love for Patrick was most obvious when the two of them discussed fashion for *De Alexia*'s line. As pigheaded and blunt as Alex could be to the rest of the world, he was sensitive and caring toward Patrick, paying special attention not to reject his suggestions too harshly. The way Alex cared for Patrick – and vice versa – was the way I always hoped someone would care for me. I sometimes felt pangs of loneliness when I watched the two of them together. Both men had experienced heartache before they found each other. I only hoped it was a matter of time before I found the right person.

"Um, mine doesn't really fit." I turned toward Dom, who was holding out his arms and staring at the t-shirt vacuum-sealed to his chest. The shirt was so tight over his large hooded sweatshirt that it made him look like an overstuffed sausage. Patrick and I exchanged glances, biting our lips to try and suppress our giggling.

"Dom, just take it off and put it under your sweatshirt," I told him, chuckling. "Maybe you'll get warm during the race – if not, no worries. There will still be three of us promoting the store." Patrick nodded in agreement.

"I think that's a great idea," Dom said, looking relieved. "I wouldn't be doing the boutique any favors looking like a grown man in a child's shirt." As Dom took off the shirt, Lindsay pulled up to the curb on the other side of the street and honked.

"Get in the car where it's warm!" She called, rolling down her window. "Hurry it up!" Calling shotgun, I ran to the car and hopped in, leaving Patrick and Dom to squeeze into the backseat. I welcomed the warmth on my face and toes, but I was afraid that thawing out would only make getting out of the car again even worse.

"Cool shirts, guys!" She exclaimed, looking at me eagerly. "Where's mine!?"

"Patience, patience," Patrick responded, throwing another shirt toward the driver's seat.

"Thanks!" Lindsay responded excitedly. "These are much cuter than the t-shirts my firm passed out yesterday. I'm glad I decided to hang out with you nerds instead of walking with the overworked and cynical lawyer population of Columbus." We all laughed. It was thanks to Lindsay's firm that we'd become involved in the walk in the first place. Lindsay had felt immense political pressure to join the walk with some of her least favorite people from work, and therefore had begged me to sign up to serve as her excuse to walk with someone else. She would sooner walk with zombies I think, than with some of her coworkers. It made me sad for her. I was incredibly lucky to work with people like Alex and Dom; I couldn't imagine working every day with people who intentionally made my day unpleasant. Life was stressful enough.

Glancing over at me expectantly, Lindsay peeked at Patrick and Dom in the rearview mirror. "So I'm going to go ahead and guess that Haley neglected to tell you guys about her date today. Am I right?" Between my misjudgment of Dom and admiring our new t-shirts, I had almost forgotten about our plans to meet Nick. My heart fluttered nervously upon being reminded.

"Now, wait just one minute," I protested, before either Dom or Patrick could chime in. "It's not a date. We may meet up before the race, but we may not."

"Um, you're going to have to fill us in back here," Patrick declared from the backseat, ignoring my protests. "Who are you meeting? And why is this the first time I'm hearing about it?" Sighing, I turned to explain the situation to Patrick and Dom, forcing myself to relive the embarrassing plane incident and giving a full rundown of my breakfast with Lindsay yesterday, sans, of course, any mention of Keegan.

"He's cute, there's no denying it," I admitted, once I'd finished describing my brief history with Nick. "But I don't know. I didn't really feel any sparks the second time around." As I turned back toward the front of the car, I noticed Lindsay glancing at me knowingly, but I ignored her. She probably guessed that my feelings for Keegan were stymieing the development of any feelings for Nick. I'm sure this displeased her, but I couldn't help how I felt.

"Nick seems pretty great," Lindsay interjected, glancing at Patrick in the rearview mirror.

"You said maybe five words to the man," I observed.

"Maybe," Lindsay admitted, "but I picked up a good vibe from him. Sometimes I can just tell about a guy, you know?" Patrick laughed from the backseat. I dismissed her with a scoff and looked out the passenger side window at the congested traffic surrounding us. We had detoured five different times in a two-mile stretch to avoid the half-marathon route and were now stuck in bumper-to-bumper traffic.

"It's crazy down here!" I observed, hoping to change the subject.

"This race has always been huge," Dom commented from the backseat. "It must be because Columbus has so many cancer treatment hospitals."

"Maybe," I mused, wondering whether we'd arrive in time for the start of the race. I was beginning to feel anxious, but I couldn't tell whether I was anxious about being late or anxious about seeing Nick. Perhaps a little bit of both.

"Don't change the subject, Haley Blythe," Patrick admonished me from the backseat. "We need to talk more about your date with Nick! What are your plans? Are we coming with you?"

"It's not a date," I grumbled, watching the traffic start to move again. "It's a walk to raise money for cancer – with his mom."

"Still . . ." Patrick replied. "You should probably decide whether you want us coming with you."

"Oh, you guys are definitely coming with me," I stated matter-of-factly. "If we even find Nick in this mess."

"Did you tell Alex about this?" Patrick's voice was low and cautious. My heart jumped into my throat from guilt almost instantaneously. I'm sure Patrick knew very well I hadn't told Alex. In fact, he was probably well aware that I hadn't talked to Alex since storming out of his apartment Friday afternoon.

"No," I started, carefully choosing my words. "After our argument Friday I needed to cool off. Some of the things he said to me were really hurtful. I figured I'd stop over sometime today to talk to him. It's been weird not having him on constant speed dial." I could have sworn that Lindsay was staring at me accusingly, but when I turned to look at her, she was concentrating on the road ahead, poised and unmoving. I wondered what she was thinking. I wouldn't blame her for judging me. I judged me.

"Well he'll love to see you," Patrick insisted. "He's been torn up about Friday. You two are too close to stop talking over something like this. It wasn't even a big deal!" I shifted uncomfortably in my seat. Patrick would have been right, but what he didn't know was that it was a big deal.

"Yeah," I agreed faintly. "It will be good to see him and talk through it." Continuing to look out the window, I felt hollow. It was strange that Alex didn't know about Nick. Frankly, it was strange that Alex didn't know about Keegan. He was always the first person I called to talk about men, but I felt too guilty and too angry to call him. I didn't know what to say. I felt distant and out of touch after not talking to him for a couple of days. I didn't like it. I needed Alex in my life. For my sanity, I had to mend what I could, even if I wasn't ready to talk about Keegan.

****

After what seemed like a century of silence, Lindsay pulled into a parking garage downtown within a few blocks from the registration tents. It had taken us thirty minutes to drive two and a half miles, leaving us an hour before the start of the race. An hour was plenty of time to register and, if we were so inclined, to find Nick's group.

"Okay team, time to wake up and get our walk on!" Lindsay announced, turning off the car. Lost in thought for the last fifteen minutes, I hadn't realized that both Dom and Patrick had dozed off in the backseat.

"I'm up," Patrick claimed unconvincingly, fluttering his brown eyes and yawning. Although Dom was stirring, he still had his eyes closed.

"Do you think they have vending machines somewhere?" Dom asked, his eyes remaining tightly shut. I laughed.

"Probably not," I responded. "You'll have to survive without your daily dose of Mountain Dew."

"Gross!" Lindsay exclaimed from my left. "If Haley's not joking, that is an awfully unhealthy habit." Dom opened his eyes to shoot Lindsay an irritated glance. They had only met a couple of times; I'm sure he didn't appreciate being scolded by someone he barely knew.

"Okay then," I interjected, trying to diffuse the tension. "We better get moving – brace yourselves. It probably isn't any warmer out there than it was thirty minutes ago."

Unfortunately, I was right. As I climbed out of the car, the cold weather instantly pierced through my clothing. If anything, it seemed colder than it had been while we were waiting in front of the boutique. Shivering next to the car as the rest of the crew followed my lead, I turned to survey the mass of people in the parking garage. Lindsay had been right about the size of the crowd attending the race. It was unbelievable. There were hundreds of people in every direction of all ages, shapes, and sizes. Some groups had matching t-shirts like ours, some groups decked themselves out in matching outfits from head-to-toe, and others carried inspirational placards with messages to struggling loved ones or in memory of loved ones passed.

As we grouped together to head to the registration tents, a small family walked by holding hands. Dressed in pink t-shirts with "Beat Cancer" bedazzled on the front, my heart melted. The father balanced his small daughter on his shoulders as she held a sign that said, "Walking for Mommy." Waddling proudly next to them was a waif of a woman wearing a camouflage handkerchief, her eyes glistening with tears. She would have been ninety pounds had she not been nearly nine months pregnant. As my eyes began to water, I felt someone grab my hand. Looking sideways, I smiled at Patrick who was biting the inside of his cheek to stifle his own tears. Winking back at me, he motioned for me to head out.

"Let's do this Hale," he said softly. Nodding in agreement I walked ahead, patting his hand as I let it go.

None of us talked as we walked toward the registration tent, silenced by the inspirational messages surrounding us. They made my trouble with men seem petty and unimportant. And it made me feel ridiculous for having been so dramatic about my situation with Keegan. I knew what it was like to lose a loved one; I could relate to that pain. No one could understand the agony and hopelessness that follows the tragic loss of a loved one until they've experienced it themselves. I wanted to hug everyone around me in support, but I wouldn't have made it a block before the race started; there were so many people walking in someone's memory.

The closer we ventured to the tents, the more people we encountered. By the time we found the registration tent the ground wasn't even visible under the sea of teeming people. "This is going to take forever!" Patrick exclaimed, appraising the line. He was right – it didn't seem as if we would make the start of the race after all.

"Not necessarily," Lindsay responded mischievously, marching toward a donation table to our right. "I know people," she said, winking at us over her shoulder. Dom, Patrick, and I followed her curiously.

"Crap. It's Kevin," I whispered to Patrick anxiously as we got close to the table, hoping he would stop and wait with me a safe distance away. Patrick raised his eyebrows in delayed recognition and nodded, waiting with me while Lindsay and Dom tried their best to cut the registration line.

Kevin was a young associate at Lindsay's law firm who she'd tried to set me up with a few months prior. He was cute, but had absolutely no interests outside of his job. He had talked exclusively about work the entire dinner, and then seemed completely uninterested when Lindsay tried to explain my job at *De Alexia*. We hadn't clicked at all, which made it even more awkward when he tried to kiss me after dinner.

"The one who kissed your ear, right?" Patrick asked, confirming that he was remembering correctly.

"Yeah," I said, cringing as I remembered how awkward it had been when I'd turned my head at the last second. I hadn't seen or talked to Kevin since our date and didn't feel the need to relive the awkwardness by saying hello.

After what seemed like an eternity, Lindsay and Dom made their way back to us. Looking at me with disapproval, Lindsay held up four race packets and handed them out one by one. "You could have at least said hello," she said, scolding me. "He really liked you."

"I know," I said, feeling bad for being rude. "But we ended the date with that awkward ear kiss." She gave me a sour look and handed me my packet. "Plus," I added, taking it from her, "I'm nervous enough to meet Nick. I don't think I could emotionally handle having to deal with the ghosts of bad dates past, too." Dom laughed, but Lindsay ignored me. At least someone appreciated my literary humor.

"Why are you nervous?" Patrick asked, looking at me suspiciously. "I thought you didn't feel any sparks." Patrick raised a good question. I wasn't sure why I felt so nervous.

"It's probably because I don't know him and I'm not quite sure why he wants me to walk with his group," I reasoned. "Five kilometers will be a painfully long distance if it turns out I don't like the guy's company." Dom looked at me curiously.

"Why meet up with him then?" He asked. "He obviously asked you to meet him because he likes you. If you aren't interested in the guy, there's no point, right?" Lindsay answered Dom's question before I could even think of a response.

"She's going to meet him because there's no harm in giving the guy a chance," Lindsay explained. "Who knows where this could lead. Haley's single, Nick seems like a nice guy, so there's really no reason not to meet him." She looked at me, almost as if daring me to challenge her point.

"Lindsay's right," I found myself saying. "We're here, he's here . . . we might as well meet up with him. Plus, I told him I would." Lindsay smiled. Although I had been resisting the idea of meeting Nick, Lindsay made a solid point. Notwithstanding what had happened with Keegan, I *was* single. And as far as Patrick and Dom knew, there was no logical reason for me to turn down Nick's offer. It was easier to meet up with Nick than to try and formulate good reasons to avoid him. "Let's head to the back of the tent," I suggested finally. "He said his group would be congregating there – it's a good place to start looking."

Dom, Lindsay, and Patrick followed me as I started weaving my way through the tent. Because of the density of the crowd, making our way proved more difficult than I'd expected. After dodging people tirelessly for a couple of minutes, I stopped to assess our surroundings. Close to the back of the tent, I spotted Nick easily. Dressed in gray sweatpants and a green faded sweatshirt, he was standing above the crowd on some steps in the back, waving to people as he spotted them. I couldn't help but notice that he looked adorable.

"I see Nick," I said, turning toward Lindsay, Dom, and Patrick.

"Where?" Lindsay asked excitedly, standing on her toes to get an easier look. "Oh, I see him!" She declared. "He looks cute, Haley." I ignored her.

"Lindsay's right," Patrick whispered from behind me. "He *is* cute." I ignored him, too. I was grateful to Dom for remaining quiet and silently thanked him for balancing out the overbearing excitement exuding from our other two companions.

"We're nearly there," I told them, beginning to weave my way through the crowd once again. "Stay together! Elbows out!"

Soon after we began walking again, I heard Nick calling my name above the murmur of the crowd. He'd obviously spotted us from his perch. "Haley!" He shouted, smiling and waving at me from the wall. When I waved back in response, he jumped down from his lookout to greet us. I stopped and waited for him to reach us, avoiding the eager looks plastered on Lindsay and Patrick's faces. Before Nick reached us, I felt my cell phone buzz in my pocket. I pulled it out quickly and looked curiously at the screen.

"Who is it?" Patrick asked me. "Is it Alex? Tell him we can't be bothered – you have a date!"

"It's no one," I stammered, shoving my phone back into my pocket as I felt my face flush with embarrassment and guilt. Patrick looked at me curiously and Lindsay shot me a knowing glance before turning to greet Nick. Although I hadn't recognized the number, there was no mistaking from whom the message came – and by the look on her face, Lindsay knew it, too:

Hey beautiful – Naresh gave me your number. Coming to Columbus first thing tomorrow and staying until Thursday. Hoping to meet Alex at some point, but more so hoping that you'll come find me at the Renaissance Hotel downtown. I can't stop thinking about the other night . . . I can't wait to see you.

9 THE CHARITY STROLL

Lindsay cornered me as soon as she had the opportunity. Stuck in a portable public toilet minutes before the race, I had no choice but to listen to her whisper urgently at me through the door. "What did it say Hale?" She asked, her voice hushed. "I know it was Keegan, what did it say?" Sighing, I pulled up my sweatpants and concentrated on avoiding every surface of the small enclosure while searching for hand sanitizer. For the first time this morning, I was thankful for the cold weather. Using a portable toilet in any kind of heat was something I tried hard to avoid.

"He's coming to Columbus tomorrow," I told her, relenting. Locating the hand sanitizer, I squirted the gel on my hands and opened the door, almost hitting Lindsay in the face. "He wants to meet Alex," I whispered hurriedly, looking around to make sure no one else could hear us. "It was just about business, Linds."

Catching Patrick's eye beyond the bathroom lines, I waved and made my way toward him. One lie to Alex, and suddenly I was lying effortlessly to everyone around me. I wasn't sure why I was hiding the fact that Keegan wanted to see me at his hotel. I imagined it was because I knew in my heart she'd disapprove. No matter the reason, however, I was in a dangerous spiral of deception. I needed to stop lying. Lindsay sighed in frustration as she followed me. I was sure that she saw right through my fib.

"I saw your face when you read that text message, Hale," she began. "It didn't seem like just a bit of business." I was right. She knew. Continuing to walk toward Patrick, I remained silent. If I didn't open my mouth, I couldn't lie. "Even if it *was* just business," Lindsay continued doubtfully, "I hope it doesn't prevent you from enjoying the morning. Nick seems like a good guy and he's obviously excited that you're here." I'm not sure how obvious his excitement really was, but Nick and his family were definitely a warm and welcoming group of people. We had been treated like a seamless part of the group, as if we were close family friends that they'd known for years. Although it felt a little like we were intruding, I couldn't help but enjoy watching Nick's family and friends interact. I didn't have any extended family or close family friends of my own, so it was nice to be a part of a bigger, more cohesive family unit for a change, even if only as an invited guest.

"Can we talk about this later?" I asked Lindsay under my breath as we made our way through the crowd. Although I knew she'd hold me to it, now was not the place or time to talk about Keegan. I was relieved when I heard Lindsay mumble in agreement behind me.

When we reached Patrick, he was standing alone next to a rambunctious group of women in their sixties and seventies. I watched as they hugged and laughed with each other, talking loudly about past memories. They weren't dressed in matching clothes, but I noticed that each was wearing a button boasting a picture of a slightly younger woman, possibly in her late forties or early fifties. I assumed she would have been laughing with them, ten years older, had it not been for cancer.

"The rest of the crew awaits us," Patrick announced as I continued to stare thoughtfully at the group of women next to us. Breaking my gaze, I turned slowly to face him.

"Where are they?" I asked.

"About a hundred yards back from the start," Patrick responded. "It's a pretty good spot. Follow me!" After weaving through what seemed like thousands of people, I spotted Nick and Dom standing at the edge of the walking group a few feet away. Nick's mother, Carol, was talking cheerfully in the middle of the group, resting her hand affectionately on her brother, Rick, as she spoke. Nick shook his head and smiled fondly as his mother doubled over with laughter.

"It's a little too early for wine," I heard him say jokingly, placing his hand on her shoulder as she tried to compose herself. Smacking him lightly on the arm, she looked at him defensively, her pretty brown eyes smiling with happiness.

"Oh stop it," she said, still chuckling as her laughing subsided. "Your Uncle Richard is trying to get me to hyperventilate before this walk, I think." She glanced at Rick accusingly.

"Don't blame me for your lunacy, Carol," Rick retorted, putting his hands up as if he had nothing to do with her laughing fit. Still smiling and shaking his head, Nick ignored them and turned his attention toward the three of us joining the group.

"I'm really glad you guys could join us," he said. Carol and Rick continued to bicker playfully in the background.

"Me too!" I said, smiling. And I was. "Your mom is mesmerizing. Her positive energy is infectious!"

"She's adorable," Patrick agreed.

"She's something," Nick said, beaming with love. "This is a pretty cool year for us. This year marks five years of my mom being cancer-free."

"That's great," Dom said, adding to the conversation. "Five years is a big one."

"Sure is," Nick replied. "I think we'll all worry a little less knowing that she's passed the five-year mark."

The event's loud speakers interrupted our conversation to announce the start of the race. "WELCOME TO THE COLUMBUS ANNUAL WALK FOR BREAST CANCER!" The voice boomed, eagerly. "THANKS FOR COMING TO SUPPORT THE FIGHT – THE WALK STARTS IN THIRTY SECONDS ON MY HORN. ARE YOU READY!?" The crowd cheered loudly around us. I watched Carol put a hand in her mouth to give a loud whistle. She was smiling from ear to ear, saturated in positive emotion. Rick stood by her side, his arm around her shoulders in affection. As I watched them, I wondered whether Nick's dad was still alive. If so, it seemed strange that he would miss such a pivotal family event.

The blast of the horn a few seconds later sent a rippling effect of movement through the crowd. People everywhere cheered and clapped as they walked, pushing people in wheelchairs or holding hands in unity. I lost myself in the masses for a while, soaking in the atmosphere around me. It wasn't until a few minutes later that I noticed Nick walking beside me, smiling and surveying the crowd in silence. Glancing quickly to my left and right, I realized that the two of us were alone in a sea of strangers. Lindsay, Patrick, and Dom were nowhere in sight.

"Crazy, isn't it?" Nick gestured to the congestion around us.

"Yeah," I agreed, peering back and forth to see whether I could spot my friends amidst the crowd. I suspected their disappearing act to be intentional. I rolled my eyes at the thought. Giving up on my search, I turned to Nick. "I had no idea this was such a popular event," I admitted. He nodded as the sound of a helicopter made me stop and peer up at the sky. "Wow," I continued, "there are television choppers and everything!"

"It seems like it gets bigger every year," Nick replied, following my gaze. "Soon they'll have to shut the whole city down to host it."

"They practically have already," I observed. "It took us thirty minutes this morning to crawl two and a half miles down High Street." Nick nodded in acknowledgment.

"I should have warned you," he said. "We made our way down here at seven this morning – figured we could hang out and claim our spot before the traffic became too insane."

"Not to worry," I assured him. "We made it, notwithstanding this crazy crowd." I shook my head in amazement and continued to people watch. I wondered how far we'd walked and whether Nick would be walking with me the rest of the way. I liked his company, but I didn't want him to feel obligated to entertain me.

"So *De Alexia* is where you work?" He pointed at my chest.

"Yup," I replied. "Almost three years now." Nick squinted in recognition.

"I think I've passed by that before," he said. "It's a men's clothing store on High Street, right?" Thrilled that he'd heard of the boutique, I nodded vigorously.

"Yes!" I exclaimed. "Alex will be pleased you recognized it. Have you ever been in the store?"

"No," he admitted. "But I'll have to come by now that I know someone working there."

"Absolutely!" I exclaimed. "I think you'd like Alex's clothes."

"Who's Alex?" He asked.

"My boss," I replied. "He's one of my best friends, actually. Patrick, who you met earlier, is Alex's boyfriend." Talking fondly about Alex conjured up feelings of intense guilt. I did my best to ignore them.

"Did he not come with you guys this morning?" Nick asked, blissfully ignorant of the feelings nagging at my conscience. If he had had any clue about my actions this past week, I doubt he would have been interested in learning anything about me. The past few days wouldn't have made a very good impression.

"No," I responded. "He had a breakfast meeting this morning." I couldn't remember with whom he was meeting, but I think it had something to do with the boutique's advertisement allocation in one of the local papers.

"That's a shame," he said. "This event is too cool to miss."

"It really is," I agreed, continuing to look through the crowd.

"It's pretty awesome you get to work with one of your best friends," Nick observed after a few seconds of silence. "What do you do there?" He listened patiently as I explained my role at *De Alexia*. He seemed genuinely interested in what I was saying. He was easy to talk to and had trusting eyes. I felt at ease explaining what I did for the boutique and how Alex's line had blossomed since its meager beginnings. "That sounds like a really cool job," he said when I'd finished. "I bet you never thought you would land your dream job at your best friend's boutique and that it would be so successful."

"I like it," I said, smiling. *But it's not my dream job*, I thought.

"It's also pretty awesome you get to travel to one of the greatest cities in the world on the company dime," he continued. "Expensing meals in New York City has got to be a huge perk."

"This is very true," I said, feeling a little silly for whining to Alex about my recent increase in travel. "Sometimes it's easy to forget how lucky you are until you step back for a second." Although it wasn't my dream job, Nick was right – I was lucky to be doing something I liked with people I loved. And wining and dining designers and boutique owners at unique, rooftop restaurants in Manhattan was definitely a perk. For the first time since the start of the walk, my thoughts turned to Keegan. I smiled, fondly remembering the first time I'd seen him emerge on the rooftop of that bustling Italian market. Thinking about his gorgeous face made my face flush with fond memories, but also made me feel guilty for being here, enjoying my morning with Nick. "So why were *you* traveling from New York?" I asked, changing the subject. Now was not the time to be obsessing over Keegan. "Were you in the city for work as well?"

"No," he said, shaking his head. "But it would be great if my job sent me to places other than middle-of-nowhere Ohio!" I smiled. "I was actually in the city to visit my sister," he continued. "I try to see her once every quarter, but it can be hard to find a weekend that works well for both of us."

"What does she do out there?" I asked.

"She moved to the city after high school to try modeling, but now she stays at home with her daughter – my niece. She met her husband in the city and did the baby thing before the marriage thing at a pretty young age." From the way he talked about her, it was clear he was protective. I wondered if she was the younger sibling; I had the same protective feelings toward my little brother.

"She must be beautiful," I said. It wasn't hard to believe, given Nick's chiseled good looks. "To move to the city to model."

"She is," Nick said confidently. "And smart. I've always told her that she gave up on the modeling gig too easily." It was sweet how much he seemed to care for his sister. I wondered whether she knew how proudly he talked about her.

"Well, what do you do?" I asked. "And why doesn't your job send you to places other than rural Ohio?" Nick opened his mouth to reply, but paused as a loud group of kids came stomping past us hooting and hollering after someone in an Elmo costume. We both laughed and shook our heads as they passed. On any other day, it would have been strange to see Elmo leading a group of screaming kids down the street. But on this particular morning, nothing seemed unusual.

After Elmo and his followers faded up ahead, Nick turned to answer my question. "Like you, I'm in sales," he explained. "But unlike you, I sell staffing services within the borders of this great state."

"What do you mean by staffing services?" I asked curiously. I'd never heard of that before. He smiled as if he'd anticipated my question.

"We provide a service to companies who need our expertise to find qualified employees," he explained. "You can think of it like an outsourced human resources department. We offer services normally performed by in-house HR, but we do it cheaper, faster, and find quality people to fill unique, skilled positions." I nodded my head in comprehension, although I still didn't entirely understand. At the very least, I understood the concept of sales.

"Do you like it?" I asked.

"I like it well enough," he replied. "I didn't grow up dreaming of selling staffing services, but I like the people I work with and I make a decent living doing it, so I really can't complain." As he finished, his voice trailed off and his eyebrows narrowed into a frown as if something disappointing had caught his eye. Following his gaze, I caught a glimpse of his friend, Mark, walking ahead of us, giving Nick an encouraging smile and a thumbs up. Although he turned around quickly when he saw me looking, it was too late. I had seen the exchange. I empathized with Nick's feelings immediately. I had seen that look from Lindsay and Patrick all too many times this morning.

At once, the previously comfortable vibe between us became awkward and quiet. Nick cleared his throat nervously and I stared at my feet in silence while we walked. Although I'd tried to resist it in consideration of what was happening (or not happening) with Keegan, I was beginning to like Nick. A lot. I didn't want Mark's interruption to end the good morning we had going. Desiring to relieve the tension, I began to admit that I'd, too, been on the receiving end of similar looks from Patrick and Lindsay. Making fun of our overeager friends would be a great way to restart the conversation.

"Look," I started nervously after a minute or two of silence, "I'm really glad we decided to walk together. This morning has been great, but . . ." Nick interjected when I paused.

"Haley," he said, interrupting me, "I'm sorry about Mark – he's just trying to help me through a tough time." I stopped talking and looked at him curiously. "I was married for seven years, but my wife left me," he continued. "My divorce became final a few months ago and since then I've been totally lost." I was shocked. He laughed at my expression and threw up his hands. "I know, I know, I barely know you and here I've asked you to walk with me at this charity event, only to share some intensely personal information with you. I guess I'm telling you because everyone wants me to move on, but I don't know if I'm ready to date. And for my ego's sake, I thought I'd interrupt you before you had a chance to tell me you weren't interested." He looked at me as if he'd predicted what I was going to say. I was totally taken aback. That's not at all where I had been going.

"I'm so sorry to hear that!" I exclaimed finally, ignoring the fact that he'd misread me. Notwithstanding my mild disappointment, I felt terrible hearing the news about his recent divorce. I couldn't imagine being married for that long, thinking you'd found your life partner, only to turn around and have to start over in your mid-thirties. I was thankful that Brayden had at least ended it before I'd wasted anymore of my life loving him.

"It hasn't been easy," he acknowledged, "but we didn't have any kids, so there are no issues there." I could tell he was still in some pain. I wanted to hug him, but thought better of it.

"That's awful," I said finally. "My fiancé left me for someone else before we were married, so I understand the pain of losing the person you think you'll be with for the rest of your life." I didn't mean to make it about me, but I hoped he would appreciate someone who could empathize with how he was feeling.

"I'm sorry," he said, looking at me with similar surprise. "When things like that happen it makes you wonder whether anyone stays together anymore."

"I'd like to think so," I replied, the strained hope obvious in my tone. Nick shrugged, indicating he wasn't as certain.

"You know, it's funny how other people in your life handle your divorce," he continued, a hint of bitterness in his voice as he reflected on what he was going through. "When you're married for that long you end up having 'couple friends' – where your friends consist solely of other couples, and you never really have any friends of your own. Did you get to that point with your fiancé?"

"No," I responded adamantly. "I can't imagine not having my own friends. How would you ever vent about your spouse's annoying habits?" Nick laughed.

"Well, you're unique I guess. Katie and I, on the other hand, had couple friends. After we were divorced, these 'couple friends' decided to continue their friendship with Katie instead of me. I suppose it would have been too uncomfortable for them to maintain both friendships. Which one of us would they have invited to monthly dinners? Which one of us would have joined them for Sunday brunch? This way, it's a clean break, and no one has to feel awkward. No one except for me." I shook my head in disbelief. He seemed like such a nice guy, even through his bitter sarcasm. I couldn't imagine anyone leaving him or ending their friendship with him for such trivial reasons.

"That's ridiculous," I replied. "It seems like they were never really good friends in the first place." I regretted it as soon as I had said it. It sounded mean, and I hadn't meant to say something so harsh.

"You're right, Haley," Nick said, rescuing me. It didn't seem as if I'd offended him too badly. "Which is what makes it even harder. I didn't even *do* anything to cause the split. She just fell out of love." He shook his head as if he still couldn't believe it. I was heartbroken for him.

"Well, I think that the first step is making new friends – *real* friends." I suggested. He looked at me and smiled. His hazel eyes twinkled expectantly.

"How does one make friends at my age?" He asked curiously. "Do you think there's match.com for finding friends?" The way he was looking at me made it apparent he was being facetious. I laughed.

"Well for starters you can ask people out on friend dates," I suggested.

"Friend dates, huh?" Nick replied, looking skeptical. "That doesn't sound like it would be awkward at all. What, should I just go up to people and ask if they'll be my friends? I can see that going over well."

"Who knows," I said, ignoring his sarcasm. "Maybe you'll meet a crazy lady on a plane, see her again in a café, ask her to walk with your mother in a charity event, and end up becoming friends with her." Nick looked at me warmly and smiled. He seemed like a good guy, and I was happy to invite him into my life, even if just as a friend. Although a part of me wished there could be a possibility for more, it was probably better this way. I didn't need my situation with Keegan to be more complicated than it already was.

"Well, gee, Haley, would you like to be my friend?" He asked.

"I'd be delighted," I responded, shaking his outstretched hand. And with that, the two of us enjoyed the last two miles of the walk as newfound friends.

10 PATCHWORK

When we pulled up to Alex's apartment, I waited for Patrick to climb out of the car and shut the door before turning to Lindsay. I was nervous to talk to Alex, and Lindsay was the only person who could fully appreciate why. "I don't think I can go in there," I said, feeling a little dizzy. "I can't listen to him apologize for the things he said while I'm hiding what happened with Keegan. It's too hypocritical." Lindsay watched me wring my hands together anxiously. She rested her head on the steering wheel for a second and let out a long, drawn out sigh.

"You know what I'm going to say," she offered softly. I did know, and thus shook my head vigorously in response.

"I can't tell him," I insisted. "Not yet at least. Like I said before, it would only cause unnecessary problems. Alex wouldn't understand."

"Well then, Hale, I have no words of wisdom for you," she claimed sadly. "I understand you're in a tough position, but you made a mistake. You should own up to it. Who knows; Alex's reaction may surprise you." As much as I wanted to believe that, I doubted it.

"No, you should have seen him on Friday," I told her, peering out of the passenger side window at Alex's open apartment door. "There's no way he could possibly understand. Even if it has no bearing on the boutique – and even if it makes me happy, he won't see past the fact that I made a mistake that could have, in the giant realm of possibility, affected his business in New York." I felt myself growing angry as I relived Alex's outburst on Friday. It took all my energy to remind myself that it was me who'd wronged him, not the other way around.

"Fine, Hale, but be careful. The more you lie, the worse it will get." I turned back toward the driver's seat, considering her point. It dawned on me that there was only one way to prevent that from becoming true.

"Honestly, Linds, he doesn't ever need to know," I suggested cautiously. She looked back at me, her grayish blue eyes wide with surprise. "I know it sounds terrible, but think about it. Even if something happens with Keegan down the road, there's no reason to tell Alex that we slept together before a deal was in place. What's the harm?"

"Other than lying to one of your best friends for the rest of your life?" Lindsay's tone was incredulous.

"Other than that," I replied flatly, annoyed that she wasn't even trying to see the situation from my perspective.

"Your friendship, your call," she said in defeat. I understood why she disapproved. It probably seemed selfish to her that I wanted to hide what I'd done. But really, my omission benefitted all of us, at least temporarily. No one needed the extra stress of a scandal before this week's big meeting, especially Alex.

I watched Lindsay as she stared at her hands, looking for a nail to bite. "Stop it!" I exclaimed, grabbing her hand in mid-route to her mouth. Her nail biting was a disgusting habit, and I couldn't get her to stop. It was like a nervous tic. Sometimes she didn't even realize her hand was in her mouth. "Gross, Linds," I admonished, "if you don't quit doing that, I'm going to start buying that dog spray that prevents dogs from chewing furniture and put it on your fingers." Placing her hands in her lap, Lindsay looked at me and motioned toward Alex's apartment.

"You better get in there," she said, ignoring my threat. "You can't avoid him forever." Puffing out my cheeks in exasperation, I turned to open the car door, my nerves switching into overdrive.

"I'm going," I mumbled, more to myself than in response to Lindsay's urging.

"Oh, and Hale?" Lindsay stopped me before I'd shut the door. I leaned back into the car. "Don't think I've forgotten about the text message this morning," she declared. "We are definitely talking about it later." Grimacing, I swung the door shut and watched as she pulled away from the curb. I had hoped she'd forgotten about the text message. Filled to the brim with her irritatingly honest advice, I was tired of talking to her about Keegan.

"The prodigal friend returns." A familiar voice called from behind me once Lindsay's car had vanished around the corner. Turning around, I threw up my hands and looked at Alex sheepishly. I didn't know what to say. He was standing in the doorway of his apartment, dressed casually in a pair of cuffed jeans and an old high school t-shirt that hung loosely from his bony shoulders. He watched silently as I climbed the stairs, both of his hands shoved deep into his pockets. "Climb those stairs any slower, and I might freeze to death," he quipped smartly. Lingering purposefully on the next to last step, I looked back at him and raised my eyebrows. Hearing him jab at me like nothing was wrong settled my nerves.

"Don't even start with me," I warned him, climbing the last step. "I've been outside in this weather all morning, wearing your fancy new t-shirt. It was at least ten degrees colder an hour ago." I stopped in front of him when I reached the doorway and smiled timidly. I know it had only been a couple of days, but I missed his face. Having cut off all communication with him the last forty-eight hours, it felt like I hadn't seen him in months.

"Everything okay with Lindsay?" Alex nodded his head toward the corner of the street from where her car had disappeared.

"Yes," I replied. "Everything is fine." We stood there for a moment in the cold, neither of us knowing exactly what to say. Alex was the more stubborn of the two of us, so I was surprised when it was he who finally broke the silence.

"Did you get my flowers?" He asked, shifting his weight nervously.

"Yes," I confirmed, not unkindly. "They were beautiful." I saw a glimmer of desperation spread across Alex's face for a moment. It was obvious that he felt like the bad friend in this scenario. My feelings of guilt rose to an all-time high and the anger I'd been feeling toward him vanished. Nevertheless, I couldn't find the words to tell him the truth about what had happened.

"I'm sorry I was such an ass Friday," Alex said suddenly, his hands still shoved in his pockets. The words fell out of him hurriedly and at an unusually high volume, as if they'd been fighting to get out for some time. "I was frustrated. You were completely uncommunicative, and then this guy ends up with you in the middle of the night . . ."

"Alex," I said, trying to interrupt his rambling.

"I freaked out, Hale. And I'm sorry for . . ."

"Alex," I said more firmly, grabbing him by his arms to get his attention. I had no desire to hear him apologize for his reaction on Friday, when it was me who had been in the wrong. While he had said some hurtful things, I'd lied to his face. The whole thing sucked. I just wanted us to patch things over and not talk about it anymore. "I acted irresponsibly last week," I began. It was a painfully true statement. "You had every right to be upset with me. I might be one of your best friends, but I'm also an employee of *your* boutique. I did not behave appropriately. There's no reason to apologize for being angry with me as a result. I know you didn't mean some of the things you said."

I loosened my grip on Alex's arms and looked at him, trying not to break my gaze. I feared that if I acted even slightly as guilty as I felt, he would somehow know something was seriously amiss. Luckily, however, he couldn't read my thoughts. Instead, he smiled and pulled his hands out of his pockets, grabbing my arms in return.

"Okay, but I'm sorry and I love you, and let's never get that mad at each other again," he said softly.

"Okay," I agreed. "I'm sorry, too. You know I love you." He hugged me hastily and turned in the doorway, beckoning me to get out of the cold and follow him into the warmth of his apartment. Right before I stepped inside, however, he put his hand up to stop me.

"Once you step inside, there's no more speaking about what happened Friday," he warned. "We both said things we shouldn't have, but it's done now." I agreed to his condition all too eagerly and made my way inside. I was happy we'd moved past our confrontation. I was especially thankful that Alex hadn't asked me about the fictitious man I'd met at the hotel bar. It surprised me that he didn't want to hear the story, but I certainly wasn't going to ask why not.

"So," Alex said, rubbing his hands together, "I'm anxious to hear about the walk. Patrick tells me you had some unexpected company this morning." I laughed as I followed Alex into the apartment, burying my lies deep into the bottom of my soul.

"The whole situation is kind of random, actually," I said, making my way toward the couch where Patrick was already sitting. He was smiling at Alex and me, obviously happy that we'd reconciled. I ignored his grin and took a seat next to him on Alex's heavenly couch. "Remember the cute guy from the plane last week?" I asked, taking off my shoes and wiggling my toes to help them thaw out. "The one I hurdled over after spilling tomato juice on my new cashmere sweater?" Sitting down across from us on a leather-tufted chaise, Alex raised his eyebrows in curious anticipation.

"Yes?" He replied inquisitively, prompting me to continue.

"I saw him at breakfast yesterday with Lindsay," I told him. Alex widened his eyes and opened his mouth in disbelief. "Oh, yes, I told you it was random. Anyway, after talking to him for a couple of minutes at breakfast, he invited us to join his walking group this morning." Leaning forward, Alex opened his eyes even wider.

"What!?" He exclaimed in reply. "I can't believe this is the first time I'm hearing about this!" Biting my lower lip, I looked at him apologetically. He waved his hand in the air and shook his head indicating it didn't matter. "Never mind, never mind," he stated impatiently. "Continue the story – I want to hear what happened."

"Well," I continued, "long story short, I walked the entire race with him and have plans to meet him for lunch later this week. It turns out he is a nice and normal guy, and not a pedophilic New Yorker like you thought." Putting his hand over his open mouth, Alex stared at me, rigid and unmoving, as if the shock of my morning with Nick had frozen him into place. His overly dramatic reaction made me laugh. His flare for drama was one of the reasons he'd excelled brilliantly in community theatre.

"Don't have a stroke," Patrick said from the opposite end of the couch. "The story doesn't end like you're hoping. They've agreed to be *friends* – nothing more." Patrick's voice was laced with disappointment. Alex looked at me to verify Patrick's version of the story.

"It's true," I admitted. Alex closed his mouth and furrowed his light blonde eyebrows into a pouty frown. "I do like him," I insisted. "But he recently got divorced and isn't ready to date. There's not much I can do about it."

"That is such bullshit!" Alex exclaimed loudly, causing both Patrick and me to wince. "If he wasn't ready to start dating, why the hell did he ask you to meet up with him today?"

"I think his friends encouraged him," I suggested, remembering the look Mark had given him during the event. "I can certainly understand doing something like that to appease your pushy friends." I looked at Alex accusingly. At Alex's incessant badgering, I'd recently agreed to try online dating. After a few weeks on the site, I still hadn't found time to fill out my profile or take a decent picture. I felt strange posing for a full body picture to put on the Internet – like a prized ham at an auction.

"He shouldn't have led you on like that," Alex replied, ignoring my reference. I wrapped myself up in a nearby blanket. My thawing limbs and extremities were giving me the chills.

"I'm actually okay with it," I told him. "Like I said, we're getting lunch later in the week. Who knows what will happen." My nonchalant attitude toward the whole thing could be at least partially attributed to my feelings for Keegan. If Keegan hadn't been in the picture, I would have been way more upset about Nick suggesting we remain friends.

"Fair enough," Alex responded, leaning back in the chaise and crossing his feet. "I'll reserve judgment until everything plays out." The three of us sat silently for a moment, each of us lost in our own thoughts. Predictably, my thoughts focused on Keegan. I was excited that he was coming into town this week, but nervous to be around him in front of Alex.

"That reminds me," I said, breaking the silence. Hesitating, I wondered why I'd said that out loud. Alex raised his head with peaked interest, waiting for me to share what had popped into my mind. "I, uh… I don't know what reminded me exactly, but Keegan Bransford is flying into Columbus tomorrow to meet with you," I informed him. Alex shot up into a sitting position, looking annoyed.

"That's a little presumptuous," he replied. "No one asked me if I was available tomorrow. In fact, I'm completely *unavailable* tomorrow. I have several things on my plate, including a meeting with Charlie and a couple of our manufacturers about recent delays."

"I'm sure that isn't a problem," I assured him. "He's in town until

Thursday. Don't get upset. I think he and Naresh are simply anxious to get the ball rolling." Alex calmed down and leaned back on the lounger.

"Okay, well I'm good all day Tuesday. If you can schedule something then, I would very much appreciate it."

"Consider it done," I said. I was disappointed he wasn't more excited about Keegan's impending visit, but I understood why he felt offended. By scheduling his flight without consulting us, it felt like Keegan had assumed we would make time for him no matter what we had going on. It was a little arrogant.

"I hate to say it, Hale, but you'll probably have the unhappy task of entertaining him Monday while I'm in meetings." I gulped, trying to portray indifference to Alex's suggestion. "I know babysitting isn't exactly in your job description," Alex continued, "but it will be worth it for the future of the boutique. I'll certainly owe you one."

"It's fine," I said, calmly. "I don't mind." I didn't think Alex intended for me to entertain Keegan in the way Keegan was expecting. I could feel my neck start to flush in embarrassment as I remembered Keegan's text message from a few hours earlier. Distracted by the morning's events, I hadn't yet responded. I hadn't even considered what to say until now. I shifted anxiously in my seat on the couch. Talking about Keegan made me uncomfortable. Every mention of his name felt like an extension of my lie. "I'm going to use the bathroom and get out of here," I announced, standing from the couch and moving toward the back of the apartment. "I have to take care of a few things today before Keegan gets into town. After he gets here, who knows how much time I'll have to myself." The comment had been harmless, but I couldn't help but wince at the thought of Alex interpreting what I had said in a way that would uncover my indiscretions. I listened, but he never bothered to respond.

When I returned to the living room, Alex had moved from the chaise to the couch to replace my spot under the blanket. Patrick was sitting beside him, focused on the television as he flipped through the channels. "I'm outta here," I proclaimed, grabbing my shoes from in front of Alex's feet and making my way toward the door. The two of them, hunkered down for an afternoon of leisure, simultaneously bid me adieu with lazy waves.

"Never go two days without talking to me again!" Alex demanded as I opened the front door. I promised him I wouldn't.

"I'd miss you too much," I gushed, shamefully ignoring the insufferable pangs of guilt in the bottom of my stomach.

The moment I stepped outside, the cold air rushed me as if it knew I hadn't yet zipped up my jacket. Bundling up hastily, I stepped into my shoes to start the short walk to my apartment. Although the walk to my place was only a few minutes long, I called my brother to distract me from the heavy guilt with which I'd left Alex's apartment. I had been meaning to call him for a few days now anyway to talk about our plans for Dad's anniversary. Lowering my face to avoid the wind, I dialed his number and waited patiently for him to answer.

"Hey, Hale!" My brother's voice rang happily through the receiver. I could hear the rumbling of people in the background and wondered if he was in the middle of hosting an art show.

"Where are you?" I asked curiously.

"At the gallery," he responded, confirming my suspicions. I was surprised that he had picked up his phone in the middle of work.

"Am I interrupting?" I inquired. "I can call back if it's a bad time."

"No, not at all," Michael assured me cheerfully. He was always chipper. His persistently happy mood had annoyed me terribly during our teenage years. Now, the sound of his cheery voice made me smile. "There are a couple of us working today and I could use the break," he insisted. "I'm not a huge fan of the artist we're displaying anyway. I'm a little tired of trying to sell her crappy art." I laughed, hoping that no one around him could hear what he was saying. There was no doubt I was talking to the same old Michael I'd known and loved for twenty-four years – never one to embellish or sugarcoat a situation. He always told the truth, no matter how harsh.

Michael's primary goal was to create and sell his own art, but he worked at an up-and-coming Nashville gallery as a way to help pay the bills. He was known throughout the local art community as a young and talented artist, but hadn't yet made it big enough to cover his living expenses. His notoriety helped the gallery's owner attract customers and sell paintings, but it annoyed Michael to be hosting art shows featuring other artists when it was his art he ultimately wanted to sell.

Notwithstanding his frustrations, I was proud of him for pursuing his dreams and refusing to settle for a more stable and lucrative job as our mother had insisted. He was fearless and determined to do what he loved; character traits I envied dearly. "So you got my message I assume?" He inquired, guessing the reason for my call. I noticed that the rumbling in the background had faded. I assumed he had moved into a back room to get away from the crowd.

"Sure did," I acknowledged. "Believe it or not, I almost forgot the date was coming up. Work has been crazy – I've been traveling a lot and trying to secure an important deal for the boutique. I guess I just got caught up in everything going on. I'm glad you called to remind me." I frowned, wondering what Michael would say if I told him exactly how I'd been trying to secure a deal with Keegan. The thought of it made me feel sick to my stomach. Seeing my relationship with Keegan from any perspective other than my own was unpleasant.

"You would have remembered as it got closer," Michael said confidently. "But I wanted to call and plan ahead because I'm actually staying in Cincinnati for a couple of days."

"Really? Any reason?"

"Just to visit some friends," he explained. "I'm coming up the night before Dad's anniversary and then staying through the weekend." Counting the days, I realized he would be in Ohio in a mere week and a half.

"That's great!" I replied. "I'll have to ask Alex whether I can hang out down there. We've been so busy lately that he may need me at the boutique."

"You're still meeting me at the graveyard, right?" Michael sounded concerned.

"Of course!" I confirmed. "Noon like always."

"Gotcha." Michael cleared his throat. "So Hale," he began hesitantly. "Have you talked to Mom lately?" Although Michael hadn't been thrilled about Mother's remarriages over the years, he had remained closer to her than I. He stayed with her whenever he was in Cincinnati and tried to encourage me to call her every so often. I wished he'd leave me alone and let me worry about my relationship with our mother. I didn't appreciate his subtle attempts to interfere.

"Nope, not really," I said curtly.

"Well you should," he said, lecturing me. "She would be happy to hear from you."

"Why?" I was becoming irritated. "So she can ask me whether I have a boyfriend? Or tell me about her latest marriage to another random dude who will convince her to get rid of even more of Dad's stuff? I don't think so." The line went silent for a second. I regretted snapping, but I didn't want to talk about Mother. I had called him to talk about Dad.

"Fine," Michael said finally, less cheerful than when he'd answered the phone. "I just hate to see you living your life effectively parentless." I huffed in response. He was my little brother. It was me who was supposed to be worried about him, not the other way around. "Changing the subject then," Michael continued, "how have your sketches been looking lately? Any new and exciting ideas pinging around in that weird head of yours?" I chuckled, thankful for the topic change.

When I graduated from college, Michael gave me a notebook in which I could write down design ideas or sketches whenever I felt inspired. I carried it with me always. It was made of recycled paper and had a thin pink binding that was now frayed from overuse. The cover boasted a copy of Claude Monet's famous *Water Lilies* painting – a painting my brother had used to create an impressionist piece shortly after Dad passed away. My brother was in third grade at the time, and the painting still hung in our elementary school. Every time I pulled out my notebook, I was reminded of the way he'd thrown himself into art to cope with his grief. He was an old, sophisticated soul, even as a child.

"I hate to admit it," I stated regrettably, "but I've been neglecting my sketching lately." It was true – I hadn't created a new sketch in months. "It's hard to clear your mind and get the creative juices flowing when you're so damn busy at work," I explained.

"I understand completely, Hale," Michael replied empathetically. "Just don't let it drift into the background. Keep your dreams a priority or else that's what they'll always be – dreams."

"My younger brother the philosopher," I taunted.

"Just sayin'," he said. I imagined him sitting in a back room of the gallery, his brown hair shaggy, but neat, shrugging his shoulders while leaning comfortably on a desk or filing cabinet. I missed him dearly and couldn't wait to see him. "I guess I should probably get back to work, huh?" He suggested finally. "It was lovely talking to you, as always."

"And to you, dear brother," I responded, walking up to my apartment.

"I love you, Haley," he said, before hanging up the phone. "See you next week."

"I love you, too," I repeated back, reaching into my pocket to grab my keys. An intense feeling of loneliness swept over me as I hung up the phone and turned the key in the lock. Despite all of the people in my life telling me they loved me, here I was again, poised to spend the rest of the day in my apartment, alone with my thoughts. I could hardly stand it anymore. I wondered painfully if there would ever come a time when I'd come home to a significant other – someone who would love me unconditionally and fill the lonely spaces in my heart. I pushed open the creaky front door and crinkled my nose in disgust as the stale, musty scent of the empty apartment filled my nostrils. Slipping off my shoes, I reached into my jacket pocket and pulled out my phone with newfound resolve. It was true that I'd have to endure my loneliness today, but tomorrow, I was satisfied in knowing that at least temporarily, I would be able to fill my desperate, lonely longing with the warm, fit body of Keegan Bransford.

11 HOTEL RENDEZVOUS

I sat on the edge of the hotel bed wrapped in a sheet, staring at the clock. The past thirty-six hours had been an incredible blur, filled with an intense level of passion I had never before experienced. Keegan and I had spent every moment together since yesterday morning, leaving the hotel for only a brief moment to grab a couple of coffees from the shop across the street. With our phones switched to silent, I felt like a college kid in love, enjoying the luxury of being with Keegan without worrying about my responsibilities to the outside world. Being with him made me feel alive and desirable – like nothing else mattered but the feel of each other's bodies between the sheets.

"So is it time?" Keegan asked groggily, rubbing my lower back lightly with his left hand. Although his touch was subtle, it sent shivers up my spine in excitement. The mere feel of him made me regret scheduling the meeting with Alex for so early in the week. A later appointment meant we could have stayed in bed for days.

"Unfortunately, yes," I responded, rolling back over in the bed to face him. His sapphire eyes glimmered as the morning sunlight poked between the curtains and caught the top half of his face. I placed my hand gently on the side of his cheek, rubbing my thumb along the roughness of his jaw. I loved the short stubble that had grown in the past day, giving him an almost burly, woodsman look. He was irresistibly gorgeous, and for the past day and a half, he'd been mine.

I pulled him toward me for a kiss, my heart racing as his hands moved behind my head, intertwining his fingers in my brown, messy hair. I wasn't sure what the future held for us, or how he even felt about me outside the walls of this hotel, but I could feel myself falling for him. Not wanting to think about the obstacles that faced a potential relationship, I concentrated on the feel of his lips and the warmth of his chest against mine. He pulled away and smiled, looking at me, with his hands still behind my head.

"We've gotta get going," he said, in a way that told me he regretted it as much as I. Groaning, he let go of me and swung his feet onto the floor, rubbing his eyes to chase away the sleep. I moved up behind him as he sat there, hugging him as I straddled his back, my gangly legs dangling off the side of the bed next to his. I never wanted to let him go, but unfortunately, we had an important business meeting to get to in one short hour. Gently breaking my embrace, he stood up and wandered into the bathroom, the door still ajar as he started the shower.

"How much time before we need to leave?" He asked, pulling back the shower curtain. I double-checked the bedside clock and heard him step into the tub and reposition the curtain.

"About thirty minutes," I shouted, still lying in bed, covered under the blankets. It would only take us fifteen minutes to walk up the street to the boutique, but I wanted to make sure we left in plenty of time so as not to risk being late. Alex prized himself on punctuality and expected those with whom he did business to do the same.

Reaching toward the nightstand, I grabbed my phone to see whether I'd missed any important calls over the past day or so. Nothing seemed to be amiss. The outside world had continued to function in my absence. I sent Alex a message letting him know that Keegan and I would be at the boutique in short order. Although Alex knew I had planned to swing by Keegan's hotel to serve as his escort to the store this morning, he didn't know I'd be spending the last thirty-six hours with the gorgeous young designer.

Placing my phone back on the nightstand, I rested my head on my pillow and sighed. Continuing to deceive Alex was becoming almost unbearable. I hoped that today's meeting would help secure Keegan's relationship with the boutique and give me the opportunity to pursue our relationship openly. I looked forward to when I could be done with all of the lies.

"Hurry it up!" I called to Keegan. He had been in the shower for at least five minutes. "I need to get in there, too!" I reminded him. I didn't think he'd heard me until I saw his face peek suggestively around the corner of the door.

"There's room for one more," he said, curling his lips up into a devilish grin. Biting my lower lip coyly I smiled back at him. It took only a couple of seconds for me to jump out of bed and rush into the bathroom to accept his invitation. Punctuality was important to Alex, that much was certain, but there was no way I was going to refuse such an irresistible offer from such an irresistible man.

****

Keegan and I started walking to the store twenty minutes prior to the scheduled start of our meeting. Even with the unplanned distraction in the shower, our timing had turned out perfectly. My hair was a little damp, but I looked fairly well put together considering. I was dressed in a cute outfit – my favorite navy blazer over a cream, flowing blouse and gray skinny jeans – and had on my trusty pair of nude pumps that gave me three extra inches of height and could carry me for miles without pain.

I was thankful I'd dressed the part yesterday, not realizing that it would be the same outfit I'd be wearing for the meeting today. The only unusual element to my appearance was the lack of makeup. I didn't wear a lot of makeup anyway, but it was a rare occasion that I emerged from my apartment sans foundation. I hoped Alex would chalk it up to my running late. I doubt he'd even notice.

Pulling my blazer together to block out the wind, I shuddered to shake off the chill of the air as we began to walk the few blocks to *De Alexia*. It wasn't as cold as the past couple of weeks, but it seemed as though the temperature was still clinging desperately to the disappearing winter air. Keegan watched me shiver, apparently impervious to cold weather himself. "I wish I could take you back to the hotel and warm you up," he said, smiling suggestively. He wrapped his arm around me and pulled me in close, using his body heat to protect me from the wind. Panicking a little, I wrestled out of his grasp and swung my head around, looking for a familiar face.

"You need to be careful," I told him quietly, easing up a little when I didn't notice anyone familiar. "Columbus is a smaller city than you realize. You never know who you might run into on the street." Keegan moved next to me closely and subtly placed his hand under my blazer, completely undeterred by my warning.

"You embarrassed to be seen with me?" He teased, pinching my skin a little. I tried not to smile as I batted his hand away, reissuing my warning once again.

"Seriously," I insisted, trying to remain firm. "You're the one who suggested we hide our involvement in the first place, remember?" Keegan eventually let go and cleared his throat, peering at me defiantly through those sexy pale blue eyes. I smirked back at him playfully, glad that he'd decided to heed my warnings.

"This is a cool little area," he observed as we walked through the southern most part of Short North and into the center of the district.

"I like it," I said proudly. I was pleased he liked it too. I had grown attached to this part of the city. No place had ever felt so much like home for me. Not even my hometown of Cincinnati. I'd finally felt as if I'd found my place in the world. It dawned on me that Keegan's place in the world existed several hundred miles away. I didn't want to think about what this meant for our future. Shaking my head, I tried not to get ahead of myself. I didn't even know if Keegan wanted a future.

"How close are we?" He asked, continuing to admire his surroundings.

"About five minutes," I estimated, searching his face for any clues as to how he felt about me. Quickly giving up, I pointed to the Italian restaurant on our left where I'd made dinner reservations for this evening. "I hope you like it," I said. "I know it's hard to compete with New York restaurants, but this place is fantastic." Keegan nodded weakly.

"You know, I'm actually not going to make dinner tonight," he revealed. My heart sunk at the unexpected news. I looked at him, confused, and a little hurt.

"Why not?" I asked. Although I'd probably already made my feelings for him rather obvious, I tried not to reveal my disappointment. "What other engagements could you possibly have in Columbus?"

"None," he admitted. "I'm going back home this evening." My heart continued to sink until it came to a sulky rest at my feet. "When you told me on Sunday that the meeting would be today, I changed my flight."

"Why didn't you tell me?" I asked, this time unable to hide my upset. "Here I thought we had two more days to spend together." I wondered in annoyance why he hadn't mentioned it before. He'd had plenty of time in the last day and a half to say something. Keegan stopped walking and placed his hand gently on my arm. He looked at me warmly, stepping close enough so I could hear him whisper.

"How I wish I could kiss you to wipe that pouty look off your face," he said, holding me a little too intimately. His breath was warm on my cheeks and his eyes gazed intensely into mine. For a brief moment, I forgot we were standing in the middle of High Street.

"Be careful," I reminded him, breaking his trance and glancing down the sidewalk again. My words told him to stop, but I hadn't moved from his grasp. Knowing he was leaving today made me want to stay in his arms – as if the longer he held me, the longer I could go without seeing him again.

It was only until he tightened his grip and pulled me in closer as if to kiss me, that I wriggled away from him. "You're impossible!" I said, giggling a little. "We only have a few more hours," I reminded him. "After you have a deal in place with Alex, you can kiss me wherever you'd like. But until then, be careful. Alex will pick up on even the most subtle of hints." Keegan's flirting halted and his face turned serious in a matter of seconds. I wondered what I'd said to change his mood so drastically.

"Haley," he said seriously, putting his hands in his pockets. "I've been meaning to talk to you about that."

"About what?" I asked him, a little worried.

"We probably shouldn't tell anyone about what's happened between us; it wouldn't look very good." I shook my head, realizing the misunderstanding between us.

"Oh . . . no, I know," I assured him. "I wasn't going to say anything about what's happened. I meant for the future. There's no harm in being openly affectionate if Alex thinks something developed between us after today . . . right?" Keegan's look of concern didn't fade in the way I'd expected.

"We probably shouldn't tell anyone, even after today," he suggested. His face was pained, but from what I didn't know. "I have a reputation to uphold and I don't want Naresh to think I sleep with people to advance my career. It's always messy when you mix business with pleasure. You know how quickly gossip spreads throughout the industry." I looked at him, not sure how to feel. He talked about his reputation, but made no mention of mine. It made me wonder whether he thought I was the type of person who *would* sleep around to advance my career. The thought of him judging me made me feel vulnerable and uncomfortable, in stark contrast to the comfort and ease with which he'd instilled in me just moments ago at the hotel.

"I appreciate where you're coming from," I replied, though it wasn't entirely true. "But continuing to hide what's happening between us means I'm lying to one of my best friends. I'm not comfortable with that." Keegan's eyes pleaded with me to understand.

"I know," he said, grabbing my arms again. "I'm sorry that it puts you in that position. But I'm just asking you to keep it between us for a little while longer." I looked at him suspiciously. I wondered how much longer he meant. I feared he meant indefinitely. I wanted to talk more about this, but now wasn't the appropriate time or place. Reluctantly, I relented.

"Okay," I agreed, looking down at the sidewalk. Keegan used a finger to lift my chin so I would look at him. His dimple flashed at me as he smiled, satisfied by my response.

"Thank you," he said softly. "Now, let's get going. Speaking of reputations, we don't want to be late."

****

Alex greeted us almost immediately when Keegan and I walked into the store. I suspected he'd been waiting at the front, pretending to fold clothes or help customers while glancing anxiously out of the windows. This was a huge meeting for Alex. He'd been looking for someone to design shoes for his line since well before Naresh was even on our radar. Today marked a big step into *De Alexia*'s bright future. It was a shame I couldn't share in his excitement, uncomfortably distracted by my recent conversation with Keegan.

"Mr. Bransford, I presume," Alex said, extending his hand toward Keegan for introductions. Keegan smiled politely and shook Alex's hand. As the two of them exchanged pleasantries, I stood there trying to appear as professional as possible, smiling encouragingly at Alex as he beamed at Keegan.

Once they'd finished introductions, Alex motioned for us to follow him toward the back of the store. "Why don't you go ahead and follow me to the office," he suggested. "Unless, of course, you'd like a quick tour of the boutique." He turned to Keegan expectantly.

"I'd like that very much," Keegan replied.

"Great!" Alex exclaimed, his voice almost giddy. "Hale, will you go back into the office and hang out with Charlie while I show Keegan around? He's been back there for a while alone. He probably wouldn't mind the company."

"Of course," I said, obliging his request. I was happy to leave them alone. Seeing the two of them together put my deceit on full display. It wasn't a pleasant feeling.

When I opened the door to the back room, I found Charlie half-asleep in one of the wooden chairs Alex had set out for the meeting. In addition to our resident red chair, we also stored two fiercely uncomfortable wooden chairs and a bar stool in the back room for gatherings such as this. We'd found the wooden chairs on the side of the street in Victorian Village almost two years ago, and had leapt at the opportunity to acquire some seating for the boutique without having to spend any money. After we'd finally started making a profit, one of the first things we'd meant to do is replace the wooden chairs. Unfortunately, however, we still hadn't replaced them.

"Hi, Charlie," I said as I walked into the room. The floor was dusty and the shelves along the walls disorganized. I was surprised Alex hadn't cleaned it better in preparation for the meeting. Not having heard me walk in, Charlie jumped at the sound of my voice, his eyes widening in a quick adjustment from daydreaming to high alert. I chuckled. "It's just me, Charlie," I assured him, permitting him to relax. "Alex is giving Keegan a tour of the store before they head back here." Charlie cleared his throat and adjusted his suit jacket, standing up to give my hand a shake. Although I'd known him for over a year, Charlie was always observant of the usual formalities. He took his job as our attorney seriously and professionally. Lindsay adored Charlie's professionalism. She liked to call him one of the 'good guys.'

"Haley, nice to see you as always," he said, sitting back down and shuffling the papers he'd laid out on the table in front of him. He was dressed in a sharp, navy blue suit, paired with a white dress shirt and a patterned red tie. His balding brown hair was short and tidy, and his black shoes appeared to have been recently polished. Alex liked to tease him about his conservative style, encouraging him to shop at *De Alexia* by offering him a sizeable discount. No matter how hard Alex tried, however, Charlie never seemed interested in purchasing the boutique's latest trends. I often wondered whether he owned any casual clothes. I'd never seen him in anything but a suit, even after hours at the local bars or restaurants.

"It's nice to see you, too," I said politely, sitting down next to him in another hard wooden chair. "How long have you been here?"

"I arrived an hour or so ago," he answered. "I wanted to talk to Alex about the type of contract he should propose to Mr. Bransford in the event they decide to work together." I nodded, thankful that Alex never asked me to deal with the more technical side of the business. I didn't mind sales, but any administrative tasks involving management, human resources, or legal decisions made my head hurt.

"I think there's a good chance they'll decide to work together," I said hopefully, crossing my legs and then uncrossing them in the same motion after realizing that neither position made the chair more comfortable. I winced and sat in an awkward, upright position, making a mental note to have Alex replace the damn chairs. "Unlike everyone else we talked to when considering hiring a shoe designer," I continued, trying to ignore my discomfort, "Keegan – Mr. Bransford – is talented and seems to understand Alex's vision." Charlie nodded and rifled through his briefcase for his blackberry.

"Do you mind if I check my email while we wait?" He asked politely.

"Of course not," I assured him, wrenching my back as I tried in vain to find a more comfortable position. The two of us sat for a few minutes in silence while Charlie tended to his other clients and I fidgeted in my chair. Eventually giving up on being comfortable, I watched him read his emails and type responses. I wondered what had prompted him to start his own law firm. Lindsay interned at Charlie's office during one of her summers in law school. I remember her telling me that she'd enjoyed the small office and respected Charlie and the other two attorneys that worked there. Charlie had asked Lindsay to come back after graduating to become the fourth attorney in the office, but she'd decided to accept the glamorous big-firm offer instead. She'd told me one night after a couple of months at the firm (and a couple of glasses of wine) that the big-firm offer had been too enticing to refuse. In an unusual temporary state of weakness, she'd admitted regretting not considering Charlie's offer more seriously. 'Had I known then what I know now,' she'd mused, 'I don't know whether I would have taken this job.'

Charlie looked up from his blackberry as if he'd read my thoughts. "How's Lindsay?" He asked curiously. "I've been trying to schedule a lunch with her, but she says she's buried under piles and piles of work." I nodded knowingly.

"Nothing new there," I said, empathizing with his inability to pin her down. "Other than being totally buried, she's good." As I watched Charlie turn his attention back to his blackberry, I found myself hoping that eventually he might consider reoffering Lindsay a position at his firm. He must have understood the reason why she'd initially taken the big-firm job. It certainly wasn't because she didn't like Charlie or his office. The amount of money she was making at the big firm was simply too hard to turn down, especially in light of the large sums of looming law school debt she'd faced upon graduation.

My thoughts about Lindsay stopped when I heard Alex's voice approaching the door. Turning toward the front of the office expectantly, I felt a small rush of adrenaline when I saw Keegan walk into the room behind Alex.

"Well, you've done great things with the store," Keegan was saying. Alex motioned for him to take a seat in the coveted red chair.

"Thank you," Alex said, smiling, moving toward the stool between Charlie and me. "Please grab a seat. Oh, and this is our attorney, Charlie Leiter," he said, continuing the introductions. "Charlie, meet Keegan Bransford, the shoe designer we've been discussing."

"Nice to meet you," Charlie said, shaking Keegan's hand.

"Likewise," Keegan responded, seating himself comfortably in preparation for the meeting. He gave me a subtle wink. I shifted uncomfortably, wondering whether Alex had seen it.

Alex didn't hesitate to start the meeting, oblivious to the nonverbal communication coming from his potential new business partner. Before long,

Alex was discussing his vision and plans for the boutique's future and giving Keegan a full rundown of his expectations for their potential partnership. My interest peaked when it finally came time for Keegan to take out his sketches to show Alex. I felt Keegan's eyes on me as Alex looked them over, but remained fixed on Alex's face as he perused them. I couldn't tell what he was thinking. It made me incredibly nervous. Handing the sketches back to Keegan, Alex turned to me for the first time since the start of the meeting, a satisfied smile creeping across his thin face. I smiled back, relieved.

"Haley told me you had hit the ball out of the park," Alex admitted, turning back to Keegan. "And because she's usually so critical, I was curious to see whether I agreed with her assessment." Keegan seemed to pick up on Alex's approval as well because he began to smile too. His dimple flashed gorgeously at the curl of his lips.

"Do you agree?" Keegan asked, already knowing the answer.

"I do," Alex confessed, nodding his head and reaching his hand out to Keegan. "I am thoroughly impressed. We'd love to have you on board."

"Excellent!" Keegan exclaimed without hesitation. I watched the two of them seal their new relationship with a firm handshake. I was happy for Alex and for the boutique, but disappointed that their solidified business partnership couldn't set me free from my prison of lies.

"If you're up for it, I'd love to jump right in and talk about what Charlie and I have conjured up in terms of an agreement."

"Of course," Keegan responded. "Although anything you give me today will have to be reviewed by my lawyer back in the city before anything becomes final."

"Understood," Alex responded, turning to me. "Hale, you don't have to sit through the rest of this stuff," he said. "It's all legal mumbo jumbo you don't need to worry about – we'll see you at dinner." I looked hesitantly at Keegan as I rose from my seat.

"I actually can't make dinner tonight," he told Alex quickly. "I rescheduled my flight for this evening. I want to get back and meet with my lawyer as soon as possible to get the ball rolling on these designs."

"That's absolutely not a problem," Alex assured him. "Haley can cancel the reservations." Alex turned to me and smiled, unaware of what I continued to hide. "Thanks Hale! I'll call you later."

"Sure thing," I responded. Though I mostly should have felt guilty, I instead found myself wondering when I'd see Keegan again. I wanted to give him the proper goodbye. I wanted to ask him when he'd be back. But I couldn't. Not in front of Alex. Looking longingly at Keegan, I forced a smile. "It was nice to see you again, Keegan. Have a safe flight back." He smiled in response as I turned to escape through the door.

I was devastated he was leaving without a solid promise of a quick return. Even after spending the most intimate day and a half of my life with him, I'd never been more confused or unsure about where I stood. I didn't know if he felt the same way; I didn't even know whether he planned to visit me again. Suddenly, I was scared that while I was falling in love, he was simply, passing the time.

"It was nice seeing you too, Haley!" Keegan called as the door shut slowly behind me. "It was a pleasure, as always," he added, his words filled with a meaning neither Alex nor Charlie would understand. Walking home alone, my head spinning uncontrollably, I wasn't sure I understood their meaning either.

12 UNPLANNED ATTRACTION

The weather was chilly, but comfortable in the late morning as I sat down on a nearby park bench to enjoy my second cup of coffee of the day. The trees surrounding the pond in front of me were blooming beautifully, uncaring that the warm weather had been late to arrive this year. I enjoyed watching the vibrant colors come alive in celebration of the end of winter almost as much as I enjoyed the orangey hues of the leaves in autumn that would eventually wither and fall in anticipation of winter's return. As much as I despised winter's bout of cold weather, there was something therapeutic and profound about the seasons. While each fall served as a reminder that all good things must come to an end, spring countered that sentiment by serving as a reminder that things would get better, no matter how harsh the winter.

Wrapped comfortably in a wool sweater and scarf, I crossed my legs and sipped slowly on the hot French Roast I'd picked up a few minutes before, thankful for this little piece of heaven amidst a busy and tumultuous week. I had hoped to feel better once Keegan and Alex had finalized their contract, but unfortunately, the christening of a deal hadn't relieved any of the guilt I'd been harboring since first lying to Alex. Instead, the contract – reached a day after Tuesday's meeting – only seemed to exacerbate those feelings, while simultaneously making me excited about Keegan's new pivotal role in the future of *De Alexia*. It was all very exhausting.

Keegan called after the meeting to apologize for not being able to properly say goodbye. He insisted that if he'd known how amazing his Monday would be, he would have never changed his flight. His phone call had done wonders to alleviate some of the doubts I'd been feeling after he'd left. I was happy that our time together had left an impression on him, and hoped it was of similar magnitude to the impression it had left on me.

Continuing to sip my coffee and reflect on the past couple of days, I watched as a woman and her dog – some type of retriever/poodle mix – went running through the middle of the park. Bounding faithfully beside her, the dog passed disinterestedly by the other park goers, concerned only with keeping up with his master's stride. *Maybe I should get a dog,* I thought to myself, taking another small sip of my coffee. The dog's obedience was inspiring and its loyalty, I'm sure, was unmatched. I had considered getting a dog before to alleviate some of my loneliness, but ultimately determined that it was too much money and effort. With my travel schedule, it would be almost cruel to get a dog only to have to leave it home all day or keep it locked away in a kennel. Besides, with Keegan now tentatively in the picture, maybe I wouldn't have to be on my own for too much longer. I almost scoffed out loud at the thought. My future with the designer was far too uncertain to be hoping for such things. I scolded myself for allowing the thought to slip unbidden into my mind.

Forcefully discarding my daydreams about Keegan, I checked the time as the woman and her dog disappeared into the park. Standing up lazily and stretching, still nursing my coffee, I prepared to make the mile trek up High Street to meet Nick for lunch at one of my favorite organic cafés. I sighed anxiously when my thoughts turned to Nick. I'd considered canceling the lunch in light of the recent developments in my relationship with Keegan, but when it came time to send the text, I couldn't go through with it. I wasn't sure whether it was because I had some feelings for Nick or whether I simply needed someone to talk to who didn't remind me of my secret love affair, but whatever the reason, the lunch was still on.

The walk from the park to the café was relaxing and pleasant. Although it was already noon, it still felt like morning, with the sun sitting low in the sky and the community barely stirring as if still trying to wake up. Crossing the street and avoiding a speeding cyclist, I darted into the café with my now-empty coffee. I saw Nick almost immediately upon entering, smiling and waving at me from a couch across the café floor. He was certainly a sight to behold. His brown hair was gelled effortlessly and his cleanly shaven face revealed a defined, square jaw. Dressed in a pinstripe suit and a handsome shirt and tie combination of navy blues and greens, he closed whatever magazine he'd been browsing and strolled over to greet me.

As I thought about how dashing he looked, I felt my chest tighten and my heart palpitate quickly with unexpected nerves. Taken aback by my physical reaction, I shook my head and reminded myself that Nick had come here as a friend and nothing more. Moreover, although Keegan and I certainly weren't exclusive (if we were even dating at all), I felt a little ridiculous being attracted to another man so soon after Monday.

Holding out my hand in anticipation of greeting him, I let out a quick, "Oh!" as I found myself enveloped in an embrace more fitting for longtime friends. Shifting awkwardly in Nick's arms, I cleared my throat and pulled a loose strand of hair behind my ear to break the hug. A little breathless, I laughed and smiled at him, trying not to appear shaken by his greeting choice.

"Hi!" I said, a little more high-pitched than I'd intended.

"How are you?" Nick replied, motioning for me to go ahead of him in the ordering line. Obliging his request, I took a step into the line and paused.

"I'm fine," I said, feeling myself settle calmly into normalcy. "Crazy week at work yet again, but otherwise, can't really complain." Nick nodded in agreement.

"Work has been tough on me too this week," he commiserated. "And with my family in town this past weekend, I didn't get much rest. What about you? Have you been doing some unexpected traveling?"

"Not exactly," I responded, thinking about whether my recent stay in Keegan's hotel could be considered traveling. "We had a big client in town earlier in the week and it zapped all of my energy." I blushed. The comment left me feeling a little dirty, although I hadn't meant it that way.

"Gotta love sales," Nick replied, grabbing a couple of the café's paper menus stacked conveniently along the wall. "Taking care of an important client can be more exhausting than babysitting."

"Yeah, it was tiring," I said vaguely. "Oh, I don't need one," I added as he stretched a menu out in my direction, "but thank you."

"A regular, I see," Nick observed, placing the menu back along the wall. His smile was infectious, just like his mom's. I smiled fondly in return, remembering our walk together, and nodded my head in acknowledgment.

"I love this café," I confirmed. "I've been here so many times that I know the menu by heart." Nick looked at me, his eyebrows raised in mild amazement. He had the kindest eyes.

"Well I've never been here, if you can believe it." He admitted. "Any recommendations?" I looked at him apologetically. I felt bad that I'd picked a place he'd never been.

"You should have told me you'd never been here!" I exclaimed earnestly. "Are you sure this is okay? I'd be happy to go somewhere else." Nick shook his head firmly and continued to browse the menu.

"No, no, I've been meaning to try it," he insisted. "Seriously, don't worry about it. Now, for my first experience, what should I get?"

"It depends on what you're looking for," I replied, still worried that I'd forced my favorite lunch spot on him without even asking whether he liked it. "Are you sure this is okay? Seriously, there are a ton of places around, we can go somewhere else if you'd like."

"No! Stop worrying about it," he assured me. He placed his hand on my shoulder for only a second, but it was enough to make the back of my neck flush. "I would have said something to you Sunday if I didn't want to try it out." Ignoring my body's physical reaction to his touch, I studied him suspiciously. Peering back at me over the menu, Nick raised his eyebrows.

"So . . . recommendations?" He asked again.

"Fine," I said, caving into the realization that we wouldn't be leaving whether he liked the place or not. "Alex – my boss," I continued, "loves the black bean burrito. It's fresh and filling and comes with some awesome guacamole. It's delicious. I, on the other hand, generally stick to their gourmet salads. Every salad is topped with something decadent like candied pecans or goat cheese. They're a little lighter, but are served with giant bread rolls to ensure you don't leave here hungry. Honestly, you can't go wrong, whatever you choose." Lifting his head from the menu and placing it back on the wall without hesitation, he clapped his hands together in excited anticipation.

"Burrito it is," he said eagerly. "That sounds really good." As I smiled at him, I found myself comparing his dark, chiseled features to Keegan's. They both had the same chestnut hair, though Keegan's was wavier, and the same infectious boyish grins. Their eyes, on the other hand – each pair magnetic in their own way – could not have been more different.

Inching up to an open register, Nick ordered his meal and beckoned me to do the same. I insisted on paying for myself, but he refused to let me order separately. It was a sweet gesture. Before I could thank him, however, a woman at the cash register next to us crossed her arms and narrowed her eyes at Nick in disapproval.

"You know, it's been several decades since the Women's Rights Movement," she told him, her face peppered with piercings and her dreadlocks pulled back into a lazy ponytail, "but small acts like paying for a woman's meal continue to perpetuate the very traditional gender roles that the movement tried to eradicate." Snatching her order number and heading for a table near the back of the restaurant, I watched as she stomped away in annoyance. My eyes wide with disbelief, I turned to Nick, who was standing at the cash register in mild shock.

Counting out Nick's change, our cashier seemed unfazed by the woman's sudden outburst. Judging by the cashier's nonchalant reaction, I suspected the heavily pierced woman to be a regular whose hostile attitude toward complete strangers was something of a normal occurrence. Given how often I ate at the café, I was surprised I'd never seen her before. Feeling myself fill with laughter, I poked Nick on the shoulder and whispered low so as not to be heard by any other nosy bystanders.

"I told you that you should have let me pay for myself," I said, suppressing a giggle. Collecting his change, Nick turned to me, still bewildered by the encounter. His eyes were as wide as saucers.

"I think you're right," he admitted. Laughing a little too loudly, I grabbed our order number and started to make my way through the restaurant in search for an open table. "Far, far away from that angry woman, please," I heard Nick whisper behind me. Nodding in agreement, I picked the furthest table from her that I could find. Almost slinking down into his chair, Nick plopped our empty drink glasses on the table and motioned toward the soda machine. Like a guard dog in a junkyard, the angry woman was sitting directly across from the dispenser, lying in wait for unsuspecting customers. I grabbed both glasses and looked at Nick knowingly.

"What would you like?" I asked. He smiled in relief.

"Thank you," he replied, wiping his brow in exaggerated nervousness. "Diet Coke – and please be careful," he warned. I laughed as I headed toward the dispenser, looking back at him as I pretended to tiptoe toward the machine. I was glad I hadn't canceled our lunch. It was turning out to be an enjoyable, entertaining afternoon.

****

Two cleaned plates, a few sodas, and a whole lot of laughing later, the two of us leaned back in our chairs, too full to move. Although this was only my second real conversation with Nick, it felt like I'd known him for much longer. Talking to him was like talking to a close friend whose every significant life experience related to my own.

We'd both experienced traumatic break-ups (though I suspected his had been worse, given the length of time he'd been with his ex-wife and the obvious agony of going through a divorce); we'd both tried living in big cities, to no avail; and we'd both lost our fathers at too young an age. As it turned out, Nick's father had left them by choice, picking up his life one day and moving across the country to remarry and never initiate contact again. I couldn't decide which loss was more painful: one in which the person you care about most in this world experiences a horrific accident and dies as a result, or one in which the person who should love you more than life itself makes the conscious choice to up and leave you forever. Either way, both scenarios made my heart ache.

Groaning and rubbing his stomach, Nick looked at his watch with disappointment. "I'd love to stay and continue to ingest large quantities of food with you, but I have a meeting at two across town." Looking at him sideways, I wondered why he needed to leave so soon – you could get anywhere in town in about twenty minutes.

"Well, what time is it?" I asked curiously.

"Almost 1:40," he replied in a tone that indicated he, too, thought the time had flown by fast.

"Wow!" I exclaimed in disbelief. "You better get out of here – I can't believe it's that late already!" Nodding his head in agreement, Nick stood up and grabbed his suit jacket from the back of the chair.

"I had a great time, Haley," he said, throwing his jacket over his arm. Notwithstanding the fact that we'd talked about some painful past experiences, I'd had a good time, too. It was nice to talk about the loss of Dad with someone who'd experienced something similar. Empathy felt more genuine than sympathy and I was grateful for the chance to commiserate with someone who truly understood. "Let's get together and do this again," he suggested. "I'm out of town this weekend, but how about sometime next week? Same day, different place? Perhaps somewhere without that scary lady?" I chuckled, but quickly stopped when I thought about where I'd be in a week. Incapable of hiding my emotions, Nick recognized the change in my expression almost immediately.

"I'm sorry," he said quickly, running his hand through his hair nervously. "I'm just suggesting another lunch. No pressure; you can think about it and get back to me."

"No, no," I said, reassuring him that my suddenly clouded mood had nothing to do with him. "Next week is just a hard week for me. It's the anniversary of my dad's accident so I'll be out of town – maybe we can get together when I get back?" Nick's face fell as he looked at me.

"I'm so sorry, Haley," he said softly. His hazel eyes were a light brown, circling his dark pupils like milk chocolate saucers. They regarded me with genuine concern. Checking his watch one more time, he stood at the table, seemingly conflicted over whether to leave me in my current state.

"It's fine," I assured him, shooing him with my hands. "You need to go or you'll be late! Seriously, go." Studying me interestedly, Nick finally gathered his keys to leave.

"Okay," he agreed hesitantly. "But are you sure you're alright? I can easily cancel." Shaking my head, I motioned him to go. I was honored that this sweet man was offering to cancel a business meeting to stay with me. I felt closer to him than I should have considering the fact that I'd only known him for a short time.

"Go!" I yelled loudly, standing up to follow him out. "I'll text you when

I get back and you can help me finish off a few pints of ice cream." Satisfied that I was okay, Nick pulled me in for another hug. This time I'd been prepared and almost excited for the embrace. I let myself relax for the short second I was in his arms. It felt really nice.

"The ice cream will be ready when you get back!" He declared, releasing me and hurrying toward the door. I followed him out. "Bye, Haley!" He called. I waved at him as he rushed down the sidewalk.

As I watched him vanish around the corner of the street, my heart swelling at the sight, I wondered how it was possible for me to feel this attracted to two men simultaneously. It wasn't common for me to develop strong feelings for one person, let alone two. This was uncharted territory, and I was hopelessly confused.

Standing on the sidewalk, I pulled out my phone to call Alex. Even though I couldn't talk to him about my conflicting feelings for Keegan and Nick, talking about Dad had conjured up unexpected emotions that required my best friend's support. It was strange: sometimes I could talk about Dad's death as if nothing would bother me, but other times I unknowingly opened an invisible door that allowed in the hurt. I wished I could find a key to that door and lock it up forever.

"Are you home?" I asked Alex hopefully when he picked up. Hanging out with Alex at his apartment and watching old VHS tapes of our community plays always put me in a better mood. Our nostalgic hangout sessions around Dad's anniversary were becoming almost as solid of a tradition as the Cincinnati gravesite tailgate with my brother.

"For a little bit," Alex confirmed. "But I have to meet with Charlie soon and then go to the boutique to screen some of the people Patrick found to replace Dom." I forgot about my self-pity for a moment when I thought about Dom's impending departure.

"When is Dom's last day?" I asked, wondering whether Alex had thought to plan a going away party for him.

"A few weeks from now," Alex responded. "He doesn't start his new job until after he graduates, but we figured we might as well hire someone now so Dom can train them."

"Gotcha," I replied. "Have you considered planning a going away party for Dom? I'd be more than happy to do it if you don't already have something in the works. It doesn't have to be glitzy, just a few close friends, you, me, Dom, Patrick and the other five employees. We could throw it on behalf of the boutique. He's been so awesome for us."

"That's a great idea," Alex agreed. "Dom *has* been a really great employee. Plus, it would be nice to get a company party together and maybe get to know the other associates better. We haven't really done anything like that before." It was hard to get to know the other sales associates because turnover was notoriously high in minimum wage retail. Dom's loyalty was an anomaly – the other five associate positions were constantly in need of being filled.

"Great!" I exclaimed. The confusing state of emotion I'd been feeling a few moments before was dissipating in the wake of our party conversation. "I'll scope out some bars and let you know what I find. It won't be anything crazy. Maybe some appetizers and an open bar for an hour or two."

"Sounds like a plan," Alex replied. He paused for a couple of seconds, making me think he'd hung up the phone. "Hale?" He inquired finally.

"Still here," I acknowledged.

"We should be good at the boutique without you until you get back from Cincinnati," he said. "Go whenever you want, stay as long as you need, and let me know when you want to relive some of our crappy old plays to get your dad off of your mind." I smiled, surprised by Alex's unprovoked mention of the anniversary. It was almost as if he had known why I'd called. Alex and I hadn't talked about me leaving for Cincinnati yet, but in true best friend form, he already had the date at the forefront of his mind. It felt good to know that the things most important to me were still just as important to Alex. Realizing how much he cared for me made the pain of lying to him about Keegan even more prominent.

"I love you, you know that?" I asked, my stomach flipping from the rush of guilt. I wanted to burst and tell him about Keegan right then and there. He deserved that much. For whatever reason, however, I couldn't bring myself to say it.

"Well, duh," Alex replied. "Who wouldn't?" Laughing and discarding the temptation to divulge my secret, I told him I'd stop by the boutique to see him later in the day. Because I didn't plan to leave for Cincinnati until after the weekend, I figured I could help him screen the potential new hires, despite the fact it was one of my least favorite tasks. "Okay, I'll see you later then," he said, hanging up the call.

When I placed my phone back into my favorite brown leather shoulder bag, I caught a glimpse of the sketching notebook my brother had given me after college. Biting my lip and smiling in anticipation, I changed my course and turned down a side street that led back to the park. For the first time in what seemed like months, my schedule was wide open and the weather was perfect. I couldn't wait to get back to the bench and pull out my notebook to sketch. It had been too long since I'd allowed myself this creative escape – an escape I needed now more than ever.

13 THE TAILGATE

I was already halfway across the parking lot when I realized the carnations had been leaking onto my new beige satin blouse. I cursed and held the flowers out to my side, analyzing the damage. It would have been better if the flowers had leaked onto my durable jean jacket, but of course, they'd leaked onto my most expensive piece of clothing. Walking slowly forward, still trying to determine whether my shirt could be salvaged, I looked up at the sound of a familiar voice calling from several yards away.

"Are those flowers for me?" My heart leapt with excitement and I forgot about my blouse immediately, more eager to wrap my arms around my little brother than obsess over a minor water spot. I looked up to see Michael standing at the edge of the parking lot, a couple of lawn chairs and a large cooler in tow, grinning at me in the same way he had for almost twenty-four years.

Michael was a couple inches short of six feet and a little chubbier than what he should have been for his frame. Although he was naturally lanky like me, his refusal to exercise and tendency to eat only processed cheeses and meats had left him on the heavy side since his early teens. His sandy brown hair was shaggier than the last time I'd seen him and his facial hair more prominent. But no matter how much facial hair he grew or how dark his hair became, he couldn't erase what remained of that sweet and innocent blond-haired little boy I'd grown up with.

Almost skipping as I made my way toward him, I laughed when I saw what he was wearing. Clothed in a flannel shirt, distressed jeans, and cowboy boots, Michael looked poised to attend a country concert or lasso a calf at a rodeo. I pointed at his clothes and raised my eyebrows, continuing to hold the carnations away from my blouse.

"So this is the style in Tennessee, huh?" I asked as I approached. Holding out his arms and making a slow, 360-degree turn, he smiled.

"It suits me, don't you think?" He inquired.

"It actually does," I said, chuckling. "You look like an up-and-coming Nashville artist in those cowboy boots." Michael smiled and beckoned me closer, his thick arms stretched out for a hug. I set my flowers gingerly on the pavement and let him wrap me in a tight embrace. Being hugged by Michael was like being hugged by a giant teddy bear. It was interesting how different Michael's embrace felt from the clutches of Alex's bony arms, although they both left me feeling loved and comforted. Letting me go, Michael asked how I was doing.

"I'm fine," I said, shrugging my shoulders. Fine was an easy way to cover up all of the real emotions I'd been feeling the last couple of weeks. "Can't complain. How are you?" Studying my face as if searching for clues as to what my response wasn't telling him, Michael answered similarly.

"I'm fine too," he said. I smiled at his equally vague response. "Painting, drawing, working – same thing, different day." Nodding, I pointed at the cooler and asked whether he'd packed all of the necessary supplies. "Of course," he responded, pretending to be affronted by the mere suggestion that he might have neglected his bi-annual duties. "Sandwiches, beer, snacks, beer, and . . . beer."

"Well done!" I responded, impressed. Michael and I switched our tailgating responsibilities every year, with one of us being responsible for flowers and the other being responsible for pretty much everything else. A few years back, he'd shown up with flowers instead of food, leaving Dad's grave decorated to the nines, but our stomachs empty. We'd only lasted an hour and a half before the both of us surrendered to the rumbling in our bellies. I liked to tease Michael every year by acting shocked when he showed up with his share of the supplies. I grabbed the carnations from the ground and held them up triumphantly, showing him that I too – like every year – had fulfilled my end of the bargain. "You ready?" I asked him, grabbing his arm with my free hand.

"Ready," he confirmed. "Let's go say 'hi' to pops." As we made our way across the graveyard, I cringed as my sandal got stuck in a muddy puddle in the grass. It was a clear and sunny day outside, but the previous night's showers had left portions of the graveyard elusively soggy. It wasn't until I'd stepped into an inch or two of mud that I realized the ground was completely saturated. I was thankful I'd worn an old pair of sandals.

Pulling my foot out with a loud squish, I crinkled my nose and hopped to the concrete path that ran through the cemetery. Although the journey to Dad's headstone was longer when following the path, I didn't feel like soaking my feet in any more mud puddles.

"Well that was gross," I said, shaking my foot to fling off the wet mud. Michael nodded in agreement and pointed to the cooler. It didn't appear as though its wheels were navigating the mushy ground any better than I was.

"Our chairs are going to sink a foot into the ground today," he predicted. Shoving my foot back through the thongs of my sandal, I waited as Michael finished cleaning the gunk off of the cooler's wheels. "You'd think Dad could help us out a little bit with the weather every year," he complained, wiping the last bit of mud off of his hands at the edge of the grass.

"He probably enjoys watching us step in mud," I replied, remembering Dad's propensity for practical jokes. Smiling and shaking my head, I found myself becoming emotional at the thought of Dad watching us trudge through the mud, pointing and laughing as if we'd fallen right into his trap. Starting down the path, Michael turned and looked at me over his shoulder.

"Probably," he agreed, amused by what I assumed were similar thoughts of Dad's humor. Speeding up to catch him, I temporarily shook my emotional memories of Dad by focusing our conversation on other things. I wanted to hear about Michael's drive from Nashville, the friends he planned to visit while in Cincinnati, and the interest he'd peaked from the community upon debuting his latest set of paintings. The community's interest in his artwork was increasing slowly, but Michael was encouraged by the increase nonetheless. I told him I was proud of him and felt confident that he'd be able to pay his bills with his own art in the very near future.

It wasn't until Dad's headstone came into view that my emotions surfaced again. I stopped and placed my hand on my chest in an unsuccessful attempt to regulate the sudden rush of grief. Michael put his arm around me and sighed, setting the cooler down on the pavement. We stood in silence for a moment, likely reflecting on the same happy, but painful memories of Dad that we would never escape.

Unwanted tears began to stream down my face and I wiped them away furiously, angry with myself for getting upset. Although I didn't want to forget my memories of Dad, I wished there was a way to remember all of the good times without simultaneously having to feel the pain of having lost him so suddenly and tragically. It was unfair that the accident had not only taken Dad, but had burdened our memories of him as well.

"Let's set up, Hale," Michael suggested, pulling himself together and grabbing the handle of the cooler once again. "I need a beer." Lost in thought, I followed Michael quietly and watched as he placed the lawn chairs firmly on either side of Dad's headstone. Opening the cooler and placing a beer in each of the chair's cup holders, he invited me to sit. I stepped off of the pavement and onto the grass, choosing my footing carefully to prevent my exposed feet from sinking into the mud.

As I passed Dad's grave to take a seat in my chair, I ran my fingers along the cold, damp stone and placed the pink carnations onto the ground at its base next to a pretty bouquet of yellow, blue, and purple spring flowers. Dad's headstone, carved with his name and a declaration that he'd been a loving husband and father, was decorated with the usual bouquets of flowers in remembrance of his anniversary. Although they'd been abundant in the beginning, the flowers that continued to show up year after year always came from the same people: Lindsay, Alex, and Patrick; Michael's best friend from grade school; Dad's assistant from work with whom he'd been incredibly close; Dad's group of guy friends I'd never really known, but with whom he'd played poker at least once a week; and the parents of the drunk driver who'd killed Dad.

At first I'd been angry and offended by the drunk driver's family's support, enraged at the injustice that their son had walked away from the accident with only minor injuries. But after years of continuing to send flowers and the eventual suicide of their son, I realized that they too had experienced a pain few could imagine. Not only had they lost their son in the end, but they also had to live with the pain of knowing that their son had killed another. At least I could revel in the memory of Dad without carrying that guilt.

"There's an extra bouquet this year," Michael observed, pointing to the flower arrangements at the foot of Dad's headstone. Peering down at the flowers, I counted them carefully, convinced that Michael was mistaken.

"I think you're right," I eventually admitted, taking the first sip of my beer before leaning down to read the cards. We hadn't received a new bouquet in years. Part of me wished they would be from Mother, but I knew better. 'Why purchase flowers to decorate for the dead when they can be used to decorate for the living?' She'd asked me after I'd confronted her about the conspicuous absence of her flowers on the fourth anniversary of Dad's death. I'd been too enraged after that to even speak to her, convinced that she had either lost her mind or her heart had turned to stone. It was that same year that she'd stopped coming to the gravesite – the same year I decided I would never forgive her for forgetting Dad.

Sifting through the flowers nearest his chair, Michael picked up a pretty bouquet of pink, yellow, and orange roses, and looked quizzically at the card as if it had been written in a foreign language he didn't understand. "Who's Nick Matthews?" He asked curiously. My heart flipped in my chest as I heard him read the name.

"Give it here," I demanded, reaching for the flowers. Narrowing his eyes, Michael stretched to hand me the flowers, looking at me with curious anticipation. Grabbing the flowers and pulling out the card, I smiled as I read Nick's message:

Haley,

Thinking of you and your family on this difficult day. Pints of ice cream await your return.

Best wishes, Nick Matthews

"So who's Nick Matthews?" Michael asked again as I sat there, smelling Nick's flowers. Shaking my head, I told him he was just a friend, although my swelling heart told me differently.

"I actually only met him a couple of weeks ago," I explained. It felt like I'd known him for much longer. "It's a long story, but last week we got to talking about our fathers at lunch and it turns out that he lost his dad when he was young, too." Michael watched me interestedly. "What's funny," I said, "is that I don't know how he found the grave. I don't even know how he knows our last name, to be honest." I was sure I hadn't provided any of those details while at lunch last week. "He must have done some digging," I mused, touched by his gesture. Stroking the dewy rose petals with my fingers, I wondered how Nick's wife could have ever left such a thoughtful man.

"Just a friend, huh?" Michael asked skeptically. I looked up to find him staring at me doubtfully.

"Yes, just friends," I assured him. My mind quickly turned to Keegan. It was him I should have been talking about, not Nick. "I'm actually seeing someone else," I quickly informed him. Raising his eyebrows, Michael looked at me in over exaggerated disbelief and threw up his hands.

"How long has this been going on?? When were you going to tell *me*?" He pretended to be offended. I laughed. I knew he was joking because the two of us rarely shared our dating lives with each other. If anything, he was probably surprised I'd mentioned it.

"Believe it or not, I never actually considered telling you until now," I admitted sarcastically. Leaning back in his chair, beer in hand, Michael dropped the act, satisfied with my answer.

"Fair enough," he replied. I laughed again. I missed my brother. I would have loved for him to live closer. He was easygoing, easy to talk to, and easily the least judgmental person I knew. "So how long have you been seeing this guy?" He asked more seriously. "What's he like?" Wincing, I realized I didn't feel like sharing any of the details. It wasn't that I was ashamed of how everything had transpired, but after experiencing Lindsay's initial reaction, I recognized that the circumstances surrounding my relationship with Keegan didn't put him in the best light. The last thing I wanted to do at Dad's grave was talk about Keegan only to have my little brother rush to conclusions or point out the obviously undesirable nature of the situation.

"It's complicated," I responded vaguely. "I don't really feel like talking about it." Although I tried to tell Lindsay the same thing earlier on my drive down to Cincinnati, she'd refused to let me go without talking about Keegan. First she demanded we talk about the text message I received at the walk. Then, after I fully disclosed the nature of the text, she asked whether anything had happened while he was in town. Albeit reluctantly, I told Lindsay everything, unwilling to lengthen the string of lies I'd already created. Her disapproval was transparent even through my cell phone, but she tried her best to be supportive. I appreciated her concern, but wished she could keep it to herself. At this point, all I wanted was for someone to share in my excitement instead of reminding me I was lying to one of my best friends. I needed the cheerleader Lindsay had already told me she couldn't be. Ironically, I needed Alex.

"Alex doesn't even know about it," I admitted finally. Michael looked at me, worried.

"That doesn't make me feel good," he said, drinking his beer. "What could possibly keep you from telling Alex?"

"It's someone I met through work," I revealed. "It's a little complicated. At this point, there's really no good reason to mix my work life with my personal life." Unfortunately, saying the words out loud didn't make them any more convincing. Staring across the cemetery at nothing in particular, Michael continued to drink his beer, relaxing in the lawn chair.

"It sounds like you've already done that," he observed. "Mixed your work life with your personal life." Rolling my eyes I reached into the cooler for some food.

"Like I said, it's complicated," I insisted. Annoyed, I grabbed a soggy peanut butter and jelly sandwich and slammed the cooler shut.

"Whatever you say," Michael responded, ending the discussion. Unlike my friends, he knew better than to probe me about something I didn't want to discuss.

Taking a bite of the soggy sandwich unwrapped in my lap, I grinned. Just as quickly as it had started, I forgot about the short discussion of my love life as I was transported back to the days when Dad, Mother, Michael, and I enjoyed picnics at the park by our house. For whatever reason, Dad always made our sandwiches soggy. 'The soggier the sandwich, the better the jelly,' Dad would say. Mother would tell us we were crazy and pack a boring sandwich with turkey and cheese. I'm sure her sandwich tasted much better, but I think Michael and I liked our soggy sandwiches simply because they were made by Dad. He could make anything great just by declaring it so.

"Soggy enough?" Michael asked, watching me take another bite of the sandwich. I nodded as I chewed.

"Just like Dad used to make them," I said, almost choking on the sandwich as I fought back tears. Michael laughed at the sight.

"Please don't choke on that," he pleaded. "I really don't want all of my family traditions marred by tragedy." I laughed as tears trickled down my face. I normally hated to cry, but laughing while crying was one of my favorite emotions. The relief from allowing my tears to escape combined with the endorphins released from my laughter created an emotional high, topped by little else.

Finishing my sandwich and gulping down the peanut butter with the rest of my beer, I asked Michael for another cold one. He reached into the cooler and pulled out the beer, shaking off the ice and water as best he could. Twisting the cap, he handed it to me and opened the cooler again to fetch one for him. We drank our beers and watched the clouds float by in the blue sky above us, sitting in silence for a while, lost in our thoughts.

I sighed and closed my eyes, thinking about Dad, trying to imagine what he'd look like after all this time. Would the sun have weathered his skin, creating deep wrinkles around his big green eyes or would he look as young as he had when he died? Would his full head of salt and pepper hair have turned a more convincing shade of gray by now? If so, would he have dyed it? Would he still be running every morning to keep his heart in shape? Would he have had those knee surgeries my mother always claimed he'd need one day in the future?

I opened my eyes, still thinking about what Dad would look like today. I imagined him sitting between us in the graveyard, cracking open a beer and laughing at the fact that we still ate soggy sandwiches in our mid-to-late twenties. It seemed silly, but the simple things he'd done when we were kids – like making sandwiches with too much jelly – were now special and cherished memories. He couldn't have known what an impact his family traditions would make on our lives today. What had seemed insignificant before his death, now became treasured traditions onto which we held, hoping to feel closer to Dad, even if only for an instant.

Sipping my beer, I allowed the serenity of the cemetery to surround me. The small breeze lightly rustled the leaves of the nearby trees and the quiet sound of traffic buzzing in the distance seemed like a lifetime away. Slowly but surely, the grief inside of me began to calm, allowing me to enjoy my memories in peace. Consumed with memories of Dad, I realized that I had found a temporary relief from my recurring thoughts about Keegan and Nick. It seemed morbid, but I was thankful to be distracted by Dad's anniversary instead of questioning my relationship statuses with the two handsome men like I had all week – statuses made more complicated by the other's existence.

Since the last time I'd seen Keegan, I'd developed serious doubts about the future of our fledgling relationship. Ultimately, I feared that the gorgeous designer didn't feel for me the way I felt for him. We'd had a couple of conversations over the past week, but nothing we'd talked about had given me any more of an idea of what he wanted out of 'us.' I was anxious to know whether Keegan had any interest in making our relationship something other than an occasional out-of-state booty call. Living in two different cities was the biggest elephant in the room, and one neither of us could address until Keegan's intentions were made more clear.

In addition to my thoughts about Keegan, I had started to overanalyze my budding friendship with Nick. I'd felt something for him at our lunch last week, hoping that we could someday be more than just friends. Nick had insisted that he wasn't ready to date, but I wondered whether his insistence was more of a defense tactic than the actual truth – a way for him to protect himself from getting hurt. I imagined that in the wake of his divorce, he was especially sensitive to rejection.

Michael cleared his throat obnoxiously as if he'd swallowed a bug, jolting me out of my daydreams. Turning to ask if he was okay, I found him sitting rigidly in his chair as if he'd been called to attention by a silent military bugle. His eyes were fixed on something in the distance and I was sure I saw a hint of fear or panic flicker across his face. Following his gaze, my heart dropped to my feet as I watched our mother making her way along the graveyard path.

"What the hell is she doing here?" I asked, suddenly furious. I looked at

Michael for an explanation. He fidgeted uncomfortably in his chair, avoiding my stare.

"I told her not to come here," he said softly, gritting his teeth and standing up. "Look, if it's okay with you, I'll go tell her we'll come to the house after we're done. She wants to talk to you and figured this would be a good place to find you. I tried to talk her out of it, but you know how she is, Hale." I stared at him accusingly as if he'd been the one encouraging Mother to come crash our tailgate. It didn't make sense that she'd come to Dad's grave just to talk. She knew that the yearly tradition at Dad's grave was important to me and that her refusal to partake in it all these years had created an immovable rift between us. What could possibly have been so important that she risked tarnishing it even more?

"What's going on Michael?" I asked suspiciously, standing up and grabbing him by the arm to prevent him from intercepting our mother. "She hasn't been here in years – what's so important that she's come to Dad's grave to talk to me?" Michael shrugged his shoulders and looked at me, well aware that his attempt to appear ignorant wasn't working. Defeated, he turned and sighed, slumping back into his chair.

"She's getting married again, Hale," he said finally. My eyes widened and my mouth dropped open in disbelief. I turned to watch Mother make her way slowly toward us, shocked that she would even dare to sully my time with Dad with news of yet another marriage.

"You have got to be kidding me," I replied, working hard to suppress the rage bubbling inside of me. "That's why she's here? To announce another marriage? She is unbelievable." Pacing, I waited impatiently until she was about twenty yards away. "Stop!" I yelled loudly, hoping she wouldn't come any closer. I wasn't about to have her talk about another man and another marriage in front of Dad. Storming toward her, Michael on my heels, I felt the tears begin to stream down my face, hot with fury. Standing calmly as she waited for me, Mother held her hands at her side and watched me approach, her thin face expressionless.

"Haley . . ." she began, ignoring my emotional state.

"No, mom!" I screamed through intermittent sobs. I had lost it completely. I was bursting with rage and grief, hurt by the timing of her wedding announcement. "You don't get to do this!" I screamed again, pointing at her angrily. "You don't get to ruin my one day with Dad by talking about someone else." Remaining calm, she tried to reach for me. Snatching my hand out of her grasp I looked at her murderously.

"Haley," she started again, "don't do this – don't punish me for trying to move on with my life. What would you have me do? Sit around holding his picture, pretending as if he were still alive?" Her comment infuriated me even more. Something inside of me snapped.

"At least I'd know you still cared about him!" I screamed, trembling. Michael stared at the two of us, unmoving, his eyes wide and filled with concern. "You are pathetic! For fifteen years I've missed Dad, wishing he could be here to watch me grow up, to watch me graduate college, get a job, to walk me down the aisle someday. I've cried and mourned, wondering why it had to happen to *my* dad – to someone who did nothing but love us with all of his heart. But YOU! You discarded him and his memory after just a couple of years!!! You forgot him like he was some guy you met once. You never cried, you never asked why, you never even cared enough to visit his grave. You're deader to me than Dad. I never want to see you again!" My words hung in the air between us when I finished. Michael stood motionless next to me. Still glaring at her, I watched as Mother blinked in faint surprise before her face turned hard and impassive once again. It seemed as if we stood there in silence for an eternity before she finally spoke.

"Well I guess that's a 'no', then," she replied quietly. She made it impossible to be kind to her. How could she stand there, virtually emotionless, talking about Dad as if he'd barely existed? In that moment, I hated her with every fiber of my being. Michael had been right – I was effectively parentless.

"Get out of here," I demanded, pointing at her in rage, trying not to yell. She sighed and tried to reach for me once again. Stepping back, I told her to leave again in a trembling whisper. She lingered for a moment, studying me like I was a puzzle impossible to solve. Her blue eyes glistened in the sun as she turned to Michael who was standing like a statue, his eyes still wide and unblinking. For a moment I thought she might cry. But the moment quickly passed when she patted him on the arm and turned toward the parking lot.

Tears still streaming down my face, I watched as she sauntered casually back to her car as if nothing had happened. I took a couple of deep breaths to regulate my emotions and wiped my wet face with the scrunched up napkin I'd placed in the pocket of my jeans. I was livid at Mother for coming to the graveyard and ruining the one-day a year I looked forward to over any other. What had she expected? That I'd be happy to talk about her wedding to another man while spending my day at a graveyard in remembrance of Dad?

"I'm sorry," I whispered under my breath, closing my eyes and picturing Dad's face. Although I always liked to think that Dad could see and hear us when we visited, this was the one time I hoped I was wrong. I wanted Dad's soul to rest easy, thinking that what he'd left behind were two loving kids and a devoted wife who loved him as much as he'd loved her. Opening my eyes again, I watched as Michael made his way silently back to our tailgate at Dad's grave. I followed solemnly, hoping desperately that if Dad did hear and see us, the committed and unwavering love of his two kids would ease whatever pain my mother had inflicted on his soul.

14 PITY PARTY

Salty caramel ice cream almost rocketed out of my nose when Alex appeared on the screen in his first appearance as Puck, the devious fairy from *A Midsummernight's Dream*. Lindsay and Patrick rolled with laughter on the couch and Alex stood up from his chaise lounger with pride, smiling and bowing as his teenage self pranced around the stage in small horns and a nude leotard decorated with leaves. Swallowing my ice cream and holding my side, I pointed at the screen.

"This was by far my favorite community theatre play," I announced, giggling. "You were *made* for this role." My soul filled with happy memories as I dug my spoon into the pint of ice cream resting in my lap. Sitting on the floor in front of the couch in sweatpants with my legs crossed, I watched as my former sixteen-year-old friend transformed into everything Shakespeare would have hoped Puck to be. We had an amazing time working on that play and I was happy to be enjoying the memory of it with my closest friends.

"Lord, what fools these mortals be!" Alex proclaimed, falling back into the chaise lounger to watch the rest of the play. Patrick laughed from behind me, amused by his boyfriend's antics.

"The role *does* suit him, doesn't it?" Patrick whispered, poking me on the shoulder.

"Just be glad you didn't know him back then," I replied, loud enough for Alex to hear. "I heard that line so many times that it almost ruined our friendship." Alex dismissed us with a flick of his hand, busy admiring his performance.

I watched him lay there, focused on the screen, dressed in relaxed jeans and a casual sweatshirt from his line. Although the rest of us had barely made an effort to get dressed and were using our Friday off from work to lounge around in sweatpants, Alex had made great efforts to appear respectable in his 'scrounge' clothes. I'd never seen the man in sweatpants, and I was confident he didn't even own any.

"I actually think I remember you complaining about it," Lindsay said from the other side of the couch, still chuckling at the screen. She was dressed in a tight, outdated velour purple sweat suit from high school. She claimed that neither she nor Trevor had had time to do laundry in weeks, but it hadn't stopped Alex from tormenting her the moment she'd walked through the door. Upon seeing her he pretended not to let her in for fear that someone may see her in his house. "I think you threatened to tape his mouth shut if he said the word 'mortals' one more time," she said, remembering our conversation from over ten years ago.

Although she hadn't known Alex well when we were in high school, I would occasionally talk about him with her. I hadn't meant to keep them separate, but for whatever reason, we never hung out as a group. Alex went to a different high school than Lindsay and I, and Lindsay didn't participate in community theatre because of evening volleyball practices. It was by sheer circumstance that my two worlds hadn't meshed until adulthood.

"She almost did, I think," Alex claimed from across the room. "But she wasn't nearly as mad at me as she was when she played Ado Annie in *Oklahoma*." Alex's eyes lit up like Christmas trees as he turned and looked at me playfully, one hand resting on the back of the lounger to keep his head propped up and one dangling off of the side.

"Don't you start singing that song, Alex," I started, trying to suppress the laughter building up inside of me. Alex's smile became wider and wider as he slowly stepped off of the lounger and started singing dramatically.

"I'm just a girl who *cain't* say no . . ." Everyone started laughing again. I grabbed a couch pillow and threw it at Alex to make him stop. Laughing maniacally, he feigned an injury and crashed to the chaise lounger, the pillow wrapped in his arms. He loved to make fun of me for singing that song. It wasn't necessarily the comedic nature of my character, but the apparently

149

ridiculous way I sounded when trying to fake a country accent that had riddled him with fits of giggling when we'd performed the musical in community theatre.

"Don't you bring out that tape, Alex Carter," I threatened, pointing my spoon at him as he rose from the lounger and started sifting through the VHS tapes in his television stand. He glanced back at me and smiled mischievously. "Don't do it!" I warned again, struggling to get out of my position on the floor. "I will end you!" Seeing me coming, Alex quickly exchanged the tapes in the VCR and turned to defend the controls, poised like a linebacker ready to strike. Throwing my hands up in surrender, I watched as a home video of *Oklahoma* began to play on the screen. Patrick and Lindsay were both behind me laughing. "Fine," I said, chuckling as I watched Alex maintain his defensive stance. "I give up – you go ahead and play it." Turning back toward my spot on the floor, I peered down at the ice cream in my hand and decided to head to the kitchen instead. It was an excellent time to put the ice cream away. I was dangerously close to the bottom of the pint and didn't wish to finish it in my grieving state of gluttony. I'd agreed to get ice cream with Nick tomorrow afternoon and didn't want to overload to the point where I couldn't eat ice cream tomorrow.

I opened Alex's freezer and shoved the pint back in, thinking about Nick and the flowers he'd sent to Dad's grave. When I walked through the door this afternoon, Alex had asked, in a heightened state of excitement, whether I'd received any surprises at my tailgate with Michael. Not knowing that he meant Nick's flowers, I told him about the confrontation with my mother. Trying to be a good friend, Alex comforted me for a few minutes and allowed me to vent until he almost burst at the seams. Unable to bear it any longer, he interrupted my sulking to ask whether I'd received roses from Nick. Confirming that I had, I listened as Alex revealed the way Nick had ventured into the boutique to ask where to send them. Alex wouldn't stop talking about how cute Nick was and how sweet it had been for him to send the flowers. I had to remind Alex several times that Nick just wanted to be friends – but even I had to admit that the gesture was above and beyond anything I would have expected from a newfound pal.

I hadn't told Keegan about Dad, but it hurt my feelings that he hadn't sent flowers or been there for me like everyone else in my life. I knew it was irrational to feel that way and completely unfair to Keegan, but I couldn't help it. Nick's flowers certainly hadn't helped that sentiment.

Behind me in the living room I could hear the tape stop, only to continue briefly and stop again. I knew Alex was fast-forwarding to the part where I sang, but I didn't care. I was happy to be in Alex's apartment, surrounded by my friends, trying to recover from my short day-trip to Cincinnati. I'd wanted to stay longer to hang out with my brother, but had decided instead to return home to keep my ice cream date with Nick. I was anxious to see the recent divorcé and to thank him for sending the roses.

Retreating from the kitchen to flee from the ice cream that still beckoned from the freezer, I almost ran into Patrick coming through the doorway. "Sorry, Patrick!" I exclaimed, releasing my grip on his shoulders. Smiling, he nodded his head toward the kitchen and whispered softly.

"Can I talk to you for a minute?" He asked, unfazed by our near collision.

"Sure," I said curiously, following him back into the kitchen. Eyeing the freezer, I took a step opposite the ice cream. "What's up?" I asked. Placing his bowl into the sink, Patrick waited for a moment until he heard Lindsay and Alex laughing loudly in the living room.

"I have something I've been meaning to talk to you about," he started quietly. He looked at me urgently before continuing. "Now's not the time, though." He leaned into the kitchen and peered through the doorway, his soft brown eyes darting back and forth nervously under his bushy eyebrows. "Can you meet me for lunch sometime this weekend or early next week?" He asked. "Even a coffee is fine – I just need to chat." I narrowed my eyebrows in concern. The mysterious way Patrick was acting made me wonder if everything was okay between him and Alex.

"Of course," I said, "but you're making me a little nervous. Is everything alright?" Patrick nodded reassuringly and reached out to touch me on the arm.

"Yes! Sorry, it's just . . . private," he replied. My eyes still narrowed, I wondered what he could need to talk to me about that he couldn't talk about with Alex. Although I was curious, I resisted the urge to ask more questions.

"I'm grabbing ice cream with Nick tomorrow around three," I said, "but I can meet for lunch before that if you'd like." Patrick smiled and nodded, revealing the gap between his two front teeth. He explained to me a while back that he'd never wanted to fix the gap because of its resemblance to Elton John – someone he'd idolized since before he could read.

"That's great!" Patrick said. "Just do me a favor and don't tell Alex we're meeting up, okay?" I looked at him, disappointed that I'd have to hide even more from Alex. Patrick sensed my thoughts immediately. "I know you and Alex share everything," he said quickly, "but this is important. Please do me this favor for the time being and you can decide after lunch whether to tell him about it."

"Okay," I said, my curiosity intensifying. He thanked me and started to leave the kitchen. Before he made it out the doorway, however, I stopped him, my fierce love for Alex getting the better of me. "This better not be about hurting Alex in any way, Patrick," I advised, ignoring the irony in my warning. "I love him and won't hesitate to protect him at all costs." Smiling, Patrick walked forward to hug me.

"I know," he whispered in my ear. "And that's why you're perfect." I stared at him as he pulled away, confused. I couldn't think of a single reason Patrick would want to talk to me outside the presence of Alex. I began to worry, wondering whether he suspected my relationship with Keegan. But how could he possibly know? Patrick hadn't even met Keegan, and Lindsay would certainly never tell anyone.

Racking my brain for any clues as to what he could want, I gave up when I heard my teenage voice belting musical tunes from the living room in crude twang. Patrick, Alex, and Lindsay were all laughing hysterically and calling for me to rejoin them. Reluctantly, I stopped worrying about my lunch with Patrick and entered the living room, braced to be the brunt of everyone's jokes. Patting the couch and continuing to laugh as I walked in, Lindsay encouraged me to sit next to her. With Alex singing every word loudly – almost loud enough to drown me out on the television – I plopped down on the couch and pursed my lips in defiance. Lindsay put her arms around me and squeezed.

"You were such a good Ado Annie," she giggled, still squeezing me.

"Yeah, yeah," I replied, dismissing her as she loosened her grip. We watched the video and gawked at Alex's uncanny remembrance of every single word.

"You know, Hale," Lindsay started, Alex continuing to sing in the background, "I always envied the way you were so fearless on the stage." I looked at her, surprised at what I was hearing.

"What do you mean?" I asked. Lindsay watched as my high school self moved awkwardly around the stage in a costume dress poorly styled for the 1940s.

"You had this incredible knack at leaving yourself behind the curtain and becoming your character without hesitation," she observed, her blond hair plopped messily in a casual bun on top of her head. She turned to face me, her light blue eyes bright above the dark circles surrounding them. It didn't appear as though she was getting enough sleep. "You never cared what people thought and you were never nervous," she continued. "You just dove right in. And I envied that."

I studied Lindsay's face for a moment, considering her observation. It was true that I'd never been nervous about theatrics before, but it never occurred to me that it was something to be proud of. Drama was fun – a way to escape reality for a couple of hours. The escape felt natural to me and I enjoyed playing the part of characters whose personalities and life stories were a world apart from my own. I wondered why Lindsay would be envious of my confidence in theatre when she possessed similar confidence in being herself. I would have traded my confidence for hers in a minute.

"Thanks for taking the day off," I said, changing the subject. "You're a great friend. It means a lot to me." She squeezed my hand and turned back to the screen to watch the end of my performance. Mercifully, the song was almost over and Alex had finally grown tired of belting it from the top of his lungs. At the end of the scene, Patrick, Lindsay, and Alex all applauded me loudly. I rolled my eyes and told them to stop. When the laughter died down, Alex turned to the three of us and asked if there were any additional requests.

"I think I've seen plenty of our old tapes," I said. We'd been at Alex's for almost four hours and I had had my fill of nostalgia as well as ice cream. Alex suggested we rent a movie to finish out the night.

"We could do pizza," he added. Lindsay agreed, offering to pick up a movie at the local grocery store. I looked around at the three of them, trying to determine whether they genuinely wanted to stay or whether they were putting on a front for me.

"You guys don't have to sit around with me all day on your day off," I interjected. I would have been perfectly happy to head back to my apartment and order my own personal pizza. It would give me a chance to relax before tomorrow and call Keegan like I'd originally planned.

"Stop it, Haley Blythe," Patrick demanded next to me. "This pity party tradition may have started for you, but I think we all enjoy a guilt-free day of watching home movies and eating ice cream." Lindsay and Alex agreed, shushing my protests. Although this meant I couldn't call Keegan until much later than I'd promised, I was happy they wanted to stay. Lindsay stood up to grab her keys in anticipation of driving the few blocks to pick up the movie, but Alex commanded her to stop when he saw her reaching for her purse.

"I cannot allow you to go anywhere in that purple-people-eater monstrosity," he announced. Lindsay put her hands on her hips and looked at him with disapproval. "Don't sass me," Alex warned before she had a chance to speak. "My house, my rules. I'll get the movie, seeing as I'm the only one who should be out in public." I laughed. It was no use arguing with him. Although I didn't place the same importance on my appearance as Alex did on his, he had a point. Patrick, Lindsay, and I looked like disheveled drifters, poised to do little else but eat bonbons and hunker down like hermits on the couch. "Besides," he continued, "it will give me a chance to call the store before closing to see how we did with our numbers today." Placing her keys on the table in defeat, Lindsay sighed.

"Have it your way," she said. "But at least let me order the pizza." Alex nodded, accepting her offer. "Cheese, please," he requested, gathering his wallet and keys. Lindsay reached for Alex's laptop on the ottoman and opened the web browser to order the pizza. Patrick and I sat unmoving on the couch, happy that neither of us was given any responsibility. I usually wasn't this lazy, but after my last couple of weeks, I was content to vegetate for a while.

I watched Alex leave the apartment on his mission to procure a good movie as Lindsay sat next to me on the couch with the computer, navigating her way through online ordering.

"What'll it be, Hale?" She asked. "I was thinking a cheese and a pepperoni to be simple." Before I could answer, Patrick cleared his throat from the opposite side of the couch. Lindsay's eyes darted from the computer screen to where he was sitting, waiting for him to speak up.

"I don't know about plain cheese and pepperoni," Patrick offered. "But if that's what everyone wants, I'll eat it." Lindsay looked at him with annoyance.

"Are you saying you'd like something other than pepperoni?" Lindsay asked, trying to be patient.

"I really don't mind," Patrick insisted vaguely. "But if you'd like something other than pepperoni I'd eat it." Lindsay continued to stare at him, obviously frustrated by his refusal to answer her question. While Lindsay was direct in an almost abrasive manner sometimes, Patrick would avoid confrontation at all costs, becoming nervous at even a hint of unpleasantness. While his refusal to be direct stemmed from an admirable desire to please the people around him, it could be maddening to have a conversation with him that required him to reveal his own opinions or desires. Their polarized communication styles made it difficult to watch the two of them make a decision together.

"Patrick, I'm not ordering this pizza until you give me a suggestion in place of the pepperoni," Lindsay stated. Patrick shifted on the couch, uncomfortable with his assigned task. I shrugged when he looked at me for help, indicating he would have to make the suggestion all on his own.

"The works?" He asked finally.

"I don't like mushrooms or onions," Lindsay replied matter-of-factly. "But we could do the works without those two toppings." Patrick looked at her, his disappointment transparent.

"If that's what you want," he replied vaguely yet again. Lindsay huffed in frustration. With the two of them in a standstill over pizza and Alex out of the apartment temporarily, I figured now would be the perfect time to tell Keegan we'd have to skip our anticipated phone date.

Excusing myself to the bathroom, I listened to the two of them suggest new pizza combinations to each other, Lindsay's frustration growing each time Patrick refused to give her a straight answer. I shook my head wondering on which pizza they would finally agree. I hoped it was something without chicken. I always thought chicken on pizza was a bit strange.

Reaching the bathroom, I closed the door behind me and took out my phone to send Keegan a text. I told him I would be getting home much later than expected and would probably not be able to call like I'd originally planned. Placing my phone on the counter next to the sink, I stared into the mirror at my appearance, giving Lindsay and Patrick a few more minutes to decide on the pizza. My green eyes blinked back at me, following my gaze to my dark bushy eyebrows that were in bad need of waxing. Running my tongue under my upper lip, I frowned. My lip needed waxing too. Having to wax my lady mustache was the only thing I disliked about being a brunette. I was jealous that Lindsay had never needed to wax her lip and could let her eyebrows grow like weeds without them being noticeable. If I missed a waxing appointment, I felt as if I needed to wear a ski mask in public to avoid stares.

Sighing, I continued to criticize myself in the mirror until my phone buzzed next to me. I was surprised to see that Keegan had already replied. It usually took him hours to respond.

That's a shame, it read, expressing Keegan's disappointment over my cancellation. I looked at my phone nodding in agreement, thinking of how to respond. Before I had a chance however, my phone buzzed again.

I'm restless for you . . . thinking about coming back into town next week. I inhaled sharply as I read the message. He'd said he'd missed me before, but this was the first time he'd suggested flying back to Columbus.

I would hate for you to spend money on a flight, I replied quickly. *Maybe you should wait for a business trip.* I regretted the text as soon as I'd sent it. I wasn't sure why I'd said something that would make him reconsider flying to Columbus, especially when I hadn't really meant it. In truth, I wanted nothing more than for him to spend his money and see me as soon as possible. Why had I lied? To seem less needy? Mad at myself, I waited for him to respond, trying not to get my hopes up.

I don't care about the money, he wrote finally. *It's worth it.* I stared at my phone smiling. It didn't seem as though my text had deterred him.

I'll try to call tonight if I can, I promised back, my excitement rising. Then I added, *I miss you – I hope you make the trip.* I stared into the bathroom mirror, my phone clutched to my chest. The fact that Keegan was even considering buying a flight to Columbus was a testament to how much he cared. Our conversations over the last week or so had been going well, but I hadn't received any confirmation of what he wanted out of us. This was the first solid indication that my feelings for him were being reciprocated.

Emerging from the bathroom, I felt like a new woman walking on air. I wished in that moment I could tell Alex about my developing relationship with Keegan. It had been a long time since dating had gone even remotely my way – he would have been thrilled to hear it. I discarded my thoughts about Alex when I entered the living room, unwilling to let my guilt distract the joy I was feeling over Keegan. Lindsay looked up at me when I entered. She and Patrick were sitting on the couch watching *Oklahoma*, which was still playing on the screen. I wondered whether they'd decided on a decent pizza, but thought better than to ask.

"Trevor's stopping over after work," Lindsay announced. I hadn't seen Trevor in over a month; I was glad to hear he was headed our way.

"I thought he was going out with the guys tonight," I said, hoping he wasn't headed over because Lindsay had made him feel guilty for not spending time with me after Dad's anniversary. Having gone to Ohio State for undergrad, Trevor had a large group of fraternity brothers with whom he hung out constantly. They loved hosting guys' nights, and Trevor rarely missed them.

"Oh, he's still going," she explained, "but he has some time to kill before heading out and figured he would come over and see how you're doing."

"Great!" I exclaimed. "Maybe we can finally convince him to come into the boutique and buy some clothes." Trevor only frequented cheap department or discount stores and stuck to a simple and safe style of khakis, jeans, and polo shirts. We'd tried multiple times to get him into *De Alexia*'s clothing, to no avail. Lindsay insisted he would never wear something from Alex's line because he hated to leave his comfort zone. He'd even refused to try on a plain v-neck t-shirt just to see whether it fit. I feared he was a lost cause. Lindsay looked at me doubtfully and invited me onto the couch to watch the rest of the play with her and Patrick.

****

I turned on the couch when I heard Alex rustling his keys outside the door. I was bored with the play, happy that the movie had finally arrived. "Look who I found roaming around outside," Alex announced as Trevor followed him into the apartment. As expected, Trevor was dressed in a light blue polo shirt and khakis, a brown belt and brown shoes. He waved and took off his jacket to hang it on the coat rack, looking curiously at the television screen.

"Lindsay told me you were watching old theatre videos," he said, making his way into the living room. "Which one is this?"

"Oklahoma," I replied, standing up to give him a welcoming hug. He looked fit and well rested; his hazel eyes were a light shade of bluish green and his short sandy hair was unmoving from his styling clay. "It's good to see you," I said.

"You too," he responded, choosing a seat next to Lindsay on the couch. Although there was plenty of room for four people on Alex's oversized sofa, I made my way back to the floor across from the chaise lounger. There was something oddly comfortable about sitting on the floor. It helped that Alex's shaggy vintage rug was soft and padded.

"So what movie did you get?" I asked Alex, anxious to get the movie started. The quicker we began, the quicker I could get home to call Keegan. Standing next to the television, Alex stopped the tape player and held up the disc in his hand to show me.

"Some Indie film that's supposed to be funny," he said dully. "It took me forever to browse through everything. There was nothing there I desperately wanted to see."

"Well that sounds promising," I replied sarcastically. Alex ignored me and placed the disc in his game console, changing the input source to the television. Waiting for him to work his magic I turned to Trevor again. "What's on the agenda for guys' night tonight?" I asked, interestedly. He shrugged and told me he wasn't sure. I liked Trevor, but he wasn't much of a talker. It wouldn't be uncommon for him to join us for dinner and say less than ten words. "Well, you're more than welcome to hang out here," I offered, "but I'm afraid that what you see is what you get. There won't be much else happening for the four of us tonight." Smiling, he placed his hand on Lindsay's knee.

"This looks like a great time," he admitted. "A lot of the guys are single, so our guys' nights are always about going out and hitting the bars. I wouldn't mind if they wanted to stay in one night to watch movies, but I don't think that's in the cards for a large group of former frat guys." We all laughed at the revelation and refocused our attention on the television as the movie began to play. Although I didn't have a huge group of friends like Trevor, I was happy to have Lindsay, Alex, and Patrick. I couldn't imagine a world without them . . . or our movie nights.

Settling in, I looked down as my phone buzzed in my pocket. Pulling it out discretely, I found a text message from Nick:

I hope you had a good day back home, he wrote. *I'm looking forward to ice cream tomorrow. See you soon!* I lingered on the message for a moment, grinning. I typed a quick response telling him I was excited to see him and put my phone back in my pocket.

Fixing my eyes on the television screen, I thought about what Keegan might say about my budding relationship with Nick. As shameful as it was to admit, the thought of Keegan being jealous made me smile. An image of the two men fighting over me flashed into my mind. I shook my head, refusing to allow myself such ridiculous indulgences. Keegan hadn't expressed a modicum of desire to have an exclusive long-distance relationship and Nick had never expressed any desire at all to be more than a friend. The thought of either of them being threatened by the other was outrageous, but I couldn't help but smile as the guilty fantasy continued to play unbidden in the back of my mind.

15 BLESSINGS AND SLIP-UPS

I eyed the clock in a panic, willing my hairdryer to work faster. Gritting my teeth, I combed my hair with my fingers as the hot air blew through the dripping strands, heating my already warm bathroom and causing me to sweat in the clothes I'd just thrown on. I ignored the heat and continued to run the hairdryer, my flushed face scowling back at me from the only part of the mirror not rendered useless by condensation. I was running late for my lunch date with Patrick, who had apparently already arrived at the restaurant and grabbed a table. Running late was stressful enough, but knowing he was sitting there waiting for me as I rushed to leave my apartment made my anxiety that much worse.

Cursing under my breath, I tossed the hairdryer onto the counter and reluctantly gathered my damp chestnut locks into a low bun. Placing bobby pins frantically behind my head to hold the stragglers in place, I snatched my new brown clutch and slipped on a pair of woven flats to head out the door. Although I'd barely had time to put on any makeup, I figured it was best not to keep Patrick waiting.

Bolting out the door and briskly covering the several blocks between my apartment and the small Thai place where I was meeting Patrick, I wondered what had possessed me to put off my shower until the last minute. I'd woken up over two hours before our scheduled lunch date – which should have given me plenty of time to get ready – but had decided instead to spend an hour and a half snacking, drinking coffee and catching up on the latest celebrity gossip through a variety of my favorite blogs.

Walking past the park, I was thankful that the season's rising temperatures remained cool this afternoon. The gentle breeze helped regulate my body temperature and prevented me from sweating through my shirt as I sped toward the restaurant. On a warmer day, I would have been sweating bullets as I bullied my way past people strolling casually along the sidewalk. Fortunately, my blouse remained dry when I approached the restaurant's front door, a mere ten minutes late. Ten minutes wasn't a completely unreasonable cushion, and I didn't expect Patrick would be too upset.

When I entered the warm, dim lighted restaurant, I was immediately engulfed by rich smells of sautéed dishes. The aroma made my stomach rumble restlessly in hunger notwithstanding the fact I'd been snacking on and off all morning. Slipping off my faux fur vest and folding it over my arms, I scanned the restaurant in search of Patrick, who I finally spotted at a small booth, waving at me gleefully. Waving back and smiling, I started toward him, suddenly anxious about our date. I'd been so focused on getting ready that I'd half-forgotten why we'd scheduled lunch in the first place. I felt like crossing my fingers as I approached the table, hoping that our talk would have nothing to do with Keegan.

Scooting out of the booth, Patrick stood up to give me a welcoming hug. He looked dashing this afternoon, dressed in smart black dress pants and a patterned, collared dress shirt of subtle pastel blues and pinks. His brown hair was parted neatly to the side, and his black dress shoes glistened with new polish. I gave him a quick hug and looked at him quizzically, wondering what occasion would call for him to look so dapper. He always looked nice, but I'd rarely, if ever, seen Patrick in business casual.

"Do you have a meeting today for the boutique?" I asked curiously, continuing to assess his outfit. I was usually the one person other than Alex who knew everything going on at *De Alexia*, but I'd been on a vacation of sorts for over a week and felt a little out of touch. Between sealing our deal with Keegan and the anniversary of Dad's death, Alex had encouraged me to relax and spend some time away from work. I appreciated the break, but after seeing Patrick dressed in preparation for a meeting I knew nothing about made me want to end my vacation right then and there and get back to my role as the store's New York liaison and Alex's right hand woman.

"No, no," Patrick said, chuckling, dissuading me of my suspicions. "I can't imagine Alex being very happy with me going anywhere on behalf of the boutique in anything other than clothes from his line."

"That's true," I replied, still wondering why he was dressed this way. I waited for him to offer an explanation, but none was forthcoming. "Well, why the business casual then?" I asked finally. "What's the occasion?" Smiling, Patrick bounced in the booth as he shuffled his feet in excitement. He was almost giddy.

"That, Haley dear, is what I want to talk to you about," he declared. I looked at him in anticipation, my eyebrows raised. When he took a breath to explain, our waiter approached the table, interrupting us with the usual pleasantries.

"Would you like anything to drink, ma'am?" He asked kindly. I looked at him impatiently, annoyed that he'd interrupted something important.

"Water is fine," I responded as politely as I could manage. I was eager to get on with the conversation, but didn't want to be rude to the unsuspecting server. As a former bartender and waitress, I knew that nothing could ruin your day like a caustic customer. Nodding, he turned to fetch my water. It didn't seem as though he'd picked up on my irritation. Turning back to Patrick, I sat in the booth impatiently, waiting for him to reveal his mystery.

"Look, Haley," he started again, focusing on his hands instead of me. "I love Alex like I've never loved anyone before." I nodded in acknowledgment, waiting for him to continue. "He is my everything," Patrick added, still staring at his hands, which were now fidgeting anxiously on top of the table, "and I know, without a doubt, that I've met the person I want to be with for the rest of my life." I smiled knowingly.

"You and Alex were made for each other," I agreed. He looked up at me, his brown eyes intensely focused on mine, his expression happy, but serious.

"You're not hearing me, Hale," he insisted, reaching into his pocket. "I want to be with Alex for the *rest of my life*." My heart started beating a little faster when he pulled his hand out of his pocket, revealing a small jewelry box covered in black velvet. He set it on the table in front of me and grinned, his eyes sparkling. I placed my hands on the table as if to steady myself.

"Is this really what I think it is?" I asked. My voice came out in barely a whisper. I was in total shock.

"Open it," Patrick insisted, beaming. I turned my attention back to the jewelry box and obliged his request, opening it to reveal a beautiful brushed silver band, plain except for the small, ornate border etched near the bottom. Looking closer still, I noticed small script inside the band, but couldn't make out what it said.

"May I?" I asked, tears stinging my eyes. Patrick nodded confidently as I reached for the band, continuing to smile and fight my amassing tears. "It's beautiful," I said, breathless. I turned it over in my hands, careful not to smudge it with my fingerprints. *Forever in my heart*, the inscription read. It was simple, but eloquent. I never knew four words could be so perfect, so romantic. Placing it gingerly back in the box, I smiled so hard that my cheeks hurt. Question after question piled up in my mind, but all I could manage was a giant smile. Patrick closed the box and placed it back in his pocket with his right hand, grabbing my hand with his left.

"I've grown up dreaming of proposing," Patrick revealed. His hand was warm and delicately soft. "Alex and I have talked about getting papers at the courthouse, but I want to propose; to have a wedding; to take the plunge in the way I've always dreamed." I nodded, still trying to comprehend what Patrick was telling me. "Haley, I want to marry the man I love," he continued. I remained speechless across from him in the booth. "I brought you here today because I want your blessing." I blinked, stunned. Patrick patted my hand and leaned closer, trying to catch my gaze. "Hale?" He looked mildly concerned. "You okay?" Continuing to smile, I turned to Patrick and shook my head in disbelief.

"Yes," I finally confirmed. "I'm more than okay; I'm ecstatic!" I moved my hand from under his and leaned back in the booth to take a breath. "I'm just completely blindsided, that's all," I admitted. "I didn't even know you two wanted to do the marriage thing." I had no idea how Alex would react to Patrick's gesture. He was more practical than traditional when it came to notions of romance. I wondered whether this was something both of them wanted. I hoped so, for both their sakes. Patrick shrugged and put the jewelry box back in his pocket.

"We've discussed it before," he told me. "But every time we do, we approach it like it's a business decision. I don't want our commitment to each other to be a day filling out papers and shaking hands. I want it to be romantic and sweet, and I want to look Alex in the eyes and ask him to be mine forever."

I understood completely. I would never want my wedding day to be shrouded in paperwork. I would want it to be about the dress, the setting, and the vows. "And Haley," he added passionately, "I want him to look back into mine and say 'yes.'" The tears that were welling up in my eyes came dangerously close to falling, but as happy as I was for Alex to have someone like Patrick by his side, I envied him. Patrick's notions of love and romance were like a fairytale. I wished, in a shameful bout of selfishness, that it was my lover sitting across from Alex in a booth, declaring his love for me in a way that brought Alex to tears. Despite all my wishing, however, I knew in my heart of hearts that people like Patrick were unique. I wasn't entirely confident that I would ever find someone who could ever be to me what Patrick was to Alex.

"Wow," I said, shaking my jealousy and refocusing on how happy I was for my two dear friends. "Alex is the luckiest person in the world to have you for a partner." Patrick smiled at me gratefully as the waiter placed my water on the table and quickly left again, this time seemingly picking up on the seriousness of our discussion.

"I wanted your blessing," Patrick explained, "because you are the closest thing to family that Alex's got. It wouldn't be right to ask him to be mine forever without asking you first if you're willing to give him away." I was taken aback by Patrick's chivalry and thrown by the realization that he considered me to be Alex's family. It was true that Alex was an only child and hadn't spoken to his mother and father in almost ten years, but I had never considered myself their replacement.

"Of course you have my blessing," I responded as Patrick watched me expectantly. "I couldn't have imagined a better man for Alex. I'm ridiculously happy for you guys and I can't believe this is going to happen!" Patrick clapped his hands together in excitement and scooted out of the booth to give me a hug.

"Thanks, Hale," he said warmly, giving me a quick squeeze. As he settled back into his side of the booth, I considered the magnitude of what he was asking. I was honored, but something didn't feel right. I wasn't the one with whom Patrick should have been talking.

"You know Patrick," I started hesitantly, "it should be Alex's parents sitting across from you in this booth, not me." For the first time since I arrived, Patrick's smile faded.

"Haley, I've never even met them," he began. I could tell he was uncomfortable with my suggestion. "Alex has written them out of his life. How could I contact them without somehow betraying Alex in the process? No, I'm not doing that – I wanted to make this special, Hale. I figured you would appreciate knowing that you're the most important person in Alex's life." I nodded, irritated that I'd ruined the moment. I should have kept my mouth shut. Who Patrick wanted to consult about proposing to Alex was his choice, and it wasn't my place to question it. Nevertheless, something in the back of my mind felt sad knowing that because of one moment almost ten years ago, Alex's parents had missed out on this special moment just like they'd missed out on so many other things in the past decade.

"I'm sorry, Patrick," I said apologetically. "It was stupid for me to say. I'm obviously thrilled about being the one to give you a blessing before you propose." I sat in the booth for a few seconds, gathering my thoughts and choosing my words carefully so as not to rock the boat any more than I already had. "It's just that I know how awful it feels, knowing that whenever someone decides to propose to me, my dad won't be around to ask. If there was anything within my power that I could do to bring him back, I would – especially for that moment. In Alex's case, he has the power to bring his parents back – at least to give them one more chance. Frankly, I don't want him to regret never trying to reconnect after all is said and done. You can't have these moments back. Once they're gone, they're gone forever." Patrick looked at me thoughtfully.

"I understand," he said, compliantly. "Don't worry about Alex. When we start planning the wedding maybe I can work on him a little. If there's any event that would bring a family together again, it's a wedding." I smiled, grateful that he understood my position. Patrick was sensible, kind, and unwaveringly caring. Alex had truly found the perfect man. "Although perhaps our wedding wouldn't be the kind of wedding that would reunite them," Patrick commented under his breath, a hint of disdain in his voice. I sighed.

"You never know," I said softly. "They may surprise you if you give them a chance." I sounded like Lindsay. It was much easier to dispense advice than receive it. Patrick looked at me doubtfully and turned back to the menu.

It was hard to believe it had been almost ten years ago – shortly after Alex's high school graduation – that he had officially announced his sexual orientation to his parents. In Alex's mind, his parents' reaction to this news had been unacceptable and had hurt him in a way he never thought possible. In later years, he admitted he hadn't really given them a chance to respond, but nevertheless claimed that his parents' disappointment had been obvious from the moment 'I'm gay' rolled out of his mouth. Infuriated by his parents' perceived disappointment, Alex told them he'd never speak to them again. And in a ruthless act of stubbornness, he'd carried out that threat now for nearly ten years.

When he'd told me he had cut them out of his life those many years ago, I'd supported him like I thought a good friend should. When you're younger, you stand strong by your friends in their convictions, and don't think about the long-term impact those actions may have down the road. Sadly, it was under those circumstances that I'd supported Alex's rage against his parents. I wished I'd had the maturity or forethought to advise Alex to talk to them and give them another chance. I was worried he had thrown away his parents too hastily. Alex remained staunchly unforgiving, no matter how many times they'd reached out to him over the years. I know they'd hurt Alex, but I desperately wished he would at least give them an opportunity to explain themselves. They'd always seemed like sweet people.

Realizing how quickly he'd cut his parents from his life made me nervous about my secret love affair with Keegan. If Alex ever found out what I'd been hiding, it pained me to think he could do the same to me.

Leaning across the table, Patrick interrupted my thoughts by talking excitedly about how he was thinking of proposing. I refocused my energy on his plans and listened actively as my thoughts about Keegan and Alex faded slowly, but not so surely, into the background.

****

It was only when I noticed my phone buzzing that I realized Patrick and I had been scheming and chatting like gossipy schoolgirls for over an hour and a half. It was already nearly two o'clock.

"Patrick, I need to get out of here," I said, interrupting him and placing my phone back in my purse. Judging by Patrick's reaction, he hadn't seen Keegan's incoming call. If anything, he seemed disappointed that his story about how he'd picked out Alex's ring had been cut short. "I'm meeting Nick in an hour for some ice cream," I explained. "As I'm sure it's obvious, I need to get back home to make myself look a little more presentable." Patrick's expression quickly changed from one of disappointment to understanding.

"You look lovely," he lied, "but go do what you need to do. And tell him I said 'hello'!" I grabbed my purse and scooted out of the booth to give Patrick a quick hug. I was anxious to get home to prepare for my rendezvous with Nick, but I was also anxious to return Keegan's call.

"We'll continue this conversation in the near future," I promised. "I cannot WAIT for everything to go down. It's going to be hard keeping this from Alex." Patrick grabbed my arm forcefully as I turned to leave, his eyes wide and intense.

"Don't you dare tell him, Haley Blythe," he warned, gritting his uneven teeth. Shaking my arm away, I looked back at him reassuringly.

"Of course I won't tell him, Patrick," I responded, surprised he would even think it. "It's just going to be hard talking to him knowing what he has to look forward to, that's all. Don't worry. I would never ruin this for him – or you." Patrick relaxed and once again motioned for me to leave.

"Okay, okay," he said. "Sorry. Of course you won't tell him. Have a good rest of the day, Hale. Let me know how your date goes!" I waved back at him and snaked my way through the restaurant. Pushing open the door and emerging into the cool spring weather, I waited until I'd turned the corner and put the restaurant a couple of blocks behind me before calling Keegan.

"Hey gorgeous," Keegan answered almost whispering. I felt my face blush at the sound of his voice and longed to have his body close to mine. I missed him terribly.

"Hi there," I said, happy that he'd picked up the phone. I reached

Keegan's voicemail more often than not. He was a busy man.

"Ready to see me in a few days?" He asked. My heart started pumping excitedly.

"Are you really coming to Columbus next week?" I hoped, my voice almost shrill from anticipation.

"Absolutely," he confirmed. "It's been too long since we've been with each other. I couldn't stand being away from you without knowing when I'd see you again." Smiling from ear to ear, I felt myself fill with happiness knowing that he longed for me as much as I longed for him.

"When are you flying in?" I asked. "Are you bringing work?"

"Wednesday," he replied quickly. "And yes. I figured I'd bring some working samples of the shoes to run by Alex before we continue with manufacturing."

"I see," I responded, slightly disappointed. I knew I'd been the one to suggest he add a business reason for his trip, but it made me feel like an added bonus to his pre-planned travels, rather than the main reason for his flight. Not quite the romantic sentiment I'd been hoping for.

"You sound a little disappointed," he said, reading my reaction. "But don't you worry. We'll have plenty of time together before I go back home on Friday. My business with Alex won't take much time."

"Oh, I'm not disappointed," I lied. "If I seem that way it's just because I miss you."

"I miss you too," Keegan replied warmly. "But my spirits are high knowing I'll be in your arms in a few short days." I smiled. I was excited to see him, but I felt guilty that I was headed to meet another man in less than an hour – a man for whom I also had feelings, though we'd never been intimate.

"Are you staying in the same hotel?" I asked, removing Nick from my thoughts.

"Yes," Keegan acknowledged. "And like last time, there'll be room for you to join me if you're interested." I was definitely interested, and hoped that his upcoming visit would be as passionate and exciting as it had been a couple of weeks ago.

"Of course I'm interested," I confirmed. Approaching my apartment, I removed my keys from my purse. "I can't wait for you to get here," I added. Turning my key in the lock, I pushed open my door and headed to the bathroom upstairs to grab my make-up. I had about thirty minutes to make my eyes look less tired and to dry and straighten my hair.

"I know, I can't wait either," Keegan agreed. "It's going to be a LOT of fun." After a short pause, his voice turned apologetic. "Well as much as I hate to, I've gotta go back to work."

"I understand," I said, rustling through my bathroom drawers. "I have to get ready to meet someone anyway. It wouldn't be very easy for me to talk on the phone and run a hairdryer."

"Okay," Keegan said quietly. "Talk to you soon – I'll try to call tonight, but no promises."

"K – I can't wait to see you!" I exclaimed.

Putting my phone to the side, I raced against the clock, scrambling to prepare to leave my apartment once again. It felt dishonest to be meeting Nick for ice cream so soon after talking to Keegan about his impending visit, but I wasn't sure who it was I felt like I was deceiving. I ignored my uneasiness, refusing to make things more complicated than they already were, and continued to get ready.

****

I made it out the door in plenty of time to walk the mile to the ice cream shop. Locking the door and turning toward the sidewalk, I placed my keys in my pocket and pulled out my impatiently buzzing phone.

"Hey!" I said, answering Alex's call. "What's going on?" I buried the knowledge of Patrick's future proposal next to my relationship with Keegan, deep, deep down in the depths of my soul.

"Oh, not too much," he responded casually. "Wanted to give you an update on what's going on with the store."

"Good!" I exclaimed, instructing myself to behave normally notwithstanding everything I was hiding. "I've been feeling disconnected lately – it will be nice to hear what's been going on. By the way, I'm going to start back up Monday, so maybe we should meet to talk about what I need to do in the next couple of weeks and when you'll want me heading back to New York."

"Sure, Hale," Alex agreed. "I'll be in and out Monday – shoot me a text before you head over to the boutique to make sure I'm there."

"Great!" I replied. "Now, go ahead and update me." I took a deep breath and sighed, my lungs filling with crisp air and the overwhelming smells of blooming trees and flowers.

"Well, first, you need to get on Dom's party," Alex reminded me. "I will send you some possible dates that work for both Dom and I. Choose one that works for you as well and we'll go from there."

"Okay," I said, nodding. "On it. What else?"

"Keegan is coming into town next week. We have a meeting Thursday."

"Right," I responded, wishing he would update me on things I didn't already know. "He's bringing shoe samples, I know, I know – what else?" Alex paused on the other end of the line and I stopped in my tracks, realizing it might seem odd that I already knew about Keegan's visit.

"How the hell do *you* know that?" He asked, justifiably confused. I searched for a lie, filling the silence in the meantime with 'um' and 'uh.'

"He called me," I finally said. I had to admit that much, at least. "Maybe he's more comfortable calling me than you," I suggested. "Anyway, I told him to call you directly and ask about your schedule. I assured him that he wouldn't be bothering you." I pressed my lips together tightly to keep my mouth shut. I couldn't keep lying with my mouth firmly closed.

"That's strange." Alex's voice was flat. "He's been calling me directly almost daily since we reached an agreement, running ideas and logistics by me. It doesn't make sense that he'd all of a sudden be concerned about bothering me." I stood in the middle of the sidewalk, wincing.

"I don't know what to tell you," I said, hoping he would let it be. I could feel my voice shaking, but I tried to remain calm. "Maybe he felt bad calling you all the time and wanted to give you a break. Technically, I am the person who schedules meetings between you and the people we do business with in New York. Naresh always calls me if he wants to schedule something, why is it weird for Keegan to do so as well?" Alex didn't respond immediately. I feared he could smell my lies like a bloodhound.

"Perhaps," Alex said. "How about you and I catch up more on Monday." My heart dropped. Judging by the tone of his voice, I was sure he suspected something.

"No more news about the boutique?" I asked, trying to sound nonchalant.

"Not at the moment," Alex replied, his voice eerily monotonous.

"Okay, well I'm off to meet Nick in a couple of minutes anyway," I said. I hoped that distracting him with thoughts of Nick would allay whatever suspicions he'd gathered during the call. "See you Monday?"

"See you Monday," Alex confirmed, hanging up. His failure to acknowledge my mention of Nick was conspicuous.

"Shit," I cursed to myself, putting away my phone and once again walking in the direction of the ice cream parlor. I was nervous that Alex had sniffed out my deceit. The way his voice changed when he'd discovered I'd spoken with Keegan was unnerving. What had possessed me to be so careless?

Torturing myself as I walked, I tried to remember exactly everything I had said. I'd admitted speaking with Keegan, but that was it. That couldn't have been enough to lead Alex to conclude we were sleeping together. Or could it? I obsessed over what Alex was thinking and began to worry about what would happen on Monday when I entered the store. Was I overreacting? Would Alex move on with business like our conversation had never happened? Or would he fire me immediately, banishing me from his life for lying to his face and messing with the future of *De Alexia*? My head was spinning. Lindsay had been right all along. I should have told Alex the minute Keegan kissed me in the park. Unfortunately, however, I couldn't go back and change what I'd done.

Reaching the street on which the ice cream shop sat, I stopped walking and turned when I heard a man's voice call my name from behind.

"Wait up!" Nick exclaimed, jogging to catch up. Seeing him instantly made me feel better. He was dressed in a pair of brown loafers, jeans, and a thin, green, long-sleeved sweater layered over a gray undershirt. As soon as he was within reach, I threw my arms around him and squeezed, thankful to be with him after what had just happened with Alex on the phone. Nick sensed my distress immediately. He lifted my head by the chin – my arms still wrapped around his waist – and peered down at me with concern. "You okay, Haley?" He asked softly, his caring hazel eyes locked into mine.

"Fine," I lied, relaxing my grip. There it was again: 'Fine.' Covering all real emotion. Brushing my hair away from my mouth, Nick placed his hand behind my head and smiled.

"Let's get you some ice cream," he suggested warmly. "Whatever's bothering you, ice cream and a friend should help you feel much better." Smiling weakly, I let him place his arm around me and guide me toward the street. He probably figured I was emotional about Dad. I wondered what he would say if I revealed the truth. I didn't dare tell him.

"Thanks," I said softly, still nestled under his arm, my thoughts and emotions swirling around in my head chaotically. "You're a great friend."

16 THE ACCIDENT

I stood inside the door of the coffee shop with my damp umbrella, thankful to be out of the gloomy weather. On a day like today, a cozy coffee shop and a hot cup of coffee was like medicine for the soul. I couldn't wait to get my hands around a thick-rimmed, steaming coffee mug, filled to the brim with a warm French Roast. Not yet seeing Patrick, however, I decided to wait to order until after he arrived.

Nestling into a brown leather chair near the fireplace, I felt better now that I was dry and comfortable in the midst of coffee heaven. The taupe walls and coffee tapestries soothed me like a fluffy blanket, and the fall hues of the furniture made me want to curl up with a piece of pumpkin pie and forget it was spring. Sifting through a stack of magazines on the table in front of me, I glanced out the window, hoping the rain would stop by the time Patrick and I had finished discussing the logistics of Dom's upcoming party. My highly anticipated meeting at the boutique with Alex was in an hour, and rain seemed like a bad omen.

I worried about meeting with Alex all weekend and couldn't believe that the time had finally come to face him. I wished I could take back what I'd said to him about talking to Keegan, but it was too late. I hoped that Alex hadn't jumped to the conclusion I feared, but from the way our conversation ended on Saturday, I was certain he suspected something. I worried about what I would say if Alex confronted me. Even then, I didn't know whether I could tell him the truth. Having dug myself a cavernous hole of deception, I feared I had no other choice but to keep digging. I'd lost too many people I'd loved in my life, that I wasn't about to lose Alex, too. Not over this.

Laying my umbrella against the table in front of me and removing my jacket, I continued to rummage through the stack of magazines, looking for a distraction. To my dismay, there was not one trashy celebrity tabloid in the midst of the wholesome, informational magazines resting on the table. I needed a mental break filled with useless celebrity gossip to calm my building anxiety – not articles summarizing the perfect way to redo an outdated bathroom. Flipping unenthusiastically through the pages of a couple of magazines, I eventually surrendered and opened my purse to find my phone. I hadn't spoken to Lindsay in a few days. A quick catch-up would be the perfect thing with which to fill my time while I waited on Patrick.

Rummaging through my purse, I stopped when I saw a bent piece of pink card stock peeking out from one of my purse's side pockets. Pulling it out slowly, I smiled once I recognized it. It was the card that accompanied the beautiful flowers Nick sent to Dad's grave last week. I'd forgotten that I'd saved it.

Placing the card carefully back into the pocket, I thought about Nick and our recent ice cream date. Spending time with him had temporarily wiped my worries away, and with my nerves currently at unhealthily high levels, I wished he could be here with me now. It was effortless to be in his company. He had an uncanny way of making me feel happy and carefree, as if nothing about life ever had to be difficult again. It helped that there were no lies or scandals clouding our time together, but something about him made me feel safe. It was different than when I was with Keegan. Not good or bad, just . . . different.

I put my phone away when I saw Patrick walk through the door in a black hooded rain jacket and a pair of dark galoshes tied above his ankles. He shuddered when he entered and hit his wet umbrella on the floor to shake off the rain. He saw me waving as he pulled back his hood to scan the coffee shop. I was happy to see him, and eager to get going on the plans for Dom's party. I could always count on Patrick to help with these sorts of things. He had a certificate in event planning from college and worked as an event planner at a local young professionals organization before quitting to help Alex run the boutique. He was great with people and wonderful at promotions and marketing, which made him an awesome addition to the *De Alexia* staff.

I rose to hug him before he sat down, trying not to rub against his freshly wet raincoat. "Hi, P," I greeted, settling back down into the chair. Patrick reciprocated my 'hello' while unbuttoning his jacket. "What can I get you?" I asked him.

"Eh, something hot, but not too caffeinated," he requested, craning his neck to look at the specials board behind him. Patrick wasn't much of a coffee drinker. The smallest bit of caffeine tended to make him jittery and wired. I was envious that it had that effect on him. I could drink coffee all day without feeling a thing. If I didn't drink it, I would get a raging headache from withdrawal.

When I returned with our drinks, Patrick had settled in by the fireplace, appearing warmer and more comfortable than he had been a couple of minutes before. I handed him his decaf mocha latte, careful not to spill it, and rested my medium French Roast on the edge of the table before sitting down. Patrick informed me that he had exciting news as soon as my butt hit the seat. "It's happening this weekend," he shared in a hushed whisper. I took a quick glance around the coffee shop for familiar faces. When I didn't see anyone I recognized, I grabbed his knee with excitement.

"It is!?" I asked happily through clenched teeth. The thought of Patrick proposing lifted my dampened spirits. I couldn't believe it was all happening so fast.

"Yes," Patrick confirmed, setting his latte down in front of him. "We're going to this adorable remote bed and breakfast out east for the weekend. I suggested it as an early anniversary celebration. Of course, Alex doesn't suspect a thing. Frankly, he's been so distracted with work the last couple of days, I'm not even sure he remembers we're going." My excitement for Patrick was strained by the mention of Alex's recent mood. I tried not to read too much into it, but it was nearly impossible not to think he was distracted by thoughts of my possible love affair with Keegan. "I'm not exactly sure yet how I'm going to do it," Patrick continued, unaware that I was panicking below the surface, "but I know I'll be popping the question at some point while we're there." I let go of Patrick's knee and continued to smile, concentrating on the happiness of his news rather than the daunting meeting that lay ahead.

"That's great Patrick," I said. "I'm happy for you. I can't wait to hear how everything goes."

"Yes, everything seems to be falling into place," Patrick mused. "The business is taking off, and if Alex says 'yes,' I'll be the happiest and luckiest man in the world." My phone buzzed in my jacket pocket. I pulled it out subtly, not wanting to interrupt Patrick's moment. I was surprised to see Trevor calling. I ignored it and sent the call to voicemail. "I'm not sure whether I should do it as soon as we get there," Patrick was saying, "or whether I should wait until the last day. Honestly, I don't know if I can wait until the end." My phone buzzed in my pocket again. Again, it was Trevor. Narrowing my eyes, I stared at it for a moment, confused by his barrage of phone calls. I wondered whether I should answer.

Placing my phone in my pocket yet again, I continued listening to Patrick, trying to put Trevor's incessant calling out of my mind. After about a minute, however, Patrick stopped chatting to pull out his own phone. Furrowing his dark eyebrows in confusion, he looked at me and told me it was Trevor. I couldn't imagine what the hell Trevor wanted.

"Go ahead and answer it," I instructed him curiously. "He called me a couple of times, too. See what he wants." Patrick obliged, answering the call with mild interest.

"Hello?" I watched him expectantly, studying Patrick's face to try and extract the reason for Trevor's call. Suddenly, all of the color drained from Patrick's face. He sat on the edge of his chair, rigid and unmoving. "Okay, okay, it's going to be okay . . ." His voice became high-pitched and frantic. My heart fluttered nervously in my chest, wondering what was happening. Something was very wrong. "I'm with Haley. We'll be there in less than ten minutes, I promise." Patrick's eyes were wide as if he'd seen a ghost. "It's going to be okay, Trevor. We'll be there." When he hung up the phone, he stared at me, frightened and on the edge of tears.

"What's going on?" I asked softly, terrified of the answer. I could feel myself starting to shake from nervous surges of adrenaline. Patrick took a deep breath and stood from his chair. "It's Lindsay," he finally managed, holding his breath after he spoke. "She's been hit by a car."

He paused a few seconds, but I continued to stare at him expressionless, shock quickly consuming my entire body. I was jolted back in time to when I was a child, my mother sitting my brother and I down at the kitchen table to tell us the same thing about Dad. This couldn't be happening to me again. "She's in the hospital downtown," Patrick continued. "That's why Trevor was calling you . . ."

"Holy shit," I said, under my breath. "Holy shit, holy shit." Patrick looked at me in a panic and began gathering his things. "Is she okay!?" I asked, almost yelling. "Patrick, tell me she's okay." Shrugging his shoulders in confusion, he looked as if he may cry, struggling to answer.

"I don't know," he said, desperately. "Trevor was freaking out – we need to get down there." I wasn't capable of thinking. I couldn't move. Patrick put on his jacket and kneeled down in front of me until his eyes met mine.

"Haley," he said, his hands on either side of my upper arms. He was shaking. "Haley, we need to get downtown. Gather your things. I'll go across the street to grab Alex. He can drive us. You stay right here. Don't move." I stared at the ground listlessly, numbing myself to my surroundings. Thoughts of the day Dad died were playing over and over in my mind.

After a period of time – long or short, I'm not quite certain – Alex was in front of me, shaking me gently. "Hale? Hi Hale," he said, calmly. "You need to snap out of it – I need you to move. Dom is out front with the car." My chest started to burn. I couldn't remember the last time I'd taken a breath. Letting the air out of my lungs, I felt myself start to shake. Alex clenched his jaw and continued to look at me. "Haley, we need to go." I began to cry, the tears streaming down my face in silent waterfalls. "It's going to be okay," Alex insisted. "Lindsay will be fine, but we need to get down there." Closing my eyes and trying to block memories of Dad out of my mind, I managed a hoarse 'okay' and stood up with Alex's help. Any worries about talking to Alex about Keegan had long disappeared. Those worries seemed petty and hollow now.

My legs felt like gelatin and the room spun violently around me as I rose. I couldn't tell whether I was going to throw up or pass out. Miraculously, I made it to Dom's car with Alex's help and shut the door behind me. My hands were shaking so intensely that I could barely guide my seatbelt into the buckle. After a couple of minutes in the car, I managed to buckle myself in as Dom drove hurriedly toward the hospital. Between reminding myself to breathe and scrutinizing the disastrous mess in Dom's beat-up Volkswagen bug, I did my best to focus on anything besides the potential loss of my friend. It was everything I could do to stay calm.

I stared out the window while Dom drove, relieved when he finally pulled into the parking garage. It was torture not to be at the hospital, knowing that Lindsay was there and not knowing her condition. Thankfully, I'd regained my motor skills over the short ride and was able to get out of Dom's car without assistance. Slamming the door shut, I took a deep breath and bee-lined straight for the hospital. Dom, Alex, and Patrick kept pace silently behind me.

None of us said a word as we rushed toward the emergency room. We were all too panicked, worried, or shocked to have anything to say besides 'this way' or 'over here' when we saw signs leading the way. My heart hammered quickly in my chest as we sped through the hospital corridors. It felt like we were running through a maze of endless, pale tiled hallways. Several of the hospital's fluorescent light bulbs flickered as we passed, as if setting the scene for our own personal horror movie. It was only until we turned the last corner and I saw Trevor pacing desperately back and forth in the waiting room that I allowed myself to take a breath. We were finally here.

Seeing us almost instantly, Trevor ran toward me and hugged me fiercely, sobbing into my shoulder. Wanting to comfort him, but also needing information, I pulled away and grabbed his arms in the same way Alex had grabbed mine earlier in the coffee shop. Urging him to look at me, I stared at him as calmly as I could and asked what had happened. "How is she?" I tried to ask patiently, but my voice came out loud and panicked. "I don't know anything." Gasping for breath, Trevor regained enough composure to tell me that a car hit Lindsay while she was crossing a street somewhere downtown.

"She was on her way to court," he explained, between gasps. His story was fragmented, but I was able to follow him without too much of a problem. "She was with some coworkers. They saw it. They called the ambulance. She's in surgery – I don't know anything else." His voice became a high-pitched squeal as he finished his last sentence, clearly devastated by his limited knowledge. He broke into a sob and collapsed in a nearby chair, holding his head against his left hand while punching the armrest with his right.

Overwhelmed with emotion, I pulled him close and hugged him, repeating that she'd be okay. The two of us rocked back and forth until I asked him whether he'd called her parents. "Of course," he said, still struggling for air. "They're on their way." I eventually let him go and slumped into my own chair, not sure of what to do or who to call. Dom, Alex, and Patrick sat silently near us in the same worn, Aztec-patterned blue chairs, staring at the other people in the waiting room or tapping their feet on the floor in unbridled anxiety.

"She'll get through it," Patrick said faintly to no one in particular. His brown eyes were bloodshot and his normally neat brown mane was disheveled from constantly running his hand through his hair. Nodding, I took out my phone and texted my brother. Then, in a move that only felt natural, I called Nick.

"Hey, Hale!" He exclaimed on the other end of the phone. The happy tone of his voice caused me to wince, as if he'd answered by running his nails down a chalkboard.

"Hey," I forced myself to respond, my voice hoarse and dry. "Something's . . . happened." Gulping down the wave of emotion clawing up my throat, I told him about Lindsay's accident as calmly as my body would allow. When I'd finished, I held my breath for a moment and closed my eyes, trying to prevent myself from breaking down.

"I'll be there in fifteen minutes," he said, without hesitation. His voice had dropped significantly from when he'd first picked up the phone. "Hang in there. Do you need anything?" I allowed myself to exhale and told him I was fine.

"You don't need to come here," I insisted weakly, not wanting him to feel obligated. "I just – I didn't know who else to call." I felt the tears welling up in my eyes and my chin quivered. I could barely keep it together.

"I'm coming down there, Haley," Nick said firmly. "I'll see you soon – everything's going to be okay." I sighed and thanked him before hanging up the phone. I didn't have the energy to protest, and frankly, I wanted him to come. With Keegan hundreds of miles away, it would be comforting to at least have Nick by my side. I looked anxiously around the room, wondering how much longer we'd have to wait for news of Lindsay's condition.

"Was that Nick?" Alex asked from his chair, gripping Patrick's hand nervously.

"Yes," I confirmed. "He knows Lindsay. I thought he should know." Alex nodded. He didn't say another word.

After a grueling and intense few minutes, a doctor finally came into the waiting room asking for Lindsay's family. Shooting up from his chair, Trevor raised his hand and almost screamed at her, identifying himself as Lindsay's boyfriend. "Her parents are on their way from Cincinnati," he offered. He spoke so fast that his words jumbled together as if he were on speed.

"We're all the family that's here right now," I added, placing my hand gently on Trevor's shoulder. Nodding, the doctor walked toward Trevor. The rest of us huddled around him, squeezing each other's arms, hands, or whatever other body parts we could reach. Holding my breath, I listened as the doctor began to explain Lindsay's condition, her dark eyes fixed calmly on Trevor's as she talked about Lindsay's injuries.

"She suffered several severe injuries," she explained slowly. "She's broken her ankle and torn most of the ligaments in her right knee." We all stared, ingesting the news in silence. "She also suffered a serious head injury," the doctor continued, "which caused bleeding in her brain." I heard Patrick gasp behind me. I squeezed Dom's hand, trying not to cry. "The initial surgery we performed was to reduce the swelling in her brain and to stop the bleeding," the doctor explained. "It appears as though the operation was successful. As of now, she remains in serious condition, but she's out of immediate danger because the bleeding appears to have stopped." Trevor collapsed into the chair behind him almost immediately. He looked like a puppet whose strings had been flung to the bottom of the stage. I reached over to place my hand again on his shoulder in comfort. It was all I could think to do. He shook as he sobbed, releasing his emotions, a part of him likely relieved, while the rest of him remained worried for the woman he loved.

"When will she be awake?" I asked hopefully. Dad had never woken up after his accident. The idea of seeing Lindsay open her eyes after surgery was something I clung to desperately.

"It's hard to tell," the doctor responded carefully. "She suffered serious head trauma. But we will be sure to keep you all updated if her condition changes in any way." Thanking her, I turned to Trevor and hugged him, telling him that it would only get better from here. Although Lindsay wasn't out of the woods, I knew in my heart she would be okay. There was never even a glimmer of hope after Dad's accident – we'd just waited and waited until we'd received the bad news.

I pulled back from Trevor to find Nick walking slowly around the corner toward the waiting area, his eyebrows furrowed with worry. Spotting me, he put up his hand in a small wave and smiled weakly, a bouquet of flowers in his arms. Without hesitation, I ran to him and let his arms wrap around me, the smell of the fresh flowers filling my nostrils with spring. "She's going to be okay," I said quietly into his chest, as if saying the words out loud would make them come true. "I just know it," I insisted. "She's going to be okay."

17 REVELATION

I walked urgently through the hospital hallways, my cold hands starting to numb from carrying the delicious, yet icy, strawberry shakes I picked up a few minutes earlier. Biting my lower lip as my hands started to burn from the cold plastic cups, I quickened my pace to a barely controlled speed-walk, trying to reach Lindsay's room as fast as possible. Turning the corner, I shuffled quickly through the doorway to find Lindsay sitting up in her bed reading the newspaper. She looked up as I entered and smiled warmly. She was looking more and more like herself every day. The bruises around the left side of her face were changing from purple to an unsavory but healing yellow, and the place where they'd shaved her head showed promising signs of fast hair re-growth. Although the rest of her was bandaged like an entombed mummy, the physical signs of her improvement were clear. She was healing rapidly and would hopefully be discharged from the hospital in a few days.

"Who reads the newspaper anymore?" I asked, hastily setting the shakes down on her bedside table and rubbing my hands together in an attempt to get back the feeling in my fingers. Lindsay watched me in amusement and raised her eyebrows as I blew warm air into my fists.

"People who care about the news, I suppose," she replied facetiously, closing the paper. Shaking my hands to distract myself from the uncomfortable tingling starting to surge through my palms, I rolled my eyes.

"You know what I mean," I said, wincing from the pins and needles in my hands. "I thought the Internet made newspapers obsolete unless you're trying to start a fire." I blew into my hands again, relieved to feel them returning to their normal state. Lindsay laughed at me.

"You gonna be okay?" She asked sarcastically. I grinned back at her. She had been in the hospital for a little over a week with broken bones, torn ligaments, and a head injury. And yet here she was asking me – whose hands were a little cold – if I was going to be okay.

"I think I'll live," I admitted. Linds laughed and reached for a shake, thanking me for bringing it.

"I'm glad," she responded, shaking her drink to break up the lumps of ice cream stuck in her straw. Pausing, she stopped fiddling with her shake to look at me, her grayish blue eyes suddenly serious. "Because otherwise, I'm not really sure what I'd do without you." Tears started to pool in the bottom of her eyes. I looked back at her lovingly and grabbed her hand to give it a good squeeze.

Standing at her bedside, I silently thanked her for being so strong. The past week had been an emotional journey for all of us, but Lindsay had definitely been forced to suffer the most. I was amazed by her strength and proud of her speedy recovery.

"You wouldn't be getting as many strawberry shakes, that's for sure," I said, steering the conversation back to a more lighthearted mood. Lindsay laughed, wiping a single tear from her cheek, and nodded as I grabbed the other shake and took a seat by her bed.

"Between you and my mom, I may gain fifty pounds before I leave this place," she said, chuckling. "My mother has been smothering me with food. Last night, she baked me vegetarian lasagna with seventy-five different cheeses. This morning, she brought me homemade chocolate muffins. She's out of control!" I laughed, thinking of all the times in high school Lindsay's mom had tried to shove food down my throat, convinced that my awkward beanpole frame was the result of teenage starvation. She was a cooking and baking machine, obsessed with making sure everyone within a mile radius of her kitchen was properly overfed. I enjoyed being her guinea pig in those days – she was a great cook.

"Oh, you laugh," Lindsay said, scooting herself laboriously back in the bed to a more comfortable sitting position, "but between the bald spot on my head and the unsightly padding of fat continuing to grow on my ass, it's a wonder Trevor sticks around!" I told her to shut up while helping her scoot. "And don't ask me where my mother found a kitchen," Lindsay added in exasperation. I looked at her thoughtfully. I was curious to know as well. I offered the use of my apartment to Lindsay's parents shortly after her accident, but they insisted on staying in a hotel room within walking distance of the hospital. The hotel wasn't a dump by any stretch, but I was fairly certain that the local inn didn't come fully equipped with kitchens in their standard rooms.

Trevor and Lindsay had plenty of space at their house – and a kitchen – but Lindsay's parents still couldn't face the fact that Trevor and Lindsay had moved in together out of wedlock. Lindsay joked that her parents' denial was a working example of 'out of sight, out of mind.' If they never saw where Lindsay and Trevor lived, the house didn't have to exist.

"Maybe your mom is commuting back to Cincinnati to cook," I suggested, trying to sound serious. Lindsay laughed out loud, closing her eyes and leaning her head back on her pillow.

"The thought of my mother making a three and a half hour roundtrip to use a kitchen – all in an effort to avoid facing the reality that Trevor and I live together – is hysterical," she said, opening her eyes again. "But entirely feasible." The two of us laughed while we suggested different places at which Lindsay's mother may have baked the lasagna. A local food shelter? The hospital cafeteria? The possibilities were endless.

It was great to see Lindsay in good spirits and hard to believe that only a week ago, she was in critical condition with significant head trauma. Nobody could tell us how serious the neurological side effects of her injuries would be before she woke up. I had hoped for the best, but certainly hadn't predicted that she'd bounce back to normalcy so quickly.

"How long do you think they'll stay in town?" I asked curiously.

"Forever," Lindsay replied, groaning. She and her parents were close, but too much exposure to them made Lindsay crazy. Her mother could be slightly overbearing and her father, while sweet, had the personality of a doorknob. The two of them were exhausting to entertain for very long. Notwithstanding their faults, however, I was jealous that Lindsay had such loving parents.

Lindsay winced and held her left hand to her head in pain. I sat up rigidly and asked whether she needed me to grab a nurse, poised to go streaming down the hall for some help. Shaking her head slowly, she put up a finger, motioning for me to wait. After a short pause, she lowered her hand and looked at me sheepishly. "Ice cream headache," she admitted. Leaning back into my chair, I threw up my hands in relief.

"You scared me half to death!" I exclaimed. "Maybe a shake wasn't a good idea after all." I was relieved she wasn't wincing from the usual bout of dizziness or pain with which she often had to contend. In addition to short-term memory loss, Lindsay continued to battle sudden episodes of confusion and vertigo. These episodes, though more infrequent as the days passed, were the main reasons she stayed in the hospital. On some days, Lindsay told me she felt as if she'd be in the hospital for all eternity.

****

Lindsay and I visited for thirty minutes, gulping down our shakes and discussing whatever came to mind. Lindsay had several entertaining stories about awkward visits from people at her firm, not the least of which included a visit from the firm's managing partner. Upon seeing her when he peeked into the room, he left his flowers in the hallway and emailed her later to tell her he'd come by while she was sleeping.

"We made eye contact," she said, between laughs. "But to him, it's less awkward to send me an email that we both know to be untrue than to come in and wish me a speedy recovery face to face." Trying to catch my breath from laughing so hard, I told her that while strange and unusual, his visit was sort of sweet.

"I mean, this guy obviously has issues with social interaction," I observed, "so the fact that he came down here to personally bring you flowers should show you how much he cares." Lindsay looked at me doubtfully, but I could tell she was considering my point. "He could have had his secretary send them," I offered. "But he came down here by himself. The man was probably petrified!" Lindsay shrugged.

"Maybe you're right," she admitted. "It can't be easy to visit someone in the hospital, especially when they look like I do." I touched her gently on the arm, my face drawn up in protest.

"Stop worrying about the way you look," I said. "You were hit by a car and still look better than I do when I haven't had at least seven hours of sleep." She laughed skeptically. We both knew it wasn't entirely true, but I think she appreciated the sentiment all the same. Plus, there was no sense in worrying about the way she looked until she received a clean bill of health from her doctors. There were bigger fish to fry than the bald spot on her head, and she knew it.

"You know," Lindsay said, changing the subject and looking down at her shake, "your mom sent me flowers." I raised my eyebrows in mild surprise. I hadn't spoken to my mother since the day she'd shown up unwelcome at Dad's grave, and I didn't have any plans to speak to her in the future. "Those blue hydrangeas in the corner," Lindsay continued, pointing. I forced a smile and told her they were nice.

"Michael must have told her about your accident," I gathered. It certainly hadn't been from me. "It was nice of her to send flowers." Lindsay nodded and stared at the bouquet of hydrangeas, lost in thought. After a few seconds she turned and looked at me, her face filled with concern.

"Are you ever going to work things out with her, Hale?" She asked. I sighed, annoyed that the conversation had turned to my mother. My nonexistent relationship with my only living parent was the last thing I wanted to talk about.

"No," I said abruptly. "I'm finished trying to work on a relationship with a woman I find to be unbearably selfish and cold." Lindsay turned back to her shake, absorbing my response.

"But she's your mother," she whispered, her voice strained in confusion. I placed my hand on her arm again, assuring her that I had thought about it at length.

"So what?" I asked her, without malice. "She's my mother. She gave birth to me, she helped raise me, and unfortunately for my future children, I have some of her genetic code." Lindsay smiled. "But that doesn't mean I have to like her," I continued. "Sure, it would be ideal if my mother and I had a fairytale mother/daughter relationship filled with laughter, gossip, shopping, and family tradition. But we don't. And for the first time in my life, I'm actually at peace with the realization that we never will."

I sat back in my chair, satisfied with my explanation. I was bound to the woman by blood, but I didn't have to be bound to the woman by friendship or pretend that the two of us could ever have any sort of relationship. I was done feeling guilty for being the 'bad' daughter. The fact that we didn't get along wasn't entirely my fault. And the fact that I felt closer to my friends than I could ever feel to her was okay.

"Are we interrupting?" A happy, familiar voice called from the hallway, interrupting our conversation about my mother. Lindsay smiled widely and waved. I turned to find Alex leaning on the doorway, Patrick peeking over his shoulder, grinning from ear to ear. I welcomed the interjection eagerly, vigorously waving my arms, beckoning them into the room.

"I can't believe you're back already!" Lindsay said happily as Alex and Patrick made their way to the other side of her bed. As they passed, Alex winked at me subtly, holding Patrick's hand. I tried to suppress my excitement with a casual cough, but I feared that if someone didn't tell Lindsay soon, I'd blow the surprise any second. Upon reaching the bed, Patrick leaned over and softly touched Lindsay's cheek before planting a gentle kiss on the same spot.

"You look even better than when we left," he said quietly, still squeezing Alex's hand. Lindsay smiled and thanked him, motioning for him to pull up a seat. While they fetched the chairs on the other side of the room, Lindsay asked about their anniversary trip.

"I'm sorry you had to postpone it a week," she said apologetically. "I hope it didn't cause you too much trouble." Both Patrick and Alex shook their heads sternly and told her she was ridiculous for apologizing.

"The only thing that matters is that you're okay," Alex insisted. "When your accident happened, none of us cared about anything other than you getting better." Lindsay smiled weakly, but I could tell she felt guilty for being the reason they postponed their weekend getaway. She hated to be an inconvenience, no matter what the circumstances.

"Think about it from our perspectives," I told her. "If one of us was seriously hurt, would you care about canceling your upcoming travel plans?" Although she didn't say anything, I'm sure she got my point.

"Haley's right," Patrick interjected. "It wasn't a big deal – in fact, it wasn't a deal at all."

"In fact," Alex added, "it turned out to be the best weekend trip I've ever had."

"That's great!" Lindsay exclaimed, looking mildly relieved. I bit my lip, forcing myself to remain calm and collected. I knew exactly what Alex meant, but poor Lindsay didn't have a clue.

"A life-changing trip, I'd say," Alex continued, beaming. The three of us smiled dementedly at Lindsay like we were high. It didn't take her more than a few seconds to realize that there was more going on than what everyone was saying. Looking at us in confusion, she narrowed her eyes and looked back at Patrick.

"What's going on?" She asked, suspiciously. Alex and Patrick looked at each other sweetly while I watched with anticipation.

"I don't know *what* you're talking about," Alex claimed, placing his left hand on Lindsay's bed to display his shiny engagement ring. Lindsay ignored his hand and looked back at him, still confused and perhaps a little bit frightened.

"What is going on!?" She asked, exasperated. "You shouldn't play tricks on a woman struggling with dizziness and confusion! Out with it!" The three of us laughed. Alex removed his hand from the bed and started shaking it in front his face dramatically.

"Well, Lindsay, we should probably call your doctor, because I just don't know *what* you're talking about," he said. It took her a couple of seconds, but when Linds finally saw the ring, she immediately started squealing. Clapping my hands together in delight, I joined in and started jumping up and down with Alex and Patrick. Together we made such awful, high-pitched noises that a nurse came running into the room as if something were on fire. We all stopped yelling for a moment when she entered, watching as she surveyed the room. When she realized nothing was wrong, she put her hands on her hips and gave us a disapproving look before walking out the door, all the while trying to hide the small smile creeping across her face. We all busted out laughing when she disappeared. Lindsay threw up her hands and looked back and forth between Alex and Patrick in shock.

"Tell me how it happened!" She insisted excitedly. "I'm in total shock – I had no idea this was happening!"

"No one did," Patrick said proudly, his smile so large across his face I feared his cheeks might explode. "I kept it a secret from everyone, except Haley." Lindsay turned to me in surprise.

"You knew!?" She asked, dumbfounded.

"Yes," I admitted proudly. I wasn't the best at keeping secrets, but I had done well with this one. "I knew for a couple of weeks – it was torture not being able to talk about it!" Alex beamed at me as I recounted the day I'd found out about Patrick's plans to propose. When I finished, Patrick chimed in, talking excitedly about the proposal. Holding Lindsay's hand tightly, Patrick covered everything from the weather, the setting, his emotions, the way the birds were chirping when he got to one knee, and the way that our strong-willed, hardnosed Alex had cried when Patrick popped the question. I looked up to find Alex still looking at me, a warm smile on his face as he listened to Patrick's story.

"You've already heard all of this," Alex said to me softly, trying not to interrupt his fiancé. It was true. I had been on the phone with them for almost an hour after they got engaged, hungry for every juicy detail. "Let's go get a coffee or something while Patrick catches Lindsay up." I nodded my head affectionately, but as soon as I moved from Lindsay's bedside, I became nervous to be alone with Alex. I hadn't spoken to him alone for over a week – since the phone call during which I feared he'd deduced my relationship with Keegan. Lindsay's accident had postponed everything for the boutique, including Keegan's previously planned trip to Columbus. Accordingly, the confrontation with Alex I'd been dreading had never come. It was as if Lindsay's accident had made time stand still, and I was nervous for the clock to start running again.

"Sounds great," I agreed hesitantly, winking at Linds before following Alex out of the room. When we were out of earshot and down another hallway, I poked at him playfully, hoping that recent events had washed away any suspicions he'd been harboring about my involvement with Keegan. "So how does it feel to be newly engaged?" I asked, grinning. Alex smiled and shook his head.

"It's amazing," he admitted. "I honestly didn't think marriage was something I wanted until Patrick proposed." I watched him thoughtfully. "It's a strange issue for us," he said after a couple of steps. "We can't get married legally in Ohio, so I always thought, why mess with it? Why make a big deal out of a commitment that isn't recognized by the country and state that we live in? Who were we doing it for when it didn't change anything in our

189

relationship? The idea of it always felt more like a political statement than a marriage – and you know very well that politics aren't my cup of tea." We continued to walk slowly down the hospital's hallways, my anger toward archaic social policies growing with each step. I wasn't exactly a soldier for social change either, but I hated that Alex and Patrick couldn't get married like everyone else.

"But then," Alex said, "Patrick was down on one knee, asking me to commit to him for the rest of my life. In that moment, I knew that marrying Patrick was the most important thing I would ever do for my life and my relationship. I don't care what anybody else thinks about it." I grabbed his arm and squeezed. It was sweet to hear Alex speak of marrying Patrick with such love and excitement. Having never broached the subject of marriage with Alex, I hadn't been sure how he was going to react when Patrick proposed. Now that Alex's thoughts on marriage were clear, I was deliriously happy for him. "After September," he added, "our lives will never be the same."

"September?" I asked, shocked. "That's less than six months away!" Alex laughed.

"Yes, well, Patrick's sure we can do it."

"That seems like a short time to plan a wedding," I said, shaking my head, "but hell, what do I know?"

"Well, we're getting married in Columbus," Alex shared. "Even though it's not technically legal in Ohio, the ceremony will be significant to us, and that's all that matters. Maybe it will make the planning easier to have everything local." I shrugged. I really didn't know anything about planning a wedding.

"Knowing Patrick, he may have already booked some vendors and locations in advance," I suggested. "I wouldn't put it past him." Alex laughed. "I'm only half-joking," I admitted, laughing with him.

"You may be right," Alex said in consideration. "But as long as he's happy with everything and we can get it planned in time, I don't even care." I smiled and put my arm through his while we walked down the hospital hallways, chatting about what color his suit would be and what type of ceremony he hoped to have. Apparently growing tired of talking about his future wedding, Alex abruptly changed the subject to ask me about Nick. I couldn't help but smile at the sound of his name.

"I've seen you two at the hospital together a few times," he observed. "I'm not trying to get my hopes up because I know he said he wasn't ready to date, but I thought maybe there was something blossoming there. I mean, the two of you do hang out a good amount these days." He was right. Nick and I *had* been together a lot. Although nothing had really happened between us, I felt closer to him every day. My relationship with Nick was beginning to make my feelings for Keegan seem distant and unreal. Keegan and I hadn't even really talked that much over the last week or so, and it hadn't even occurred to me until now.

"Oh, I don't know," I responded, my head in the clouds. "He's an incredible friend. Nothing's really happened, though." Alex looked at me suspiciously as if I were hiding something. "Trust me," I said, trying to reassure him. "If anything was happening romantically in my life, you'd know about it." I hadn't intended to lie. When I said it, it seemed like the truth. But I regretted saying it instantly, annoyed that my involvement with Keegan hovered over my friendship with Alex like a dark cloud. Alex, of course, didn't pick up on my pathetic fib. He simply shrugged his bony shoulders and continued walking down the hall quietly, oblivious to the toxic waste seeping effortlessly out of my mouth.

After taking a couple of agonizing steps, I stopped and looked at my loyal, caring friend and employer. I was insufferably pained by my continuing deceit; I couldn't stand it anymore. I'd lied to Alex for weeks now, all at the suggestion of a man whose intentions remained entirely unclear. I'd been brazenly selfish, and for what? A racy hook-up? A chance at a relationship with someone I'd known for a month? If Lindsay's accident had taught me anything, it was that the most important things in life were the people I loved. For too long I'd been putting Keegan's needs – someone I barely knew – ahead of one of my most cherished friend's. If deceiving someone I held in such high regard continued to come so easily, what kind of person did that make me? The lies had to stop now.

"I lied." The two words didn't come out of me easily. My tongue felt swollen and stuck to the roof of my mouth, like my body was doing everything in its power to keep me from telling the truth. I clenched my jaw as Alex stared back at me, justifiably confused. Even now, when the words were out in the open, I couldn't bring myself to explain.

"About what?" Alex pulled his arm from mine and stood in the hallway, narrowing his eyes at me as if trying to uncover my secrets through telepathy. I looked at him apologetically, not sure of what to say. A feeling of dread crept over me as I searched my mind for the right words.

"About New York," I started cryptically, "about my life – about Keegan." I took a deep breath and found the strength to divulge the information I'd been disgracefully hiding from Alex for weeks. "Alex, I've been sleeping with Keegan." Even though the words were my own, they cut through my dropping heart like a knife. A group of nurses came walking by us chatting, oblivious to the bomb that I'd dropped in the middle of the hospital. I wanted to apologize. I wanted to cry. I wanted to tell Alex that I had never meant to betray him and that, if I could, I would take back my deceit a hundred times over. But I couldn't. All I could do was stare back at him in the hospital hallway and watch his eyes burn steadily and unreadable into mine.

18 THE SANCTITY OF MARRIAGE

I was paralyzed in a chair in the hallway, my head in my hands as I leaned forward in my seat. "I'm sorry," I said in a soft whisper, repeating myself for the hundredth time. I was desperate for something to say to Alex that would make everything okay, but all I could manage was 'I'm sorry' over and over again. At least it was true. I *was* sorry. I was sorry for jeopardizing the boutique's future business. I was sorry for lying to his face for well over a month. I was sorry for choosing my own selfish desires over everyone else. I had been acting like a fool, and only in the face of my betrayed employer and friend could I see just how foolish I'd been. I wondered painfully what this all meant for the future of my relationship with Alex. I was scared that in the end, the two of us would never be the same.

Alex hadn't said much. To my surprise, he hadn't yelled at me, scolded me, or even left me in a huff in the middle of the hospital. Instead, he sat down next to me in eerie silence, his hands calmly folded in his lap, presumably waiting for me to regain my composure. When he realized I had little else to say, Alex broke the silence in an unexpectedly calm and patient voice.

"I've known you for a long time," he said, taking a deep breath. "Did you really think I wouldn't realize that something was going on?" I pulled my head out of my hands and turned to him, surprised. "Haley, give me some credit," he scolded. "I knew there was something happening between the two of you, I just didn't know exactly what. I'm not blind." I shook my head in disbelief.

I'd been right to suspect that he knew about Keegan after all.

"If you knew, why didn't you say anything?" I asked. I was shocked that he hadn't confronted me about Keegan before now. It was very unlike Alex. He shrugged and stared at his bony hands.

"I don't know," he admitted. "I guess I wanted to give you a chance to deal with it in your own time." The maturity with which he was approaching the situation smashed my heart into tiny, shameful bits. It somehow made my lies more childish and pathetic. "I mean, what the hell happened, Haley?" Alex asked, his voice remaining calm, but frustrated. "I don't really need to know the details, but why did you feel you had to lie to me? What is it about this guy that made you act this way?" I blushed in shame. I wanted to explain so it would all make sense, but there was nothing to say. No excuse could justify what I'd done or make my lies less blatantly self-serving. I threw up my hands in surrender.

"I don't know what to say other than 'I'm sorry,' Alex." I wished I had more to offer, but I was utterly incapable of appropriately expressing my feelings of regret. Tears streamed down my face in frustration. The more I sat there, the angrier I became at myself for what I'd done.

"He was the guy that night, right? At the hotel?" Alex looked at me hopefully, as if there was a small chance I'd tell him it wasn't. But we both knew the answer.

"Yeah," I admitted. Alex sighed when he heard the answer he'd feared.

"What you did was insanely selfish," he said. I nodded my head in disgust.

"I know," I acknowledged.

"You not only lied to me as your friend, but you gambled with the future of my business."

"I know," I said again. I felt like a wretched human being.

"I should fire you." I looked at him suddenly, catching his eyes for the first time since we sat down. The words hurt, but I knew he was right. I had acted unforgivably. I couldn't keep my job after what I had done. "But I'm not going to," he revealed. I looked at him, confused. I didn't understand.

"Why not?" I asked. I didn't want him to fire me, but I knew that I didn't deserve to be let off the hook. I squinted my eyes at him. "I lied to your face. I slept with a potential business partner. No employee could possibly do any worse." Alex winced. Hearing it out loud put what I'd done in rather harsh perspective. I put my head in my hands again and rocked back and forth. I felt like an idiot – a classic moron. I couldn't believe how many times I'd dismissed Lindsay's advice. If I had only had the maturity to listen . . .

"Do you have serious feelings for him, Hale?" Alex inquired. "Are you dating him?" I shook my head.

"I don't know," I admitted, feeling painfully foolish. I'd lied to one of my best friends for a man who lived hundreds of miles away and had given me no true indication that he wanted a real relationship. The tears welled up in my eyes and the air escaped my lungs as my body prepared for a complete meltdown. After a few seconds, I started to sob. Weeks of pent up guilt, anxiety, and stress flowed out of me like a waterfall. Alex grabbed my arm and pulled me toward him in a bony embrace. Putting up little resistance, I let him wrap his arms around me as all of the emotions I'd been suppressing rapidly escaped me.

"You screwed up bad," Alex said, when I eventually calmed down. He looked at me firmly, but kept his eyes soft and caring. "When I first suspected something was going on, I did want to fire you. I wanted to scream at you, tell you I would never forgive you, and punish you cruelly for what you had done." He wiped the wetness off my face with his jacket sleeve and continued. "But Patrick made me realize that everyone makes mistakes." I scoffed at him, but he ignored me. "You've been my best friend for so many years . . . I'm not willing to just throw that away."

I stared at my feet, terrified that I'd tarnished our friendship forever. Alex was speaking patiently, expressing more understanding than I would have ever expected, but there was no telling how deep my deceit had cut him under his even-keeled exterior. I didn't think either of us knew whether he would trust me again, or whether we could ever be as close as we were before this all happened. It was heartbreaking, but I tried to find solace in the fact that he was giving me a chance to repair what I'd broken.

"Everything happened so fast and spiraled so quickly out of control . . ." I said finally, barely able to focus through my swollen eyes. I rubbed my throbbing temples, more frustrated with myself than I'd ever been. "I don't even know if Keegan wants to be with me – the whole thing seems so ridiculous now." Alex reached out his hand as if to pat my back in comfort, but decided against it. I couldn't blame him.

"Yes, well we can talk more about the status of your relationship later," Alex suggested, a hint of disdain in his voice. "But I think we've both had our fill of this mess for now." Alex stood up and encouraged me to do the same. "The best thing we can do at the moment," he said, "is get you cleaned up and back to Lindsay's room. She's the one who's really going through some shit."

I grabbed Alex's hand and stood up, placing my other hand on his shoulder to steady myself. My sobbing outburst had left me lightheaded and woozy. It took a few seconds for me to get my bearings. "At least we're in a hospital," Alex said as we started making our way to the bathroom. "No one will be fazed by how awful you look." Nodding weakly in agreement, I ignored his harshness. Having been patient with me up to this point, I figured he was more than entitled to an unwelcomed jab. It was the least I deserved.

Leaving Alex at the entrance of the women's bathroom, I walked toward the sinks along the wall. Finding myself alone, I let out a long sigh, hung my head over a sink in the corner, and closed my eyes. The bathroom walls muffled the noisy hospital hallways, giving me a temporary place of peace in which to think. Not even the unpleasant aroma of bleach and toilet water bothered me as I rolled my head back and forth across my chest, trying to work out the tension that had caused monstrous, uncomfortable knots at the base of my neck.

Raising my head and opening my eyes, I took the first brave look at myself in the grainy mirror hanging on the wall in front of me. Alex was right. I looked awful. My eyes were swollen, puffy, and red – cruelly disguising their usually prominent green hue – and my cheeks were covered in red splotches, overpowering whatever makeup I had put on before leaving the house. My appearance sickened me. Who was this sad, selfish woman, staring back at me, feeling piteous for reaping consequences she herself had sown? I splashed cold water on my face repeatedly, but the red splotches remained, stubborn and unwavering. The splotches were like my red scarlet letter, identifying my sins for all to see.

Leaning over the sink to grab a paper towel, I felt a light buzzing in the pocket of my jeans. I thought I had left my phone in Lindsay's room with the rest of my belongings, but apparently, I'd taken it with me. Wiping my hands dry, I pulled my phone out to see who was calling. In true ironic fashion, Keegan's name flashed across the screen in big capital letters. Completely unprepared to speak with him, I shoved my phone back in my pocket with force. I know I couldn't blame him for my mistakes, but thinking of him now made me angry. Alex's question echoed in my head. What was it about this guy that had caused me to act this way? Was love leading me to make these stupid decisions or was it something more toxic? I wasn't quite sure.

Pushing Keegan out of my mind, I exited the bathroom to rejoin Alex. Leaning against a wall with his arms crossed in boredom, Alex opened his eyes widely when he saw me and lifted up his jacket sleeve to look at an imaginary watch on his bare left wrist. "All that time, and you still don't look any better!" He exclaimed. I shrugged and walked back with him to Lindsay's room, glad to hear him joking like nothing was wrong. The two of us had a long road ahead, but his sarcasm, no matter how mean, was an encouraging sign that we may be okay when all was said and done.

When we returned to the room, Patrick was still sitting next to Lindsay on the bed, chatting charismatically. Lindsay looked at us in exaggerated shock when we walked in, wondering where we'd been. "I was beginning to worry that the two of you had fallen into the hospital's infamous black hole!" She exclaimed. Alex laughed from behind me.

"That might have been more enjoyable," I muttered, frowning. Lindsay's tone quickly turned more serious when she saw me. My swollen face was hard to miss.

"What happened, Hale? Are you okay?" She asked in concern. Patrick shifted his seat on the bed and sat up, looking worried. I shuffled my feet uncomfortably until Alex spoke up to explain.

"Everything's out, now," he said, matter-of-factly. "She told me about Keegan." The room grew silent. Lindsay and Patrick glanced at each other nervously. I looked at them in confusion, wondering what silent message was being passed between them.

"Wait a minute," I started. "Have you all talked about this together?" When no one said anything, I pointed my finger at Lindsay accusatorily. "You *told* them!?" I suddenly felt very foolish.

"We asked her a couple of weeks back if she knew anything about Keegan," Patrick offered, before Lindsay could respond. "We told her that we knew something weird was going on. We wanted to know what you weren't telling us." Lindsay didn't say anything. She didn't even look at me. I couldn't believe what I was hearing. I'd told her about Keegan in confidence, and she'd used that information to talk about me behind my back. I wondered how much she'd shared of what I had told her.

"Well that's great," I said angrily, feeling betrayed. "You knew how much my guilt was eating at me, but you said nothing?" Lindsay still wouldn't look at me. I felt sick to my stomach imagining the three of them sitting around and watching me, taking bets on when I'd offer Alex the truth. "Why didn't you just tell me Alex knew so we could all move on with our lives!?" I asked Lindsay desperately. "Did the three of you want to teach me a lesson? Let me suffer while you watched me from your front row seats?"

I marched over to grab my purse and coat and turned for the door. Tears started to well up in my eyes again, my tear ducts having miraculously replenished from my earlier bout of sobbing. "I'm not a goddamn social experiment," I said as I left, holding in the tears for as long as I could. "You should have told me." The three of them remained silent as I turned down the hallway. Nobody followed. I walked hurriedly toward the parking garage, furious that the three of them had watched me agonize over my mistakes for weeks. Although I'd been the one to screw up, I was the one left feeling hurt, embarrassed, and betrayed.

When I made it to my car I sat paralyzed in the driver's seat for a moment, calming myself in preparation for driving. I had experienced so much emotion in the past few weeks – and especially the past hour – that I didn't know how much more I could take. Turning the key in the ignition and glancing into the rearview mirror before I reversed, I paused when I got a look at my swollen face for the second time. Seeing the hurt and pain in my eyes made me want to share what I was feeling with someone who could understand. Throwing the car back into park, I pulled out my phone to dial Keegan.

"Hi, Haley," he said casually, after three long rings. I was relieved to hear his voice. I was tired of carrying the burden of our mistake alone.

"Hi," I said, trying to mask my pain. Apparently, I hadn't done a good enough job.

"Is . . . this a bad time?" He asked hesitantly. "You don't really sound like yourself." He was certainly perceptive. All I'd done was said 'hi.'

"It *is* a bad time," I admitted, "but that's what I want to talk to you about."

"What do you mean?" His question was reluctant, like he wasn't sure he wanted to know the answer. I could feel myself starting to become upset again, so I took a deep breath. Keegan sat in silence on the other end of the phone for a few seconds, waiting for me to explain. "Keegan, Alex knows. Alex knows about us." I heard Keegan's breath escape him on the other end of the line.

"He does?" He was clearly not thrilled by the news. It hurt my feelings to hear him so disappointed, but I'd expected as much.

"Yes," I confirmed. "And my conversation with him was completely awful. I can't believe I lied to him about it all this time. We should have told him right from the start." I waited for Keegan to agree, but when he didn't say anything, I continued. "Shockingly enough, he's not firing me, but he should. I can't believe we decided to hide it, Keegan. That was so stupid."

"How did he find out?" I was taken aback by his response. I was hoping he'd be a little more concerned for my feelings.

"Well, I told him . . . but Keegan, that's not really why I called. I need your support right now. I feel so alone in this mess."

"You told him!?" His voice was hushed, but I could tell he was having trouble masking his anger. "Why did you do that?!" His accusatory tone and conspicuous lack of empathy began to irritate me. I couldn't understand why he was being this callous and unsupportive.

"Because my friends mean everything to me, and I should have never lied about us in the first place!" I replied loudly. I could feel hot tears gathering at the bottom of my eyes.

"I understand, Haley," he insisted, his voice temperate and delicate, "but I need to know: do you think he's planning on telling anyone? Like, Naresh, for example?" I huffed in disgust. It was apparent that Keegan was only concerned about himself.

"I don't know, I didn't think to ask him." My voice was flat and angry.

"In fact, when he was confronting me about hiding it from him, the furthest thing from my mind was whether he'd help me hide it from other people! I was a little busy concentrating on not losing my best friend." I heard Keegan sigh into the phone. His tone was soft, but frustrated, as if he were dealing with an unreasonable child.

"Haley, calm down. I don't mean to be insensitive." I didn't believe him. "I just don't want this getting out," he stressed. "I know I've tried to explain it before, but it could really hurt my reputation. Please, try to understand." His words were like a punch in the gut. I understood that sleeping with someone with whom you were involved in business wasn't ideal, but I didn't understand how his involvement with me would hurt his reputation.

"No," I said, becoming angrier. "No, I don't understand. What about me would sully your reputation, huh? What about me could possibly be so embarrassing, that it would hurt your business in New York City!?" My hands shook, causing the phone to almost vibrate against my ear.

"Haley . . ."

"No!" My anger turned to pure, unadulterated rage. "What happened between us has obviously meant nothing to you!" I screamed. "I've been running around like a fool lying to my best friend and jeopardizing my job because I thought there was something between us. What a load of bullshit. I might not be your ideal woman, but don't insult me by suggesting that your involvement with me would somehow hurt your reputation." The tears began to run down my face in fury and pain. I sat on the phone for a moment, convinced he'd hung up. But then I heard his voice reach out to me, slow and defeated.

"Haley, it's hard to explain." I sat there, wondering how I could have so terribly misinterpreted what I thought had been a connection between us. "Haley," he said again, more softly. "Haley, I'm married." His statement echoed in my ears like a gong. I couldn't fully comprehend what he was telling me. It was all too much. "Haley, please. You must understand. I can't let what's happened between us get out. Please . . ." I sat there for a moment, looking back at my reflection in the rear view mirror. I blinked twice to clear my vision from the rush of tears springing from my eyes, concentrating on my gaze. My green irises flashed back at me for a second, reminding me of Dad.

"I'm sorry I ever let you kiss me, you son of a bitch." I said quietly, and hung up the phone.

19 MY ROCK

Flowers bloomed in vibrant colors across the pond. The trees rustled their newly grown leaves proudly, as if rejoicing in the new season. It was a beautiful spring day, and I was thankful to at least have the weather on my side.

Picking up my sketchbook on the bench beside me, I breathed deeply and opened it, willing my creative juices to start magically flowing. After flipping the pages for a few minutes and staring at the blank ones in the back, I slammed the book in frustration and leaned back on the hard bench. Normally, I could sit in the park and sketch for hours, blocking out anything else going on in my life. It was my go-to stress reliever – my way of keeping my thoughts off of the outside world. Today, however, I couldn't seem to stop replaying yesterday over and over in my mind. It was as if I expected something to change the more I relived it. Perhaps I would learn that I hadn't lied to Alex about Keegan. Perhaps I would discover that I hadn't told Alex about my deceit. Perhaps I could rewind the clock so that Keegan would never tell me he was married.

Crossing my legs and arms, I searched for a suitable distraction. An elderly couple walked by hand in hand, taking small, measured steps around the pond. They had serene smiles on their faces as if thinking fondly of the same private memory. I stared at them as they shuffled past, wondering how long they'd been together. After a few seconds, I found myself envying the life I imagined they'd had. I longed for a husband to grow old with. I longed for a family. When I was little, I dreamed of where I'd be in my late twenties. In none of my dreams, was I sitting alone on a bench, wondering how everything had gone so wrong.

I shook my head to prevent my piteous thoughts from getting the better of me. Convinced that my sketchbook would be of no help today, I grabbed my phone and called the only person I knew who could make me feel better and who thankfully, wasn't involved in any of the latest drama.

"Hi there!" Nick's friendly voice lifted my spirits immediately.

"Hi," I said, relieved that he'd picked up the phone. "I'm sorry for calling you while you're working. I'm having a royally bad day and needed to talk to someone." I could hear Nick's car in the background. It sounded like I caught him on the road.

"You can call me at any time, you know that," he said genuinely. "Sorry to hear about your day, though – what's going on?" I sighed and rested my elbows on my crossed legs.

"Everything," I muttered vaguely.

"Sounds serious," Nick said. I couldn't help but smile at the way he said it. He had a way of making light of a dark situation without cheapening or under appreciating the way I was feeling. "Sounds like you need a friend, some greasy food, and a pack of light beer," he suggested. "Gluttony and companionship always turn the tables for me." I laughed.

"I think you're right," I agreed.

"How about I come over tonight after work and hang out? I'll bring the beer and the greasy food – all you have to do is sit on the couch and pick something for us to watch." I smiled as I sat on the bench, peering up at the sunny sky. Hanging out with Nick sounded like a great idea. He would be a welcome distraction from my agonizing thoughts and memories of Keegan. I couldn't wait to see him.

"That sounds great," I said, trying not to let the pain of what happened yesterday touch my voice. "You're amazing. I'll see you in a couple of hours."

"Bye, Haley."

I hung up the call and leaned my head against the bench. I was looking forward to seeing Nick. Although I'd only known him for a handful of weeks, he had been by my side, comforting me, through some relatively heavy stuff: The anniversary of Dad's death, Lindsay's accident – he'd been there through it all. And now he was coming to my rescue to soothe my heartbreak after the devastating news of Keegan's marital status, albeit unknowingly. He was a rock. *My* rock, it seemed.

I was especially thankful for Nick this morning, considering the way I exploded on Alex, Patrick, and Lindsay yesterday at the hospital. After the way I'd acted, I had no right to call any of them and ask for their support. I grimaced, imagining what I must have looked like yelling at them and storming angrily out of the hospital. While I was hurt that they'd talked about me behind my back, I was guilty of so much deceit on my end, that I didn't really have a right to be upset. Moreover, they had more important things to worry about than my hurt feelings. Alex was dealing with the fact that I'd slept with his new business partner and lied about it for over a month, while Lindsay was stuck in a hospital still recovering from a life-threatening accident. My outburst yesterday must have appeared childish and selfish in light of everything else going on. I felt ill at the thought.

Sauntering slowly down the sidewalk in the weak breeze, I began to feel lucky that Alex, Patrick and Lindsay continued to stick by me, notwithstanding my recent selfishness. Like Nick, all of them supported me through Dad's anniversary and Lindsay's accident, eager to lend a helping hand or comforting word. As I reflected on our friendships, it dawned on me that I'd done little, if anything, to be there for my friends like they'd been there for me. Uncomfortable at the thought, I pulled out my phone to text Alex, determined to make things right in the morning.

We need to talk. I'm sorry for storming out on you yesterday – can I stop by first thing tomorrow? Alex responded in a couple of seconds.

Yes. I gulped at the terseness of his text, wondering whether he would supplement his response to assure me he wasn't too upset. When no assurance was forthcoming, I sighed, realizing that rightfully so, Alex was probably pretty pissed.

Okay, I responded. *Be by around ten.* When Alex didn't reply, I sent a similar text to Lindsay, apologizing for my outburst and telling her I'd stop by tomorrow after lunch. Unlike Alex, Lindsay sent me a sweet reply, encouraging me not to worry about what had happened yesterday at the hospital.

It's okay, Hale. Don't worry about it. I understand why you got upset. I'll see you tomorrow, babe. I smiled, undeserving of her kindness.

You're too good to me Linds, I admitted. *See you tomorrow.* I placed my phone back in my pocket, trekking slowly along the sidewalks the rest of the way home.

****

Lost in reflection and reality television, it wasn't until Nick texted me on his way to my apartment that I realized I hadn't moved for hours. Moving my legs from underneath the raggedy cream throw with which I'd covered myself, I sat up from my cushiony red couch and responded that I was excited to see him. *Do you remember which apt is mine?* I asked over text. Nick had only been to my apartment once and I wanted to make sure he remembered where I lived. He responded quickly that he did.

Of course I remember! He exclaimed. *I was there a week ago!* I chuckled. He acted as though it was silly for me to think he could have forgotten. He apparently wasn't aware that I had a terrible sense of direction.

Your memory is obviously much better than mine, I told him. *See you soon!* Once my text had been sent, I threw the cream throw on the opposite end of the couch and headed to the bathroom. Checking my appearance in the mirror while washing my hands, I frowned in disappointment. I didn't look very nice. My eyeliner had smudged and my foundation had faded, revealing the unsightly combination skin of my round face underneath. Not wanting to spend time throwing on a thick layer of makeup, I shrugged my shoulders in defeat. The way I looked would just have to do.

Shuffling back past the kitchen and onto my couch, I told myself that at least I looked better than the last time Nick had been here. After Lindsay's accident, it had taken a lot of insisting from a lot of people to get me to leave the hospital and come back home to get some rest. Being the incredible person that he is, Nick demanded that I let him come over and keep me company until I fell asleep. I'd begged him not to worry about me, but he wouldn't take 'no' for an answer.

For hours into the night, he planted himself next to me on my couch, occasionally rubbing my back in comfort and telling me that everything would be okay. I woke up the next morning to find him sleeping in my living room chair, his hands folded peacefully across his chest. I remembered thinking how lucky I was to have him in my life. He always made me feel as if everything really would be okay. And here he was again, racing to my side for comfort.

Taking off my boots and pulling the throw back over my legs, I started to worry that Nick may be growing weary of coming to my rescue. In the month that I'd known him, I'd been an emotional, whiny mess. Other than a couple of lighthearted lunches and our walk to raise money for cancer, our friendship had centered entirely on *my* problems. I sighed, realizing that my relationship with Nick served as yet another example of the selfish way I'd been treating all of my friendships. It was about time to turn the tables and start concentrating on the needs of my friends instead of my own. Nick's visit was the perfect time to begin.

I sprung off the couch in excitement when I heard Nick knock on the door, determined to prove to him that I could be more than a self-pitying, wet blanket. Rushing to greet him, I flung the door open with a giant smile and hugged him tight. Bracing himself, he laughed at my enthusiasm, nearly dropping the beer and food he was carrying. "Sorry!" I exclaimed, apologetically. "Come in!"

"It's quite alright," he said, slipping off his loafers and walking into the apartment. He headed to the kitchen and placed the food and beer on the counter. "I don't mind being greeted like that – I just wasn't ready for it." I followed him into the kitchen, peeking over his shoulder as he dug into the brown paper bag he was carrying. He had changed out of his work clothes and into some casual jeans and a hooded sweatshirt with a team crest on it I didn't recognize. Not wanting to reveal my embarrassingly limited knowledge of sports, I decided not to ask him about it.

"What did you bring?" I inquired, suddenly aware of how hungry I was. Peering back at me as he unloaded the bag, he held up a container of fried rice.

"Chinese," he answered, grinning. We'd had Chinese food together on a couple of occasions, and he knew I was a sucker for sesame chicken and fried rice. Rubbing my hands together in anticipation, I watched as he unpacked the food and reached into the case of light beer to pass me a drink. Realizing I'd done nothing to help, I turned and opened my kitchen cabinets to grab a couple of plates.

"Thanks!" I said, and took the beer he was handing me. I passed him the plates in exchange. Opening the can and leaning against the counter, I thanked him for coming over and bringing the meal.

"You're very welcome," he said, handing me a plate of food. "Chinese food and bad television on your red couch is pretty much my ideal Monday night."

"Of course it is," I said sarcastically, easily seeing through his attempt to be modest about his intentions. I had no doubt he had better things to do on a Monday night than spend them wallowing in bad food and television with me. Walking to the couch, I sat my plate down on the coffee table, eager to start eating.

"Go ahead and eat," Nick called from the kitchen. "I'll be over in a second." Grateful for his permission to dive in, I began shoveling the deliciousness into my mouth ravenously. Watching him as he joined me in the living room, I almost choked on my food when I saw his reaction to the way I was eating. Swallowing quickly, I burst out laughing as Nick sat down in the chair, staring at me like a zoo animal. "You know, I'm not trying to race you," he said, jokingly. "And you can have all of the leftovers."

"I'm hungry!" I said defensively.

"Hey, I'm not judging," he claimed, holding his hands up innocently. "I've just never seen someone shovel such large amounts of food in their mouth so rapidly." I leaned over and smacked him playfully on the arm before purposefully shoveling another enormous bite in my mouth. Nick shook his head and begged me not to choke. "I'm serious," he said, pointing his fork in my direction. "I don't want to have to say 'I told you so' while giving you the Heimlich." Struggling to swallow, I leaned back and pointed at his fork. Nick pulled it away quickly, giving me a defensive look. His hazel eyes tried to remain defiant, but they flickered at me playfully. "I don't care what you think," he said. "It's more practical and efficient to use a fork. Using chopsticks makes no sense." I giggled, still chewing. Each time we ate Chinese, I made fun of Nick for not using chopsticks. He claimed that he liked to use forks better, but I knew the real reason he used a fork was because he couldn't use chopsticks to save his life.

"I'm going to have to see it sometime," I insisted, swallowing the last bit of food in my mouth. "This is a mystery that can be easily solved." Nick looked at me, raising his eyebrows.

"It could be," he said. "But I don't think I'm going to give you the satisfaction of knowing whether or not I can use them." I gave him a dirty look and continued to eat my food. We laughed and poked fun at each other as we ate, enjoying each other's company until we'd finished the last grain of rice on our plates. When we'd both finished, I grabbed Nick's empty dish to take it back into the kitchen. He unzipped his jacket as I placed the plates in the sink, revealing a casual gray soccer t-shirt underneath.

"Man, it is *hot* in here!" He exclaimed as I returned to the couch. "You really do hate being cold, huh?" I looked at him sheepishly. I still had my heat set to seventy-five degrees. I realized that for most people, it could be a little toasty.

"I can turn it down," I offered, not wanting to smoke him out. Nick shook his head, and said it was okay.

"I'm comfortable," he insisted. Throwing his jacket across the back of the chair, I pointed at his t-shirt.

"What's MSD?" I asked, referring to the monogram on the front.

"Oh, my soccer club when I was in high school," he said. "It's been my favorite t-shirt for well over a decade."

"I can tell," I said, looking at the holes starting to form in the seam of his collar. "I didn't know you played soccer." Nick shrugged.

"Yeah, I played in college, too," he shared. I was immediately impressed.

"Wow!" I exclaimed. "That's incredible! Why is this the first time I'm hearing about it?" Nick looked down at his hands and told me it wasn't a big deal.

"I played at a Division III college, it's not that impressive."

"You're being ridiculous," I told him. "It's very impressive. You should be proud!" He looked at me, seemingly appreciative of my support. "So does that crest on your jacket represent your college team?" I asked, curious again. Nick shook his head.

"Oh, no," he said. "It's an English professional soccer team. One of the best in the world." I nodded, slightly embarrassed I hadn't known. Nick sensed how I felt immediately. "English soccer is big worldwide, but not necessarily in America," he told me. "It isn't something a lot of people would know." I guessed that wasn't entirely accurate, but I appreciated his attempt to make me feel less ignorant nonetheless. Changing the subject, he turned to me and suggested we pick a movie. "What do you feel like watching?" I told him I didn't care.

"You really don't have to stay," I said, offering him an escape. "I feel silly about complaining about my day earlier. I feel like you're always here, making sure I don't jump off of a bridge or something." Nick laughed. "I'm serious," I said, smiling at him affectionately. "Don't feel obligated to stay and watch a movie thinking that I'm some lonely, emotional loser that needs some company." Nick stopped laughing and leaned over, looking at me seriously.

"I definitely don't think you're a loser," he said. "I *want* to stay." Meeting his gaze, I noticed that the mixtures of greens, yellows, and browns in his hazel eyes were especially fiery tonight. His eyes were usually soft and kind, but tonight, there was an undertone of fiery passion in them that caught me off-guard. I immediately felt my heart beat faster. "Unless you want me to leave," he added. Looking down at my hands, I shook my head.

"No, I don't want you to leave," I admitted softly. Nick held his gaze for a few more seconds. I could feel his eyes on me as I avoided his stare. Suddenly feeling hot myself, I stood up from the couch to browse through my DVDs. Gulping, I cleared my throat and asked him what he wanted to watch. "Is there anything you're itching to see?" I asked. I turned to look at him as he leaned back in the chair and smiled.

"Up to you," he said, getting comfortable. Scanning the movie titles, I picked one of my favorite comedies and held it up for him to see. My heart was pounding and wouldn't calm down. "Perfect," he said. I popped the movie into the DVD player and grabbed the remote on my way back to the couch. Neither Nick nor I said a word as we waited for the movie to start. In that instant, I felt an undeniable electric charge surging between us. I wondered whether Nick felt it, too.

****

"I wish I could stay for a double feature." Nick groaned as the credits began to roll on the screen. He stretched and stood up from the chair. I nodded my head. I still felt some unspoken tension between us, but certainly not as much as I'd felt before we'd started the movie. I wondered whether I'd imagined it.

"Well, thanks for coming over," I said, turning off the television. I was disappointed he had to leave. "I had a great night."

"You're welcome," he responded, leaning his head forward and scratching his neck. "Now, before I leave, do you want to talk about anything or are you good?" I sat up on the couch and pursed my lips in a side smile.

"I'm good," I said confidently. And for the first time in a while, it was true.

"Okay," Nick said, grabbing his jacket. I watched him affectionately, wondering whether I'd ever feel that electric charge between us again. I hoped so.

My phone buzzed on the coffee table with a text. Nick walked into the kitchen while I checked it.

I'm coming back into town to meet with Alex on Wednesday. I would like to see you. I think we should talk about this, Haley. Please.

Keegan's message caught me off-guard. I stared at it for a moment, reading the text again. My chest constricted as I remembered the way I had felt a few weeks ago with Keegan in that downtown hotel. Our brief affair felt distant and unreal, as if it had happened in a previous lifetime. I angered at the memory. What kind of married man would spend thirty-six intimate hours making love to another woman? And what kind of woman would fall for such a man? I shuddered, not daring to venture a guess.

"Is everything okay?" Nick was standing at the sink looking back at me with concern. I panicked a little, upset that he'd picked up on my sudden mood change.

"Everything's fine," I assured him, but the shakiness in my voice gave me away. Nick narrowed his eyes suspiciously.

"I don't believe you," he said. "I can tell something happened. What is it?" I frowned, irritated by his prying. I felt comfortable confiding in him for most things, but not this.

"It's not worth going into," I said, trying to brush it off. I set my phone back onto the coffee table, hoping he would leave it alone.

"Seriously, what's going on? I'm here; talk to me." I shook my head. I did not want to talk about Keegan anymore, especially not with Nick. Why wasn't he letting it go? "Haley," he said, almost scolding me. "You can tell me. Please, that's why I'm here." I shot him an angry look. I thought he was here to hang out, not serve as my therapist.

"I was seeing someone and it didn't work out. The end." I stated it bluntly, my voice flat. I hoped my succinct explanation would end the inquiry. Nick took a step back from the counter, looking unpleasantly surprised.

"I didn't know you were dating someone," he said. I could sense the hurt in his voice. He had no right to be upset. I wanted to remind him that he'd been the one to suggest we stay friends, not me. I'd always hoped for something more.

"We weren't really dating," I insisted, feeling as though I needed to explain myself. I sighed in frustration. I couldn't believe we were talking about this. "It was someone I met through work. He lives in New York, we saw each other a couple of times, but we were never dating and certainly never exclusive. He wasn't worth mentioning, and to be honest, he still isn't." Nick walked around the kitchen counters and into the living room to sit back down in the chair.

"Well, you're obviously upset about it, even if he wasn't worth mentioning." His voice was warm and soothing, but his eyes looked pained and curious. I sat back down on the couch in defeat, angry that Keegan was once again affecting the other relationships in my life.

"It's hard to explain," I insisted. How could I get out of this without sharing more details?

"Did you love him?" I sat up rigidly, reeling from his question. He'd taken the conversation to a whole new level.

"Uh, no . . . that's not why I'm upset," I looked at him defensively, shocked that he'd asked me something so insanely personal. "Nick, can we please drop it?" He shook his head adamantly.

"Haley, talk to me." I shook my head equally adamantly.

"Not about this."

"I'm not leaving until I know you're okay." I stared back into Nick's eyes.

They were plagued with curiosity and concern. I took a deep, frustrated breath and broke his gaze, intertwining my fingers in my lap. Fine. He asked for it.

"He told me he's married." The words shot out of me quickly but quietly. Nick sat there, his eyes wide and unblinking. He looked like he'd been stunned. His reaction made me angry. I hadn't wanted to talk about it with him, and this was exactly why. "I told you I didn't want to talk about it," I snapped. "It's embarrassing. I feel like a fool."

"And you had no idea?" I shot him a furious look.

"Of course not," I responded, defensively. I'd made many mistakes over the past few weeks, but I would never have knowingly slept with a married man. I couldn't believe he would ask me that. "Look, maybe you should go."

"Haley, I'm sorry," he said, easing up a bit. "Don't be upset with me. It's just a lot to process." Nick leaned forward. I watched him run his hands through his brown hair, wrapping his mind around what I'd told him.

"Right. You can understand why I'm upset, then," I said, taking a deep breath. I was angry with him for not letting it go. Our night was now ruined.

"I can," Nick agreed. His playful flirting from earlier had retreated behind a steady frown. My heart sunk to my feet. "Do you want to talk about it?" He asked. "I mean, that's heavy stuff." I shook my head.

"No," I stated firmly. "I told you I didn't want to talk about it in the first place." My voice was hard and mean. Nick looked at me sadly.

"I'm sorry, Haley," he whispered. "I was only trying to help." I watched him stand and head to the front door. My heart melted a little. I shouldn't have been so angry. It wasn't his fault that he had tried to be supportive. He couldn't have known what was wrong. Standing up, I followed Nick through the hall.

"I know you were trying to help," I told him more softly. "Thank you. I'm sorry I dragged you down with all of this. I envisioned our night together going much differently." Nick looked at me and gave me a weak smile. I'm sure he'd had different expectations for tonight as well.

"Don't worry about it," he said kindly. "I'm just sorry that you didn't feel comfortable enough telling me all this before now." I followed him to the door, thanking him for coming over and apologizing again for the way our night had ended. Nick put on his shoes and stood in the doorway.

"It was my pleasure," he said softly. He leaned forward to give me a light kiss on the forehead. It felt nice. I wished desperately we hadn't talked about Keegan. "But don't apologize. I want you to feel like you can tell me anything."

"I do feel that way," I admitted, looking into his eyes. "But honestly, this wasn't something I wanted to talk to *you* about, of all people." I prayed he would understand. I had feelings for him. The last thing I wanted to talk to him about was another man. Nick looked at me impassively, giving nothing away.

We said our goodbyes and I closed the door behind him, defeated. I was convinced that any feelings Nick may have had for me at the beginning of the night had quickly evaporated in the blackened, smoldering devastation that Keegan left in his wake. Somehow, Keegan had successfully tainted every loving relationship I had. Feeling even more frustrated than this morning, I turned down the hall to warm up the leftovers, prepared to eat my feelings. Dishing out what remained of the Chinese food, I stopped when I heard a small knock on the door. Curious, I walked back down the hall and opened it to find Nick standing there, looking at the ground.

"Haley," he said, hesitantly. "This guy is an idiot . . . you are incredible." I stood motionless, taken aback by the gesture. Nick raised his head to look at me. The passion in his eyes had returned, even more furious than before. It took my breath away. "You are amazing," he stated. My throat locked up, preventing me from gulping. "You are beautiful, smart, funny, and unassuming. I know we're friends, and I'm not trying to make things weird between us. But this guy – he's a loser." He shuffled his feet before continuing. I was too stunned to say anything back. "Haley, you are the first woman I've met since Katie . . ." he paused midsentence. My heart began to race. Sighing he looked back up at me and smiled. "Meeting you has made me confident that I can be happy again. You've made me realize that I haven't missed my chance for love, and you can't possibly know what that means to me."

He took a step back and placed his hands in the pockets of his jacket. I still couldn't bring myself to speak. "Don't let this guy bring you down, Haley. I'm positive you will meet someone someday who will appreciate you for all that you are and treat you in the way that you deserve." Turning away from the apartment, I watched in silence as Nick made his way to the sidewalk and across the street to his car. He turned before getting in and shouted back at me. "Have a good night, Haley. And like always, call me if you need me. I'll always be here for you."

20 BEST WOMAN

I stood nervously at the door of Alex's apartment. It would take more than an eloquent apology to repair the damage I'd done to our friendship, but I had to say something that would at least get us started down the road to recovery. Closing my eyes, I leaned my head forward and took a deep breath, trying to release some of the tension building at the base of my neck. I had so much to atone for and so much to prove. Thinking about the long road ahead was overwhelmingly daunting. Opening my eyes, I raised my fist to the door and knocked. It didn't take long for Patrick to open it.

"Hey, Hale," he said, smiling warmly, not the least bit surprised to see me. I reciprocated his greeting and followed him into the apartment silently, my nerves growing with each timid step. Alex had been forgiving and understanding at the hospital – something for which I was very grateful. But given my overreaction in Lindsay's room later that day, I was sure I'd exceeded the limits of his patience.

My nerves increasing rapidly, I sat down on the couch in the living room as Patrick called up the stairs to announce my arrival. Crossing my legs and placing my clammy hands in my lap, I bounced my leg up and down in a nervous twitch. Feeling uncomfortable and awkward in Alex's apartment was strange, and only increased my anxiety. This was usually a place I felt comfortable and safe. I had sprawled across the couch a hundred times before, always feeling loved, comforted, and supported. Today, however, I felt like I was visiting an apartment in which I'd never been. After years of building love and trust in my friendship with Alex, I had wounded it severely in just a few short weeks. I could only hope now that those wounds, someday in the future, could be healed.

Patrick walked into the living room and sat down next to me on the couch. Leaning against the armrest opposite from where I was sitting, he studied me in silence. Patrick always had comforting, loving things to say, even in the darkest of times. When I began to worry that not even he could extend a kind word, he smiled and asked how I was doing.

"We were worried about you after you left the hospital," he added before I had a chance to respond. "I told Alex I didn't think you should be alone." I opened my mouth to assure him I was okay, but Alex's stern voice traveled loudly from the bottom of the stairs to cut me off.

"I told him you were a big girl and could take care of yourself," Alex declared. "You made your own bed; I thought it would be best to let you lie in it for a while." I turned red in shame and lowered my head, disconcerted by Alex's confrontational attitude. Patrick shot him a heated glance in disapproval, but I shook my head.

"He's right," I acknowledged. Patrick softened his glare and turned toward me on the couch. I uncrossed my legs and stood to address Alex, who was standing at the bottom of the stairs, his thin arms crossed in defiance. My heart thumped loudly in my chest, but for the first time in a long time, I knew what I had to do: acknowledge the truth. "You're right," I repeated. He stared at me, unmoving. "I have done nothing over the past few weeks but think about myself," I said sadly. "It was about time I realized how isolated and lonely my life could be if I lost you to my selfishness." Alex's thin face remained hard, but I could tell he was listening. "I lied to you," I said, as if he didn't already know. "And my actions threatened to undermine your dream of becoming a big designer. For that, I am truly sorry."

I paused to gather my thoughts. "You have done so much for me over the years, and lately, I've reciprocated your love and kindness with nothing but selfishness and deceit." The sternness in Alex's face began to melt as I continued. "When I returned from Manhattan, broken and alone, you gave me a job. You let me live with you until I got on my feet. You've extended me this amazing opportunity, and I've paid you back by sleeping with the one

designer who could supplement your line in ways we never thought possible."
Tears began to stream down my face unexpectedly. I wiped them away,
determined to get through what I needed to say. "I lied to you to protect my
own interests, Alex. And unfortunately, I can't take that decision back. But," I
said, trying to hide the desperation in my voice, "I know I can do better. I can
be the friend and employee I should have been through this whole mess. I
want to show you honesty and support, and I want you to feel as safe and
loved in our friendship as I do." Alex bit his lower lip and walked toward the
living room. I stood in front of the couch, crying, feeling exposed and
vulnerable.

"I do feel that way," he said quietly, stripped of any anger or bitterness.
"You're a great friend – the best." When he reached me, he pulled me in tight
and whispered in my ear that he loved me. "I don't think you're selfish," he
said, gripping me hard. "Everyone makes mistakes. I know that you love me
and I understand why you kept it from me. Admittedly, I probably wouldn't
have handled it all too well."

When he released me, we looked at each other, wiping our faces and
smiling. A huge sense of relief washed over me as we basked in our
reconciliation. I was starting to believe that, notwithstanding my selfish
mistakes, my friendship with Alex would be okay.

Satisfied that he'd given us enough space, Patrick practically leapt from
the couch to give me a hug. Kissing him on the cheek, I thanked him for
being supportive over the past few weeks, and, eager to change the subject,
asked whether he'd made any more wedding plans in the past twenty-four
hours. Patrick nodded affirmatively and encouraged me to take a seat on the
couch.

"I have a binder," he announced excitedly, flashing the gap in his teeth.
"Let me go grab it." Smiling, I turned toward Alex, who had propped himself
up in his usual spot on the chaise lounger.

"Why am I not surprised?" I asked, trying to ease back into our
friendship. Alex shrugged.

"Because you know my future husband all too well," he said. Shifting on
the chaise to a more comfortable position, he stared back at me, his expression
once again serious. "I know you were trying to change the subject, but I think

you and I should talk about Keegan before we move on," he suggested. I frowned. "I'm sure you don't want to," he recognized, "but we need to. I've been working with him a lot and he's coming into town tomorrow afternoon. I need to know what's going on to be properly prepared for his visit." I swallowed, disappointed that our brief moment of normalcy had been so short-lived.

"I'm really not sure what to say," I admitted, "but I guess the most important thing to know is that we're over. We won't be seeing each other anymore." It was Alex's turn to frown.

"What happened?" He asked. "More importantly, how is this going to affect work?" I cringed at the thought of having to work with Keegan. I hadn't even considered that part of the equation until now.

"I honestly don't know how it will affect work," I told him. "I'm sorry." Alex rolled his head to the side and stared blankly across the room in thought. I decided not to tell him that Keegan was married. With everything else going on, Alex didn't need the added distraction. It really made no difference to the boutique's business whether Keegan was married or not. It only made a difference to me.

"I'm not really sure what to do," he finally said. "He is an integral part of our deal with Naresh – a deal on which I need the help of my New York liaison. I can't handle all of this by myself." I nodded with understanding.

"I know," I said, frustrated with myself for putting us in this situation. "I can put my personal stuff to the side, Alex, and do whatever you need." He seemed doubtful, and rightly so. It probably wasn't realistic to think I could work with Keegan and ignore what had happened between us.

"It's going to be awkward either way, I think," he predicted flatly. "Does Keegan know I found out about your relationship?" I nodded. "Oy vey," Alex said dramatically, placing his head in his hands. Patrick raced down the stairs behind me having found the binder. Sitting down on the couch, he picked up on the seriousness of our conversation immediately. "I'll meet with him alone tomorrow," Alex eventually decided. "You don't need to be there. But Haley, we're going to have to figure this out. As it stands, the situation is not acceptable." I agreed, shamefully relieved that he didn't want me to come to the meeting. I didn't think I could face Keegan again so soon.

Patrick cleared his throat and opened to the first page of the binder, trying to steer the conversation back in the direction of the wedding. Noticing his partner, Alex switched gears and insisted that he show me a draft of their ceremony program. I figured it was his way of giving Patrick the go ahead to change the subject to a more pleasant topic.

"They're really beautiful," Alex said in reference to the programs. "Patrick spent a lot of time on them." Scooting toward Patrick's side of the couch, I smiled, excited to be talking about something other than Keegan. Patrick flipped a few pages and placed the binder in my lap, revealing the draft of the program through a clear plastic cover. Alex was right. The program was beautiful.

"Wow," I said, impressed. "It's perfect!" I ran my hand along the plastic cover, admiring Patrick's work. The program's colors were a stunning combination of reds, oranges, and other warm, fall hues, appropriate for the season in which they'd be married. A border wrapped around the pages in the shape of an old tree, its roots extending along the bottom in intricate detail. "You did this all on your own?" I asked, impressed. Patrick was creative, but I hadn't realized he was such a gifted artist. He smiled sheepishly and shook his head.

"Actually, no," he admitted. "It was your brother. I told him what I was looking for and he scanned a color copy of his design to me yesterday. I think it only took him a few hours, but I'm in love with it." I smiled knowingly.

"Now that you mention it, this has Michael written all over it," I said proudly. "He did a nice job." When I looked up from the binder, I caught Patrick and Alex giving each other knowing, sneaky looks. Catching me watching them, Patrick turned back toward the binder and suggested I continue to look at the program.

"What do you think about the way everything's laid out?" He asked. I narrowed my eyes suspiciously and turned to browse the program in more detail. Scanning the program carefully, I wasn't even halfway down the first page when I saw it: "*Haley Blythe Simpson*" it read, in an elegant script font, . . . "*Best Woman.*" I looked up excitedly at Patrick and then over at Alex, searching for confirmation of what I'd seen. Grinning, Alex stood up and walked over to the couch to sit next to me. I was over the moon.

"I want you to stand up there with me," Alex said, placing his right hand on my shoulder as he sat down. "Despite everything that's happened, you're still my best friend, and I love you with all of my heart. I can't imagine anyone else being there as my person of honor." I almost shrieked with delight as I wrapped my arms excitedly around Alex's scrawny neck.

"I can't believe it!" I exclaimed. "I'd be honored to be . . ." I paused and looked down at the program, searching for the correct title, "your Best Woman!" Alex leaned in to hug me again. Once he released me, Patrick grabbed my hand from the other side and pulled me in for another gleeful embrace.

"As much as we'd like to be traditional," Patrick said, letting me go, "not much is traditional about the joining together of two grooms. That's why we chose to name you, 'Best Woman.' If gay weddings break the traditional mold, we figured, why not take some creative liberties?"

"Well, it's your day and you can do whatever you want," I told him. "Plus, like I said before, I love it." Leaning forward, I continued to study the program's contents to see who else they'd chosen to assume roles in the ceremony. Muffling another girly squeal, I pointed happily when I saw Lindsay's name as one of the readers. Alex stood up from the couch while I continued to peruse.

"We've gotta get going," he interrupted, looking at Patrick while pointing to his watch. "Patrick has interviews in thirty minutes and I have to get ready for Keegan's arrival." Overtly disappointed, Patrick snatched the binder from my lap and closed it with a huff.

"Of all the mornings," Patrick complained. "When Haley and I are finally able to sit down and talk about the wedding." Alex laughed.

"You'll have plenty of time to talk about the wedding," he insisted. "But we don't have plenty of time to find Dom's replacement." Groaning, Patrick rose from the couch in obligation and saluted Alex sarcastically.

"I know, I know," he said. "Mush, mush." Alex rolled his eyes as Patrick ran back upstairs to put away the binder and grab a coat.

"As you can see, he's getting really excited about the wedding," Alex said as he made his way to the front door to put on a pair of casual sneakers. I smiled, imagining how excited I would be if it were me in Patrick's shoes. Who could blame him? Planning a wedding and getting married was a childhood dream. It was only natural for Patrick to be excited to finally see it coming true.

"I know he's excited, but are you?" I asked, looking to make sure Alex wasn't getting lost in the plans. He responded with a disapproving look.

"Of course I'm excited," he said. "I'm just not as excited to plan the damn thing as my party planning fiend of a partner." I laughed.

"Understood," I said, getting up from the couch to leave. Zipping my jacket and grabbing the handle on the front door, I turned to Alex to say goodbye. "So I'll see you later?" I asked hopefully, unsure as to when exactly that would be.

"Yeah," he said vaguely. "In the meantime I'll think about what to do with Keegan going forward. We'll talk about it later." He sounded less annoyed about the situation than he had a few minutes earlier, but I felt guilty that I wasn't able to fulfill my job duties for Alex's biggest client account.

"Okay," I acknowledged, a hint of apology and sadness in my voice. Alex's upcoming meeting with Keegan shed light on the fact that although Alex and I had reconciled, some obstacles still remained for us to overcome.

****

I reached over the hospital bed to help Lindsay put on a thick wrap-around sweater. She got cold in the afternoons after her body temperature recovered from the vigor of physical therapy. Like clockwork, she'd started shivering upon my arrival, having had a particularly tough physical therapy session while I was at Alex's apartment. She grimaced as I draped the thick wool over her shoulder. It was obvious that the recent decrease in her pain medication was causing her to suffer more than usual. I wished there was something I could do to make her feel better.

"Thanks, Hale," she said, lying back against her pillow to rest. I told her I was more than happy to oblige. Sitting next to her bed, I watched while Linds took a moment to catch her breath. When she turned her head toward me, her face was long and solemn, and her pale blue eyes lacked their usual lively spirit. "It's pathetic how exhausted I get after the simplest tasks," she said sadly. I reached my hand toward her face and gently tucked a strand of her blond hair behind her ear. She smiled at me weakly.

"You had physical therapy today," I reminded her. "That always takes a lot out of you." She rolled her head away from me and sighed, puffing out her cheeks in frustration. "Plus, look on the bright side," I added, trying to cheer her up. "Your recovery from your head injury has been lightening fast and the doctor said you'll be home in time for Dom's party on Saturday!"

Lindsay smiled faintly, but didn't say anything. Like me, she probably doubted that she'd have the strength to endure that kind of event. I sat next to her on the bed, searching for more to say. Eventually, I resigned myself to the fact that the best thing I could do for her was keep her company. We sat in silence for a minute while I rubbed the outside of her hand with my thumb. Her hands were icy cold. I hoped that the gentle friction from the rubbing would help warm her up. Breaking her trance, Lindsay rolled her head back to face me.

"If you've been such a horrible friend lately," she said, referring to our conversation when I first arrived at the hospital, "why is it that you've been by my side in this damn hospital from the very beginning, no matter what?" I squeezed her hand in response.

"I didn't say I was a horrible friend," I reminded her. "Just a self-centered, needy one." Lindsay shrugged.

"Well I think you're being too hard on yourself," she suggested. I patted her hand lightly, hoping to avoid a total rehash of our earlier conversation. I hadn't been as nervous to talk to Lindsay as I had Alex because I hadn't betrayed her in the same way I had him. Nevertheless, I still owed her an apology for falsely accusing her of revealing my relationship with Keegan. "I would like the record to reflect that I don't think you've been selfish," she added. "You've always been there when I've needed you."

"Alright," I replied, laughing at her refusal to fully accept my earlier apology. "It's on the record. Now let's talk about something else." I glanced at the flowers and chocolates littering her room, wondering from whom they all came. Most of them were probably from work. "Have you talked to anyone at work lately?" I asked her, moving on to a more lighthearted topic of conversation. Lindsay sighed. It didn't seem as though my attempt to change the subject had helped lift her spirits. She was as depressed as I'd ever seen her, and I didn't know how to bring her out of it. This was uncharted territory.

"I don't talk to people at work much," Lindsay shared, back to staring out the window. "I guess the accident put my life into a bit of perspective. Getting better just to have my soul sucked away at that horrible job seems a bit pointless." Her voice was monotonous and distant. Again, I found myself searching for things to say to make her feel better. All I could think about was how much better Lindsay was at this kind of thing than me.

"You don't have to go back there," I suggested. "You can do a lot of other things with your law degree." Lindsay grunted, unimpressed by my logic. "Well, I know Charlie would hire you in a heartbeat," I told her. "He asks about you all the time. He thinks you're great." Lindsay turned away from the window and pointed at a pretty bouquet of spring flowers tied together by a brightly colored 'Get Well Soon' balloon.

"Those are from Charlie," Lindsay told me, her voice still lethargic and hollow. "He's emailed me a couple of times, asking if I receive visitors. I lied and told him that I don't. I'd rather people not see me like this."

"I think you should let him come see you," I said. "He cares about you. It might be a good way for you to start talking about expanding your career options." Lindsay turned back toward the window.

"Give it a rest, Haley," she snapped. The tone of her voice was mean. "The last thing I want to talk about is work. Why'd you even bring it up?" I gulped, trying not to let her attitude affect me. The doctor warned us that the residual effects of a head injury such as Lindsay's often manifested in atypical mood swings, but none of us had really been ready for them. No matter what the circumstances, Lindsay had always treated her family and friends with respect. Even when upset or frustrated, her tone remained gentle and kind. Post-accident, however, a part of her had changed. There had been a few times Lindsay had been uncharacteristically rude or harsh. Knowing that her unusual moods were a result of the accident helped us cope, but also saddened our hearts to know that something inside of her had been permanently altered.

"Hale, I'm sorry." Lindsay's chin started to quiver. "I don't know what's wrong with me. I didn't mean to bite your head off." I watched her, heartbroken, as a single tear ran down her cheek. If the police ever found the person who hit her and left her lying there, broken, in the middle of the street, I hoped I'd get the chance to give them a hard, bare-knuckle punch to the face.

"Think nothing of it," I said softly, trying to hide my anger. I didn't want her to see my rage toward the person who hit her and think it was in any way directed at her. "I'm pretty sure anyone would be cranky if they were stuck in a hospital for almost two weeks," I added. "Can you imagine how awful I would be as a patient?" Lindsay turned to me and smiled, silently thanking me for understanding. I smiled back and leaned forward to kiss her on the forehead as Trevor entered the room. The sight of him brought some life back to her eyes instantaneously.

"Hey babe," he said, ignoring me for a moment to give her a kiss. He winked at me and waved before pulling up a chair on the other side of her bed.

"Hi," I replied. I was glad he was here. Scooting as close to the bed as he could, Trevor grabbed Lindsay's fingers and gently put them up to his face in a loving caress. Lindsay watched him affectionately before asking about his day.

"You're here early," she said, concerned. "You've taken enough time off of work already – you need to be careful." Trevor gave her a look that indicated she shouldn't worry.

"The doctor called and said you had a particularly tough PT session this morning," he said. "I know how hard you are on yourself. I wasn't going to let you sit here alone and worry about it." Lindsay closed her eyes and quickly burst into a waterfall of tears. I watched her sudden breakdown in concern and continued to hold her hand until she gently pulled it away to wipe her eyes. Trevor, continuing to hold her fingers, stood and placed his other hand on the side of her face in comfort. She turned toward him, still crying.

"I don't want you to miss work because I'm lying here feeling sorry for myself over a bad physical therapy session," she said, sobbing. "Your boss has already talked about how much work you've missed – you can't afford to miss any more." Trevor let go of Lindsay's fingers and put both hands on the sides of her head to calm her down.

"Shhhhhh," he whispered softly, stroking her hair gently. He waited for her crying to slow before speaking. When he finally did, his tone was serious and quiet. "There is nothing," he said slowly, "*nothing* that will keep me away from you when you need me." He brushed the hair out of her face with his thumbs, continuing to hold either side of her head to keep her eyes focused on his gaze. "The only thing that matters in my world is you," he said. "You are the love of my life and my best friend. I almost lost you. You're out of your mind if you think that something as insignificant as a job can keep me from this hospital room." I watched the two of them stare at each other. Their love in that moment was magnetic. I shifted uncomfortably in my seat, wondering whether I should leave.

"I love you," Lindsay whispered, the corners of her mouth curling up into a small smile. Trevor leaned in and gave her another kiss.

"I love you, too," he said, looking at her in a way that made me melt. Even with Lindsay's bandages, shaved patches of hair, and splotchy skin, Trevor looked at her as if she were the most beautiful person in the world. I had never considered Lindsay and Trevor's love to be the kind of sweep-you-off-your-feet, movie star love of which I'd always dreamed. But seeing them in this moment made me realize how special their love truly was. Lindsay and Trevor's love may not have been fit for a feel-good romantic comedy, but it was better. It was real. And although it came with the occasional fight or blasé night of television and sweatpants, I realized that Lindsay and Trevor's love was capable of remarkable things that a movie – no matter how well written or acted – could never possibly portray.

21 PARTY PLANNING

I cursed in frustration when the other side of the banner I was holding fell from the ceiling for the third time this afternoon. Turning carefully on the bar stool so as not to lose my balance, I peered down at Alex. He was standing on the ground next to me rifling through the bags of decorations we'd picked up from the store. "Alex, this tape is *not* working," I told him. He looked up at me and winced apologetically.

"I think it might be Patrick's scrapbooking tape," he admitted. "I'm sorry. It's not as good of an adhesive as regular tape because it's designed not to ruin pictures." I rolled my eyes, pretending to be annoyed. "Well, in all fairness, you didn't specify what type of tape you needed," he claimed, opening a bag of party confetti and spreading it around the bar. "You said, 'grab some tape,' so that's what I did."

"You may be right," I said, shaking my head at him, "but this tape is totally useless." I climbed carefully off of the barstool and laid the festive 'Farewell' banner on a nearby high top table.

"You want me to go grab some?" Alex offered. I shook my head.

"No, I need your help here. We only have forty-five minutes to finish decorating before people start arriving. I'll ask Linds to bring some." I dug my phone out of my purse and dialed Lindsay. It only took Trevor a couple of rings to answer.

"Hey, Hale," he said, greeting me. "What's up?"

"Hey Trevor," I responded. "I know you guys are picking up the cake, but is there any way you can get here sooner and bring me some tape? I'm trying to hang the decorations with a spool of useless scrapbooking adhesive and it's not going well."

"I don't know, Hale, we're running late as it is," Trevor replied. "Getting ready has been . . . slower than we anticipated. Linds is already stressed enough about being late with the cake." I hung my head in disappointment, but told him not to worry. I was just glad Lindsay was able to make it. It was hard to believe she'd recovered so quickly from her accident when in the beginning, we didn't know whether she'd wake from that first surgery. Her possible attendance at Dom's party today seemed like a miracle.

"I understand," I said reassuringly. "I'm sure I'll find some. Tell Linds not to stress about being late. Not having the cake before Dom gets here is the very last thing anyone should be worried about."

"I'll tell her," Trevor confirmed. "Why don't you have Patrick or Alex run out and grab some tape from the small pharmacy a few blocks from the bar?"

"Yes, well that would normally be a good idea," I agreed. "However, Patrick had to run home this morning to tend to a family emergency and I need Alex's help with the rest of the decorations."

"Is everything okay with Patrick?"

"Yeah, he's fine," I assured him. "His grandmother fell and broke her hip this morning, so he went to Dayton to see her at the hospital. She should be okay, but Patrick wanted to see for himself. He's really close with her."

"That's a shame," Trevor mused. "I think we've all had enough of hospitals for the time being."

"No kidding," I commiserated.

"Well, keep us updated on how Patrick's doing," Trevor requested. "I'm gonna go help Linds finish getting ready. We should be on our way soon enough."

"Okay, no rush," I responded. "See you guys in a bit."

After saying goodbye to Trevor, I hung up the phone and stared at my screen, contemplating my next move. At this point, calling Nick was my best option, but I was nervous to hear his voice. Other than a few lighthearted and friendly texts, I hadn't spoken to him since he left my apartment on Monday. I was worried that things may be weird between us after the way the night had ended. Exhaling nervously, I nevertheless decided to call. I'd be seeing him soon at the party anyway, and I really needed some tape.

"Hi, Haley," Nick said, answering almost immediately. "Shouldn't you be getting ready for the party?" I laughed. My nerves faded at the sound of his voice. There was nothing awkward between us at all.

"Well that's exactly what I'm doing," I told him. "But I've run into a teensy little problem with the tape. Any chance you can head over here early and bring me some?"

"I think I can manage that," Nick replied warmly, without hesitation. I smiled widely.

"Thank you!" I said, relieved. "You're a life saver – oh, and Nick? Bring normal tape. Nothing weird. No scrapbooking tape." Nick chuckled on the other end of the phone.

"What makes you think I own scrapbooking tape?" He asked. I laughed.

"Nothing," I assured him. "Just – bring normal tape. I'll see you soon." When I hung up the phone, I found Alex grinning at me from across the room.

"What?" I asked, defensively.

"Oh, nothing," he said, turning to open another bag of confetti. "I'm just happy that Nick was around to save the day." His implication was impossible to miss.

"Oh, shut it, Alex," I replied, unable to keep from smiling myself. My growing feelings for Nick were hard to ignore. I just hoped that our uncomfortable discussion about my short-lived relationship with Keegan hadn't sullied whatever feelings Nick may have had toward me before Monday.

Thinking about Keegan's unwelcome interference in my night with Nick made me frown. His attempts to contact me hadn't stopped there. Keegan texted and called me incessantly all week, desperate to ensure I wouldn't divulge his precious secret. Disgusted with his very existence, I ignored his constant efforts to get me to talk. I'd even successfully avoided him while he was in town this past week conducting business with Alex.

Although it pained me to have ended our affair so abruptly – especially after the way I'd felt about him the last time he'd been to Columbus – it was easier to cope, knowing that Keegan was a remorseless cheater. My anger toward him adequately masked whatever romantic feelings I may have previously harbored. His infidelity could not have been less desirable or more abhorrent. At bottom, he sickened me – and I was furious to be the other woman in his extramarital affair.

I grabbed a bag of silly string cans to distribute amongst the tables, trying hard to keep Keegan's infidelity from creeping unwanted into my thoughts. While I distributed the cans, I saw Alex dump half of a bag of confetti on the table I'd cleared for the food. I tried hard not to laugh. "Alex, maybe it's time you lay off the confetti," I suggested, smirking. I didn't think anyone would be keen on eating appetizers covered with tiny, plastic shimmering squiggles. Looking around the room, I noticed that confetti covered almost every inch of the tabletops. Alex's confetti spreading had gotten entirely out of control. "It's beginning to look like a paper shredder exploded in here," I said. Pretending to ignore me, Alex reached slowly into the bag and grabbed an oversized handful of confetti. Raising his hand slowly, he turned toward me, a mischievous look on his face.

"Lay off the confetti, huh?" He asked playfully, holding up his fist as if it were a dangerous weapon. I tried to give him a threatening look in response, but instead, I started to giggle.

"Alex," I said, fighting to remain serious. "Alex . . . don't. We don't have time to mess around." Alex took an exaggerated step toward me, laughing like a cartoon villain. I stared at him, silently begging him not to throw the confetti, when suddenly he broke into a run. Screaming like a child, I ran from him desperately, looking over my shoulder as Alex held up his fist and ran after me like a maniac. Sprinting past the table with the decorations, I managed to snatch my own bag of confetti and open it mid-run, preparing to fire back.

****

When Nick arrived, he found Alex and I sitting in the middle of the room laughing breathlessly, covered head to toe in confetti. Alex was the first to notice him walk in. "Hey, Nick!" He exclaimed, picking confetti out of his hair carefully. I spun around on the floor and looked at Nick sheepishly as if he'd caught me playing paintball in the middle of my mother's formal dining room. Nick laughed, shaking his head.

"You two look like you're having a good time," he observed. Embarrassed that he'd caught us acting like children, I picked myself off of the floor and walked over to give him a welcoming hug.

"Hi, there," I said, wrapping my arms around his bundled torso. I felt a small surge of adrenaline course through my body as we touched. When I pulled away, I noticed some of the confetti had stuck to his jacket. "Sorry," I said, brushing it off.

"That's okay," Nick replied, gently picking some pieces of confetti out of my brown hair. "*I'm* not the one covered in it." Once Nick had been cleared of confetti, the two of us started picking it out of my hair and off of my clothes. Turning around, I let Nick brush the pieces off of my back. "Okay, turn back around," Nick demanded, taking one last swipe at my shoulder blades. When I turned to face him, Nick moved my hair behind my shoulder. His finger ran lightly across my collarbone in the process, giving me the chills as he looked down at me with his fiery hazel eyes, smiling.

"I'm going to the bathroom," Alex suddenly announced. The sound of his voice startled me. For a split second, lost in Nick's stare, I'd forgotten he was here. "I need a mirror to get this crap out of my hair." Turning to face him, I stifled a giggle as Alex sprung from the floor and stormed to the men's bathroom in annoyance. His hair had grown fast in the past month, requiring him to use gel to tame his usually short mane. It appeared as though the gel was causing the confetti to stick stubbornly to his blond strands, forcing him to pick out one piece at a time.

"I should help him," I said to Nick, reluctantly. I knew how obsessive Alex could be, and I didn't want him to stand in front of the bathroom mirror all afternoon and miss the whole party. Nick agreed, staring after Alex sympathetically.

"Sounds like he needs some help," he replied. I took a step toward the bathroom, but stopped when Nick grabbed me gently by the arm. "Really quickly, though," he said, reaching into his jacket pocket. I raised my hands in the air in exaggerated praise as he emerged holding a pack of magnetic tape.

"Hallelujah!" I exclaimed. "We finally have tape!" Nick smiled, pleased that he'd brought what I needed.

"While you're in the bathroom picking through Alex's hair, is there something I can do to help you get ready? Perhaps by using this normal, certainly not weird, tape?" I laughed and grabbed his hand to lead him to the banner I'd left on the table.

"There certainly is," I responded. After showing him where I wanted the banner hung, I grabbed his hand once again and led him to another bag of decorations. "If the banner goes up and we're still purging Alex of confetti, can you start hanging these swirly, streamer-like thingies from the walls and ceilings?" I asked. Nick nodded and laughed.

"I've never hung a swirly, streamer thingy, but I'll do my best," he said. I hit him lightly on the arm for making fun of me, but thanked him for his help. "No problem," he said genuinely. "That's what I'm here for." I paused before heading to the men's room and looked at him seriously.

"Don't think I'm not aware that I am way behind on favors in this friendship," I said, thinking of all the times Nick had come to my rescue. Nick took off his jacket and rested it on a nearby chair.

"That's not how friendship works," he said. "I'm not keeping a tally, so you should stop keeping yours." I smiled at him in appreciation and headed to the bathroom where I was sure to find a frustrated Alex. As I opened the men's bathroom door, Nick called to me as he picked up one of the banner's ends.

"One more thing, Haley," he said. "Would you like me to spread some confetti when I'm done?" I laughed.

"Absolutely," I replied, sarcastically. "Just try not to get it everywhere." Nick chuckled and turned to hang the banner. Although we were still running behind on time, I felt at ease as I entered the bathroom, knowing Nick was here to lend a helping hand.

****

It took Alex and I fifteen minutes to pick the gel-encased confetti out of his hair. When we were finally done, there were only ten minutes left before people were scheduled to arrive for the party. "Hurry up and get the confetti off of your clothes so you can come help," I told Alex frantically, before leaving the bathroom. "We only have ten minutes!" Pushing open the door, I rushed into the room to see what Nick had left to do.

"What do you think?" Lindsay's voice caused me to stop in my tracks. I gaped around the room in amazement. It was nearly finished. Trevor and Nick were standing on bar stools, hanging the final set of streamers from a window in the back. The bar's employees were beginning to carry out silver trays of appetizers to place around the cake, which sat prominently in the center of the food table. I stood in the front of the room, my hands on my hips, taking in the view.

"It looks great," I told Lindsay, happy to see everything done. The banner hung perfectly at the entrance and the colorful hanging streamers added a pop of color to the bar's normally dreary, darkly painted walls. The room's wood floors were still covered in confetti, but it looked as though someone had spread it around to make it look intentional. "I can't believe we actually got it all done!" I exclaimed. "Thank you guys so much." Lindsay started to make her way over to me in her wheelchair, using her left hand to propel herself awkwardly forward. I put up my hand, motioning for her to stop, and walked over to give her a hug. "Thanks," I said, whispering in her ear. She shook her head and pointed in Nick's direction.

"We got here five minutes ago," she said. "Nick had already pretty much finished everything." Nick winked at me from across the room. I mouthed a 'thank you' in his direction, my heart swelling. Once again, I felt lucky to have him in my life.

Alex emerged from the bathroom at the same time Charlie walked into the room with his wife, Jody. "Hey Charlie!" I called, releasing Lindsay's hand. "Come on in and grab some food and beer!" I pushed Lindsay across the room to greet them while Trevor, Nick, and Alex chatted and disposed of the remaining trash from the decorations. "Hi, Jo," I said, hugging Charlie's wife. "It's been a while!" She smiled, her pretty blue eyes crinkling in their corners.

"I know," she said. "It's good to see you."

"How are you, Lindsay?" Charlie turned his attention almost immediately toward Linds. Lindsay smiled and shrugged.

"I've been better," she replied, making light of her injuries. "But I've been out of the hospital for a few days, so I'm feeling good in spite of it all! I can't wait for my arm to heal so I can get out of this wheelchair and onto some crutches." Charlie and Jody extended their well wishes, but it wasn't long before the three of them were discussing the latest happenings in the legal world. Glancing around the room, I noticed more people were arriving and excused myself from the conversation.

"I hope we aren't chasing you away with lawyer stuff," Jody said, as I moved to leave them. Like Lindsay and Charlie, Jody was a lawyer, too.

"Of course not," I assured her. "I'm just trying to be a good hostess and work the room." Bidding them a temporary adieu, I made my way to the front and began greeting people as they walked in.

Over a matter of fifteen to twenty minutes, the upstairs bar space we'd reserved was nearly filled with Dom's college friends, new work friends, and even some new sales associates from the boutique that I hadn't yet met. Before long, the room was teeming with people chatting, drinking, and eating, waiting patiently for the guest of honor to arrive. I didn't even notice when Dom walked in. The crowd was substantially larger than I'd expected, and I found myself worrying about running out of food instead of paying attention to the front of the room. It wasn't until I saw Dom ordering a beer from the bar that I realized he'd arrived.

"He's here, everybody!" I yelled loudly, trying to encourage people to cheer and douse him with the silly string like I'd instructed. Drowned out by the noise of the room, I was disappointed when the only can of silly string spraying in his direction was my own. Turning around and laughing at me, Dom shook his head as I stood in the middle of the oblivious crowd. I threw my hands up and made my way toward him. "I imagined that going a bit differently when I bought all that damn silly string," I insisted, giving him a hug. He had cut his hair since the last time I'd seen him at the hospital, and was wearing a pair of well-fitted jeans and a beige v-neck casual sweater. It was strange to see him without his usual grunge t-shirt and pair of *De Alexia* skinny jeans. He looked good.

"Thanks for the party, Hale," he said raising his beer and nodding. I raised my beer and clinked it against his in cheers.

"Thanks for everything you've done for the boutique!" I replied. "But I have to say, this new engineering job does a body good. You look great!" Dom blushed.

"Well, I'm not sure if it's the job or my new girlfriend," Dom said, practically glowing.

"Girlfriend, huh?" I asked. "Well, that's great! Is she here?" Dom nodded and pointed across the room at a short brunette in flare-legged jeans and a long-sleeved, thin striped sweater. She was adorable. "She's cute," I told him, elbowing him in the side. "Nice work." Dom smiled and continued to watch her as she talked to a group of his college friends.

"She's pretty cool," he acknowledged, taking a swig of his beer. Before I had a chance to ask him how they'd met, I spotted Nick across the room, talking alone with a young, busty blonde. They were leaning casually against the wall, chatting. Every now and then, the blonde touched his arm flirtatiously as they spoke. I felt myself frowning, but quickly shook my head to snap out of it. I had no right to be jealous; Nick and I weren't together. Nevertheless, I watched the two of them like a hawk, mentally yelling at her to leave him alone.

"This party is such a success!" Alex moved into my line of sight and slapped me on the arm. Dom raised his beer at Alex in 'hello' and made his way across the room to put his arm around his girlfriend's waist.

"Uh, yeah, it's going well, I think," I responded, trying to reposition myself so I could continue watching Nick's conversation. Alex waved his hand in front of my face obnoxiously.

"Stop it, Alex!" I grabbed his hand and reluctantly refocused my gaze on him. Alex turned around to see what I'd been watching.

"Oh, I see . . ." he observed. I blushed. As he turned around to taunt me, I felt my phone vibrate in my jeans with a call. I pulled it out, but shoved it back into my pocket immediately upon seeing it was Keegan. I was frustrated that he refused to accept the fact that I had no interest in ever talking to him again. Although I could have put an end to his badgering by telling him I never intended to share the details of our salacious affair, I didn't want to give him the satisfaction. Letting the slimy bastard squirm made me feel better about what I'd done. Alex shot me a curious glance. I reciprocated with a fake smile and took a sip of my beer, hoping he wouldn't ask about the call.

"Who was it?" He asked, looking at me as if he already knew. I shook my head in frustration.

"Who do you think?" I asked. Alex frowned. "I don't get it, Alex," I complained. "He won't stop calling me. It's madness."

"He must really like you," he observed, not amused. I avoided his eye contact. It felt strange talking to him about Keegan.

"Ha, no – that's certainly not why he keeps calling me . . ." Alex studied me with mild interest.

"Well why else would he be calling you?" He asked. I shrugged noncommittally, leaving his question hovering in the air unanswered. "You never told me why your little tryst ended," he added. "Is it because I found out or is it because of Nick?"

"Neither," I admitted. *It's because he's freaking married.* "Keegan's not the guy for me," I said vaguely. "It's that simple." Alex turned his body toward the bar and set his beer down on its wooden surface.

"I feel like you're not telling me something," he observed, fiddling with the label on his bottle. I sighed and took another sip of my drink, studying Alex's face. "I thought we had moved past hiding things from each other." He looked at me seriously. I was frustrated we were talking about this in the middle of Dom's party.

"Now is not the time to talk about it, Alex." He set his elbow down on the bar and balled his hand into a fist on which to rest his head. I couldn't tell whether he was upset, interested, or annoyed.

"Out with it, Haley," he demanded. "I'm serious." I ran my hand through my long hair and sighed again.

"Fine," I relented. "But you have to understand I didn't tell you because it has no bearing on you or the boutique. I didn't want to add more drama to what you were already dealing with." Alex stared at me, unsympathetic. He didn't want to hear excuses. He wanted to hear the truth. I dropped my head to my chest and whispered, "He's married, Alex." Alex's mouth dropped and his eyes nearly shot out of his head. Like I had been, he had been wholly unprepared for this news.

"Are you kidding me!?" He asked, his voice shrill. I regretted telling him immediately. I told him to calm down and that I'd handled it, but he was furious. "Did you know!?" I shot him an angry glare. Why did everyone keep asking me that?

"No!" I exclaimed. "That's why I ended it! When he told me he was married, I told him to go to hell! Come on, Alex, give me a little credit!" I was yelling in a hushed whisper so the people around us couldn't overhear what we were saying. I was thankful for the loud buzzing of conversation that filled the room and helped drown out my voice.

"Sorry – I just had to ask." Alex put a hand to his forehead, as if the news of Keegan's marital status had blown his mind. "This is . . . heavy, Haley." He sounded like Nick. Shaking my head, I tried to assure him it was quite the opposite.

"No, actually," I said. "It's nothing. It was upsetting when I found out, sure. But it's over and has absolutely no bearing on the merit of his designs. It should have no affect on you or the boutique whatsoever. Total nonissue."

"Total nonissue!?" Alex looked at me in disbelief. "Haley, how the hell am I supposed to even look at this guy after knowing what he did to you? Would you be able to work with someone who did something like that to me?!" I wanted to argue, but the answer to his question was obvious.

"No," I admitted. "But this situation is unique. Keegan isn't just some guy who screwed me over. He's your business partner and he's critical to the boutique. You *need* him to design shoes for the line. Alex, please. I would never forgive myself if you ended your business relationship with him over something that's ultimately my fault." Alex looked at me, as if searching for a better solution. I tried to think of what I could say to make him understand. "Please, Alex," I begged. "Please don't overreact. Maybe we should take some time and talk about this later when we aren't drinking and in the middle of what's supposed to be a fun party." Alex ripped off the rest of his beer label in frustration. I watched, my eyes silently pleading with him to drop the subject, at least for the time being.

"Ohhh, Haley," he said, groaning. "This is crazy." I nodded, agreeing heartily with his sentiment. "But you're right. This isn't the time or place for this conversation." I took a deep breath and placed my hand on his shoulder affectionately.

"I'm sorry about all of this," I said softly. "I promise, some day in the future, I will make it all up to you." Alex laughed sardonically and patted my hand.

"You can make it up to me by no longer dating losers." I forced a laugh in response.

"I'm not doing it on purpose," I assured him. I paused when the busty blonde with whom Nick had been talking walked past us to order a drink from the bar. Alex saw her, too. "So are we good?" I asked him, hopefully. I wanted to take the opportunity to snag Nick before the blonde returned with her beverage. "Are we done talking about this?" Alex nodded and motioned toward Nick, who was now chatting with Trevor and Lindsay at the other end of the bar.

"Yes, go," he insisted knowingly. I smiled.

"Thanks. I'll talk to you later."

I left Alex alone to make my way through the crowd, smiling as I watched Nick talking. Standing next to Trevor, Nick looked especially tall. He must have been three of four inches over six feet – I wondered why I hadn't noticed it before.

"Well, there you are!" Nick exclaimed when I joined the group. The uneasiness I was feeling after my discussion with Alex dissipated. Once again, Nick effortlessly made me feel better, just by being in my company. "You disappeared when the party started and I haven't seen you since! I've been looking for you everywhere," he claimed. I looked at him doubtfully.

"Oh, you have, have you?" I asked him suspiciously. I wondered how hard he'd been looking for me during his conversation with the perky blonde. He looked back at me, confused, picking up on the unusual hint of abrasiveness in my voice. I regretted letting my jealousy get the best of me. I tried to lessen the effect of my snarky undertone with an innocent smile. Lindsay poked Trevor and asked him if he wanted some food.

"No, I'm actually not that hungry," he said. Lindsay poked him harder and told him that she wanted to try the bacon wrapped scallops.

"I hear they're delicious," she said, clenching her teeth, obviously trying to leave Nick and I alone. Trevor finally picked up on her underlying message, as we all did, and bid us an awkward farewell. When they left, I turned to Nick and chuckled.

"She seems to be back to her old self," I said.

"Yeah," Nick observed, laughing. We both watched as Trevor wheeled Lindsay slowly through the crowd toward the table of food. "She seems to be doing really well," he observed. "I can't believe it."

"I know," I agreed. "She recovered so quickly – it's amazing." I turned around to see the blonde walk by and give Nick a flirty look. She was circling him expectantly, probably waiting for an opportunity to get him alone again. My thoughts of Lindsay's miraculous recovery were quickly replaced by my fervent dislike of this woman. I wanted her to leave Nick alone and go away. Nick started to laugh.

"Do you know that woman?" He asked, referring to the blonde. I realized I'd been glaring at her. I blushed in embarrassment, caught again in my moment of jealousy.

"No, do you?" I tried to ask innocently.

"I met her earlier," he replied, narrowing his eyes at me. "Her name is Stacey. She's Dom's friend from college."

"Oh, so she's like, eighteen?" I raised my eyebrows at him. He laughed.

"Ouch," he said, leaning back as if I'd thrown a punch. I relaxed my attitude and shook my head, embarrassed.

"I'm sorry," I said, blushing. "I saw you talking to her earlier and I have to admit, I was a little jealous." Nick smiled at me knowingly. I was telling him something he already knew.

"Jealous, huh? Why would you be jealous?" I blushed again. I didn't have a good answer. Nick moved in closer and leaned his head toward me so I could hear him whisper. "I'm glad you were jealous," he said quietly, looking at me in a way that made me weak in the knees. My heart started to beat faster as I stared back at him, remembering what he'd said at my apartment a few days earlier. "But Haley, you should know by now, that she's the one who should be jealous; not you." I bit my lower lip in shy anticipation.

"Oh, yeah?" I asked, shuffling my feet. Nick placed his hand behind my neck affectionately.

"Yeah," he said softly. "I'm only interested in one woman at this party, and I think you already know that." I felt his hand start to pull me in close. I shut my eyes, opening them up again as our lips touched. Nick's hazel eyes sparked wildly with an intoxicating fiery passion that made Keegan's sapphire eyes seem hollow and weak. In the deepest depths of my heart, wrapped passionately in Nick's comforting arms, I knew that this was where I had always been destined to be.

22 THE PHOTO

I ran my hand along the inside of Nick's arm, weaving my fingers gently over his elbow and down to his wrist. He stirred and opened his light hazel eyes, smiling when he saw me staring. I leaned forward on my pillow. "Good morning," I said, grinning. Waking up next to Nick filled me with happiness.

"Good morning." Nick lifted his arm, beckoning me to rest my head on his chest. I curled up next to his warm body gladly, basking in the glory of the morning. My head fit perfectly into the contours of Nick's body, as if I had been made for this exact spot. I draped my arm around him, gently rubbing his pale skin as we laid there in silence. I breathed in slowly, my thoughts drifting back to our night together. Our passion had been raw and fiery, but there was something else between us – something indescribable – that made the night more intense and special than I could have ever imagined.

I rested on Nick's warm chest, wondering what it had been. Whatever it was, it made me feel different than when I was with Keegan. On paper, the two situations were the same. Here I was again, waking up next to a man, finding myself falling head over heels in what I thought could be love. But what I felt for Nick this morning was a world apart from what I'd felt for Keegan within the walls of the Renaissance Hotel. I wondered if the difference meant that love could never feel the same way twice. Perhaps I'd never been in love.

"Are you hungry?" I glanced up at the sound of Nick's voice and clutched him tightly, temporarily shelving my thoughts about love. I admired his disheveled brown hair and sleepy features, happy to be in his arms.

"Yes," I told him, "but I don't ever want to leave this spot." I nestled my head comfortably into his chest. He brushed my hair to the side and kissed the top of my head.

"It's not going anywhere," he assured me. I looked up at him again. He placed his hand on the side of my face and tucked my hair behind my ear. In that moment, I believed him. Even after all of the heartache and deceit I experienced in my past relationships, I truly believed that the spot on his chest was mine forever. "You're beautiful, you know that?" I blushed and broke my gaze. Nick lifted my head, forcing me to look at him. "You are. I can't tell you how happy I am that I met you on that plane." This time, I laughed.

"I'm just glad you gave me a second chance," I admitted. "After that horrific plane ride, I never thought I'd see you again." Nick rubbed my cheek with his thumb.

"Something kept drawing us to each other," he said. I wasn't one for believing in higher powers or mysteries of fate, but it was nice to think that the forces of the world wanted Nick and I to be together.

"Maybe," I mused. Nick leaned over and kissed me, his morning scruff rough on my face. I groaned when he pulled away. I didn't want him to get out of bed.

"If we stay here much longer, we'll starve," he joked, pointing at the clock. It was almost noon.

"I don't care," I insisted, leaning back on my pillow, pouting. I pulled the sheets up to my chin to stay warm. Without Nick's body heat, the room temperature felt cold on my naked skin. Ignoring my whines, Nick threw back the sheets and rose from the bed. His body was even more defined than I remembered. It made me smile. He turned to me and pulled up his sweatpants, picking a t-shirt off the floor.

"You take your time getting up," he insisted, pulling the shirt over his head and trying in vain to tame his tousled hair. "I'll go down and brew us some coffee."

"Okay," I agreed, reluctantly. He leaned back into the bed to give me another kiss and smiled. I watched him happily, studying his every move until he disappeared into the hall.

I sighed and sat up, wrapping the bed sheet around me so I would stay warm while looking for my clothes. I peered thoughtfully around Nick's room. The walls were painted a light beige, and the only hanging decoration was a black and white canvas painting of Wrigley Field in the 1940s. The red bed sheets clashed miserably with the blue and orange patterned duvet cover, and the windows were devoid of any dressings. It looked as if he'd just moved in. One lone dresser stood in the corner, covered with a messy pile of clothes. The bedroom screamed bachelor pad. There were no hints of a woman anywhere. I wondered how differently his home had looked when he'd been married. The thought of his previous life with Katie was strange. I wasn't sure how I felt about it.

I eventually located my clothes on the bedroom floor. They were lying haphazardly in a trail leading to the bed, painting a scandalous picture of last night's activities. Smiling as I remembered the night, I picked up the pieces of clothing one by one and got dressed.

When I was fully clothed, I emerged from the bedroom into a long carpeted hallway. Like the bedroom, the hallway's walls were bare, giving it an almost hospital feel. I wondered whether Nick owned any frames with which to decorate them. Once again, I found myself imagining his former life with Katie. The walls in their home had probably been peppered with pretty frames of their wedding, the two of them smiling and kissing, unaware in that happy moment that the life they planned to share would be broken. Although their divorce had ultimately led Nick to me, it made me sad for him. I wondered whether the bare walls in his condo served as a painful reminder of the pictures that once existed. I hoped that someday he could decorate his halls with pictures again; confident that the growing bond between us would never be shattered.

I descended the stairs and turned into Nick's kitchen, watching him pour coffee beans into his grinder. Like the other rooms in the condo, the kitchen was spacious, but the sparse decorating and neutral-colored walls made it feel sterile and cold. The kitchen boasted newer, stainless steel appliances and beautiful black and white granite countertops that extended beyond the dark, modern cabinets to form a casual breakfast bar. The breakfast bar served as a natural separation between the kitchen and the open family room, which housed a matching leather couch and chair, a television, and two side tables with a couple of black picture frames. For some reason, I was happy to see the frames. It was good to know that Nick had at least a couple of memories worth displaying.

"Take a seat," Nick suggested, pointing toward one of the stools at the bar. Obliging, I sat down as he bustled around the kitchen, grabbing creamer and coffee mugs.

"You're always taking care of me," I observed. I asked if he wanted some help.

"I like taking care of you," he insisted. "Stay seated." I crossed my legs and leaned my forearms on the counter. I'd never been with a man like Nick. He was caring and sweet, and even in our friendship, had treated me like a queen. I felt so lucky, especially after everything that had happened with Keegan. "Your phone is on the table over there," Nick said, pointing to a small breakfast nook in the corner of the kitchen. "It's buzzed a couple of times since I've been down here." I rolled my eyes and swung around in the barstool to retrieve my phone.

"I guarantee you the buzzing is all Alex," I predicted. "He's probably desperate for details from last night." Nick turned to me and leaned against the counter.

"Details?" He asked. I realized he probably wasn't comfortable with the level of sharing to which Alex and I were accustomed.

"Don't worry," I assured him. "I'll be vague. Alex doesn't have to know everything." Nick looked at me doubtfully and turned back to what he was doing in the kitchen.

"Something tells me there won't be a whole lot of privacy when it comes to Alex." I insisted he was wrong, but Nick shook his head and laughed. "I really don't mind," he claimed. "He's your best friend. I understand."

I carried my phone back with me to the counter. I didn't want Nick to feel as if our relationship would be open to the outside world. I wanted him to feel safe and comfortable, knowing that our intimacy would stay as private as he wanted. "I will never share something intimate with Alex unless you approve," I told him. I knew it would be difficult, but I wanted to respect his wishes in the same way I imagined he would respect mine. "What shall I tell Alex about last night?" I'd been right about the morning's texts. All of them were from Alex, begging me to call and let him know what happened with Nick. Nick walked over to me as the coffee began to brew and leaned onto the other side of the breakfast bar.

"Tell him whatever you'd like," he said, smiling. I set the phone down on the counter and crossed my arms. In that moment, Nick was irresistible. His messy do and scruffy facial hair gave him a manly, sinewy look, and his sweatpants hung loosely around his waist, daring someone to tug them to the floor.

"Alex can wait," I said, leaning over the bar to kiss him. When our lips met, I felt a surge of excitement ripple through my body as if his touch had created an electric shock. I knew I hadn't imagined it that night at my apartment. Nick pulled me closer and held me tighter until he was picking me up from the barstool and laying me on the counter. One of his hands rested behind my head to protect me from the hard surface, while his other hand ran up my shirt. I extended my arms, allowing him to pull my top over my head. I reciprocated the favor, pulling Nick's t-shirt off feverishly and wrapping my legs around his waist. Wrapped around his upper body, Nick pulled me from the counter and carried me to the living room couch with ease. He kissed my neck and my collarbone, once again sending a tingling sensation through my entire body. His mouth ran down my stomach and stopped when he reached the top of my jeans. He looked at me as he unbuttoned them slowly, never once breaking his gaze as he pulled them off. I closed my eyes as he threw them to the floor, reveling excitedly in the heat and intense passion of the moment.

****

"Well, now I'm really hungry," I admitted. Resting on top of Nick under a blanket from the couch, I laid my chin on the palm of my hands, staring up at him from his hairy, muscular chest. He nodded, tired from the last twenty minutes.

"Me too," he said softly. "You're going to make me drop twenty pounds at the rate we're going." I smiled and asked if he wanted me to bring him some coffee. Groaning, he told me he'd get it. "You wrap yourself up in this blanket and rest. I'll bring you some coffee. Do you want any cream?"

"Yes, please," I requested, wrapping the blanket around me as I sat up to let him move from underneath. I sank back into the leather couch and watched once again as Nick gathered and put on his clothes. It was an enjoyable sight. The leather on the couch was damp with sweat, but I didn't care. It would have been strange to worry about lying in his sweat after what we'd just shared.

Fully clothed for the second time today, Nick returned with a hot mug of coffee and a pile of my clothes. "Here you are," he said, setting the mug beside me on the table and handing me the pile. I thanked him. "How about an omelet?" He proposed. "I hear I'm a rather decent omelet chef and I have a ton of ingredients: cheese, green peppers, sausage, ham, onions, you-name-it."

"I'd love one," I told him, my stomach rumbling at the thought. "Cheese, green peppers, and ham, please." Nick returned to the kitchen and began to take the food out of the refrigerator while I got dressed. Again, I asked if he needed any help.

"No, ma'am," he insisted. "You go ahead and curl up on that couch and relax. If you'd like to watch TV the remote is on the table behind you."

"Okay." I walked toward the kitchen to fetch my phone. Gladly climbing back onto the couch, I wriggled my body into the corner, grabbing the thick brown blanket that I'd wrapped myself in a few minutes earlier. "This couch is a little piece of heaven!" I called to Nick. "I would lay in it all day if I could." I watched as he shut the refrigerator door before turning to me to respond.

"Well then do it!" He exclaimed. "I have no plans – we can watch movies and be lazy all day if you want." I grinned, reaching over to grab my coffee. The table was positioned behind my head, making it awkward to grab it without spilling. I sat up for a moment to avoid making a mess and held the coffee mug between my hands, sipping it cautiously so as not to burn my tongue.

"I was supposed to hang out at Alex's today, but I don't think he'll mind if I ditch him," I said. I pulled out my phone to text Alex. I was confident he would be ecstatic to hear why I was bailing on our lazy Sunday plans.

I'm at Nick's. Last night was incredible. I'm staying here to hang out. Details will follow ☺. Not surprisingly, it took only a few seconds for Alex to respond.

YAAAAYYYYY!!! I can't wait to hear!!! Call me as soon as you can! I told him I would.

Alex, this is just what I needed. He's ten times the man Keegan could ever be. I'm happy. I couldn't imagine being in the living room of a more honest, more caring, more sensational man.

I'm over the moon, Hale. He's exactly the kind of guy I have always pictured for you. Have a good day and seriously, call me as soon as you can. AS SOON AS YOU CAN. I smiled at Alex's enthusiasm.

I will, I promise. BTW, is Patrick back? Everything okay? Alex confirmed that Patrick was home safe and that his grandma would be fine.

Later, Hale. I put my phone on the side table, happy with the state of the world. My friends were healthy and safe and I was in the midst of relationship heaven.

"Is Alex upset you're changing your plans?" Nick called from the kitchen when he saw me put down my phone. I shook my head, unable to wipe the giant grin off of my face.

"No, he understands," I said. "He's happy I'm here." Nick smiled.

"Good," he said. "I like you here."

"You may change your mind before long," I warned him. "You may never get me to leave. I could get used to this service!" Nick laughed.

"I hate to burst your bubble, Haley, but the personal cooking service ends after breakfast," he joked. "If we get hungry later, we're ordering pizza." I pretended to be outraged.

"Well, that is unacceptable!" I exclaimed. Nick laughed again. I heard the burners on his gas-stove click on as he began my breakfast. "Are you 100% you don't need any help?" I asked.

"Yes!" Nick assured me. "Relax – I'll be ready with your omelet in a few minutes."

I crossed my legs and took another sip of my coffee, continuing to grin like a demented clown. The coffee was still too hot, so I leaned over the side table to put down my mug and let it cool.

As I set it down, however, the grin on my face suddenly vanished as I caught a glimpse of the picture sitting next to the coaster. Letting go of my drink so hastily that it almost spilled, I grabbed the black picture frame with two hands and held it close to my face to make sure I wasn't hallucinating. I stared at the picture and started to shake. Smiling in the middle of the photograph – one arm holding a small child and the other wrapped around a strikingly beautiful woman – was Keegan Bransford. My eyes bore into the picture as I tried to comprehend what I was seeing. Almost forgetting where I was, I jumped as I heard Nick call to me from the kitchen.

"That's my sister and her family," he offered, seeing that I'd grabbed the picture. "I'm not the biggest fan of her husband, but he seems to make her happy. I guess that's all I can ask for." I felt like I was going to be sick.

"*This* is your sister's husband?" I asked, trying to keep my voice from cracking as I held up the picture and pointed at Keegan. Nick peered across the room and wrinkled his nose.

"Unfortunately," he said, refocusing his attention back on the omelets he was making. "His name is Keegan – stupid name, don't you think?" The room spun violently. This couldn't be happening. After all of the drama Keegan had already caused in my life, here he was again, poised and ready to ruin the one relationship I thought he could never affect. "Haley, are you alright?" I looked up at Nick, who was watching me with concern from the kitchen. I must have looked like I'd seen a ghost. I had to get out of here so I could wrap my mind around what I'd discovered.

"Uh, I don't know," I said, struggling to speak. "I suddenly don't feel very well." Nick studied me. I was scared he'd uncover my secret if he stared any longer.

"Are you hungover?" He asked, justifiably confused by my sudden change.

"Uh, no . . . no," I stammered. "I mean, maybe. Nick, I'm going to have Alex come pick me up. I'm sorry. I really don't feel well." Nick turned off the burners and walked over to the couch to sit next to me. He put his hand across my forehead to check my temperature, a look of confused concern on his face. I was still clutching the picture frame tightly, unable to let it go.

"You don't have a fever," Nick observed. "You sure you don't want to wait to see if food and some rest will make you feel better? I'd hate to have you go home so soon." I shook my head. Nick reached for the picture and slowly pulled it from my sweaty grip to set it back on the side table.

"No, I want to go home," I insisted. Nick squeezed my knee and continued to study me with curiosity. I wanted to cry. How could this be happening? Of all the men that existed in the world, why did Keegan have to be Nick's brother-in-law? It didn't seem real. It wasn't fair.

"Okay," Nick finally agreed. "But I'll take you. Don't worry about bothering Alex." I nodded and allowed him to help me off the couch. How was I going to tell him about Keegan? The thought devastated me beyond words. I knew now that Nick and I would never be what I'd hoped. The fantasy I'd woken up to this morning was over. As quickly as it had begun, it had been replaced by the hard, cold, reality that I'd soon face the world again, broken hearted and alone.

23 LAWN BRAWL

Alex paced around the room with nervous energy. I sat on my big red couch, my hands on my head, trying not to be sick. Patrick was sitting on the edge of the living room chair, looking tired and distraught. I had just finished telling them about the picture of Keegan at Nick's condo and what it all meant. Not surprisingly, the news sent them into a mild shock. The three of us hadn't spoken for almost a minute.

"I deserve this," I said, breaking the silence, my hands still pressed against my head in disbelief. "After all of the lies and sneaking around . . . it's karma." Alex shook his head vigorously and continued pacing. His slim, bony frame shook with nervous energy. Patrick sat expressionless on the chair as if he couldn't process the information I'd relayed.

"No," Alex said firmly. "No, you don't deserve this." I stared listlessly at the ground.

"Well whether I deserve it or not, it's real and I can't take back what happened." Patrick started fidgeting with his hands.

"And Nick has no idea?" He asked, still trying to comprehend the situation.

"Nope, he has no idea," I confirmed. I was devastated. It was bad enough to find out that Keegan was married, but to find out his wife was Nick's sister – someone who Nick cherished and loved – was impossibly terrible. I couldn't believe my bad fortune. I knew that sleeping with Keegan had been ill advised from the beginning, but I could have never predicted how far-reaching the consequences of that mistake would be. An hour ago, I was on top of the world, falling in love with a man who I thought might feel the same for me. Now, I was faced with having to tell that same man that I'd unknowingly slept with his sister's husband a few weeks earlier. It was an unimaginable situation and one for which I was completely unprepared.

Alex gave me a look of helplessness as he searched for comforting words. "Don't tell him," he suggested desperately, whispering. "No one needs to know – you're innocent in all of this, Haley. You didn't know Keegan was married and you broke it off when you found out. You certainly didn't know he was married to Nick's sister. You didn't do anything wrong." I grabbed Alex's hand and looked at him lovingly.

"I know you're trying to help me," I responded gratefully, "but you of all people should know the damage that can come from lying to the people you love." Alex's eyes filled with panic. He knew I had to tell Nick about Keegan, but also knew that I'd lose Nick as a result. None of us wanted that to happen, but I didn't have much of a choice. "Plus," I added softly, "Nick deserves to know. His *sister* deserves to know." Alex closed his eyes and hung his head. We all knew I had to tell him. It was inevitable that he would find out eventually anyway.

We sat in silence again, absorbing the weight of the situation. My thoughts turned to Nick's sister and her little girl. I hated Keegan Bransford in that moment more than anyone in the entire world. He was scum, and I was ashamed to have ever been with him.

Alex began pacing around the room again. "When you told me Keegan was married last night, I was furious," he recalled. He put his fingers to his temples in frustration. "But this . . . the situation is now completely out of control." I nodded weakly in acknowledgment. "Hale, I may not know how to fix things with Nick, but I do know that Keegan needs to be out of our lives. We have to cancel his contract. There's no other way." I didn't have the energy to panic, but canceling Keegan's contract would be disastrous. I had to convince Alex not to make any rash decisions. Keegan was essential to the boutique. We would never find a designer to replace Keegan in time to meet our already pressing deadline for Resh+001. I hated to think what Naresh would do if we didn't have shoes for the line. Determined not to let Alex harm the future of his business because of my mistakes, I mustered as much energy as I could to protest.

"No, that's not the answer." I tried to sound adamant, but my resolve was weak. I was too overwhelmed to be very persuasive. "Like I said last night, Alex, the fact that Keegan's married – albeit to Nick's sister – doesn't change what he brings to the boutique. Breaking his agreement will only cause us more heartache and jeopardize your account with Naresh." Alex didn't respond. "I don't know about you, but I don't need any more freaking heartache." Alex stood next to the television, chewing his bottom lip with nervous energy.

"I understand this isn't what you wanted, Hale," he replied delicately, "but I cannot work with this guy. How could I after all the hurt he's caused? It's a done deal. He's not designing for us anymore. We'll have to face the consequences of that decision, but there is absolutely no other way." I leaned my head back and closed my eyes. Everything around me seemed to be falling apart, all because of sleeping with one stupid man.

"Haley, I know you don't want this to affect the boutique," Patrick said from beside me, "but think about what happens after you tell Nick the truth." I glanced at him for a second in confusion, wondering what he was trying to say. "Nick's obviously going to tell his sister," he continued, "and she's going to confront Keegan . . . he'll know it all came from you." I stared back at him. "Point is, as much as you don't want this to affect business, it will. I doubt Keegan will want to honor his contract after you ruin his marriage."

"HE ruined his marriage," I snapped angrily, tears beginning to stream down my face. Patrick looked at me apologetically.

"I know, honey, I didn't mean it that way." My anger quickly dissipated as I began to break down. There was too much going on to focus on Patrick's point, or anything else for that matter.

"I can't think anymore," I muttered, sobbing. "I know I made a mistake, but this . . . this isn't fair." Patrick and Alex quickly converged on the couch, sandwiching me between them. Alex wrapped me up in his beanpole arms while Patrick rubbed my back in comfort.

"We'll get through this, Hale," Alex whispered, hugging me. "Whatever we face, we always get through it together."

All three of us stopped and looked toward the hallway as we heard a faint knock at the door. "Who's here?" Patrick asked, as if Alex and I would have the answer. Neither of us responded, sitting in silence, listening again for the door. Sure enough, we heard another soft knock. I felt myself begin to shake.

"It's probably Nick," I said, frantically through my tears. "He said he might stop by later to see how I was feeling. I told him not to, but knowing him, he probably came anyway." Patrick and Alex glanced at each other, trying to determine what to do. "Alex, I can't face him right now," I insisted desperately. "Will you answer it and tell him I'm sleeping? Please." Alex nodded sympathetically and told me to lie down on the couch. I complied by burying myself into the cushions, Patrick continuing to rub my back. I felt ashamed to be hiding, but I wasn't physically or mentally prepared to face him. I needed some time to calm down before I could imagine telling him the truth about Keegan.

"What the hell are *you* doing here?!" I looked at Patrick in confusion when I heard Alex open the door and greet the visitor with alarming harshness. Patrick reciprocated my look of alarm and whispered that he'd check it out. "I don't give a shit that you flew all the way here," I heard Alex yell, as Patrick rose from the couch. "You shouldn't have come. In fact, you should never come back to Columbus again, you piece of shit!" I jumped from the couch in a panic and ran down the hallway to see what was happening. I nearly toppled over Patrick as I ran, desperate to know what the hell was going on. I stopped in my tracks and dropped the cream throw I was wrapped in when I saw Keegan standing in the doorway, looking tired and distraught. He saw me freeze in the hallway, standing on the tips of his toes to peer at me over Alex's head.

"Haley, please," Keegan begged pathetically. His sapphire eyes, once passionate and seductive, were now faded and desperate. Alex turned to me in surprise, not having realized I'd come to the door. "We need to talk," Keegan continued. "You won't answer my calls, you won't respond to my texts . . . I knew this was the only way you would listen." I stared at him as if he were a ghost. I was numb to emotion in that moment. I felt nothing.

"Haley, go back to the couch," Alex commanded. "I can handle this prick." Keegan ignored Alex and continued pleading with me to listen.

"I made a mistake," he said desperately. "But you have to understand.

Everything happened so quickly between us; I didn't have time to think about what we were doing before we were doing it. You remember. Please, I want you to know that I didn't mean to hurt you. But Haley, I love my wife. I just . . . I would die if she found out. Haley, please. You *must* understand." The numbness I'd been feeling vanished as I watched him beg for my silence. I couldn't believe he'd come all of this way to cover up his infidelity. Watching him grovel to save his marriage made me intensely angry. He didn't deserve his family, and he had certainly never deserved me. I couldn't believe I'd ever convinced myself to care for this pathetic excuse for a man.

I stormed the hallway, marching past Patrick and Alex determinedly. When I reached Keegan, I pushed him violently from my doorstep, hitting him with every fiber of strength in my being. He barely budged. "You have ruined my life!" I screamed angrily, shaking with rage. "You have single handedly screwed up everything that's important to me. You are a lying, cheating, sack of shit, and I hate you!" Keegan took a step back, surprised by my outburst. I wanted to give him another shove to try and inflict on him the same amount of pain he'd inflicted on me, but stopped when I heard a car door slam behind him on the street. Once again, I felt myself freeze when I saw Nick standing in the street, staring at the two of us in shock.

"What's . . . what's going on?" He asked quietly, glancing between Keegan and myself, dumbfounded. Keegan seemed equally surprised, glancing between Nick and I in similar confusion. I shook my head, looking desperately at Nick. This wasn't the way he was supposed to find out about Keegan. It looked so scandalous – like I'd been trying to hide it from him all this time.

"Nick, I . . ." I started to speak, but stopped when I couldn't think of what to say. Nick's look of shock morphed into one of furious rage as he began to put the pieces of the puzzle together. He stared at Keegan, who was now shifting nervously in the front lawn of my apartment building.

"You two?" He asked, almost hissing, glaring viciously at Keegan. His hazel eyes flickered with fury.

"I was going to tell you," I insisted, panicked. "When I saw the picture earlier I was too shocked – I couldn't think." Nick ignored me, continuing to shoot daggers into Keegan with his eyes.

"You . . ." he said, pointing at Keegan and shaking. "YOU . . ." Before I knew it, Nick had dropped his keys in the middle of the street and was sprinting at Keegan like an angry bull. Still shocked by Nick's sudden interjection in the situation, Keegan put up his hands in weak defense, bracing himself poorly for Nick's imminent attack. My heart raced in my chest as I watched the two men collide and topple into the grass. Nick was yelling, but I couldn't make out his words. All I could hear were the grunting of the two men as they fought, fists flying through the air. I turned to Alex, who was standing in the doorway, watching the melee like a deer in headlights.

"Do something!" I pleaded hysterically. Alex looked at me, utterly lost. "Stop it!" I screamed at the two fighting men, crying uncontrollably. Keegan eventually managed to get himself out from under Nick's hold through the scuffle and distance himself from his enraged brother-in-law. He staggered across the lawn, disheveled and muddy, holding his hands out again in defense. He still hadn't said a word.

"Nick, I never meant for this to happen," he finally managed, straining for breath. Nick stood up straight, his eyes glaring venomously in Keegan's direction. He breathed heavily as he wiped a small amount of blood from his bottom lip. Recovering from their brawl, both men stared at one another in tense silence.

Nick eventually broke his glare and turned toward me, his eyes filled with anger, but now also mixed with hints of betrayal and sadness. "I can't believe this," he muttered, almost whispering, shaking his head in disgust. I watched his reaction helplessly, desperate to explain.

"I didn't know he was married to your sister . . ." I insisted earnestly. "I didn't . . . ." Nick turned toward me and put his hand up to stop me from continuing. The irises of his eyes had turned a bright green, clashing with the bloodshot red that filled his eyes' normally white corners. His expression burned with confused pain.

"You should have told me the minute you saw that picture," he said angrily, brushing the mud and grass from his shirt and turning back to the street. He was right. I had nothing to say in my defense. I watched him in silent agony as he picked up his keys from the curb and walked toward his car. Keegan stood on the lawn in disbelief, watching the situation unfolding before him. "Do you know what I did when you left?" Nick asked me, opening the driver's side door. I shook my head, tears continuing to stream down my face.

"I called my sister," he told me, his normally calm, soothing voice shaking with emotion. "I called my sister to tell her about *you*." He emphasized the last word with a mixture of anger and disdain. He stared at me. I didn't want to imagine what he was thinking.

"Nick, I'm sorry," I claimed softly between breaths, not knowing what else to say. "I wish . . . I wish I could take it all back." Nick shot me a pained look before turning to glare at Keegan one more time.

"Me too," he said, more defeated than angry. "But you can't." I watched helplessly as he opened his car door and raised his eyes to look into mine one last time. "Goodbye, Haley," he said firmly, his hazel eyes peering into my soul and stopping my heart. My mind screamed at him not to leave, but all I could do was stare back at him as he lowered his head and climbed into his car. I sunk into a crouching position in my doorway, hugging myself while I cried. Alex wrapped me in his arms once again and pulled me inside as Nick pulled away from the curb. Alex slammed the door behind us. Keegan stood motionless in the front lawn of the apartment, watching as Nick's car disappeared down the street and out of our lives forever.

24 WEDDING INVASION

I held my lips together firmly, trying to keep from laughing at the sad, saggy green bow Trevor had tied to the edge of one of the place cards. Lindsay looked across the table at me, similarly attempting to stifle her laughter while tying a yellow bow to a place card herself.

"That is *not* going to work." Patrick's voice boomed matter-of-factly as he approached us from the living room. Trevor frowned. "The bows need to be pretty," Patrick explained, his hands flat and rigid as he spoke, "while also indicating whether the guest is to be served a chicken, beef, or vegetarian meal." He hustled hurriedly over to where Trevor was sitting and snatched the place card rudely out of Trevor's hands. Untying and retying the bow quickly in one fluid motion, Patrick widened his eyes with anxiety. "Like this," he demonstrated, almost hissing his words. He flung the place card to the center of the table once he'd finished and scurried out of the kitchen to make sure the programs were being assembled properly in the dining room. Trevor looked at Lindsay and me in mild annoyance.

"Are neither of you going to say anything to him?" He asked, frustrated. "He's out of control." I shook my head.

"Not a chance I'm saying anything," I told him, laughing. Lindsay agreed, giggling as she continued to tie bows to the hundreds of bowless place cards piled neatly on top of the table. Patrick had been his sweet, calm and collected self throughout the entire wedding planning process, but with only a week before the ceremony and a seemingly endless list of things to do, his anxiety had suddenly turned him into a classic bridezilla. Groomzilla, to be exact. Trevor sighed and threw up his hands.

"Well, I can't sit here and do this anymore, especially if he's going to bother redoing everything anyway!" Lindsay set down the ribbon in her hand and touched Trevor lightly on the wrist.

"Don't get upset, babe," she requested. "A wedding creates a lot of stress. I'll probably be the same way next summer." Trevor frowned at her, disappointed at the prospect.

"Wonderful," he grunted.

A couple of months ago, after the last cumbersome cast was removed from Lindsay's healing limbs, Trevor took her out to dinner to celebrate her miraculous recovery. Upon toasting her and telling her he couldn't imagine life without her, he dropped to one knee and proposed. The waiter caught the whole thing on video, giving Trevor and Lindsay an opportunity to share the moment with family and friends. The proposal was intimate and sweet – and after over five years of being together, a long time coming.

I was looking forward to planning another wedding, now a veteran in my responsibilities as the maid of honor. I even planned to host a bachelorette party for Lindsay like the one I'd thrown for Alex – similarly equipped with ridiculous and raunchy bachelorette games; a couple of hot, gay strippers; and a cabaret tranny show to round out the night. Weddings caused a whole lot of stress, but man, did they also create a whole lot of fun.

"I don't *really* plan on acting like that," Lindsay reassured Trevor, trying to keep him from stressing over their upcoming nuptials. "I'm just trying to make you understand that Patrick's overwhelmed." Trevor didn't look convinced.

"Oh, don't worry, Trev," I told him, "you won't be involved in your wedding plans anyway, so even if Lindsay does act like a crazy bitch, you won't have to know!" Lindsay widened her grayish blue eyes.

"Says who?" She demanded. "He's been involved in picking the venue and colors already. I'm going to need his help! I can't do it all on my own." I looked at Trevor sheepishly and mouthed an apologetic 'sorry' for his plight. Once again, he threw his hands up in frustration.

"I'm getting out of here," he said. "This is stressing me out." Lindsay and I watched as Trevor escaped from the kitchen and out the front door in a matter of seconds. I giggled, but felt bad that we'd chased him out of his own home. In the past forty-eight hours, we'd transformed Trevor and Lindsay's house into wedding ground zero, and it didn't look like it would be returning to normal anytime soon. We had place cards to ribbon, programs to construct, favors to assemble, and an innumerable array of other things to do before next Saturday. Neither Alex's apartment nor mine could have housed all the projects at once.

"He'll be happy to have us out of here," I guessed, looking at Lindsay. "I feel bad we've invaded your home." She waved her hand, unconcerned.

"He's fine," she assured me. "You know how men can get. I'm surprised he lasted this long. I was sure he'd take one look at the ribbon project and bolt." I laughed and looked behind me to ensure the coast was clear.

"He was probably scared of what Patrick might do to him if he didn't help." The two of us sat amongst the ribbons, laughing and joking about Patrick's recent personality change. We would have normally been offended with how he'd been treating everyone, but we knew the stress of the wedding was getting the best of him. It would all be over soon, and likely, with a giant apology from Patrick.

I stopped tying my bows and looked down as my phone started ringing at the end of the table. "Oh, it's work," I told Lindsay, excusing myself to answer it. We'd recently shipped the clothes and accessories from Alex's winter line to Resh+001. I expected it was Naresh calling to let me know he'd received them.

"I remember having to answer those incessant weekend calls," Lindsay reminisced from the table. "I'm so happy to be done with that stage of my life." I was happy for her, too. After seeing her at Dom's party almost six months ago, Charlie called and insisted that Lindsay return to work at his small, boutique firm. It hadn't taken much convincing for Lindsay to quit her big firm job and take Charlie up on his offer. Returning to work in a normal, nurturing office environment had probably helped make her transition from the hospital to the real world relatively seamless. Lindsay was still the same hardworking lawyer we all knew and loved, but now, she was happy, well rested, and available to hang out with her friends. It was as if her accident had truly been a life-saving event in disguise.

"Haley Simpson." I answered my phone by announcing myself, standing in the corner of the kitchen.

"Hi, Haley," Naresh replied. "I received everything, and am once again amazed with how it all turned out. The two of you never cease to impress me." I smiled. I was relieved to hear good news from our biggest, most fabulous client.

"That's wonderful," I said. "But you know, the one you need to be impressed with is Alex. It's all his doing." Naresh clicked his tongue against the roof of his mouth, scolding me for being modest.

"I know it's you who's been designing the shoes," he declared. "And I also know that while Keegan may have left behind designs for the summer and fall lines, you had to construct these new winter shoes all on your own." I blushed on the other end of the phone, undeserving of his compliments.

"It's not that impressive," I explained. "I simply started from the previous patterns and made some changes to suit the season."

"Oh yeah?" Naresh seemed unconvinced. "How simple was it to change a wing-tip lace-up Oxford into a rugged hand-sewn work boot?" I sighed through my nose and shrugged.

"I'm glad you liked everything," I said, refusing to resist any further. Naresh laughed.

"That's what I thought! Well done, Haley." I thanked him for his kind words and asked if anything was wrong or missing with the order. "No," he assured me. "Everything seems to be here and intact. I'll let you know more on Monday when we start readying it all for display."

"Okay, have a wonderful weekend, then," I said. "Thanks for the call."

"You, too," he replied. "Send Alex my regards and good luck with all the wedding preparations! We'll talk soon." I hung up the phone and walked through the house to find Alex. He'd be happy to hear that despite the absence of a qualified shoe designer, the two of us had pulled off a successful winter line.

When Keegan's relationship with the boutique was suddenly severed half a year ago, Alex and I had little choice but to continue with the shoe designs in-house. With Alex staunchly refusing to even try, Keegan's former design responsibilities fell unceremoniously into my lap. Although I'd sketched my own designs for years, I had never been forced to design men's shoes to fit a specific style, for a specific time of year, under a looming deadline. It was by sheer luck that I'd fallen into a rhythm and somehow helped Alex supply shoes now for three seasons running. We owed Naresh a big thank you for sticking with us through our time of crisis. As it turned out, his loyalty rested with good people and good business. When we delicately explained what happened with Keegan those many months ago, Naresh luckily determined that his loyalty rested with us.

I found Alex sitting at the head of the dining room table looking annoyed. Patrick's mother was sitting beside him, helping him put together the programs that Michael had designed for the ceremony. When he saw me waving at him, he was quick to abandon his post. "I'll be right back," he assured Patrick's mother, patting her on the hand. Following me out of the room and into the living room, Alex grabbed my arm and thanked me for saving him. "I'm tired of preparing for the wedding," he moaned dramatically. "I know this sounds terrible, but I can't wait for it all to be over."

"I understand," I related, checking each corner of the room for Patrick. I didn't want him to hear his groom complaining, especially given the state of insanity in which he was currently operating. "So good news," I announced, changing the subject. "I just got off the phone with Naresh. He called to say he received everything and is happy with the merchandise. No complaints or extra requests thus far!" Alex rolled his eyes in the back of his head in relief and hugged me with crippling force. I winced.

"No offense, Hale," he said, "but I was really worried about what he'd say this time around because of the shoes." I put my hands up to assure him I wasn't offended. "I mean, I loved them," he explained, "but I had no idea if they were hot with the line. That's why I don't design shoes, Hale, I just don't have the same eye and creativity like I do with clothes!"

"No offense taken," I said. "You think *you* were nervous, take your nerves and multiply them by a thousand, and you may begin to understand how I felt." Alex hugged me again and slumped into a nearby couch looking exhausted.

"Will life ever slow down?" He wondered out loud. I slumped next to him on the couch and stared at the ceiling. Our business with Naresh had opened a lot of doors, inundating us with new accounts and new orders. The new business was like a dream, but it had buried us now for over three months. Scrambling at all hours of the day and night, we were barely keeping up. We needed more staff – including, of course, a more qualified, full-time shoe designer.

"I don't know," I admitted. "But I'm sure things will be less stressful after the wedding." I turned to look at him, our heads resting comfortably on the back cushion of the sofa. "I know you're ready for the planning and stress to be over, but are you excited for the actual wedding?" I asked. "Are you nervous? Anything?" Alex turned his head to face me and smiled.

"Excited," he said. "Unbelievably thankful that I've found the love of my life. And unbelievably thankful that he loves me back." I smiled at him and returned to staring at the ceiling.

"Good," I said. I was happy to hear it. "I'm glad you realize how lucky you are to have found each other." Alex put his hand on my thigh and squeezed.

"How are you doing with all of this?" He asked, softly.

"What do you mean?"

"You know," Alex continued. "With all of the wedding stuff. Me and Patrick, Lindsay and Trevor; you're surrounded by it. I know you love us and you're happy for everyone, but how are you doing – how do you feel with all of this constantly around you? Are you okay or does it make missing Nick more difficult?" It had been six months since I'd last seen or spoken to Nick, but the pain of losing him still hurt. I'd considered contacting him a couple of times, but knew that what had happened between me and Keegan was too big to overcome. Besides, if Nick had wanted to talk, he would have reached out to me, and he never did.

"I'm fine," I said reassuringly, grateful for his concern. "I'd be lying if I didn't admit that I occasionally wished I had him by my side, but that's not how it turned out. And really, I'm okay." Alex sighed.

"Do you think you'll ever see him again?" He asked. I knew I'd just said I was okay, but I didn't want to talk about Nick anymore. It was easier to ignore the subject entirely. Talking about him reopened old wounds. I preferred that they remain closed.

"No," I said confidently. Alex sat up from the couch and gave my thigh one last squeeze. He sensed the finality in the tone of my voice. We were finished talking about Nick.

"You'll meet someone soon, Hale, I just know it," he said lovingly, standing and readjusting the waist of his jeans. I watched him thoughtfully as he smiled and returned to the dining room to assume his wedding prep duties. I wished Alex did know that there was someone out there waiting for me, but he didn't. No one did. Such was the unknown agony us single women bore. We were cursed with living for the rest of our days, waiting and wondering whether tomorrow would be the day on which we would meet that special someone we were always promised. Standing up from the couch to return to my own duties in the kitchen, I decided not to wait and wonder. I refused to sit around in sorrow, as if the only thing that made life worth living was the accompaniment of a man. After what had happened with Nick six months ago, I had succumbed to the realization that playing the role of bride may never be in the cards for me. And I was slowly teaching myself to be okay with the prospect. I was surrounded by a loving and supportive group of incredible friends, that not everyone had the opportunity to claim. I was one of the lucky ones, and I didn't need a man to remind me.

25 GIFT FROM A GROOM

I peered patiently out of the third story window at the leaves floating like feathers in the gentle breeze. They freckled the sky with the red and orange hues of autumn, adding a naturally elegant element to the already beautifully decorated soiree outside. Placing my right hand on the windowsill, I stood on my toes in an attempt to catch a glimpse of the bustling below. Some of Patrick's younger cousins were chasing each other on the outskirts of the crowd, their parents warning them loudly not to dirty their tuxedos.

Although I couldn't see them, I could hear the string quartet playing somewhere out of view, delighting the crowd with an upbeat and classical movement from one of Mozart's famous compositions. I took a deep breath to settle the butterflies in my stomach and moved away from the window, fussing with the skirt of my burnt orange dress nervously. The day, the weather, the decorations . . . none of it could have been more perfect. In this moment, waiting anxiously for Alex's arrival, I couldn't have been happier.

"Hale? Can I come in?" I whipped my head toward the door when I heard Alex's voice calling to me quietly from the hallway. Rushing across the room in my bare feet, I swung open the door and smiled at Alex proudly, restraining myself from toppling him with a giant hug. I stared at his black, crisp tuxedo in awe. He looked amazing. I was filled with so much love and excitement in that moment, I could barely speak. Taking another deep breath, I loosened the grip on my bouquet of orange calla lilies and roses and touched the side of Alex's thin face lightly with my other hand.

"You look incredible," I said, trying to prevent the tears welling up in my green eyes from falling. I had no intention of testing the limits of my waterproof mascara this early in the evening. "Dashing," I added, whispering. Alex placed his hand over mine and smiled, displaying his high cheekbones.

"You look pretty amazing, yourself," he replied, nodding at my dress. I removed my hand from his cheek and entertained him with a curtsey.

"Do I look like a good Best Woman?" I asked, grinning. He nodded and pointed at my bare feet.

"Yes, although I do remember that the outfit came with shoes." I held my finger up and turned, trying to remember in which corner of the room I'd left them.

"I was saving the best for last," I told him, finding them lying next to a wooden chair by the fireplace. I held them up happily, displaying my first pair of Manolo Blahniks to Alex with pride. Patrick and I picked out the pair of muted gold, strappy heels, which complimented the autumn colors of the wedding nicely. Naturally, I'd used the grandeur and importance of their wedding day as an excuse to purchase overpriced designer shoes of which I'd always dreamed. As Alex's Best Woman, there was no doubt in my mind that I deserved to splurge. The gold designer pumps were an iconic, classic, Best-Woman-worthy pair of heels. I wouldn't have dared to wear anything less. Alex smiled and shook his head.

"They're fabulous," he observed. "Perfect for my Best Woman." I smiled at him affectionately.

"Are you ready to do this?" I asked him. I sat down in the wooden chair to put on my shoes. Alex cleared his throat and nodded, watching as I slipped my cherished heels onto my feet with care. When I'd finished, I rose from the chair, pleased with the way the shoes became instantly molded to my feet. Walking toward the window, I peered down at the scene below for the last time. Patrick's cousins had stopped running, and the soft murmur of chatting from the crowd had lulled. All I could hear now was the melodious, classical styling of the talented string quartet. Turning away from the window, I walked steadily toward Alex and placed my hands on either side of his arms, my bouquet of fresh flowers hovering inches from his face. It was time.

"I would hug you," I started, "but I don't want to get my deodorant on your newly pressed tuxedo." Alex laughed and shuffled his feet nervously. It was endearing to see. "I would kiss you," I continued, "but I don't want to leave a giant lip print on your cheek for the ceremony." Alex laughed again and thanked me for being so thoughtful. "You're welcome," I responded, chuckling. "So," I concluded, "instead of hugging or kissing you, I'm going to stand here, hold you by the shoulders, and tell you that I love you very much and could not be happier to be standing by your side today." I pursed my lips together firmly, trying again to hold in my emotions. Alex looked back at me with watery eyes and mouthed, 'I love you, too.' We stood for a minute in silence until we regained what little composure we had left. Shaking his head and taking a deep breath through his nose, Alex held up his right arm, encouraging me to take it.

"Let's do this," he said, confidently. I nodded and followed Alex into the hall, the two of us arm and arm, smiling uncontrollably. The level of happiness I was feeling was like nothing I'd ever experienced. I didn't think I would ever stop smiling, no matter how much my cheeks began to hurt.

As the two of us made our way down the rickety staircase, I whispered quietly in Alex's ear. "This place is beautiful," I told him, admiring the history that surrounded me, "but I wish it had an elevator." Alex laughed quietly and patted me on the arm as we began to descend the second flight of stairs.

After a lot of thought and planning, Patrick and Alex decided to move their Columbus wedding north into Amish country to get married on one of the state's scenic wineries. The main building on the winery was a three-storied old mansion, built sometime in the late 1800s. Classic wood floors shone throughout, and glamorous, hand-carved woodwork surrounded each window and door at least three inches deep. Every nineteenth century detail of the building was intact. Even the hinges on the doors were made of black, plated metal, boasting several unique designs. The stairs creaked with each step down; I couldn't have imagined a better setting for Patrick and Alex's fall, sunset ceremony. Like their relationship, the winery was classic and timeless – the makings of a fairytale.

When we descended the final staircase, I heard Alex draw in his breath sharply. Following his gaze, I saw Patrick standing alone in the entryway in a similarly classic black tuxedo, waiting patiently for his groom. I squeezed Alex's arm as we walked down the last couple of steps and reminded him quietly to breathe. When we reached the bottom of the stairs, I let go of Alex's arm and watched him happily as he slowly approached his soon-to-be husband. Patrick looked lovingly at Alex and sighed, grabbing him by the hands without a word. Leaning in, Alex placed his forehead onto Patrick's and whispered something only the two of them could hear. Shaking my head to prevent from tearing up yet again, I walked passed them and opened the front door to take my place with the rest of the wedding party. Before I closed the door behind me, however, I paused to catch one last glimpse of the grooms. Noticing me in the background, Alex winked as he and Patrick held each other in a long embrace. I smiled back and nodded, my heart filled with happiness and love.

When I walked outside, I was amazed at how beautiful everything had turned out. Although I'd helped Patrick and Alex plan the flower arrangements and decorations for months, nothing could have prepared me for how incredible everything would look. The sun was beginning to set, lighting up the sky with an array of gorgeous colors no painter could ever replicate. The leaves from the giant red maples continued to fly through the air majestically as the guests sat patiently in rustic, wooden chairs that had been decorated with orange and red sashes. A large gazebo covered in multi-colored organza ribbons sat prominently at the front of the terrace, poised and ready for the start of the ceremony. And behind it all, the rolling hills of Amish country stretched for miles, untouched by modern construction and decorated naturally with colors from the changing season.

The breathtaking scenery and the weight of the moment gave me chills as I organized myself behind the rest of the wedding party. Waiting patiently for the string quartet to begin the processional, I looked anxiously at the back of the crowd for some familiar faces. I recognized some of the boutique's sales associates sitting together in the last few rows, and smiled widely when I caught a glimpse of Dom's more-tamed, but still-wavy, mane bouncing as he talked to a person on his right I didn't recognize.

Craning my neck a little, I spotted Lindsay and Trevor holding hands in the middle of a row toward the front. Lindsay smiled sweetly as she spoke to Trevor, fidgeting with the vintage diamond ring glistening proudly on her left hand. Her light-blonde hair, cut into a fashionably short bob, was pretty against the brown ribbon she was using as a headband. Charlie and his wife sat next to them on their left, studying the ceremony programs. In that moment, as I got ready to join the processional, it seemed as though the stars had aligned and life had finally become everything I'd ever dreamed. I told myself that I didn't need or want anything else. Most importantly, I didn't want or need *anyone* else.

Last to make my way down the aisle, I smiled nervously when it came my turn to walk. I felt awkward as I proceeded down the aisle alone, locking eyes with familiar faces to help get me through my uncomfortable moment in the spotlight. As I neared the front of the crowd, I caught my little brother looking happily at me from the second row, our mother sitting properly at his side. I would never have a close, loving relationship with my mother, but I was happy that we'd at least managed to reconcile enough to hold a polite conversation.

When I passed them to step onto the gazebo, Michael pointed subtly at Alex's parents sitting in front of him in the first row. He looked at me with pleasant surprise. I nodded back at him in self-satisfaction. It had taken a lot of convincing, but after several serious conversations, Alex had eventually agreed to extend an olive branch to the two people who had brought him into this world. The three of them had a long way to go, but seeing Alex's parents sitting there, smiling contently as they watched me pass, I knew that they'd have a longstanding relationship with their son for years and years to come.

Walking the couple of steps into the gazebo, I turned as the sun continued to set at my back, painting the sky with deep oranges and yellows. I gripped my bouquet tightly in anticipation, excited to catch the first glimpse of the grooms walking together down the aisle. My heart stopped beating in my chest when, unexpectedly, the string quartet began to play an elegant version of Coldplay's *Reign of Love*. The crowd stood in reverence. Tears began to well up in my eyes as I listened to the instrumental introduction of Alex and Patrick's favorite song. Then, like out of a dream, the two of them came into view, hand-in-hand, smiling widely as a male vocalist, sounding eerily like Coldplay's lead singer, Chris Martin, began to sing. They strolled together slowly toward the gazebo, gripping each other tightly. Smiling and nodding at their guests, I watched as the two of them stepped to the front and turned to face each other for the ceremony. Waiting patiently for the music to fade so the vows could begin, I leaned toward Alex and whispered softly at the back of his head.

"I'm so happy for you," I told him quietly. "I hope today is everything you've ever dreamed." Without turning, I heard Alex respond, almost as if he were speaking directly to Patrick.

"It's more," he whispered, clutching Patrick's hands. "Much, much more."

****

I hobbled across the wooden floor to take a long-awaited seat at one of the deserted reception tables. I had made it through the ceremony, the dinner, and even my Best Woman speech before my golden new heels had started to take their toll on my feet. Taking them off and placing them under the table, I rubbed my toes, watching in contentment as the remaining wedding guests started to party under the disco ball, prepared to dance their way into the night. I breathed in slowly, trying to freeze the moment and take it all in. Everything had gone by so fast that I was scared I would forget the important details. I wanted to remember it all: The way I felt when I saw Alex in his tuxedo for the first time; the way Patrick's voice shook with emotion when he read his vows; and even the nervous way I laughed during the delivery of my speech. All of it was so special – so near and dear to my heart – I wished I could bottle it up and carry it with me so that the night could last forever.

I giggled when I saw Patrick in the middle of the dance floor starting to move in ways I never thought possible. The crowd was forming a circle around the spectacle, clapping and yelling words of encouragement as Patrick completed an interesting choreographed dance to Michael Jackson's *Beat It*. I had just started to look for Alex, secretly hoping he would intervene, when I heard his voice pipe up behind me in amusement.

"He loves Michael Jackson," Alex said, laughing at the man he'd just married. I turned and looked at him over the tall floral centerpiece, which was set carefully on top of a brass candelabrum.

"Where'd *you* come from?" I asked him, surprised to see him taking a break from the festivities. He walked around the table and pulled out the chair next to me.

"I was looking for my Best Woman," he told me, patting me on the hand as he sat down. "It's traditional to get each member of the bridal party a gift – and if you don't mind, I'd like to give you yours right now." I smiled at him eagerly as he pulled out a small box from behind his back. I reached out to grab it, looking at him suspiciously.

"This better not be expensive," I warned. Alex shrugged.

"This is for more than just being by my side today," he said, taking my hand. "This is for everything you've done for me *and* for the boutique in the last few months. We've been through a lot together, and I want you to know how much you mean to me." I paused before opening the box, touched by Alex's sentiment. Alex nudged me impatiently. "Open it!" He demanded. Breaking my gaze, I turned my attention toward the box in my lap and opened it. I almost squealed when I saw the orange and pink striped Henri Bendel business card holder lying importantly at the bottom of the box.

"Alex – I love it!" I exclaimed, throwing my arms around him in a big hug. He nodded, but pointed impatiently at the box as if I'd missed something.

"Look inside," he said anxiously. I looked back at him with curiosity and reached inside. Not surprisingly, I discovered one of my business cards. "Take it out and read it," Alex said, impatiently. My curiosity heightening with every second, I took the card out and held it up to read. It looked like all of my other business cards, except for one important distinction. Instead of *Haley Blythe Simpson, Account Manager*, the business card read: *Haley Blythe Simpson, Designer*. I stared at the card, waiting for the information to register.

"But Alex," I said, shaking my head in disbelief, "I thought this was only going to be temporary . . ." Alex reached out his hand and placed it on my arm to stop me.

"Hale, if this isn't something you want," he said gently, "you can assume your former role as an account manager for our New York clients. But I've talked about it extensively with Patrick and some of the other employees, and they all agree. What you've done with Keegan's unfinished designs in a time of crisis . . . it's nothing short of incredible." I continued to stare at the business card in shock. I'd assumed Keegan's responsibilities only because we'd had no other choice. I never considered myself the right person for the job, nor thought that my design responsibilities would extend past Alex's winter line.

"Alex, I have no qualifications," I replied, trying to wrap my head around his offer. Alex chuckled at me.

"You went to school for design," he pointed out. "And you know my style better than anyone. You are dedicated to the boutique, you're creative, and as it turns out, you're a brilliant designer." I stared back at him, my eyes wide. Just when I didn't think the night could get any better, *my* dreams – dreams I never thought possible – were suddenly coming true. I had nothing left to say besides 'thank you.'

"You're welcome," Alex replied slapping his hands together and standing up. "But don't thank me yet – I have one more gift." Still reeling from the giant opportunity that had fallen into my lap, I looked at Alex curiously without saying a word. He smiled sheepishly and turned to the side to give me a better view of the person walking up to the table. Without explanation, Alex squeezed me on the shoulder and walked past me toward the dance floor to join his party. I gaped stupidly, my mouth wide open, as I watched Nick take the seat Alex had vacated.

"Hi," Nick said, looking at me, as if he also couldn't believe he was there. I scrunched my eyebrows together, trying to understand. His hazel eyes regarded me tentatively as he fidgeted with his fitted gray suit.

"What are you doing here?" I asked, utterly shocked to see him in front of me. We hadn't spoken since the day he found Keegan at my apartment. I never thought I'd see him again, let alone in northern Ohio at Alex's wedding. Nick stared nervously at his feet before he replied.

"Your friend over there," he said, nodding in Alex's direction, "is . . . persuasive." I smiled cautiously, still not sure what was going on.

"Did he bribe you to be here or something?" I asked. I was only half-kidding. Nick laughed anxiously and smiled, shaking his head. I missed his smile. Seeing it now after so many months of its absence made my heart hurt with agonizing longing. "Well, that's a relief," I muttered, under my breath. Nick leaned forward in his chair and looked at me. It wasn't the fiery way he had looked at me before finding out I'd slept with his sister's husband, but there were hints of hope and kindness in his eyes.

"I've missed you," he admitted, hesitantly. I tried hard to maintain eye contact, but the wounds I'd suffered from losing him several months ago had never quite healed. It was hard to look into his hazel eyes again and suddenly feel the emotions I thought had been permanently shut away in the basement of my heart.

"I've missed you too," I told him quietly. "But why are you here?" I repeated. "Not that I'm not happy to see you, but we haven't spoken in months." Nick sat up and sighed, straightening his pink tie nervously. "Why didn't you call?" My voice cracked as I asked him the question I'd wondered painfully for months. I understood why he hadn't contacted me – what had happened between Keegan and me was difficult to bear. Nevertheless, I had often wondered why he hadn't at least given me a chance to explain my side of the story. It made me fear that he'd never had feelings for me like I'd thought.

"I had trouble getting my mind around what happened at first," he said, looking away. "When I finally did digest it, so much time had passed that I didn't think you'd want me to call." He couldn't have been more wrong. I never stopped wanting him to call. "Haley, I'm ashamed that I didn't fight for you those many months ago. I'm not trying to make excuses, but with everything that happened with Katie, it was hard for me to process another devastating heartache so soon. I didn't handle it well." I clenched my teeth together, finding some solace in the fact that his heart had been broken, too.

"I understand," I said softly, but I still wasn't sure why he was here. Was he here to apologize? Find some closure? I searched his face for clues. He grabbed me by the hand and caught my gaze, his eyes burning faintly with the fire I'd missed so dearly.

"Haley, I know it seems crazy with everything that has happened and all the time that's passed, but I want to start over," he said. I let his words resonate for a moment before responding. I wanted to believe we could be together, but I shook my head, remembering the reason he'd left in the first place.

"Nick, what about your sister? Keegan? Time can't erase what I've done." Nick shook his head back at me and squeezed my hand.

"I know, Haley, but my sister's the one who helped me realize that as betrayed as I felt, you did nothing wrong." I listened doubtfully. "Keegan's the one that lied to everybody," he explained. "My sister doesn't want him to ruin all of our lives, and neither do I." I swallowed hard. I didn't want that either, but moving past it seemed impossibly difficult. "I want you back in my life, Haley," Nick insisted. "I know it may take weeks, months, or even years before we figure out how to be us again, but I want to try." His words were everything I wanted to hear, but it was hard for me to believe a future with him was a realistic possibility. I didn't want to open my heart again to all that hurt.

"But Keegan," I protested again. "He's your niece's father – he'll always be in your life. I don't know if I can handle that . . ." I shot my eyes to the floor as the music in the background changed dramatically to a slow song by Jason Mraz. Nick didn't say anything to alleviate my fears. We sat in silence, the reception proceeding obliviously in the background. I was counting down the seconds, expecting him to leave at any moment. After about a minute, however, Nick sighed and stood from his chair, still holding me by the hand.

"You want to dance?" He asked, gesturing toward the dance floor. I didn't know what to say. Pulling gently on my arm, Nick beckoned for me to follow him into the crowd. I nodded silently and stood from my chair. We didn't speak as we weaved through the tables, but before we approached the dance floor, I hesitated.

"I don't know about this," I said, my voice laced with trepidation. "It's going to be so hard . . . so complicated. I don't want go through losing you again." Nick stopped walking and turned to face me.

"Me neither, Haley," he shared. His expression was calm, but determined. The nervousness he'd exuded upon first arriving had vanished behind a willful look of confidence. "And you're right. It will be hard," he said, repeating my sentiment. "I don't know what the future will hold after tonight, but there is nothing more we can say to change the past. Our only two options are to quit and go our separate ways again, or to move forward, one step at a time. I know how it feels without you in my life. I'm willing to risk being hurt again for the chance to have you in it." The stone casing around my heart fell to pieces. I grabbed his other hand and smiled. His profession of feelings and willingness to move forward helped me find my own bout of confidence and strength. If he was here, willing to give us another chance after all that had happened, I was willing too.

"Okay," I said, poised to take the plunge and open up to him again. "I'm in." Nick let go of one of my hands to brush a piece of hair out of my face.

"Then let's dance," he said, softly. Without another word, we made our way under the glittering of the disco ball. My heart beat quickly as he pulled me close to him, remembering the incredible night we'd spent together last spring. As we started to sway, I saw Alex, Patrick, Lindsay, and Trevor dancing around us on either side, watching intently. I smiled widely at Alex in gratitude. He nodded, a single tear running down the side of his face. I closed my eyes and followed Nick's lead. I didn't know where we were going or how long it would take us to get there, but I was happy to be in his arms again, pressed closely to his chest, navigating our dance together one step at a time.

ABOUT THE AUTHOR

Life in Plan B is Jennifer Vessells's first novel – one of what she hopes will be many. Having practiced law for nearly three years, Ms. Vessells decided, at the age of twenty-seven, to quit her practice and pursue her dream of becoming an author. Only a year and a half later, with the support of her family and friends, that dream is now being realized with the publication of this book.

Ms. Vessells lives in Columbus, Ohio with her husband, Michael. The couple is expecting their first child, a daughter, in December 2013.